ROY F. CHANDLER

THE BOSS'S BOY

A NOVEL OF PERRY COUNTY, PA

Iron Brigade Armory, Publishers
100 Radcliffe Circle
Jacksonville, NC 28546
Tel: (910) 455-3834

www.ironbrigadearmory.com

Printed in The United States of America

Book Number four
Of the
Iron Brigade Series

The Boss's Boy by Roy F. Chandler
Copyright © 2007 Katherine R. Chandler
All rights reserved

This is a work of fiction. The incidents in this book and the situations depicted are the author's creations. They do not and did not exist or happen.

ISBN 1-885633-28-9

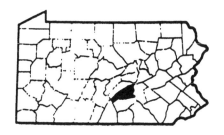

PERRY COUNTY

Dedication

To

The People of Perry County, Pa.

This book is written for the people who have, for more than thirty-seven years, so generously supported my writing efforts.

Sixty-two books! Who would have believed it? My work is now read throughout the English (and French) speaking world. Who would have believed that either?

You have been a generous audience, and I have been honored to write for and about you.

Additional titles from this author will be few, if any, but I am satisfied with what is out there, and I am grateful for your unflagging interest that made most of it possible.

My fondest hope is that future generations of Perry Countians will discover my books and be made more aware of the marvelous land in which they live.

Introduction

Every author would like his book to sell a million or so copies, but *The Boss's Boy* has been written for Perry Countians. If my Perry readership enjoys the book, but I do not sell a single copy beyond the county, I will be content.

Of course, being a Perry Countian is a state of mind more than a place of residence. My Perry County frontier series is being read all over the world, and people come from distant places to walk the ground written about and, perhaps, to suck in a little of the Perry flavor.

When I began writing about Perry County (in book form in 1968), readers beyond the county could be remembered by name, and I had lists recording who bought books and where they lived.

No more! Anyone who checks E-bay or Amazon can discover that Chandler Books are sometimes offered from exotic locations and are bought by English speakers around the globe.

I describe *The Boss's Boy* as a story about a youth who simply likes to fight. Have you known young men like that? I have, and to bring it home to some who will remember, my pal Bussy Thebes of Bloomfield was that sort of guy. Bussy got into fights at every baseball game and occasionally on the town square. Bussy did not drink, and he was not really mad. *He just liked it.*

Bussy Thebes is gone now, but my guess is that among the young guys of the county there are others who carry on the street corner fisticuffs tradition.

In this book, the youth grows to manhood and becomes sober and responsible—a man of business who is still willing to let his fists fly if needed. Yep, I could name a couple of those types as well.

All of that is in the Perry County tradition. About half of Harrisburg's citizenry still believe that Perry Countians are wild characters who lack teeth (especially in front), go to one-room schools, sell hoop poles to subsist, and get "lickered up" and fight with knives and guns at the drop of a slur—like calling it PURRY County.

The Perry County frontier era was memorably violent, and it may be true that genetic imprints of that time are cherished a touch more by our people than they are in some other places.

Good for us! Let the wimps live elsewhere. We should be careful not to have too much of that thinner blood transfused when we go outside for emergencies.

Now you have hints of how *The Boss's Boy* will run. I chose the subject matter because I wished to write a bit about the early canal era (1827 to 1834) and I needed to position the story in Duncannon—a town I have neglected a bit in earlier volumes.

As canals are prominent herein (although this is not a yarn primarily about canals) I have attached a sort of canal summary following the text. If a reader would like to know something about the Pennsylvania canals before he tackles the story, turn to pages 394-406. That is not necessary (and there will be a bit of repetition of material within the book), but some will be glad they did.

Historians will recognize that I have condensed time a little to make the story more inclusive. A few incidents occur before their historical dates, and some in the book happen a touch later than in real life. A novel is storytelling. I am not recording actual history.

As usual, this is a book that anyone can give to anyone without fear of embarrassment or insult. There is no sex and no swearing, the good guys win, and the bad guys get what they deserve—and maybe a bit more. I hope that when a reader finishes the book, he will lay it aside with a sense of satisfaction and a wish that it were longer.

RFC

The Boss's Boy

1

1826

Young Matt Miller backed away and ran his tongue across his split lip. Blood was salty in his mouth, and he spit it away, glaring at Mickey McFee with hunger in his eyes.

McFee, too, paused to rub at his head where it had collided with Matt's jaw, indicating that the butt had been accidental. If the head butt had been deliberate, McFee would have taken advantage of Matt's momentary hesitation and been on his opponent like a coat of paint,

The difference was that this was a friendly fight to prove who was toughest, who had the heart, and who, until they met again, could claim to be the cock-of-the-towpath.

McFee had strutted up to Matt betraying his intentions by a pugnacious, outthrust jaw and balled up fists.

He said, "Hear you're moving out." He waited for Matt's answer, grinning in delight at what he expected was about to happen.

McFee was like that. He liked to fight, and he and Matt had battled twice before to inconclusive decisions.

Mickey McFee was a year older and built like a brick. He worked beside the toughest nuts in his labor gang and pretty much held his own. He smoked a short Irish pipe, drank himself stupid on occasion, sang loudly when soused, and fought with anyone his size or a little larger. McFee was sixteen years old.

Matt had watched McFee swagger along the horse-manured towpath paralleling the new canal and had easily guessed his intentions. He felt a lift to his spirit and could have acknowledged a growing excitement, for if the truth be known, young Matt Miller liked a good fight about as much as did tough Mickey McFee. Furthermore, he was still unsure whether he could properly lick McFee or whether the more-than-willing young fist fighter could put him down for a count.

Matt's answer to McFee's query was quiet, but his eyes challenged, and the Mick did not miss the set of feet or the unblinking return of his stare.

Miller said, "We'll be gone for a while, but we'll be back."

McFee said, "Guess I ought to lick you once more before you go so's you won't forget how it feels."

Matt found himself grinning in anticipation, and excitement ballooned somewhere inside his body.

"McFee, they couldn't melt you down and pour you on me." Matt tried to look speculative.

"The fact is, I think I'll beat on your thick skull like I did the last time you came looking for a fight."

The words came routinely because that was the way men talked to each other. McFee was already laying his hat aside, and when Matt dropped his alongside someone began yelling, "fight."

Matt stepped squarely onto the towpath and got his hands up. The excited shouting came clearly through a sudden buzzing in his senses, and he heard a voice bellowing, "Come on, McFee's going to whip the Boss's Boy."

Other voices took up the cry. "McFee and the Boss's Boy are going to scrap." A burly worker was ready to bet. "I'll put two pence on McFee. Anybody, taking?"

Nobody accepted, and that raked Matt's nerve ends. He squared off and quick as a flash, McFee made for him.

The Mick came in swinging. He grunted with every punch and intended that each knock his enemy as cold as frozen mackerel.

Matt Miller met McFee head on, and their blows thumped along heads and into bodies. Crude blocking forced misses, but just as many wallops thudded home. Matt felt an ear turn hot, and his vision blurred a little from a powerful whack.

When stung, each fighter instinctively swung harder and faster. Attack was met with fiercer attack, and men gathered to watch the battle, cheering more or less equally, more interested in the small war itself than who was actually winning.

Then McFee's head had come up hard under Matt's chin and rattled his senses. His lip split and burned like fire, and McFee had stepped back to rub at the pain in his own skull. The Irish boy's grin was nail-hard, and his body was gathering to resume the battle, so Matt punched him straight in the middle of his face.

Mickey McFee took the smash, which bounced his head and flattened his nose, spraying blood onto his upper lip. Shaken, he swung like a gate. The wild right hand got through, thudding solidly against Matt's ear, and Miller felt his feet lift and his rump hit the ground. Slightly dazed, he lunged erect, getting close and grabbing fistfuls of Mickey's clothing.

They wrestled about trying to topple the other, and a foreman decided he had seen enough. He signaled a muscular helper, and they moved in to separate the youthful brawlers. The still-gathering crowd hooted and demanded the fight go on, but the company paid for work, and youths hammering at each other was only entertainment.

Matt found his arms pinned from behind, and he was unceremoniously hoisted off his feet. An instant before he was hurled off the towpath and into ungraceful flight, he glimpsed Mickey McFee struggling just as fruitlessly in someone else's more powerful grip.

He smacked face first into the canal and went under. The long Swatara Creek cut had only recently been refilling after its winter sleep. The water was fresh off still thawing hillsides and felt colder than ice.

Matt got erect in chest deep water and stood on the smoothed bottom searching for the best climb up the canal bank and out of the freezing cold.

McFee surfaced nearby snorting water and blood from his nose and looking for the villain who had thrown him in.

The foreman who had roughly treated the Boss's Boy picked up their hats and examined them thoughtfully. "You two want to fight, do it after hours. We'll get in a ring and take bets on who'll miss the most times."

He shook his head in apparent disgust. "If a man's going to fight, he ought to know how. I doubt I've ever seen clumsier work in all my life." His words were cutting and meant to slash through any heroics the youths might harbor.

"You two should hike over to the girl's school and take lessons afore some full-grown man whomps your brains into mush."

He chose a head-sized stone from beyond the towpath and pushed the caps into nesting. The stone fit inside nicely, and he lobbed the weighted hats into the canal upstream from Mickey McFee where they immediately sank.

"Get yourself out of there and back to work, McFee, or I'll dock your pay for the whole morning!"

"And, you, young Matt. Quit picking on my men or you'll spend most of your time crawling in and out of this canal."

McFee shook his fist at the foreman's departing back. "If he wasn't the head bull I'd pile out of here and punch his face till he couldn't yell no more."

"Sure you would, McFee. That man would pound you into the ground like a tent stake." It would not do to gouge holes in the clay lining the canal walls, and Matt Miller was still hunting the best route out.

McFee was already thinking about other things. "You mark where my hat landed? I sort of lost track."

Young Matt answered wearily. "Yeah, it's to the left of where you're heading. Go a little more. Now they should be about under your feet." He watched McFee's leather-clad rump appear as the boy dove for the hats.

It took three dives before Mickey surfaced triumphantly waving his soggy cap. "Right where you thought it was, Boss's Boy." He clapped the water-streaming hat to his head. "Yours got washed away or something, but I reckon you'll find it after a while."

Like hell it did! Matt knew as sure as it was cold that McFee had tromped his hat into the mud, and it would be the very devil to find. Matt gritted his teeth and plowed through the canal toward the grinning Irish youth.

McFee let him get close before he lifted his other hand holding Matt's soggy cap. "Actually, I found yours right off, but I wanted you to worry a little." He tossed the rag in Matt's general direction.

They studied the steep bank guessing they might have to bottom-walk to the nearest sloping bank, which was too far away to be pleasurable.

McFee said, "Look, I'll hold you on my shoulders 'cause I'm the strongest. Once you get on the bank, you find a good grip on something and lower an arm for me to grab onto."

The cold was biting deep, so Matt was willing. He warned, "Don't go dumping me head first or something, McFee." He got a knee on Mickey's shoulder and pressed on the Irish boy's hat while he worked the other knee onto the second shoulder. McFee tottered toward the bank where the bottom rounded upward following the general shape of a canal boat's hull.

"Damn it, boy, lean forward or you'll pull us both backward. Cripes, ain't you ever balanced anything?" McFee paused just out of reach of the embankment. "You wouldn't get out and just leave me here in the water would you, Boss's Boy?"

"Of course not." Matt made his voice indignant, but he had considered just that. It would be funny and deserving, but as sure as the sun shown, when he finally got out, Mickey McFee would come looking for him, and he was tired of fighting just now

Matt got his balance on the towpath and found a mostly buried root to hang onto. He draped his body back over the bank, his feet almost touching the water, and McFee clawed his way upward gripping clothing and finally his rescuer's shoulders.

McFee rolled to safety on the towpath and immediately reached back to grip the collar of Matt's shirt and haul him onto the security of flat ground.

McFee twitched his upper body and complained loudly. "Damn it, you didn't have to pick a spot with fresh horse manure on it. I rolled right in it."

Matt did not care. "Why don't you just jump back in the canal and wash it off, McFee? This is all your fault, anyway."

"My fault? If it was anybody else, they'd have let me finish you off. You're lucky you're the boss's boy. They didn't want to see you get really whipped or you'd be pretty badly licked about now."

They clambered to their feet studying each other and making sure the other didn't get in a sneak punch.

Matt said, "If I was losing, how come your nose is flat and you're going to have two big black eyes?"

McFee shrugged it off. "A nose isn't nothing to a real fighter. Your lip's another thing. Hell, it's sticking out so far I could hang my hat on it." He grinned maliciously. "Hurts, too, don't it?"

Matt lied, "I can't even feel it." Then curious, "Why'd you come after me, anyway? I haven't laid eyes on you for weeks and here you come stomping along looking for trouble—which you surely got about all you could take."

McFee appeared uncertain. "Damned if I can recollect. Somebody suggested I knock you around a little lest you start thinking you were tough or maybe important." His voice sagged away in confusion before he rallied.

"Anyway, I'm glad I licked you, and if I didn't have to get back to the job, I'd polish you off here and now just 'cause it feels good." He turned away hoping to have had the last word.

"That beak of yours doesn't feel so good, and I'll bet you won't smell anything for a month." Matt considered starting the fight all over again.

McFee turned and said, "You're moving away now, Boss's Boy, but I'm going to fight for money. I've got me a trainer, and if we meet again you'd better walk soft 'cause by then I'll likely be a champion." McFee again turned away.

Matt got in the last dig. "Well, if you see me somewhere along the pike just remind me, and I'll make you the ex-champion." He saw McFee's shoulders hunch a little, but the foreman had stepped onto the towpath and was looking in their direction. McFee kept walking.

Matt headed toward the camp headquarters wondering if his father had heard the fracas. It might be best to slip in a side door and shed the wet clothes. Big Matt had requested he quit fighting the workers' sons, and he was willing, but what was he to do when some hard head like McFee came hunting trouble?

Damn, it had been a good scrap until they'd gotten thrown into the drink. Working full days, McFee was getting terrible strong while he, the Boss's son, was sitting in school trying to learn mostly useless stuff.

He pondered Mickey McFee fighting for money. A lot of young men did that, but not many made anything useful. Klubber Cole was always around the workmen's camp training somebody. The Klubber had been a hard fighter, but he was a little old now.

Most professionals adopted tough names, and Matt wondered what McFee would pick. Probably something like Hurricane McFee. Matt grinned to himself.

He licked at his hugely swollen lip. Damned thing was still bleeding, and it couldn't be explained away other than fighting. He might as well go straight in and get it over with. He knew his father's first question would be, "Did you win?" Big Matt put a lot of importance on finishing first.

Had he won? No, he couldn't claim that he had. A draw, maybe. That flash knockdown didn't count for anything. Those happened, and he had landed a lot of good punches. His fists were sore and he saw swelling on a knuckle. He tried sucking on it, but his mouth hurt too much. Fighting was exciting, and he liked it, but afterwards a man surely did pay for his pleasure.

2

When Mickey McFee marched up the towpath, China Smith called big Matt Miller over to watch.

"Young McFee is going for little Matt, Skipper, and we've got the best seats in the house."

They stood in the headquarters' door, and Brascomb Miller went to a window to watch.

All Brascomb saw was a worker boy standing in front of little Matt with his fists planted on his hips.

"How do you know they are going to fight?" Brascomb asked what big Matt would not have thought to question. If China Smith said it was so, that settled it for Matt Miller.

"Just watch for a minute, Mister Miller, and you'll see." Smith never addressed big Matt's younger brother as anything other than Mister. If Brascomb noticed, he never commented, and Brascomb certainly preferred that an employee like China Smith did not take personal liberties.

The fight started, and big Matt twisted and grunted as if he were down there and part of it. When young Matt went down, China heard the father mutter, "Get up, boy," and little Matt did.

Big Matt's laughter led China's when both fighters were thrown into the canal, but Brascomb turned away, his lip curled. Brawling with the help demeaned the family, and when he ran the businesses—the younger brother stifled the thought. That happy circumstance was unlikely to be. Big Matt was hale and hearty and, in fact, they should both have decades ahead.

Still, if the time ever came that he, Brascomb controlled the Miller companies, a great deal would be different. A more disturbing reality entered Brascomb's mind.

Big Matt owned the business. If he passed away, his son, the brawling boy they had been watching, would inherit, and Brascomb would still be under the thumb of his brother's side of the family.

This unchangeable fact had galled Brascomb since young Matt had been born. He did the books, paid out the money, and counted everything that came in. He deserved his chance at the Miller helm—and how he would change things. That worker boy, for instance, who dared to punch at a Miller, would never work for them again.

Deep within his mind, Brascomb changed the thought. If he ever gained control, there would never be a "them." The companies would be his, and his alone. The bookkeeper tore his mind from such improbabilities and concentrated on his ledgers.

Matt Miller turned to Smith with amusement in his voice, but China also heard a deeper concern.

"Well, he about held his own, wouldn't you say, China?"

"Just about is all, Skipper."

Big Matt turned toward his desk, then hesitated, watching his son start the climb to the company's field office.

"I've told him to quit fighting those boys, but what's he to do? They come at him because of who he is, and it wouldn't do for him to turn down too many. Some day he will have to lead these same boys, and they will remember how he stood up or laid down when they were young."

Brascomb interjected. "They call him the Boss's Boy as if it were a pugilist's nickname. You should put a stop to that as well."

Neither Smith nor big Matt bothered to answer, and that soured in the soul of Brascomb Miller. They always did that, as if he hadn't even spoken.

Matt scrubbed at his thick mop of brown hair and thought about it. "Well, if we can't stop him fighting, the next best thing is that he do it right. God a'mighty, China, those two just swung at each other like they didn't have any brains at all. If anybody blocked or dodged a punch I didn't see it."

Smith chuckled. "That's the way boys fight, and if they don't learn better, that's how they'll hammer when they are men."

There was a certain grim satisfaction in Smith's next words that brought Matt Miller's head around.

"There's one thing different about those two though, Skipper, and I reckon you could see it clear enough. Both of 'em like it. Lumps and a little blood don't slow them, and little Matt was back up before his rump hardly hit the ground."

"You admire that, don't you, China?"

"Admire it? Don't know that it's quite like that, Skipper, but I respect it. When they're grown, those two won't be afraid to do whatever comes along, and that is a thing to look for in any man."

"You're hinting that little Matt will be fist fighting for years to come, aren't you?"

Smith was mildly surprised. "Well, that wasn't actually in my mind, but that is what'll be happening. As long as he's the boss's son and stays out with the men, others will try him for size."

"'The Boss's Boy.' What a hell of a name to hang on him."

Smith laughed aloud. "Nothing wrong with it, Captain. For a fist fighter the name has a certain balance. It will stick, as sure as I'm standing here. Like it or not, little Matt will get called Boss's Boy long after you and me are looking at the sky."

"He'll be the boss then, China."

"Won't make any difference. When fight talk or just plain remembering comes up, those men that were urging on him or McFee and their sons and their son's sons will call him by his fighting name. It's always been like that."

Big Matt sighed in resignation. "You are right, China, so that leaves only one sensible solution, doesn't it?"

Smith nodded immediate understanding. "I teach him so that he won't be taking unnecessary beatings from the likes of that McFee."

Brascomb muttered just loud enough for them to hear. "Of course, turn him into a better brawler."

Matt Miller considered his brother for a long moment, but spoke again to China Smith.

"We'll be leaving for Perry County in the morning, so you will be able to start right away. We will probably settle in Baskinsville or Petersburg near where the Susquehanna and the Juniata Rivers join, but I won't know for sure until we've looked things over.

"Little Matt won't have much to do until he goes back to school in the fall, so you can work hard with him—assuming that he takes to the teaching, of course."

Smith nodded acceptance. "He'll take to it. Just like I told you, he likes fighting. He isn't afraid, and he sort of glories in having it out with someone trying to put a lot of fists on him."

Smith's laugh was rueful. "You'll remember that I happen to know how that feels, Skipper."

Little Matt tried to know a lot about China Smith, but there were so many stories that he couldn't tell for sure which were real.

Smith had appeared nearly four years earlier. Big Matt had been at Brascomb's office in Philadelphia, and the two had connected like long separated brothers. Now China stood at Matt Miller's right hand, and if you saw one, you were likely to encounter the other.

Beyond personal appreciation and special understandings, China Smith was important for his wide knowledge and occasionally remarkable insights. In the city, China had advised his new friend to avoid investing in a Far Eastern shipping venture because, he said, that despite its bright paint and new sails, the vessel was rotten in the bottom and would be unlikely to survive the voyage. Miller had held off, and the ship had sprung a plank and foundered in Delaware Bay with its cargo spoiled and investments lost.

China Smith had been to China. It seemed sometimes, that he had been everywhere. Smith claimed only ten years at sea, but they had been adventurous years, and the Miller enterprises profited from his accumulated knowledge.

Smith had also been a successful prizefighter, and his bouts in little known ports on other continents had given him his nickname.

Smith was called China because of his delicate hands, not for his distant travels. China Smith had never lost to anyone at or near his weight, but China's hand bones were delicate, and he had suffered breaks and fractures in too many bouts. Table china dishes also broke easily, and so the nickname China-hands Smith had appeared but was quickly shortened to the more convenient China.

As a fist fighter, Smith had relied on skills discovered in foreign lands, and his fighting styles were virtually unknown among the American pugilists he had encountered. Because his hands broke so easily, Smith could not fight often, but when a purse was too large to refuse, China went in and while dazzling his opponent with movements others did not have, he carefully picked his shots and avoided bashing his tender fists on thick skulls and iron jaws.

In effect, China Smith wore his opponents out by pounding their bodies and by twisting face punches so that skin split letting blood flow into eyes, and broken noses and slashed lips made breathing laborious. Not until he had his man well softened did China throw the few brutal blows that knocked men unconscious.

Little Matt Miller looked on China Smith as a sort of older uncle who could be relied upon to know the best ways. Smith willingly imparted his knowledge and his humor but did not seek a close relationship with the boss's son. China Smith knew his place in the order of things, and big Matt Miller had already raised his new friend far above any expected social stature.

Experienced but uneducated men like Smith were usually destined to labor hard but progress little. Even in this new nation, life was rarely fair or easy. Some prospered, but most men struggled in the pits and shops eking out enough to survive but rarely forging far ahead.

Matt Miller placed China Smith at his side and saw that the former seaman, ship's carpenter, and professional boxer invested his few dollars wisely while living the style of a man of at least medium prosperity. Smith made his appreciation known, and Matt Miller grew to trust his companion in things both personal and business.

As expected, big Matt asked his son, "Did you win?"

"Not this time. The towpath foreman broke us up. I was fighting Mickey McFee, and he's tough. If I could have landed one or two more I'd have had him."

Big Matt nodded seriously, but the boy could not see China's approving nod. Every fighter worth watching believed if given just another few moments he would land the big one. That confidence and self-assurance went with being a battler.

Matt's father said, "I caught the end of it when you got thrown in the canal. Looked like you and McFee helped each other out."

Young Matt was a little embarrassed.

"Yeah, McFee is all right. He's learning to be a money fighter and thinks he's tough. I'll get him next time."

As soon as he said it, young Matt regretted his words. He'd been told to quit fighting, and here he was talking about the next time. He wished China Smith was standing where he could see him, but China often took a position behind whomever was facing big Matt. His father had explained that having someone from the other side just out of your sight made anybody uneasy and therefore gave him an advantage. That was particularly true if the someone was known to be dangerous.

Big Matt never told Smith where to stand, China just knew. Right now, little Matt understood exactly what his Pa had meant. If he could see China's expressions maybe he could tell how his words were going over.

Big Matt took another tack, which gave his son momentary relief.

"We'll be gone from here for many months and maybe we will never come back to this particular canal, but McFee's father is one of my best workers, so he will go where the crews go, and we will see them all again."

Big Matt scrubbed at his jaw in thought.

"So, you're likely right. You will run onto young McFee again, and he will probably want to take up where you two left off." Again the older man paused.

He raised an eyebrow in question. "You say he's learning to be a prize fighter?" At young Matt's nod he turned to China Smith.

"You heard anything about this, China?"

"I know that Klubber Cole is picking up a few coins and more than a few drinks teaching anybody interested the finer arts of self defense, as he sees them. McFee is probably with him."

Big Matt snorted. "Defense? I didn't know Klubber knew the word. Ten thousand fists must have bounced off his noggin before he quit."

China smiled, "Klubber did lean toward getting him afore he got you, but he does know what being in there is all about."

"So, that means that the next time you two square off Mickey McFee will have learned a lot more than he knows now." Little Matt nodded ruefully, and his father added, "And seeing that you barely held your own this time, he will undoubtedly knock your block off."

Little Matt wanted to bristle, but his Pa had it right, and the awareness did not sit well with him.

Big Matt let him stew for a long moment before he announced his solution.

"Well, I don't see any sense in letting some bog Irish kid whip up on one of us Millers. Do you, son?" Little Matt knew he didn't.

His father went on. "What we'll have to do is either ship you out to some distant place or get you trained so that McFee and others like him won't have an advantage.

"That means that China here will have to take you in hand and teach you how to fist fight. How's that sound to you, son?"

Little Matt could barely contain himself. Nothing could have suited him more. "I'd like that, Pa." He turned to China. "That is, if Mister Smith is willing to teach me how he does it."

China knew the answer big Matt wanted.

"I'll train you, boy. I'll teach you things these locals never dreamed of, but I'll only teach as long as you stay with it. You've got to go through hard work and some painful lessons to make progress that is real and lasting.

"I'm not interested in wasting my time showing someone how to hold their hands or move their feet. With me, you either learn all your brain can hold and all your body can rise to, or I'm not even starting."

The youth was enthusiastic. "I'll stay with it, Mister Smith. I'll work just as hard as you want, and I don't hurt all that easy."

Smith nodded approval. "I like hearing brave words, and I figure you mean them—right now. Question will be, how much heart you'll show when the going gets real tough and pains like you've never felt before arrive real often."

Smith turned to big Matt. "You think he's up to it, Skipper? I'm not interested in wasting both our time."

The Skipper looked to his son. "If you say you will see it through, I'll believe you, but, Matt, I'll be highly disappointed if you let me down on this.

"China is right. We all have better things to do, but as much as I'd like to see you prepared to stand your ground against the river rats and wood choppers we hire, you have to admit that you haven't worked at your studies in school. I'm therefore inclined to ask why this education will be any different from book learning?"

Little Matt hated the comparison. Couldn't everybody see the difference? In school you sat on your behind and tried to be interested in what somebody long dead said about something. In fight training you would be moving and working with your muscles and your mind at things that would keep a slugger like McFee from lumping your skull.

All he could say was, "It would be a lot different to me, Pa, and I won't let you down. I want to learn what Mister Smith has to show me, and I will stick with it no matter if it does hurt."

What could hurt, after all? Some punches along the head or in the gut? They would be worth anything he might get better at like faking or dodging punches. He had never seen China Smith fight, but big Matt had said it was beautiful to behold.

Little Matt Miller thought some about being beautiful in a real fight. He could see himself sliding like he was on ice, left and right hands working so much faster than the other guy that he'd hardly get hit at all. He was anxious to get started, and he hoped China would begin teaching him even before they got to wherever it was they were going.

3

They sat around their evening fire while hired men worked at camp chores. Big Matt was backed against a wagon wheel, willing to listen in because with encroaching dark he could no longer study the paper piles he had brought along.

China Smith said, "Your fight training will begin with conversation. I will talk and you will listen."

China Smith was not physically intimidating. He had no real size to him. He stood average height and was said to weigh about one hundred and sixty pounds. Big Matt claimed the best fighters to watch were close to that weight because they could hit hard like bigger men but were lightning quick like the flyweight battlers. Big Matt also pointed out that China's ordinary size had lured many a gambler to bet against him, which allowed unusual profits when Smith pounded out the tougher looking opponent.

Smith's features showed the wear of many conflicts. There was scar tissue above his eyes, and his nose was wide and crooked from being repeatedly broken. Cheekbones were prominent, as though calluses had packed beneath his skin. China's ears were flattened, and one sagged slightly from having been nearly torn from his head and crudely doctored by tightly wrapping the injured member within a rag around his skull until reattachment was well along.

It was China's hands that caught the eye. His fingers were crooked, and the joints were huge and distorted, but they had healed so that their owner could still make tight fists. Smith had explained that when he broke a hand he folded it into a fighting fist and wrapped it tightly. Unless he fought, he did not use the broken hand for six weeks.

Smith laughed that when both hands were broken at once he wasn't worth a dead rat to his shipmates, but they covered for him because when he fought, he stood for them and their vessel, and their bets on China Smith always paid off.

The backs of China's hands were worse looking than his fingers. Those hand bones that he enjoyed describing as metacarpals, rolling the word as if savoring its sounds, had healed poorly too many times, and they jutted at odd angles, some clearly overlapping their broken ends.

China was want to flex his seemingly destroyed fingers and hands, marveling that they opened more or less fully, and remarking with undisguised awe that his hands never hurt even a little. He would wonder how that could be possible but swore it was so. Young Matt Miller looked at the fighter's hands and hated the thought that his might someday suffer similar batterings.

China said, "Fist fighting is a dirty business. Respectable folks will have nothing to do with it, and a fighter gets marked so that there is no denying what he has been."

Smith pointed to his own battered features.

"If you fight enough, you will gather in all of the gashes and lumps you see on me. My hair covers dozens of scars, and look at my lips."

Matt looked closely, and he could see the healed over splits that thickened and twisted both upper and lower lips.

The old fighter pointed to young Matt's swollen and discolored split lip. "You've already collected your first marking, boy, and you will get them regularly if you follow the fight game. This time you were lucky, and the cut is inside your mouth, but others will come, and if you care about how you look you will do two things. First, you will not fight when you don't have to."

Smith stopped and almost glared at his student. "I don't care how good it feels, young Matt. I don't care how exciting it can be or how strong and powerful you feel if you put someone down. I know those feelings, and they are dangerous to play with. What I am saying is, don't fight if you don't have to. Is that clear?

"The second point is that you must listen very very closely to what I am telling you and what I am going to teach you. You've got to go past understanding all that I say until you can actually feel the things I am talking about.

"Now, that will take time, but it will come if you work at it. If I had known what I am going to tell you during my early years I would not be wearing most of these scars. My jaw would not have been broken twice, my teeth would not be splintered and broken off, and I would not have busted one half as many ribs."

Big Matt said, "He's not been thinking about being a professional fighter, have you, Matt? I just want you to be able to handle yourself when fights do come."

China gave his student no time to respond.

"It's all of one piece, Captain. Little Matt already has a fighting name and at least a small reputation for being willing. You do not have to be fighting for money. A man's face can get torn apart in a single bout. You know that, Skipper."

They sat for a while staring into the flames, each weighing his thoughts. Finally, China was ready to continue.

"Serious fist fighting, and that means anything more than boyhood squabbles like you've been doing up until now, demands as much thinking as it does punching. Having both fighters plant their boots and swing until one drops is exciting to watch, and that is exactly the way most men fight."

Big Matt snorted in disgust. "Most of those fights beat more air than faces, China, and most of the time both brawlers get exhausted and stand there panting and trying to get enough strength to throw another punch."

Smith chuckled. "True, and most of them are drunkards who won't remember what they were battling about come morning, but we've all seen the result of even those stumble-bum squabbles. Men get slashed-open eyebrows and split lips—like little Matt is wearing. If the men are big enough, noses get flattened almost every time, and it seems like big men fight a lot more than physically smaller men."

Smith chose to look across the fire at little Matt. "You've no doubt heard people say that a good big man can lick a good little man every time?"

The student nodded assent. The statement was often made in arguments about who would lick who.

"Well, take it to heart because it is true." Smith again studied his student. "My guess is that you may not be as tall as your father, young Matt. That means that you will be fighting men larger than yourself as often as you battle opponents your own size."

Smith smiled coldly. "There will also be a few feisty small men who simply cannot believe that their stature won't let them evenly compete in fist fights.

"Watch out for those kind. They have to be almost killed before they will quit, and just as likely they will be at it again with someone else as soon as they recover. Small people sometimes substitute attitude for size, and in fights they can be very hard and determined."

There was a pause while kindling was added to their fire.

Smith continued, "The point to remember is the word 'good.' Few fist fighters are good. Many are willing or even anxious, but good? Not many.

"What we will be trying to do is make you a good fighter, little Matt. That means being able to think while you fight and know what to do when you think about it.

"Then, of course, there is the matter of being able to accomplish what you have discovered."

China smiled as much to himself as to his audience. "I guess that is only gibberish at this point so here is an example. Suppose you pound at your man's head, and he covers up with his hands high along his face—sort of like he was peeking between his fists. Well, if you saw that and were clear-headed enough to think about it, you might decide to hit him in his belly because with his hands high his gut should be open."

Little Matt could see the sense of that.

China said, "On the other hand, might not your man be expecting that or maybe even hoping for it, and when you dropped a fist to come in low he might smash his knuckles straight into your face?"

Smith gave them a short moment to consider how that could go. "So, suppose instead of trying to punch in under or between his elbows you took a step to the right and drove a hard punch into his kidney, and when he turned and bent to cover, you came across the top with a whistling left hook smack into the side of his jaw?"

He watched little Matt's eyes judging his ability to follow the punches. "Some call that combination punching, young Matt. What they mean is a series of pre-planned punches that have been practiced and drilled at so long they are as automatic as breathing. When the fighter senses a hole, off goes a combination without hesitation, and if he has figured right, down will go his man. Maybe to stay, but at least stung and probably hurt."

The Boss's Boy liked what he was hearing, and he went to his blankets with his mind weighing combinations he could work up and have ready next time someone came at him.

Young Matt Miller knew that this was going to be the best summer ever. He loved summer as much as he despised the winter months when he huddled over his books with the professors ready and willing to lay their hickory switches across his shoulders.

His father had promised that he would have to endure school only until he was sixteen, so he had one more winter to go. He wondered idly if he might not later return to the school to use his soon to be acquired fighting skills on the unfeeling teachers who hardly let him even look up from his studying.

This summer he would learn to be a fighter. Maybe not as great as China Smith, but he should be able to give that Mickey McFee the drubbing he deserved.

Little Matt sometimes wished he and McFee could be more friendly. They had worked side by side on occasion when big Matt had his son in the clay pits or behind a team learning how it was to labor with your back instead of your head.

McFee was interesting to be around. He smoked, like most Irish boys did, but he swore that after this summer he was giving up hard liquor forever because he acted foolish when he had been drinking. Matt asked him why he was waiting until after the summer, and McFee had claimed that he didn't want grown men thinking he believed himself better than they were, but once he was about through his sixteenth year he would be looked on as a man by everybody, and he could do whatever he wanted.

McFee had nudged Matt suggestively and hinted that in pretty girls' minds he already was as much of a man as anyone around. That impressed little Matt more than anything else Mickey McFee had said. Girls were of increasing interest, and he knew next to nothing about what they thought or expected.

Then, just two days past, up the towpath had come McFee all huffed and puffed looking for a fight. Everybody knew the Irish liked to fight, and once in a while, little Matt admitted that he didn't mind it too much either. Thunder! He wished he had licked McFee properly once and for all and could forget it.

Now, here they were off to the west, and he would not get another crack at McFee until the fall, and maybe not then if they didn't happen to come across each other. Matt mused that if they clashed he would have to watch McFee closely because of Klubber Cole's training. He planned to keep that in mind, and it would make him work harder at whatever China Smith had for him.

Big Matt Miller was going west to examine new business possibilities. The Pennsylvania Canal Commission might (or might not) be planning to extend the canal system west even over the Allegheny Mountains to Pittsburgh.

The venture seemed barely possible. If completed, it would be a tremendous engineering feat and vast sums of money would change hands during and following the effort.

If a canal system could be opened from Pittsburgh in the west all the way to Philadelphia in the east, much of the trade now flowing down the Ohio and Mississippi Rivers to New Orleans could be diverted to Pennsylvania ports and the Commonwealth would be tied together—almost as if the mountains did not exist.

Big Matt had explained that the Millers' interest would not necessarily be in digging canals but more in the opportunities opened by construction.

Big Matt claimed that logging and milling lumber would be extensive. Clay for lining the canals would be in demand. If large deposits could be found and purchased, that trade would prosper.

Land for the rights of way would be bought and sold, and water rights might offer interesting accommodations as threats to dams or diverting streams and rivulets along the canal routes appeared.

Herds of horses, mules, and oxen would be needed. Forage, harness, and blacksmithing would be required. Buildings would go up, boats would be built, and wagons would truck odd tonnage everywhere.

Those smaller less spectacular businesses had been the meat and potatoes of the Millers' successes. Matt Miller moved ahead, found the opportunities and started things moving. On occasion, Brascomb Miller came out, set up his desks, and kept the ventures profitable, but mostly he stayed in Philadelphia overseeing city contracts.

At Matt Miller's insistence, the Millers tried to hire the same crews as they moved along. As a canal or turnpike section was completed, Miller operations closed shop, and some of those already employed were moved on to big Matt's latest ventures.

Brascomb Miller did not approve because new men could be hired at cheaper rates, and common laborers were available everywhere. Brascomb claimed that, with minor exceptions, all men could be made to work hard, and there was nothing to choose between Matt's favored workers and cheaper labor anxious and waiting to be employed.

Big Matt's answer was that loyal men deserved reward by re-employment and that he grew to understand his men. They, in turn, learned his likes and dislikes and therefore produced more and better work.

Brascomb snorted and pointed to bottom lines. Cheap labor saved money, he argued, but Matt held the reins, and the Miller labor force moved as big Matt led. Little Matt was very likely to again see Mickey McFee.

Vast canal surveys were being undertaken, and Commonwealth money was being acquired for mighty engineering attempts. Still, no one knew for sure which canal routes would be approved or when more construction might begin.

Big Matt Miller had studied his maps and concluded that unless the canals swung down into Virginia to avoid some higher mountains—which was ludicrous to even consider, as that would open Baltimore or even Washington as competing ports, the canals would have to pass the joining of the mighty Susquehanna and the lesser Juniata Rivers.

That was Perry County—the sparkling new Perry County, barely six years old and, the Skipper suspected, flowing with unrecognized opportunity.

The key spots would lie near the rivers' junction. Matt Miller decided to arrive early and see what could be seen. He expected he would find business or investment. Some ventures might be highly speculative with profits far down the road, but he came cash in hand. In a land constantly money short, that would be hard to ignore.

Big Matt thought a little about his son—the Boss's Boy. What a nickname. Leave it to the Scot Presbyterians (or maybe the Irish Catholics) to hang something like that around a youth's neck. It would stick. China was right about that, and Matt would have to live with it until he grew and became his own man.

Not for the first time, big Matt thought about that time, now only a handful of years away. Young Matt would grow, and he would be worked into the businesses. At first, he would lead small crews. From them, he would gain experience and hopefully wisdom. His leadership, if he had any, would be tested, and big Matt and China Smith would watch and judge his progress. Somewhere, far down the line, when both he and China grew ancient, young Matt would take control.

Big Matt smiled openly at that distant imagining. He hoped his brother had retired before then because Brascomb Miller lacked the necessary humility or sense of place to make that transition. Brascomb would be unable to take orders from the Boss's Boy.

These days, Brascomb was often in Matt Miller's thoughts. The brother managed the accounts and did them well. Money was there when needed, men got paid on the dot, and the books balanced as far as Matt could tell. No one else got a look at them, of course, because how well the Miller companies did or did not do was no one else's business.

Still, Brascomb had stealthy ways about him. He had always been secretive with schemes brewing and unannounced sidelines that he hoped would turn personally profitable.

Brascomb's envy of his older brother had been clear since they were boys working for their father, but everyone, except Brascomb, had recognized that Matt had the ingenuity and the intuitive business insights that made money and moved the Millers ahead. Brascomb would be a company man, and he would be well rewarded because he was family, but he would never lead. Not in Matt's lifetime and never during young Matt's tenure.

Big Matt sensed Brascomb's hunger to be boss, but he was used to it. China's seldom mentioned but detectable distrust of Brascomb's intentions encouraged big Matt's closer consideration of his brother.

Despite his willingness to accept calculated business risks, Matt Miller kept his personal house in order. His paperwork was up to date, and he looked ahead—even to the time when he would no longer be in charge. Unexpected things happened. Accidents occurred. Men got kicked silly by horses or knocked off canal boats. Matt kept China Smith, his strong right arm, informed of how he wanted things to be—just in case. A man could never know what the future held, but he could prepare.

Little Matt had made his expectation known. He ached to finish at the academy and hungered to get into the field to do real work and to earn big money, like the Irish workers got.

His father knew better. Once little Matt's fists gripped a shovel or a pick for six days a week and when he was paid the seventy cents a day workmen received, the Boss's Boy would quickly lose marvelous expectations. Big Matt would let him discover those hard facts of life. Only then would he begin moving his son into small bossing jobs.

Leading his workmen would teach the boy more in a month than he would learn in a year elsewhere. The Irishmen were always up to something. They tested a foreman's determination, they challenged his knowledge, and they always questioned his abilities to stand man to man beside them in their rough and ready lives both on the job and within their social circles.

The prickly Scotch-Irish and the real Irish (Big Matt had given up deciding who was what and thought of them all as Irishmen) demanded loyalty before they gave their own, and the Boss's Boy would have to prove himself to gain the trust and respect he would need.

The more stolid German workers that comprised some recently hired work crews followed orders more comfortably, but they, too, responded to a foreman's recognition of their worth.

Most businessmen ignored all of that. To them, their workers were almost faceless and certainly nameless drudges who heaved and tugged and sweat and sometimes bled for the reluctantly paid pittances that kept them alive and able to labor on.

Brascomb Miller was that type, but big Matt knew his workers, and he believed they knew him. He trusted them where others did not, and he believed that, in return, they gave him more honest work and more willing efforts.

Lately, some of the Miller workers were being called Miller Men because they had worked for the same boss on many jobs. Big Matt liked that, and he suspected his Irishmen enjoyed the distinction. It was obvious that they appreciated the security of being rehired for Miller jobs rather than again being thrown into the overcrowded labor pool and simply hoping that some foreman would pick them out for some kind of work somewhere—for whatever wage was being offered.

Studying his fifteen-year-old son, big Matt often wondered how little Matt would measure up. China believed that, in time, he would stand tall. So did the father, but not yet. Not until the professors finished with him and maybe another year with Brascomb on the bookkeeping.

The Skipper's smile turned grim. If the Boss's Boy survived Brascomb's winter of misery, he should make easy work of running a work crew on any job.

4

1829

On this, his third summer trip to the western office, young Matt Miller liked what he saw. It seemed as if all of the Millers' planning and constructions were coming together.

Big Matt Miller was putting down roots. The boss saw opportunity all around him. He believed that the canal developments would lift rural towns into special affluences from which he could prosper.

Canal building was well underway, and the older Miller had been right in believing their routes would pass and perhaps meet at the Juniata River and Susquehanna's blending. The planning was completed and the Miller companies already had men employed.

Because of the new canals, the world of young Matt Miller was changing at an astonishing rate. Returning from Philadelphia, he had been transported by a horse-drawn railway to Columbia on the Susquehanna. There he had transferred to a boat, and via a combination of canals and the river, he had floated past the growing city of Harrisburg, on up the river, and then across the Susquehanna at Clark's Ferry to the Juniata joining at the tip of Duncan's Island.

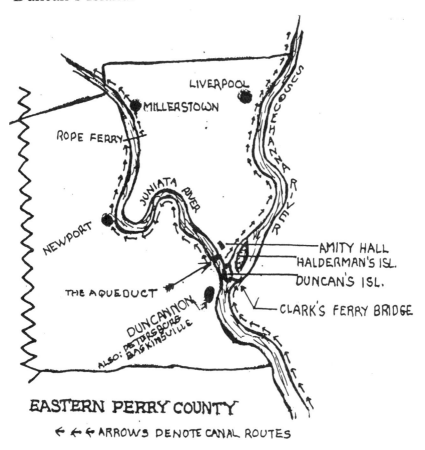

EASTERN PERRY COUNTY

← ← ← ARROWS DENOTE CANAL ROUTES

The journey had seemed long, but if compared to the bruising road travel, the horse-railroad and the boats were luxurious and allowed time and comfort to consider all that was being passed.

Riverbank changes, with isolated cabins transforming almost overnight into named towns, were astonishing enough, but the increasing size of opened fields with growing crops was more amazing.

Two years before, most farms produced barely enough to feed those living on them. Now there were cash crops to be sold at market. Matt suspected the farms along the river could feed Philadelphia—if the produce could be efficiently moved to markets.

That, of course, was what the new canals were doing. Harvested crops and salable goods were loaded onto barges that were towed to the railhead at Columbia. The loads were transferred to the railroad's horse-drawn iron-wheeled wagons that pulled them directly into the heart of the city.

Not much continued downriver to Baltimore, the way it once had. Young Matt could see the canal system as a wise, if expensive, investment by the Commonwealth of Pennsylvania.

A mile to the south of the rivers' junction lay the small villages of Baskinsville and Petersburg. There, too, was his father's new headquarters.

Little Juniata Creek separated the communities with Baskinsville to the north and Petersburg to the south. Both villages were growing, and residents were blending the towns under the Petersburg name.

Water Street in the upper town, which big Matt claimed was too low and too close to the river, appeared to be sprouting buildings.

Front Street, the next road up the hill had become the main thoroughfare, and a higher-on-the-hill third road, although little more than a path, was being called High Street.

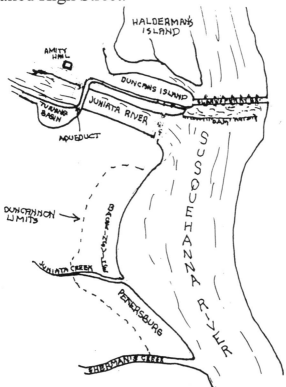

A local carter had met Matt's packet boat at the Juniata Ferry and transported him along a barely smoothed road nearly a mile to the beginnings of Petersburg.

The cart driver was a loquacious man, eager to talk, who knew about bare fist fighting. He spoke about it as if certain of his passenger's interest. Matt was not surprised. His summer training with China Smith had always been of interest to local men, and although uninvited, those with time to spare were want to drop by to watch and comment on the training.

Still, his training was just exercise. The Boss's Boy had fought no one, except a few untrained young men who simply wanted to fight—as young men sometimes did.

Matt had flattened his little-skilled opponents without difficulty, but those had not been the formal bouts that the driver preferred discussing.

The carter observed that some real fighters were developing along the rivers, and, in fact, someone like Mickey McFee, the Irish Hurricane who was taking on all comers, was a fist fighter to watch. Klubber Cole, the man said, believed McFee could be a champion.

Matt asked, and the man answered that China Smith had not expressed an opinion on Mickey McFee's potential, but many wished that Smith would come out of retirement and allow them to judge how McFee would handle himself against the once great fighter.

Matt smiled inwardly at that desire. If Mickey McFee could raise enough money, China would give him a bare fisted lesson that would end any speculations that he had big time potential.

Then Matt wondered if the time might be right for him to take up where he and McFee had left off four years before. Maybe he should whip McFee until the so-called professional knew who really was tough and who was not.

Matt judged that was idle imagining. Too many years had passed, and they were not young boys. A fight now would be brutal and damaging. Big Matt would never allow it, and Matt knew his father would be right. He was now part of the company, and fighting with a workman just for the hell of it was not the way to act.

Still? If McFee got too challenging or maybe a bit disrespectful . . . ?

The carter had dropped Matt and his traveling baggage short of the village square, and he had labored uphill to his father's new building on High Street. The door was open, but no one was waiting his arrival.

Matt supposed both his father and China were living at the new hotel on the square and might be there, but the log building that had been their office and sleeping quarters stood behind the new headquarters, and Matt dropped his bags at the foot of the cot he had always used.

In the office, papers lay openly on the two desks, so Matt expected that someone had merely stepped away and would shortly reappear.

That would be soon, he hoped. He was hungry but unsure of what eating arrangements big Matt would have made. Probably, they would still dine at Mrs. Black's restaurant less than a block away. Matt hoped so; the widow Black offered an excellent table. Mrs. Black cooked in an outside shelter, and the inside dining room boasted windows that were opened to help remove summer heat. A large cast iron stove that Matt had never seen working promised warmth and comfort during the bitter Pennsylvania winters.

Matt stepped onto the headquarters' narrow porch to study the handsome view of river and the burgeoning bustle of the town. Considering the new and permanent office building, Matt judged that his father's interests in the area had not diminished. He also suspected that the eastern operations would be left evermore often to Brascomb Miller.

The eastern Miller businesses were more settled, more staid, without the bustle and profit-risking of the western ventures. Brascomb far preferred that more predictable atmosphere and viewed his older brother's entrepreneurial western excursions as risky and more than a little demeaning to his vision of the dignity appropriate to Miller enterprises.

After completing his schooling, young Matt Miller's required winter with his uncle and the company accounts had been stretched into a second winter. Both seasons had provided endless sufferings amid paper and ink within the cavernous warehouse Brascomb preferred as an office.

The second winter of misery had resulted because of big Matt's dissatisfaction with his son's accumulated knowledge. The father decided that his boy had wasted the winter instead of learning, so he was returned to Brascomb's ministrations until he absorbed what a Miller had to know.

The Boss's Boy did not repeat his mistake. He buckled down and forced the book learning into his mind as hard as he could pack it. By May, Brascomb Miller had tired of young Matt's pointed correcting of insignificant minutia in his bookkeeping and had shipped the young man back to his father.

This summer had begun auspiciously, and Matt had been sent east with money in his pocket and directions to discover all that he could about the suddenly developing but little understood steam railroads.

Matt's travels had taken him to the coalfields between the Schuylkill and the Susquehanna Rivers. He had examined the massive stationary steam engines being used to move coal, and he had seen similar engines put on wheels to haul railcar loads longer distances. He believed he understood almost everything about the transporting of coal that big Matt would want to know. Now he was back, ready to tell what he had learned . . . and darned if that wasn't Mickey McFee and other men marching toward him along High Street.

Mickey McFee! The man showed up everywhere. Well, Matt shrugged the muscles of his shoulders, McFee had better watch his smart Irish mouth—and it wouldn't be a draw like the last time.

If McFee was looking for a fight, and unless he had changed he would be, the Boss's Boy would help him swallow some teeth.

The men came on, marching home from a day's labor, Matt assumed. As he watched, a slender, better-dressed man came uphill, probably from the hotel, and joined the group. Matt recognized him as the company's western clerk and bookkeeper.

There was distant talk and head bobbing among the workers, and Matt was pleased to see that the bookish clerk was accepted and included. There had been talk that a delicate man like the clerk might be resented and unmercifully taunted, but it appeared that the studious young man had found his place.

Matt sought the clerk's name and finally came up with it—Lukey Bates. Bates had attended a new academy in Bloomfield and could do bookkeeping. The Boss's Boy was pleased to find him still employed, as he greatly feared such tasks would otherwise fall upon his shoulders.

John McFee said, "That's young Matt up there on the porch."

Mickey said, "I see him, Pa."

"I know you saw him, Mickey. You all of a sudden began rolling your shoulders and tucking your chin against your chest." The father looked closer at his son. "Now you're sticking your chin out as if you were daring somebody to take a punch at it."

"I'm just letting him know that I'm ready any time he is, Pa. He hasn't been doing all of that box training with China just for show. One of these days he'll come at me." Mickey grinned, "And I can't hardly wait, Pa. I've been planning to paste him good since we were little kids."

John McFee frowned at his pugnacious son. "I've heard you speak well of young Matt, boy. Now you are practically picking a fight with him."

Mickey sounded a little confused. "Oh, Matt's all right, Pa, but he thinks he can lick me. I'm just ready to straighten him out a little."

One of the men said, "You could whip him one-handed, Mickey."

"Who'd he ever fight?" another chimed in agreement.

John McFee brought the group to a halt. He included everybody but directed his words to his son.

"Now, you look here, Mickey. Young Matt is our boss. We are Miller Men, and you keep that in mind. The Boss's Boy don't own the company, but he will some day. Young Matt is your boss, and that is how you will address him. There'll be no smirking or strutting, Mickey. You are not children anymore, and if Big Matt found you pounding on his son he would send you down the road, and you know what that would mean."

Mickey McFee knew. He would be hanging around the edges, trying to pick up work anywhere he could get it. There would be no Saturday night dollars placed in his hand, and he would most likely not be allowed to stay in the rooms that the family rented from the Miller companies.

Work of any kind was hard to come by, and strong and willing workers often got paid with chickens, slabs of hog meat, or quarts of some kind of grain because there was just not enough money to go around. His irregular boxing matches could not provide serious income. A man needed a regular job that paid every week—especially during the winter when work slowed.

With John and Mickey fully employed by big Matt Miller at seventy cents a day each, six days a week, and only ten or twelve hours a day—usually, the McFees were doing better than most. Mickey's mother and sister kept their house and added to the family income by sewing and patching clothing, but if either Mickey or his father lost their jobs, living would change from decent to very tight. Being a Miller Man meant reasonably steady employment, and any worker would be a fool to let it slip away.

John started them forward again, but he said, "When you speak to Young Matt, you address him as Boss or Mister Miller. Do you understand that, Mickey?"

"I can do that, Pa, but if he wants a fight, I'm the guy he will call out."

"I doubt he will do any calling out, son. Young Matt is an educated young man on his way to being boss of big companies."

The father smiled a little. "I expect he's heard more than a little about The Irish Hurricane, and I expect he'll be hesitant about trying his luck."

Mickey said, "If he's as smart as you think he is, Pa, the Boss's Boy will be real careful about raising his mitts to a professional like me."

A companion was certain. "You could hammer him without working up a sweat, Mickey."

Men chimed in to agree with the speaker, and John again warned them. "You'd best all forget the fight talk, or you're likely to say something that could be taken wrong and be looking for work."

McFee added sincerity. "I could imagine big Matt putting a few of you to work with the Germans over on Sherman's creek."

A man muttered, "I ain't workin' with no Germans."

The senior McFee was unsympathetic. "Oh you'd work with Germans or beside those African slaves that come through now and then, O'Leary. If you get laid off, your wife and those stair-step kids you've got will get hungry mighty quick."

O'Leary spoke softly because they were nearing the headquarters building. "You've made powerful points, John, but the biggest you ain't mentioned. The fact is that, if I ever got let-go because of my own doin', my Maggie would beat me with our ax handle all the way down to Harrisburg—and then back again to make sure I got the message."

There were understanding chuckles from his companions who were turning their attentions to young Matt Miller looking down on them from his two-step high wooden porch.

John McFee tipped his ragged cap and said, "Glad to see you back, Mister Miller."

Matt said, "It's good to be back, Mister McFee."

The Boss's Boy sounded respectful of the older man, and the workers noted it.

Matt turned his eyes to the younger McFee, and Mickey thought a slight smile touched the corner of the Boss's Boy's mouth. Challenging? McFee could not be sure.

Matt said only, "Mickey?" But there was questioning in the word. Challenging? McFee could not tell.

His father's warning fresh in his mind, Mickey said, "Boss," and added a big Irish grin that could be seen as pleasure or . . . about anything anyone chose to read into it.

The other men touched their caps, and the group moved on. Mickey McFee felt the Boss's Boy's eyes on his back, and he could not resist hunching his shoulders and throwing a few quick and short hooks at an imaginary opponent.

O'Leary said, "We'll miss you around here, Mickey."

Fearing he might actually have gone too far, Mickey said, "Aw, I didn't mean anything, and young Matt'll know it."

His father said, "You're on your own when you meddle with the powerful people, Mickey. The Boss's Boy never did take any foolishness from you, and I doubt he will now. Maybe you will have to learn the hard way, and don't expect any of us to try bailing you out if big Matt shows you the road."

Mickey McFee snorted at the improbability of being canned—for nothing, after all, but inwardly he cringed and resolved to keep his mouth closed and his hands open and at his sides—assuming he still had a job to worry about.

Damn, throwing those air-hooks had been dumb, but . . . if he got away with it this time, he would not falter again. God, why did he do such stupid things, anyway?

Young Matt Miller watched the workers move by. He saw Mickey McFee's swagger and judged the competence of the swift and hard thrown hooks.

The Boss's Boy found himself grinning. The cocky Irishman had not changed, and he had not forgotten. Matt found his own fists bunched and tapping together at his waist. Maybe . . . but Lukey Bates had stepped up onto the porch, and Matt got his mind back on what was important.

5

Big Matt and China Smith sat across the desk, and Lukey Bates pulled a high stool close so that he could see little Matt's sketches without stretching. The Boss's Boy found the arrangement interesting. He was used to facing off opposite China and his father, but Bates was new to the conferences.

Lukey had placed his stool so that he peered over little Matt's shoulder—so that he could read right side up, or did the clerk see himself as a Boss's Boy supporter?

Matt inwardly smiled at his measuring and evaluating. He had picked up the habit from his too many months with Brascomb Miller who saw everything as him or them. Still, if not carried too far, judging and evaluating was important to a man of business—which Matt intended to be.

Big Matt had sat them down and said, "So tell me about the steam engines, Matt."

Young Matt began with the mining of coal itself because, unless that was understood, the locomotive engines would not be appreciated. He quickly sketched river routes, a few villages, and the coal mining areas.

"They dig coal two ways, Pa. If the coal is near the surface, they scrape away the worthless dirt or rock and break the coal loose by blasting or simply pick and shovel work. If the coal veins are deep, they tunnel, leaving the surface untouched.

"Next, they move the coal to a crusher and grading mill that smashes big coal into smaller lumps and filters all of the coal through wood and metal screens so that they end up with different size piles. Some coal is best for big furnaces and other sizes are more suitable for use in ordinary stoves.

"Before coal is shipped, it is washed using big leather hoses that dump stream water stored behind earth and wood dams. A lot of slate passes through the graders, and gangs of boys are hired to toss out what is not wanted. Coal is sold by the ton, and buyers do not like paying for a lot of dirt that won't burn."

Matt paused to gather his thoughts, and his father said, "We see the result of that washing every time we look at the river. The mines wash the coal, and all of the filth, including a million tons of coal grit, floats down the creeks and finally into the Susquehanna. I expect you noticed on your way here."

Matt had noticed. In places, the river was almost black, and there were bars of sand-sized coal appearing here and there.

China put in. "Wait till you see the coal shallows filling up just north of here. The bottom over near Liverpool is rough stone. The coal hits, slides off and settles. The river is black with it."

Matt was awed. "My lordy, those mines are a hundred miles away. It must be really foul above Shamokin and . . ." A thought came to him.

"Pa, is that coal worth anything? It ought to be easy digging, if it will burn, and all."

Big Matt and China exchanged glances with raised eyebrows.

The boss said, "Now that is something to consider, Matt, and I'm surprised that we hadn't even thought about it."

He scratched his clean-shaven jaw thoughtfully, and China Smith asked, "You notice any coal bars forming south of here, Matt?"

"More than a few, China, but I didn't think about them, except to notice how dirty the river had become."

China's disgust showed. "Yeah, fish are dying, and you don't jump in the Susquehanna to get clean anymore."

The older Miller was more interested in the value of the river's coal, but his words seemed to veer from the subject.

"Did you know that there is iron in the ground just a little way up the Juniata, Matt?"

Iron was news. "Are there mines, Pa? Are they dumping into the Juniata?"

"No, no mines yet, but there might be. There are a number of simple furnaces starting up that are able to get pig iron from the ore, so probably. . .?" Big Matt let the thought run.

The Boss's Boy returned to his story telling. "The mines are using their own coal to run their steam engines. The coal crushers and the graders are all steam powered, and they're claiming that stationary engines on wheels can haul loads that horses can't manage."

Dead serious, Matt added, "They point out that an engine doesn't eat when it isn't working, and although engineers and mechanics have to be hired, they need only a few of them, and all of the wranglers, the animals, their feed and their farriers are gone for good.

"The way I understand it is that they get a fire started under a boiler by using wood. When the flames get hot, they dump on coal and it catches. They claim the coal burns really hot and lasts a long time.

"Compared to wood, coal doesn't take much storage space either, and it can sit out in the weather—which isn't good for wood at all. Most of the trees are gone for miles around the mines, anyway—used for shoring up mine tunnels, mostly. By using coal, most firewood chopping and hauling is eliminated."

Matt paused to shake his head. "Those coal regions are really ugly, Pa. Everything is destroyed and dug up. I doubt anything will ever grow up there again.

"Anyway, once you have steam coming out of the boiler, you pipe it to whatever you want to turn. On some engines, the steam enters against a piston that gets pushed to its end. A valve opens when the piston strikes it, and the steam enters from the other end and pushes the piston back. On other engines, the piston is pushed by the steam but gets moved back by the weight of a huge fly wheel that keeps things moving until the piston shoves again. They even have engines that have more than one piston, and they have tremendous power.

"Hook wheels or some kind of gears to the revolving piston shaft and you can move heavy things including the engines, or so they claim. The rolling engines I saw didn't work all that well, but those engine-men believe in what they are doing, and the bigger mines are turning from horses and waterpower to steam.

"Most of the engines on wheels that move coal have been fired by wood, but everyone up there believes that coal is coming on strong. One of the foremen loading along the Schuylkill River told me that there were a hundred barges shipping coal to Philadelphia, and a canal, and maybe a railroad, were being opened so that coal could be sent cross country to New York.

"The same foreman said that big ships were carrying coal from the Pennsylvania fields to cities down south. It turned out that Uncle Brascomb already knew about it. He said the Feather Company had everything sewed up, and there was no room in the coal shipping business for a small company like ours."

The older Miller pondered, "A hundred barges? Did you see any of them, Matt?"

"Well, I didn't see most of them, but there are coal barges running up and down both the Schuylkill and the Delaware."

China Smith said, "Baltimore would love to have a steady coal source. Once the Susquehanna canal is in, we'll get some of that trade from the mines. Until then, the river is too shallow with too many rocks for most of the year. All we'll get for now is the filthy runoff."

"You are a believer in the future of coal, China?"

"I know something about it, Captain. There is coal in Cathay, and they use it for metal working. England has been using coal for heating buildings since long before I went to sea. I expect coal-burning engines on wheels will develop and be useful before too long. If they've got some working now, a few years will see better ones, and even better after that. Yep, coal will get important."

Matt had an offering. "Some coal is being moved on that railroad from Philadelphia to Columbia and then down the river to Baltimore and even to Annapolis. There are two engines that will run on rails coming in from England. They burn wood and maybe coal and are going to be tested on the Columbia railroad in place of the horses."

Miller said. "We'll talk more about coal, but I will add that China and I have been looking into the possibility of opening an iron furnace along one of our local creeks where we would have waterpower to turn bellows. Most furnaces melt ore using charcoal, but maybe coal will be a cheaper answer. We'll look into it more later."

China said, "I don't see how enough iron can be made to use railroads all over the country—whether horse-drawn or steam pulled. And, how can a whole bunch of furnaces make rails that will be so much alike that they will all fit together, and . . .?"

China shook his head doubtfully. "Railroads will likely stay local." He shook his head again. "I can't imagine what it would cost to put in railroads through this mountain country."

Matt said, "A man told me that the railroad engines can't pull uphill because their wheels skid on the smooth rails, but another claimed that eventually railroads will win out over canals because a railroad will be able to run all winter."

Smith was skeptical. "A steam engine that can't run uphill will be able to hold onto rails frozen with ice and maybe buried in snow? Something is not right there, little Matt."

With just a slight trepidation, little Matt chose to change the subject. "I noticed a lot of logs floating down the river, Pa."

"Yep, they come by all the time. Men out fishing have to watch out for the floaters, and almost every day logs get stuck behind the dam just below the Clark's Ferry bridge and have to be cleared away before they make too big a tangle."

China picked up the story. "Whole mountains are being logged out up along the west branch of the Susquehanna. In the spring, log rafts pass here by the dozens. Some of 'em are huge with men camping on them so that they can be ready with push poles and sweeps to help the rafts get positioned before curves or spots too shallow to float over. The rest of the year, the river is too shallow, and only smaller rafting makes it through. The cut logs are stored upstream and dozens get loose and come down—serious hazards to the ferries, and big logs moving fast can damage bridge pilings, but there's nothing that can be done about it."

Matt had raised the subject so that he could present an idea that had come to him while riding the canal boat.

"Pa, why couldn't we put a man or two in a small boat. When likely logs come floating into the slow water above the dam, we could hook a line to them and muscle them to where we can use them?"

China was doubtful. "And what would we do with them, Matt? We could only store so many along the bank before we would have to make our own log-float all the way to Baltimore, and that doesn't sound very profitable to me."

Matt broke in. "We could just pull them into the slack water behind Halderman's Island, China. We could keep them there until we get our own sawmill going . . . "

Big Matt said, "Whoa, son. Just what sawmill are you talking about? Are you and Brascomb opening some businesses that I haven't been told about?"

Little Matt laughed along with his father.

"That'll be the day, Pa, but seeing all that timber going downstream for somebody else to salvage got me to thinking about how easy it would be to throw a dam across a handy creek, put in an overshot waterwheel hooked to one of those new round saws, and . . ."

China cut in. "A round saw? What's a round saw?"

The Boss's Boy had to pause to gather his wits. The talk was going beyond gathering river logs, and he had planned to sort of ease into his overall plan. Too late now, he would have to lay it all out for his father's consideration.

"Well, there's a new kind of sawmill, or maybe it's just one I haven't seen before. Instead of hooking a ram to vertical saw blades, the mill wheel's shaft is fitted with an iron disk that has saw teeth all around it. The mill wheel turns the saw, and you just feed logs into it making planks about as fast as you can get the logs in place."

Matt had to stop to smile at his simplifications. "At least that's how the rig I saw worked." He shook his head in recognition of limited knowledge. "I'm sure there is more to it than that, Pa, but I never saw a vertical mill that could begin to turn out perfectly straight planks the way the round saw did."

The boss asked, "Where did you see this saw-mill, Matt?"

"Over on the Delaware, Pa. It was run by some Germans, but I don't know who owned it."

Then with renewed enthusiasm, "Why they just adjusted some stops behind a sort of edging guide and changed the cut to any thickness they wanted. It caught my eye, but I didn't see us getting into the business. Getting logs would take the profit, but if we got our logs darn near free, it could be another thing. So, when I saw the river logs just floating by I thought there might be a new business there."

Big Matt was nodding interest, but it was China who spoke first. "Captain, we'd better ship this boy out to some distant place. He hasn't been home two hours, and he has already lined up a pair of businesses that need looking into. By tonight we'll have to hire another clerk just to keep track of the schemes young Matt has laid out."

The father slid back in his chair, so Matt and China did the same. Lukey Bates quit leaning over Matt's shoulder and went to his desk.

Matt had not expected that much attention would be paid to his ideas, but he had seen his father move fast when others would have pondered and weighed—like Uncle Brascomb always did. That kind of quick, on-the-spot decision-making was what put big Matt Miller out in front and made the Miller's most of their money. So maybe?

Big Matt seemed to be studying his son, and that made young Matt nervous, but the waiting held hope that the older man really was considering the river coal and sawmill ideas.

Finally, the Boss got to it. "If we went ahead with the river coal idea, what would we do with the coal, Matt?"

Matt flushed a little because he did not have that answer well worked out. "We could sell some of it around here, Pa, but I know that locally there isn't much money to buy anything, so we would have to ship most of the coal down the canal to either Philadelphia or Baltimore where people have cash."

Big Matt nodded agreement. "That is why state contracts for canal building are best. We get cash money without someone wanting to trade for something we will still have to sell.

"Paying our workers takes regular cash outlays that can put pressure on a business, son, and you keep that in mind. Making sure that we do not get cash-short is Brascomb's specialty, and he earns his pay doing it. Keep that in mind as well when you are thinking hard thoughts about your uncle.

"So, where will you get men to dig out river coal? And Matt, don't be looking at our regulars. They cost real money and have to produce even more money or they get let go."

Matt was ready for that part. "I figure we could hire some of the old men that can't work hard anymore. All of them want to help their families, and a lot of them can work as long as they do not have to push real hard. What I would do is provide the boats to work out of and a couple of flats, sort of rafts, to pile the coal on. The coal diggers would get paid by the ton delivered to our balance scales, and they could set their own hours and work or not work as they saw fit."

China groaned. "I can see it now. I'll have to build the boats and the rafts or nothing will float right."

Matt grinned. "That was part of my plan all along, China." Matt kept his grin as he added, "If we had a working sawmill, we would have any kind of planks we would need for boats, Pa."

Big Matt again nodded. "And if we had cheap coal, we might fire iron furnaces with it, mightn't we, son?"

Little Matt nodded his own head. By golly, his father *was* thinking of going into the iron business.

His thoughts turned. Let Uncle Brascomb choke on this kind of risk taking. He hoped his father would let him help with some of it. Matt dreaded the thought of being anchored to books beside Lukey Bates while the interesting and moneymaking stuff was going on up and down the rivers.

6

When he came to the office, Big Matt could hear the shuffle of feet and fists hitting China's old sea bag. The bag had been stuffed with tanbark and hung from a tree limb, but over the years, young Matt had pounded the canvas into shreds, and Mrs. John McFee had first patched and finally completely covered the bag with cowhide.

Big Matt could see China's mind following the sounds and judging the work and movements by what he heard.

The boss turned to Lukey Bates who was deep into his ledgers. "What's little Matt doing out there instead of helping in here, Lukey?"

Bates turned on his stool and made his thoughts plain. "Matt is about as useful as somebody who can't even read, Mister Miller. His mind wanders, and he makes mistakes—when he doesn't shove everything aside and want to talk about a scheme he has to dig down to Florida or maybe fly to the moon. I make more progress when

he is out there dancing around than I do when he is ·
at his desk."

Big Matt's neck began to swell, so China
Smith stuck in a soothing oar. "Lukey's not telling
us something we didn't already know, Captain. Matt
is not rigged for office work—any more than you
are." China's opinion was a clincher, but he went
on.

"You ought to decide he knows enough about
the bookkeeping end of the business and send him
out where he can sweat and work on ideas. The
Lord knows that he has a bucket of them, and some
are not too bad."

China saw the older Miller weighing his
words, and Lukey, who would be pleased to have
Matt somewhere else, added weight to the
argument.

"Matt could use more experience out on the
jobs, Mister Miller. Sooner or later, that is where he
will be, and we all know that he won't ever settle
down behind a desk."

Big Matt grumbled as he thought about it.
"There isn't much for him to learn out there
handling a pick or an ax. He's done all of that
already. So . . ."

China said, "Why don't I turn him over to a
different foreman every few days and have them
explain what is going on and where his gang is
heading."

Big Matt could see sense in the idea. "That
would be smart, China, and while you are setting
that up, tell him to stop this boxing exercise. The

idea was to teach him enough to defend himself, not to become a pugilist."

China grinned, "A pugilist? Damn, Skipper, you've got the language down pat—although most of the riffraff in the fight game call us Pugs not . . ."

"I've got it, Smith, just straighten him out, and get him to doing something useful." Big Matt thought for a long moment, "And see that he doesn't get into a battle with John McFee's boy. That should have ended years ago."

China turned toward a new scuffle of shadow boxing. "They haven't fought since they were boys before either of them began learning to be *pugilists*, Captain." Smith rolled the *pugilist* word as if it tasted good.

The boss was already turning to other things, but he paused to add, "I've been thinking of making John McFee foreman of a small gang to keep around here, China. Small jobs pop up unexpectedly, and we have to scramble to find workmen. McFee could pick men that can do about anything, and when there is no work waiting we could keep them busy—maybe starting that boatyard up near Benvenue you are so hungry to get to."

China liked that. The tiny community of Benvenue was perched on the point of Duncan's Island, and with the canals developing, the old seaman figured there would be a demand for well-built canal boats and certainly for boat repairs. If the Miller Company got started now, they would have a leg up on everybody else. There could be some money in the venture—which the Captain recognized or he would not waste time and labor on it. China headed for the training lot thinking about the boat works and wondering who he should send Matt to.

As China came into view, Matt hammered three hard left hooks into the heavy bag that buckled the leather-bound cylinder in the middle. Although the tanbark filling had packed solidly and more had been added, the Boss's Boy hit hard, and China thought that the bag needed more weight—maybe sand in the bottom?

The Captain's order that young Matt quit boxing drifted from his thoughts. Young Matt Miller liked it. So did China Smith, and unless the senior Miller twisted their arms, the training would continue—perhaps less openly and probably not during a workday.

China said, "Nice hooks, Matt, but unwrap your hands. We're going upriver for the day."

Matt was pleased. He had little idea how the canal building had advanced over the summer. The Millers had crews working along the canal line, and there were other interests he would like to look into.

He said, "Let me change my pants, China. Pa will kill me if I tear up my decent clothes."

As Matt hurried off, China thought about that. Most men owned two pair of pants. One pair they wore for work. The other was part of their suit and kept for Sunday meetings and funerals. Children were equipped the same, and women wore wash dresses year in and year out.

Everything everybody owned was mended and patched. If something wore completely out, women sewed new clothes from whatever cloth they could find. Only the three of them, the Captain, little Matt, and himself had store bought clothes. Decently fitting clothing made them stand out, which could be good or bad—depending on the circumstances.

Success in life, which to most meant having money, was both admired and resented. Wealth was respected but almost universally envied. A young man like the Boss's Boy would do well to dress much like the workers. Envy created hard feelings, and as easily as young Matt Miller fought, a wrong word here or there could have him squaring off against men he would not really wish to fight.

Matt reappeared in a worn and patched pair of work pants that he had used the summer before. The pants were short in the leg, but almost everyone wore hand-me-downs, and the length would go unremarked.

They walked the short mile to the Juniata crossing where the community of Benvenue and the first canal lock lay on Duncan's Island. The canal was dug the length of the island, and the great wooden aqueduct that crossed the Juniata River was already filled with water. The new canal turning pool was upriver and across the Juniata aqueduct.

A boat could depart Columbia, far down the Susquehanna, and, never leaving a canal, work its way up the east side of that great waterway to the

Juniata where the boat crossed and the canal resumed on the smaller Juniata River.

Eventually, a canal boat would be able to travel all the way to Pittsburgh—or so engineers claimed, although few could see how a canal could cross the high mountains in between.

The Matt Millers knew how the boats would cross the heights of the Allegheny Mountain, and that scheme had, in part, inspired Big Matt's launching of his son on his steam engine examinations.

Crossing the mountains would probably not involve the Miller companies, at least directly, but knowing what was coming and how things were done offered opportunity.

When they arrived at the great mountains, canal boats would encounter a railroad that angled up the major mountain. The loaded canal boat would be floated onto a railcar and a huge steam engine at the top of the rail line would attach a new kind of rope called a cable to the car. The engine would turn, and the car would rise. At the top end of the rail line, a new cable would be attached, and a steam engine higher on the mountain would take over and haul the load up a second inclined railroad. Those engines burned wood, but even the great mountains were getting chopped out. Eventually coal might do better.

The inclined-plane railroad lifting procedure would continue until the canal boat reached the top where it would descend on the Pittsburgh side much as it had risen. The scheme was revolutionary, but both the Captain and China Smith believed it would work.

The cable being used was of special interest. Instead of twisted strands of hemp rope, the new cable was to be made from lengths of metal wire twisted until the mass became large and stunningly strong. The word cable would be forever changed to mean wire rope, and Miller and Smith could see a thousand uses for the extremely strong line that did not stretch like ordinary rope. The world they had all known was changing in marvelous ways, and it would profit them to know and be ready to take advantage of the changes.

The Boss's boy knew Alex Donovan. Donovan was the foreman who had thrown him into the canal when he and Mickey McFee were trying to settle things once and for all.

When China turned him over to Donovan for the day and probably longer, Matt took careful measure of the man. There would be no fist fighting or any other uncooperative actions from the Boss's Boy. He was not being guided around to show off how smart or tough he was. Donovan knew almost everything about everything the Millers undertook, and little Matt was sent to learn. He was hungry to discover all that the foreman knew, but it was natural for any man to judge how he would make out if he and the bull of the towpath came to blows.

Not so good, Matt estimated. Alex Donovan had fists the size of splitting mauls and the body to go with them. Donovan was more than forty years old, and he had been running work gangs for big Matt for nearly twenty years. That meant Donovan was smart and tougher than a hickory plank. The Boss's Boy perked up and paid complete attention.

Donovan asked, "So what do you know about canals, Matt?" There was no suggestion in the foreman's voice that the Boss's Boy was any more than any other young man trying to learn.

"I know how they work, sort of, and I know where and why they go where they go, Mister Donovan. I'm afraid I do not know much about building canals, if that is what you mean."

"That is what I mean. To make sure that we don't miss anything, I'll pretend that you never saw a canal before, and as I think of things, I'll describe them to you. If you've got questions, ask 'em. That's what you are here for, and that is what I've been pulled off serious work to explain."

Oh, oh, Alex Donovan was not exactly thrilled by his assignment. Matt resolved to stay humble and interested. Actually, he was interested, so that part should be easy. Humble? Listening to a man as knowledgeable as Donovan, humility should come naturally.

Donovan began on Duncan's Island.

"A canal can be no better than its surveying, Matt. The trick is to lay out long runs of canal where the water level will be flat. That means that the canal neither rises nor falls, but because we are following a river, the canal is either moving uphill or downhill. When we have stretched a flat water canal as long as can be done, we raise the canal water level to a new height by building a stone box with a wooden door on each end. The box is large enough to hold a boat."

They had arrived at the familiar lock on the island that boats entered leaving the canal to cross the Susquehanna or returning from that river to proceed up the Juniata.

Donovan introduced details Matt had been unaware of. "For some reason I have never understood, this part of Duncan's Island—here on the west bank—belongs to Dauphin County that is, otherwise, all on the east shore of the Susquehanna.

"Common sense would say that a county line should run at the center of a river, but this lock, all of the Clark's Ferry Bridge, and the dam below the bridge, are in Dauphin County.

"So, this lock belongs to the Dauphin canal section although it stands on what should logically be Perry County ground. From here on past Newport, about twenty miles, I would guess, the canal runs flat, and the next lock is at Old Ferry almost at Millerstown. Canal builders like those long runs, as do the boatmen. Canals running through flats like these are easiest to build and fastest to move through."

They examined the lock, and Donovan resumed his description as though Matt lacked eyes and had little brainpower. The foreman had apparently forgotten that Matt had hauled stone and mixed mortar, helping to build this very lock.

Or, maybe Donovan was just continuing his explanation pretending that Matt did know nothing and needed everything from the beginning—to make sure that nothing was overlooked.

The foreman said, "We call this stone box a lock, and once through a lock, the canal and the boat are either higher or lower than before the lock." Matt wanted to groan.

Donovan paused to adjust a tobacco chew and to spit aside. He resumed his explanation in a resigned tone that indicated he was aware that Matt understood these simplest of descriptions that had to be covered anyway.

"So, if a boat is going upriver via a canal, it will eventually reach a lock. The lower lock gate is opened, and the canal boat is floated inside. The lower door is then closed and the upstream door is eased open allowing water from the higher canal to flow in and fill the box. When the water level in the box reaches the new canal height, the boat is floated out and continues on upstream in the flat water."

Matt suspected everybody in the whole world knew all of that, but Donovan continued as if his student were the most uninformed child ever talked to.

"Now, the flat water is the important part, Matt. That is the real canal. The locks are just gimmicks to lift or lower. Because the canals never rise or fall but just run perfectly flat, a team of horses or mules on the towpath never has a harder or easier pull. The boat always slides along as easy or as heavily as ever. Animals pulling level on the smoothed out canal towpath can work for years where the same team pulling loads up and down roads would wear itself out in a few seasons, and a canal team can easily move a gigantic load on a boat that it could never budge if it were on a wagon."

Donovan chose to sit on an immense flat-topped log placed near the lockmaster's building for resting, and Matt was pleased to sit alongside his instructor.

"Canals move goods cheap and they move steadily, so a man can make a reasonable guess of when his purchases will arrive. Canal boats are gentle on manufactured things, and people like to ride on them because they do not beat you half to death the way a horse or carriage does."

"They are slower than molasses, though, Mister Donovan. A horse can make better time even on bad roads."

Donovan nodded. "Mostly true, although fast packet boats will go long distances moving whole groups of people—as they will between Philadelphia and Pittsburgh when we are done—better than any teams of horses pulling coaches ever could. The people will arrive rested and comfortable, and the horse teams pulling the boats will hardly raise a sweat. The canal teams will be moving on flat ground and at an unchanging pace. That makes for speed and comfort, young Matt."

Matt Miller agreed with everything the foreman said. The canals would open the mountain communities to the outside world as never before. A farmer raising grain deep in the middle of

Pennsylvania could have his crop safely to market in the nation's biggest cities within a week or two. The world was moving ahead at an amazing pace.

Donovan chose to rest himself on a sitting-log closer to the canal edge.

"When the diggers hollowed out the canal we are looking at here on Duncan's Island they encountered mountains of Indian bones. Seems that some of the tribes had a huge battle here about the time we whites were moving in. It's said that the island was littered with skeletons and broken weapons. The most interesting and mysterious find was a large, stone Christian cross buried about three feet deep that looked to be very old. Where it came from nobody knows, but . . ."

Matt interrupted, "Where is the cross now, Mister Donavan? I would like to see it."

The foreman sighed. "At the bottom of the Susquehanna. Some professors down in Philadelphia wanted to study it, so the cross was put on a supply boat and shipped down, but the boat had a load of black powder aboard that blew up on the way. The whole rig is on the bottom somewhere down river."

Donovan got back to his history. "The point I was making is that this land is not the untouched soil we like to think it is. A lot of generations of people have lived here, and when we look close, their marks show. The canal diggers raked the Indian bones into piles and buried them in the canal banks. Now, they'd be hard to find."

Donovan chose a stick and swiped a clear space on the flat ground at their feet.

"I know you've seen canals full and empty, Matt, but I doubt you've studied them closely. Canal shape doesn't just happen, and some shapes are better than others."

The foreman drew in the dirt with his stick.

"A canal cannot be straight-sided. Any numbskull will know that straight sides will cave in and have to be dug out again.

Most canals have banked sides and almost flat bottoms. Like this:

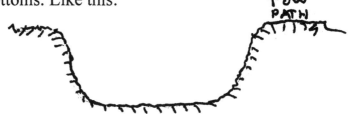

"The trick is to have slanted sides on the canal that match the slant of a canal boat's sides. That way, when a boat scrapes a side it just slides along and does not gouge holes in the canal walls.

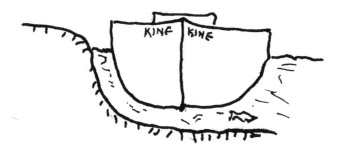

"Unfortunately, there are only loose rules on boat shapes, and box-ended boats get launched that just eat the hell out of canal banks. The reason we worry about that is because a lot of the ground in this part of Pennsylvania has shale in it, and shale does not hold water well. So, we have to line the canals with a few inches of clay. Lining canals is expensive and takes time. Having the sides ripped open by cheap boats costs a lot, and the Commonwealth does not like having to provide those kind of repairs when they should not be necessary."

Donovan appeared thoughtful before continuing. "I hear that you and China are going to build canal boats out at Benvenue, is that right?"

Matt was surprised that the idea had spread.

"Well, it is China's idea, but I would like to be part of it. I don't think the plan is for certain yet, but it sounds profitable to me."

Donovan nodded approval. "Boat building will make some money for a while, but for the long run, boat repair will make more. A proper boatyard ought to have handy skids where boats can be easily drawn from and relaunched into the canal so the repair can be more or less overnight. That way, canal traffic that develops leaks or needs work can plan ahead and get it done without delay."

A thought popped into Matt's mind. "Then, our boatyard should be along the canal and not in Benvenue. Maybe right up against the turning basin just past the aqueduct would be the place."

The thinking prompted another concept and Matt added, "You know, Mister Donavan, we could dig a length of canal off the basin and put our skids and maybe a dock or two along it. As I recall, there is a run of water off the mountain right along in there that just might give us enough fall to run a sawmill for our river logs, and . . ."

Donovan asked, "What logs?"

"Oh, I suggested that we could salvage free logs from the river by towing them in behind Halderman's Island for our own sawing. Then, . . ."

Donovan was clearly amazed. "Matt, boy, you're just full of ideas, aren't you." He again pondered. "I like the log claiming idea, but I don't remember any stream coming down near the basin. Could be, though, and any stream can be dammed."

Flooded with enthusiasm, Matt said, "Oh we wouldn't have to put in much of a dam, Mister Donovan. We could just channel the flow into a chute and put an overshot waterwheel under it. All we would need would be enough weight of water to turn the wheel at a good rate."

The foreman held up a restraining palm. "All right, Matt. You take that up with your father. Let's get back to the canal building.

"Now, here's a trick we've been using where shale ground is the worst. What we do is put a sort of bustle in the bottom edge of the canal. When one of those brick–shaped boats touches, it just digs into the bustle and doesn't start leaks. Seems to work pretty well, and it keeps all but the best-shaped boat from scraping along the sides. Boat pilots get lazy and let their crafts ram the banks all of the time.

"Your Pa has a team employed full time repairing those kind of accidents. Pilots tell the repair crews where the damage is—that's always claimed to have been caused by some other boat, of course—and Miller Men go fix the leaks. Steady money and regular employment for that crew—paid for by the Commonwealth, which is the most certain money there is these days."

A workboat came off the Clark's Ferry Bridge (the new Susquehanna river covered-bridge crossing) and resumed its walking pace up the canal. Donovan hailed the pilot who knew the Miller foreman and welcomed them aboard for the remainder of the journey to the turning basin.

As they waited out the canal lock's cycle, Donovan kept explaining. "Now, Matt, a boat like we are on is made for easy maneuvering. I'd judge this craft to be about forty feet in length, and it only needs a single animal to move it along. The boat has a rudder-man who is also the captain to keep the boat in line and a horse or mule handler who controls the towpath.

"In this case, we have a mule, which I favor, incidentally. Mules pull heavier loads and last longer. The only special thing to know about mules is that they are smarter than horses, so they can be stubborn and downright pestiferous in nature—especially if foolish demands are placed on them. A cantankerous mule should be traded away.

"Mules also tend to choose their own pace. Hurrying a mule is not often profitable, but if you let the mule use his good sense, he will probably get you and your cargo there just as fast with a lot less wear on himself.

"Canal boats vary a lot in length, and we will have a few that will be one hundred feet long, and many as short as twenty-five feet. Most boats do not longhaul, and their cargoes do not travel to the sea. As a practical matter, canal boats must be short enough to fit in locks, which limits them to less than ninety feet long on most canals, and they must be able to pass each other in the canals.

"A canal boat is rarely more than ten feet wide, and a typical canal is forty-five feet wide. There is a square footage rule involved in these measurements. A canal should be six times the square footage of a cross section of a boat. We tend to add a few inches of canal width just to make sure.

"The area rule is important as it helps control boat momentum and currents within the canals. The waves, even the little ones created by the slowest moving boats, force other boats out of line and encourage canal wall erosion."

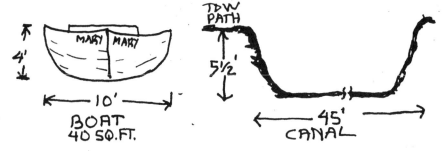

Donovan's sketch of a boat's cross-section and a canal shape demonstrated the square footage rule.

Most of the details were new to Matt, and he believed them important. He spoke his appreciation.

"I never knew this stuff, Mister Donovan. Even this much makes me feel ignorant and not ready to go ahead with some of the plans I have been dreaming up."

"There is nothing earthshaking to know, Matt. It is small knowledge that once heard is remembered, and you will automatically apply it whenever you need it.

"How much water a boat draws is also controlled, and it is important. By drawing, I mean, how deep in the canal the boat sinks when fully loaded. As a rule of thumb, the Commonwealth requires a boat to have eighteen inches of water beneath her bottom. A canal bottom being passed over creates drag on the boat, unless about a foot and a half of water separates the two. Most canals are dug for boats that draw four feet. That means that most of them have a five and one half foot water depth.

"That sounds shallow, but men can drown in water that deep." Donovan chuckled in memory.

"When we threw you and Mickey McFee into the canal those years ago, we took note that the ditch was still refilling, and there was about four feet of water for you to wallow around in."

Matt was amused by the revelation, but he was looking ahead to examining the Petersburg side of the turning basin where he thought he remembered a small stream trickling down and where he could visualize a working sawmill and their boatyard.

Matt asked, "If we put in a sawmill, could we float our logs through the basin to the mill do you think, Mister Donovan?"

Donovan snorted disdain. "Not a prayer, Boss's Boy. If you were allowed, everyone would try dragging something. Canals are for paying customers, and there are no exceptions. State inspectors would shut you down in a minute—or less."

Matt Miller was not dismayed. So, they would build a pair of flatboats that would draw less than four feet and use "A" frame hoists to load their logs onto the crafts. Coming out from behind Halderman's Island, they could simply turn their loaded boats into the river-level canal, ease through the lock, and tow them to the mill. Of course, that would cost locking fees.

There was another way that Matt had seen while in Philadelphia. It was called warping, and great ships were moved to docks using the method.

He could float his logs from behind Halderman's Island to the mouth of the Juniata. He could place an anchor or a piling upstream in the Juniata. A rope attached to the front of his log and around a pulley on the piling would run to an ox on the shore. The log would be pulled to the piling, and then reattached to a piling further upriver. It might even be possible to loop the rope through a pulley and back to his rowing boat that would head downstream. Aided by the current and by rowing powerfully, they might propel the log upstream until it was positioned to haul from the river and used in the mill.

It couldn't be easier. Young Matt wanted to begin immediately.

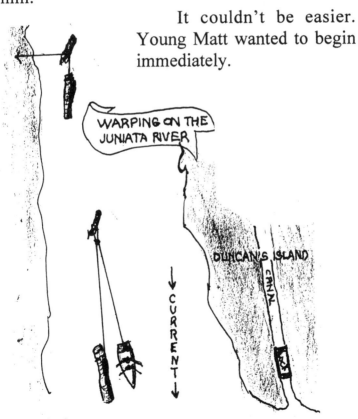

WARPING ON THE JUNIATA RIVER

DUNCAN'S ISLAND

CURRENT

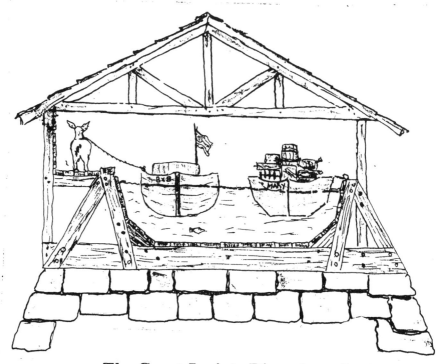

The Great Juniata River Aqueduct

Aqueducts continued canals across rivers and large streams. Most were built on stone piers (pilings) that could resist high water, ice floes, uprooted trees, and fires. The canal boats floated onto the aqueducts, which were canals made of wood. Most aqueducts, including ours a mile and a half upriver from Clark's Ferry Bridge, were covered as if they were road bridges. During the winter the canals were drained and the aqueducts were caulked and made watertight as if they were boats.

7

Matt Miller, the younger, examined his domain with satisfaction. With China and his father gone far up the Juniata and not due back for days, he, the Boss's Boy, ruled the vast Miller empire.

On a whim he could send men scurrying. He could launch cargoes, he could command teams of workers, he . . . Lukey Bates' firm tones interrupted his gratifying contemplations.

"You going to the milling tonight, Matt?"

Matt shook his mind into the real world. "Milling? Where? I hadn't heard about it."

It was Bates' turn to enjoy a headshake. "The fights have been the talk for nearly a week, and you hadn't heard?"

Matt had a valid excuse. He had been up the Susquehanna most of the week smoothing out the river coal mining, which had somehow become his alone to deal with.

Just because he presented an idea did not mean that he should be stuck with the day-to-day details of the scheme, but big Matt had said, "It's your plan, son. Make it work," and that had been that.

And it was working. Matt had found his older men and put them into flat-bottomed work boats that tonged and shoveled aboard the coal bars before poling ashore to unload onto piles that grew astonishingly high.

Even before he had enough coal to ship, a buyer arrived at the Miller headquarters. The man had a coal-fired iron foundry well downriver from Columbia, and the cost of coal coming in from the fields via the Delaware and across land to his workings was devouring his profit.

River coal was trash compared to the graded tonnage from the usual sources, but it should be cheap, and it would burn—if Mister Miller could provide enough of it on schedule and for a tolerable price.

It happened that, among other products, the ironmaster was a maker of round saw blades—of a temper not to be found elsewhere, he claimed. The iron man called his blades circular saws. The younger Mister Miller agreed to barter payment—coal to blades for a sawmill. Less money changing hands—good business.

The Boss was away, but young Matt guaranteed delivery, closed the deal, and immediately headed north to the best coal bars at Liverpool. The Susquehanna branch of the canal passed the small town, and Matt needed not only more coal but also a dock and hoist to transfer his cargo into their canal boats—as soon as he could get a canal boat.

Passing through the Irish workers' camp on Duncan's Island, he had arranged for three more two-man crews to obtain boats and tools from the turning basin boatyard to join the miners already at work.

As he had before, Matt hired older men who needed work badly but who could no longer manage the usual ten-hour days. Working at his own pace, a worn-down laborer still produced steadily, and he worked for less money.

The miners moved to Liverpool vicinity and lived together in a single barrack kind of housing. When he had time, Matt intended looking into that end of things. There could be a dollar in providing living places for workmen—Millerstown, two dozen miles up the Juniata, had twenty-nine so-called hotels for just that purpose. A perfect arrangement, Matt believed. Everybody was satisfied, and everybody got ahead.

Of course, it was not quite that easy. Before he had been able to provide flat boats, logs salvaged from the river had to be sawed into boards, and the sawmill itself had to be built.

An Irish sawyer had been found among the Miller Men, and using John McFee's crew, they had constructed a decent round-saw mill. Overseen by China Smith, the sawyer now ruled a burgeoning boat building and repair yard that was paying handsomely. Lumber sales were also growing as towns along the canals rapidly developed.

From the Maryland Iron Works, big Matt had received a pair of three foot in diameter saw blades that ate through any wood fed into them like hot knives through lard. The coal-buying ironmaster had not exaggerated. His saw blades held their edge.

Even saw-milling became more complicated as other opportunists sought the suddenly valuable floating logs, and Matt made arrangements to buy as well as salvage the formerly free floaters, but business expanded, and the Miller companies were getting their share.

China Smith designed and oversaw the Miller Company's boat building. The first canal boat had been built from green lumber because the craft was needed immediately. That boat was not expected to endure lengthy service, but China had built before, and he planned on shrinkages and warpings that few freshwater builders anticipated. From the first to their current offerings, Miller boats gained sterling reputations.

Young Matt's flat-bottom workboats could be turned out virtually overnight. China had insisted on creating full-size wooden patterns of various shapes of small boats—the way it was done in New England where boat building was a major occupation.

Lumber was laid against the pattern of the boat piece wanted, drawn around, and sawed out. Flat boats were nailed together, often coated with boiled pine pitch, and launched.

Matt considered the savings possible if there was a Miller nail factory in operation, and with iron on the hill, that might be practical.

Still, they might do best by dealing with one of the local furnaces that could easily produce nails and spikes. Until then, he swapped coal for nails from the Maryland works. Return cargo for the empty coal boat was always difficult.

For working the coal bars, Matt insisted on doubled bottoms and extra thick gunneled boats. The boats were often run aground or scraped over rock ledges, and digging tools knocked regularly against the gunnels—the top edges of the boat sides. When the boats were new, a bailing bucket was provided until the wood swelled and the flat bottomed crafts became watertight. Those boats also sold well along the rivers.

As the coal business developed, large flat boats were towed into position against profitable coal bars and coal was piled on. When loaded, the flats were towed ashore, attached to lifting booms that swung the load over a canal boat, and dumped into the cargo hold. China Smith knew how to rig those kind of contraptions, and once seen, everybody else knew as well.

Inevitably, but astonishingly fast to Matt's eyes, other men got into the river coal business, but none of the others had Miller outlets to canal boats or distant iron works. Their profit came from selling cheaply to young Matt Miller's operation. Big Matt liked that kind of moneymaking.

So, there were to be fights. Was he going? Matt could not have considered otherwise.

Matt asked, "Who's milling?"

Lukey Bates was not a genuine fight fan, but the clerk had the contacts to know about nearly everything going on.

"The big fight is between someone called Frederick The Great and our man Mickey McFee, the Irish Hurricane."

Matt's interest leaped. "Are the Irish fighting the Germans?"

"That's the idea, as I understand it. Some other mills are to be fought, but I do not know the names."

Bates frowned to himself, "Why do they call it milling, Matt? Why not stick to fighting or boxing? Milling sounds as if they were going to grind flour or something."

"Milling comes from England, Lukey. The great champions like Tom Cribb or Tom Spring, Harry "Kid" Furness, and Jem Ward, the current champion, are all known as millers. Sounds more civilized than fist fighters for the ladies and the gentle folk, maybe."

"There is nothing gentle about any of it, to my mind. Fist fighters are identifiable as soon as you see them. Most can't breathe through their noses, and they have face scars that are painful to look at."

"Yeah." Matt's voice sounded distant. His thoughts were on the evening's battles. He wanted to see Mickey McFee in action again. The man was becoming a ferocious hitter, but, to Matt's eyes, he lacked almost all of the skills China taught. Who else would square off against the Germans?

Actually, some of the German workers were as much Miller Men as the Irish. Except for their native language differences, they were all much alike, anyway. They were young men who worked almost until they dropped, who believed they were tougher than anyone else around, and who were ready to prove it almost any time and any place.

The millings provided outlets for men to escape the mind-numbing drudgery of day in and day out work. The fights raised a battler above the common mob, and men admired and respected their fighters. A little money could even be made—if a fighter won.

China said the fights pulled the different groups together and gave the men something to belong to.

If Miller Men were battling, Matt wanted to be there to lend support. Maybe? . . . Young Matt Miller let that thought run.

8

China and the Captain reached the new canal-side village of Newport late in the afternoon. Beyond the canal docks and convenient river crossings, the town had little to offer, but Big Matt had been lacking vigor in recent weeks and chose to call it a day. They checked into lodging a half block from the canal bank. While the boss rested before supper, China drifted about the docks arranging for a morning boat ride to Petersburg and picking up bits and pieces of information that might prove of later interest.

Word of the Saturday evening fights scheduled for their destination grabbed China's attention. Many Newporters were German, and their hopes lay with a battler known as Frederick the Great. Another recognized German combatant was called The Baron, and Smith gathered that the workman—whose full title included Von und Zu

Dieter Haas of Haasburg in Bavaria—actually was of noble lineage.

The Irish Hurricane would meet Frederick. Other Irish fighters? To their knowledge, no one had stepped forward—but some would! They always did, and the talkers and spitters wished they could get downriver to enjoy the milling.

China checked the sun and considered that he and the Boss could rent a carriage and easily make the fights. Both would like to attend, but . . . big Matt was sort of worn out, and China began to weigh just who else might plan on stepping into the square while the big dogs were away.

Young Matt was aching to try organized fist fighting. Big Matt's wishes had squelched the hungers so far, but with neither father nor China about, little Matt really might seize the chance to test his skills.

China let time run while he thought about it. The truth was, he also wondered how Matt would do if squared off against a tough and determined opponent.

Big Matt, on the other hand, might plow on in and order his pugnacious son out of the square. That would prove mortifying to the youth, and it would weaken him in many eyes and minds.

Of course, the Boss might stay quiet and in the background waiting to applaud his boy and perhaps, secretly, as interested in the outcome as anyone.

It could go either way. China suspected it would be safest to let the milling go by undiscovered and to arrive about noon to determine if little Matt had been involved.

Damn, the Boss's Boy would get into it as sure as he, China Smith, sat on his duffle ten miles away. The old fighter wished he could be there to wrap his protégé's fists, to whisper advice in his ear, and to make sure that he fought smart and damn sure won without getting his head knocked out of shape.

Although the law claimed a boy was not a man until his twenty-first birthday, young Matt was almost twenty, and that was old enough to take his chances in life. Most youths were married, working, and raising children well before that magic birth date.

Big Matt was aware of his son's coming of age, and he was making moves toward that time.

He had said, "I am separating all of our western businesses from those in the east, China. Everything will eventually come to Matt, but I think it would be wise to divorce what we have out here from Brascomb's projects. My brother has a jealous streak, and it surfaces often enough for me to wish to make sure that Matt has a solid grip on things in case Brascomb outlives me."

Smith nodded understanding, and the Captain continued. "As you know, I have sent to Philadelphia for the biggest safe we can get. I won't announce it to Brascomb, but we will begin salting cash away in quantities large enough to be meaningful but small enough not to make our books look bad. It will take a year, but thereafter, if anything goes wrong in the east, we will be able to function out here without interruption."

China believed that move to be wise, although it was unlikely that the father would ever willingly hand over all of the reins to his son. A man like big Matt Miller thrived on power and control of successful business. As long as he breathed, he would want the final word on important decisions.

Even if he wished, big Matt could not endow his son with ownership until he was twenty-one, but he could surrender some control and decision making to young Matt. If little Matt hungered for ultimate authority, he would have to wait a few more decades. His father was still increasing his workforce and expanding his influence.

Young Matt had projects of his own, and the boss tolerated and approved of his son's varied operations. River coal mining was turning out well, and the circular sawmill became busier each month. Although boat building was steady, lumber for house building promised to become the mill's most important product.

With cold weather again approaching, Young Matt was storing every river log he could acquire. When the earth froze, the canals would be drained for the winter, canal construction would stall, and workmen of all skills would be idle. Matt had not announced his plans for the burgeoning log piles, but China and the Captain expected he would keep the mill working as long as the wheel had water to turn it.

Over the cold months, the mill could convert mountains of logs into salable boards and planks. Until the stream froze, the mill would keep some of the men working, and in the spring, their seasoned lumber would be barged downstream and sell for high prices.

Young Matt's interest extended beyond coal and milled lumber. He had noted that the shingles roofing the almost new Susquehanna River bridge were already failing. Instead of good split red cedar shingles, the bridge contractor had slapped on pine shingling that could not last. At young Matt's insistence, Lukey Bates was already in contact with a Commonwealth purchasing agent. When the bridge needed reroofing, the name Miller would be high on the agent's list.

Which meant that Matt had to create a shingle factory. China was not sure just how a shingle-works operated, but the Boss's Boy had been making drawings.

Big Matt approved that direction as well. Houses also needed good roofs, and there might be a market for shingles downstream—or even along the canals where towns were sprouting like mushrooms.

Within a year or two, canal building would be finished, and although there could be profit in maintaining the waterways and their boats, other businesses would be needed. The Millers thought of bricks and iron and, of all things—stump-pullers.

Young Matt was responsible for that interest as well. Everywhere he looked, Matt saw stump-dotted fields. Immense stumps loomed in the middle of roads and made meadows discouraging to scythe. Men ripped their plows apart on giant roots, and they labored endlessly chopping and hauling the stumps of trees their fathers had felled half a lifetime before.

An influential man back of Bloomfield had an iron screw machine that sucked out stumps using a single ox. Matt intended to contact the stump man during the colder months when they would both have time to discuss the machine and how the Millers might come onto one or more.

The fights were being staged at the German camp almost alongside the Little Juniata Creek. Irish Miller Men had hiked en masse from their encampment north of the town, and more than a few spectators were from Petersburg itself.

Unlike some millings, this was an almost friendly gathering. There were no bitter emotions threatening to boil over into general brawling. Both German and Irish contingents described themselves as Miller Men, and increasingly often they worked together.

Their champions would hammer at each other, and challenges from the crowd might induce others to step into the square to advance their personal standing or support their never deeply-buried national traditions as mighty warriors prepared to take on all-comers.

Men fought. It was as simple as that. Men longed to prove who packed the hardest punch or had the strongest chin. To be knocked flat held no disgrace. That too was part of being a Donnybrook Irishman or a battling Bavarian.

Men judged other men by how well they handled themselves, and more than a few placed great value on another's willingness to square off against anyone challenging. Fortunately, for this night's activities, there was no money available for hard liquor, and the scheduled bouts had no serious money bet either way. Although voices would be loud and the cheering and jeering confrontational, a good time for all was expected.

Matt and Lukey Bates had brought a tall bench for sitting on during the melees. They wanted to be high enough to see over heads in front of them, but standing could grow wearisome, and the gathering could be lengthy.

Where to sit required a bit of thought as Matt wished to appear neutral without leaning toward either side. The Germans had claimed the best rising ground for seats. Lukey placed their bench almost between the battling contingents. Matt figured no one could fairly claim the Boss's Boy and his clerk were choosing sides.

Rough joking greeted their presence. Some suggested the Boss's Boy ought to take on the winner of the Great Frederick and Irish Hurricane fight. Matt responded that meeting the loser might be more his level.

A German announced that he had heard that the Boss's Boy was putting up a purse of five dollars to the main event's winner.

Matt responded by stating that he would if someone would change his fifty dollar gold piece. As anyone present would have had a hard time producing a dollar, probably including the boss's son, the offer was recognized as extremely safe.

There were announcements before battlers took to the squared-off flat spot along the creek. A man running for public office explained his qualifications, and a committee that had formed to encourage renaming the town of Petersburg as Duncannon made its pitch.

A pair of the Shuler brothers who made guns at Liverpool passed examples of their work for comment and appreciation, but eventually the side shows ended, and the audience settled for what it had come for.

Klubber Cole would referee most of the bouts, and there were fighters on both sides who had worked with the old fist fighter.

Matt thought some about the Klubber. Cole had been around for as long as he could remember, and he seemed to travel with the Miller projects.

When the headquarters moved to Petersburg, Klubber came along. Men who barely made enough to feed their families managed lessons for their sons with Cole. Matt expected Klubber was most often paid with meals and even nightly shelter, but somehow the once famous fighter held on. Cole was always around, and Matt wondered if he, too, considered himself a Miller Man?

Mickey McFee was Klubber's current prospect, and together they made a little money on

Mickey's fights. Cole had a dozen other acolytes, however, and some of them expected to demonstrate their skills at this milling.

There appeared to be enough fighters to go around, and the only qualification or restriction seemed to be that the pugilists be about the same height. Each fight lasted until a man could not or would not stand up. If the fighters wore themselves out, the crowd would complain, and Klubber declared a victor, a draw, or no contest. The indecisive draws were the most common as untrained men could not last long, and if a smasher of a blow was not landed, the exhausted pair often ended leaning against each other.

It was a good show, and for a major bout of the evening the German's Baron made his appearance.

Until the Baron, there had been no technique for Matt to evaluate. Fighters shook hands, squared off, and began to swing from as far back as they could reach. Most bouts had been knockouts, most scored by the German side, and Matt suspected that the methodical Germans had prepared and planned their milling campaign against the more volatile and less organized Irish.

The Baron's sterling performance added weight to young Matt's preplanning suspicions and fueled his barely banked hunger to get into the game.

Baron Dieter Haas looked . . . well, baronial. He stood tall, held his chin high, and appeared to examine his opposition as if studying insects of suspect origin. Every Irishman in the gathering wished to punch his arrogant features. In fact, as the Baron entered the square, two Irish Miller Men grappled for the right to pound the German's face as flat as a skillet bottom.

One struggler broke free and entered the square. His friend immediately began shouting encouragement for him to, "Hammer his lordship all the way back to Paris."

Lukey Bates asked, "Paris?"

Matt said, "Geography is not a major study in the Irish camp, Lukey," but the Boss's Boy's attention was on the fighters.

They seemed a physical match, the Irishman wider in the shoulders, the German more finely muscled, and about the same in height. Klubber Cole brought them together at square-center and introduced them to each other and the audience.

The Baron made a significant moment of their handshake, but Germans shook hands at every opportunity anyway.

The referee ordered, "Fight!"

The Irish fighter stepped away, to gather himself for a rush, Matt supposed, and the German assumed his stance. The Baron's fighting style grabbed Matt Miller's attention because it was something new. The Baron turned sideward and crouched. His strong right arm was held forward with his elbow almost into his ribs. His back was very straight, and his right foot and knee pointed at his opponent. The left fist was held high protecting that side of his head. Matt thought the position stiff and inflexible.

The Irish fighter came in like a whirlwind. His fists swung when he was still too far away, and he grunted with every swing—each of which was expected to demolish anything it hit.

The Baron edged straight back, keeping his weight on his rear foot, then, like a lightning strike, his right arm straightened, his body lunged, and his glove-clad fist splatted into his opponent's features as if it were the butt end of a clothes pole.

The Irishman was stopped in his tracks. His head snapped back, blood spurted from a smashed nose—and the Baron struck again.

The blow was the same. The right arm stabbed straight with the German's body behind it, and the result was similar—only this punch staggered the Irish fighter and turned his legs into willow wands.

Before the Boss's Boy or the audience understood what was happening, the third blow was en route, another straight and perfect, jabbing punch.

Matt's appreciation of how the Baron was fighting did not help the unfortunate Irish battler. The Baron's third blow dropped him like a discarded shirt, and although he was struggling to his feet, the dazed fighter was facing away from his opponent, and Klubber Cole was quick to end the bout by stepping between the still willing combatants.

Lukey Bates said, "What a slaughter," and Matt had to agree. The still woozy Irishman was escorted back to his seat and a large rag was provided to hold against his seriously altered nose.

The defeated Irishman's companion was already in the square, demanding he be next and against the Baron. He declaimed for all to hear that, unlike his friend, he was ready for sneak punches.

Lukey asked, "Sneak punches?"

Matt laughed aloud. "They probably taught those sneaky blows over there in Paris."

Mickey McFee was seated to his right, and Matt caught his eye. The Mick smirked, perhaps with the same knowledge the Boss's boy was still absorbing. Before he could think more about it, Klubber Cole called the fighters to the center, the handshaking took place, and the command "Fight!" started them at it.

The second fight was longer but much the same. The Irishman charged, the Baron drew straight back, then he countered with his stabbing and astonishingly accurate right hand. If the Irishman withdrew, the Baron was instantly on him, and his blows were weighty and swift.

When they grappled, The Baron did not do as well, but neither had come to wrestle, and the instant they parted, Baron Dieter Haas's fist resumed its stunning splats and thuds into his opponent's bloodied features. This fight would clearly not be long in duration.

Matt said, "He's a sword fighter, Lukey. He moves straight in and straight back out. Look at his stance. That is the way sword fighters duel and fence. I watched a lot of them at the University in Philadelphia. He does not go sideward well. He has no left hand at all. His sword arm, the one he is jabbing with, is his only weapon."

Then Matt added, "But it's a good one, and a fighter is stupid to stand there and get hit by it."

Matt started to say, "What you have to do is . . ." but just then the Irish battler landed on his tailbone. He struggled to regain his feet, but the referee had seen enough. These were almost friendly bouts, and no one should be permanently injured. He waved the fight over, and the Germans howled in triumph.

Von Haas turned smiling to receive their accolades, and the Boss's Boy stood up.

Matt wondered a little if he had planned to fight even before they had come to watch. The desire had been in his mind, of course, but seeing two of his men go down to ignominious defeat tripped something, and suddenly he was standing.

Then he was walking into the square, ignoring Lukey Bates' somehow distant calling, brushing figures aside, and receiving encouraging slaps on his shoulders. The thought came that both his father and China would kill him for this, but the worry instantly passed, and he found his unwrapped fists clenched waist high and ready to go. The Boss's Boy was no unpolished slugger, and he expected that he knew how to fight the obviously skilled Baron Dieter Haas.

Klubber Cole said, "I wondered how long you'd sit there, Boss's Boy," and introduced him to the confident-appearing Baron.

They shook hands, and Von Haas included a short bow of recognition that he was engaging an employer in combat. Matt returned the bow and stepped away to shed his coat and shirt.

Mickey McFee pushed to the edge of the square. "You know how to handle him, Boss? He hits hard with that one hand."

Matt said, "I'm going to knock him colder than a fish trapped in ice." Matt's voice was cold and hard—a fighter's voice, just like his own, Mickey realized.

McFee was sobered and a trifle bemused by the Boss's Boy's intensity. This was not the overheated youth of canal-side scrapping from years past. Matt Miller meant what he said.

If he could do it! McFee was not so sure, but he recognized that, even if he lost, the Boss's Boy intended to put serious marks on the other man.

Klubber Cole introduced the fighters to the crowd. The Boss's Boy received a thunderous ovation from the Irish side but little from the Germans. Concentrating on what he was going to do, Matt barely heard, but a corner of his mind recognized that, at least for the moment, he had placed himself in the Irish camp. He would have to fix that later. Right now, he just wanted to whale the tar out of the fighter called the Baron.

The fighters toed Klubber's line in the dirt, and Cole said, "Fight."

As ready as he thought he was, the Boss's Boy instantly absorbed a mind-rattling thump just above his left eye. The Baron was explosive, but Matt was away before he could be hit again.

Wondering if the stiff jab had sliced him open Matt swiped a hand across his brow—and barely escaped a second stabbing right fist that was followed by another and another, so swiftly that they almost flowed together.

The Boss's Boy's concentration tightened. The crowd, the referee, and all else disappeared from his mind. Only the crouched and sliding forward Baron Von Haas lay within his focus. He saw the cocked right fist and moved to his left. The Baron's front foot edged to follow, and Matt knew what would be next and what he would do about it.

Edging to his left, the Boss's Boy moved away from the Baron's left cross—if he even had one. More important, he disturbed the German fighter's comfortable forward-and-back balance.

Swordsmen fought in straight lines. Unlike children dancing about while swinging wildly with their wooden swords, masters of the saber, the epee, or even the foils shuffled in and out in straight lines that wore grooves in the stones of the older academies. They did not train to shift out of line and into varied angles of defense or attack.

China Smith did. He swiveled, ducked, bobbed and wove. He slipped close from a side and shifted instantly to strike from a different location. So, the Boss's Boy fought the same.

Young Matt Miller drifted left, dropped his left hand almost to his side—and the Baron saw the opening. The swordsman stabbed into the space left by his opponent's lowered fist. He thrust into it and his feet followed as they had to, leaving him crouched, tightly balanced and ready for his next straight ahead stab.

The Boss's Boy let the expected jab through, but he leaned his head out of the way, and the Baron's fist passed close to his ear.

It was not a new move, and the riposte from the Baron's opponent would be either a left hook over the extended jabbing arm or a countering right cross. The German had seen them both, and he was ready for either.

Instead, Matt's dropped left arm rose outside the Baron's thrusting right arm and slammed downward with almost crushing force onto the German's forearm. The weight of the blow held the Baron's entire right arm lower than planned, and powered by the momentum of his own slamming punch, Matt came in over it with the straightest and most classic right cross he had ever thrown—aimed exactly and delivered with all of his whippy body behind it onto the point of Baron Von Haas's chin. There was no instant for the Baron's head-protecting left hand to block. Unobstructed, Matt's fist went in deep, and the Boss's Boy felt his knuckles grind and everything ahead of those knuckles folding and giving way.

The impact of Matt's clenched fist sounded sodden, as if he had punched the side of a horse, but the result was thunderous. The Baron dropped as if struck by a sledge. He collapsed straight down and lay as if dead with his face buried in the dirt of the fight square.

The Irish crowd exploded in a mindless shout while the Germans sat silent and barely believing.

Matt's had been a tremendous punch, planned and perfectly executed, and if he had been present, China Smith would have joined the crowd's enthusiasm.

Leaving the opening to tempt the Baron's almost certain lunging jab had been routine, but turning the fighter just enough to degrade his swordsman's balance, denying instantaneous retreat or dipping sideward for the crucial instant, had left the Baron stuck in place as if nailed to the ground.

The mob of spectators on both sides would recognize no such refinements. To them, only the blow had really counted. China Smith would have appreciated the opening created by Matt's downward smash of the Baron's jabbing arm, and he would have especially approved of the straight-as-a-string right hand that detonated against the Baron's jaw, knocking the sword fighter unconscious.

For all of their years together, China had preached that the shortest distance from point to point was always a straight line. The straight punch got there first, and if the fighter rolled his shoulder behind the punch, as the Boss's Boy had, the impact could be magnified into a knockout blow.

Shaking the pain from already swelling knuckles, young Matt Miller felt the enthusiastic adulation of the crowd envelop him. Klubber Cole held Matt's fist aloft in victory, and German companions knelt to help revive the barely moving Baron Von Haas.

Within the crowd, Mickey McFee shook his own fist in excited approval, and Matt was especially pleased by that. He saw Lukey Bates standing with his jaw still agape and his head twisting, as if he could not accept what he had seen.

Germans approached with hands outstretched for shaking. As he completed those rounds and survived the heavy backslapping of the Irish contingent, the Baron got himself erect and pushed aside helping hands.

Von Haas presented himself with grace and dignified congratulations. The Boss's Boy filed the Baron's graciousness in defeat as a proper way to act—if his own occasion ever appeared.

An immense swelling was already forming near the joint on one side of the Baron's jaw, and Matt expected bone might have broken.

Klubber Cole shortened their handshake to turn the defeated fighter to his handlers and to suggest that the swelling be immediately soaked for some hours in the coldest water they could manage and that the jaw be immobilized by wrapping tightly until swelling went down and the damaged jaw bone properly examined.

Before Mickey McFee entered the square for the big fight of the evening, Matt got his own battered hand into a bucket of stream water. Caring for his swelling knuckles allowed him to calm after the adrenalin rush of the fast and furious battling.

The Baron's single punishing stab had landed high enough not to swell Matt's eye, and the Boss's Boy was grateful for that. He would have an undisguisable lump for a day or two, and Big Matt would be angry enough without the sight of his son with a blackened and swollen eye. Matt tried to hope that China might blunt the sting of his father's exasperation at least a little, but China, too, might not think much of his fighting unprepared, wearing work boots, and with his fists unwrapped.

Matt resolved to enjoy the rest of the evening and leave tomorrow to whatever came. If the boss and China were real late, Matt thought he might be absent visiting the upriver coal operation, even if it was Sunday.

Mickey McFee met Frederick The Great at ring center, and Matt doubted that either man took a step backward. Frederick was tough and threw punches from all angles, but McFee right-handed him until Matt feared the German's head might fall from his shoulders.

McFee punished his opponent until the man collapsed. Mickey took his own licks as if they had never landed, but the Boss's Boy knew that China Smith would have shook his head and claimed that win or lose, if McFee took many such batterings he would be fit only to carry heavy things.

Mickey sure could hit, though, and Matt Miller found himself wondering how he would stand up to such hammer blows launched one after another until his opponent folded?

Something to consider, if he really ever expected to meet Mickey McFee in the so-called square circle.

9

It was not that bad. The Boss was late coming, and China had worked at smoothing young Matt's path.

Matt had not slipped away to other duties. Lukey Bates was at church, and Matt had considered that escape option as well. Instead, the Boss's Boy worked at odds and ends—killing time until his father appeared.

When he arrived alone, China had planted his feet and examined his charge's swollen temple.

"They claim the Baron did that with a single jab. He must have power."

Matt was not defensive about it. "Hardest jab I have ever seen, China. Haas is a sword fighter, and he stabbed his best hand straight out with body lunges as if his arm were a sword and brought his back leg forward so that he was set to jab again. He is very practiced and well balanced.

"Every time he landed, the punch was dazing. The two Irishmen he flattened ahead of me ate

116

enough jabs to last a lifetime. They couldn't get away from the Baron's punches, and their only chance was to land a lucky punch—which never happened." Matt gently touched his swelling. "He only got to me once, but I felt it clear to my toes.

"I guess they told you that I knocked his jab downward with my left forearm and kept going with a straight right to his chin. His whole body was moving forward behind his jab, and he walked right into it."

Matt shook his head grimly and fingered a pair of swollen knuckles. "If the Baron has a left hand punch, I never saw it."

Then with a grin, "I'd hate to meet Von Haas with a saber in his fist. My guess is that wherever he came from he was known as a ferocious sword fighter."

China stayed sober. "I asked around—as you should have before you jumped into the square. Fist fighting a man you never saw before and know nothing about is a sucker's game."

Matt said, "I got a good look at him while he was knocking out our Irishmen."

Smith sighed and explained what he had learned. "Deiter Von Haas has a town named after his family. They are richer than Midas, but Deiter, who is now the family head, has a wandering streak. For the moment, he lives and works with the other Dutchmen living along the creek, but he will move on to see what he can see.

"Did you notice the scars along his hairline? Haas attended a university in Heidelberg, Germany.

The German I talked with does not know the details, but Von Haas dueled in some ancient clubs they have. Those sword fighters get scars like Haas has."

Matt interrupted, "Here comes Pa up the path, China. I've got to get ready for him. All I've got to add about the Baron is that I hope I won't be fighting him again." Matt considered for a minute.

"The fact is, I sort of like Von Haas. He has a personal dignity that makes a bout more of a contest and less of a fight to the finish. I like that attitude."

Smith leaned out the office door to judge the Boss's progress up the hill. "When your father gets here, you be quiet and humble. I've softened him up by explaining how you almost had to jump in to defend the Irish Miller Men who were getting whipped one after another. I made it sound like an honorable team sort of thing, Matt. Don't mess up my story."

If China Smith had softened the Boss, young Matt would not have wished to sit through his father's stronger commentary. Matt Miller senior laid his tongue powerfully on his wayward son.

Low class, stupid, trashy, and a complete embarrassment to Miller Enterprises were included before big Matt really got down to it.

Young Matt had fought his last bare knuckle mill, and young Matt had better damned well turn in some serious profit from his lackadaisical, half-baked poking around with coal and plank-making or he would find himself bent over a pick and shovel until hell turned cold. Furthermore . . . the Boss's Boy got the idea.

Lukey Bates did not appear after church, and the two Millers and China had the office to themselves. It was mid-afternoon before young Matt believed the office temperament was right to draw his father and China Smith into conversation about a new idea or two that he wanted them to consider.

Matt said, "I was out at the work camp early this morning, Pa."

He was interrupted. "Basking in glory from having punched another man's face?"

"No Pa." Matt thought it best not to pursue that direction.

"I was studying on how they are living out there because I have an idea that could make a profit as well as improve some other things harder to measure."

Profit always interested big Matt. The Boss's Boy felt able to continue.

"Most of those people are living poor and winter is closing in. Their tents and shanties are shabby protection against the cold, and none of them could afford better lodging, even if there was any around here."

China interrupted. "Most of them will leave when the freeze comes, Matt. There won't be any work here and little anywhere else. They go down to the cities and pile in with relatives or friends. If many of them have been able to put away money to hold them over, I will be surprised."

"I know that, China. When I was helping Uncle Brascomb, I watched poor people flood into the city every winter, and that was the beginning of my idea."

Big Matt's eyebrows rose, before his eyes squinted at the "helping" part, but he said nothing.

Little Matt decided to back up a little and develop his explanation about as he had been working at it.

"I've been stacking every log I could get from the river. You've no doubt noticed."

Of course they had. Lukey Bates complained about money going out to men dragging river logs behind Halderman's Island and nothing coming in from it. It was clear to everybody else that little Matt would run the sawmill most of the winter, and their profit would come in the spring. So?

Matt continued in a rush. "My plan is to talk the Irishmen into building themselves hotels where they can live for very little money all of the time."

The boss began to bristle, and Matt guessed he had better hurry on.

"My idea is that I—we, that is—would make the mill available to them to saw the lumber they will need for their lodgings. They will mill and carpenter without pay, but when they get shelter built, they will be able to live inside for almost nothing—maybe a nickel or a dime a day.

"For Miller Men, we could hold off on the rent money until they are working for us again in the spring. Other people, if the Irish build enough places for others, would have to pay as they go—by the week maybe."

No one said anything, but Matt could tell that his father was churning the numbers in his mind.

"Pa, you own that land just upriver. It's flat and there are already two wells dug there, so we know water will be handy. That is the perfect place to put in a row of workers' hotels.

"We will make some profit from the workmen paying for their lodging all winter, and if we opened a little Miller Company store where they could buy flour and meal, maybe bread, bacon, and other necessities—all to be paid in the spring when they are at work again, we might find some real profit."

Still no one said anything, and his father was quick to shut down ideas he did not like. Matt thought the silence to be a positive sign.

He quickly added, "Remember that we will own the hotels and that we got them almost for free." Big Matt should like that part.

Matt added more. "Keeping our Miller Men close will be valuable when the cold leaves, Pa. If we don't hold them here, some of the best will find other work—like they do every year, and the rest will straggle back in no order at all. That could delay starting early when the best deals can be made—like before-filling canal work, and . . ."

Big Matt said, "Go on," but the son had almost run out. He sought clinchers, but he had proposed the heart of his plan. If that didn't sell? Well, he did have a few more points.

"I was talking to Mrs. Black off and on." China moved as if uncomfortable, and Matt wondered about that, but he continued.

"I suggested that if—just in case you understand—we built hotels like I have been describing, we might hire her to do some cooking out there. Men come up with a dime or two for decent meals now and then, and providing a hot supper might do best.

"If it didn't work out, no one would be out anything, but I suspect the restaurant business could work along with our store and make a profit. If the store had a warm stove that men could come in and sit around during the cold months, we might stock plug tobacco for them and crackers and cheeses, and maybe . . ."

Big Matt raised a hand, and Matt stopped in mid-sentence. The father dragged out his watch. "How long is this explanation, Matt? Your mention of Mrs. Black's cooking awakened my appetite."

"Only a little more, Pa." Matt hurried on. "The rivers will not be frozen most of the time, and that means logs will keep coming down. If I can have my men on the river, we will get all of the logs because everybody else will be gone to the city or holed up keeping warm. If we can't get them, the high water will take the logs over the dam, and they will be gone.

"If other people do collect logs, I could even refuse to buy them, and they haven't anyone else to sell to—so, I will at least get their logs really cheap. If some of our men are paid this winter for gathering logs, they will spend most of their money in our new hotels or in our new store, and we will get a lot of it back.

"And Pa, as long as I can keep the mill stream flowing, we can cut and store boards for spring shipping, and . . ."

This time it was China who held up a restraining palm. "The Captain can work out the rest of it, Matt. Let's go down to Mrs. Black's and eat. That will give us all time to think about your scheming, and we can talk about it later."

Matt had about run down anyway, but he, also, would think while eating, and when the other men were ready, he would be again armed with powerful arguments.

His plan was sound, and, except for pure stubbornness (and maybe a little exasperation at his box fighting), his father would have no counter-arguments. Instead of wasted months, the winter began to sound interesting.

10

Before the hotels proposition could be further discussed, the Captain's immense safe arrived. The vault was a monster of a steel box; rivets lined every joint, and the entire mass was banded with a dozen thick, wrought iron straps, each of which was forged into an endless box pattern re-enforcing the safe on all sides except the door.

Both Millers were impressed. The safe lay on its back, but they judged the massive recessed door to stand nearly seven feet high. Because of its weight, the door's thickness could not be examined until the safe was upright, but a brass-faced combination lock and an inch-thick steel opening handle promised that the door would also be nearly impregnable.

The safe had been shipped via canal boat, but John McFee's crew levered the immense weight onto a flat-decked barge and maneuvered the awkward load down the Susquehanna River until it was beached below the Miller Headquarters.

Boat anchors were planted uphill from the boat, and China Smith oversaw the rigging of ropes and pulleys to be drawn tight by a number of oxen. Planks were laid to guide the great safe ashore. When the oxen leaned into their yokes, the iron mass slid easily onto the bank and, assisted by multiple log rollers, began plowing its way across Water Street and almost to the buried anchors.

The remainder was routine. The anchors were repositioned further uphill, the oxen pulled, and the safe moved ever closer to the headquarters building. Once on site, the laborers worried the safe into its final rest using iron wedges to tip the safe before heaving mightily against long steel wrecking bars until the vault edged ahead.

Limestone foundation stones had been long in place waiting for the safe's arrival, and workmen heaved the massive box erect and carefully leveled while a removed wall of the building was being replaced. Only then, did the Captain twirl the brass knob and apply the secret combination.

The Millers and China Smith were privy to the opening, and only the three would know the combination. Lukey Bates was trusted, but big Matt saw no reason for the clerk to be involved. Bandits had been known to kidnap officials and force them to open their vaults. The fewer who knew the combination of the Millers' safe, the more secure the contents would be.

Big Matt allowed everyone interested to examine the inside of the vault. The three-inch thick door with steel rods that turned into the adjoining steel walls would be noted and spoken about. Casual attack by some fool with a keg of blasting powder might be deterred.

It had been an exciting day with many visitations and shared admiration for the strongest safe any had ever seen. Before they closed for the night, a number of Petersburg residents had asked to have their money and important papers stored in the new vault.

The Captain agreed in principle but required that they wait a few days until he had determined the proper—if small—charge he would levy for the protection of people's valuables.

Little Matt realized that by most measures, they had just become bankers. His father had a knack for making money, and the son wondered if he could perform similarly. He supposed that with his river logs, his mill, and his coal, he, to some small degree, already had.

Maybe some of big Matt's entrepreneurial traits had been passed to him. That awareness felt good, and the Boss's Boy went to sleep comforted that the future held possibilities yet undiscovered.

Then it all went bad.

John McFee died in his sleep. There was no understandable explanation. Mother McFee had turned to her husband, and the family head was simply dead. In an instant, the McFee family had moved from comfortable living to the edge of poverty. Young Mickey McFee could not yet earn the wage of his father, and he was now the family's only provider. The mother and sister's sewing and patching pittances suddenly loomed important.

Winter was coming, and work would be scarce. Some of the best workers would be kept on, of course. Young Matt Miller hoped his father would count Mickey McFee among them.

There was Mickey's income from bare-fist fighting, but unless a fighter was a champion in a large city, there was little money to be made. The Boss's Boy doubted that Mickey, the courageous slugger, could rise to those heights.

There was nothing more to add.

Most came to see John McFee properly interred in the local cemetery, and someone was chipping at a stone to be placed at the gravesite.

Life was difficult for laborers. All lived close to the bone with few resources to fall back on. Young Matt wondered if the McFees could now afford their comfortable two-room lodging near the hotel.

He resolved to purchase new pants and a winter coat from Mother McFee. His father gave him little money because he had not needed or cared much about having cash in his pocket. Maybe he should carry a few dollars, so that he could pitch in where it might really be needed.

As work was already slowing, big Matt brought Alex Donovan in to boss the suddenly leaderless headquarters gang. Donovan was known as a driver, but the Miller Men would work extra or harder to stay on over the frozen months.

There was no greener grass just over the horizon for laborers. Men usually moved on during the summers when work could sometimes be plentiful, and a workman had opportunities to find a job and adjust to a new situation.

Irish workers were notorious for always moving west. Men who had seemed settled in and part of the Miller team too often shouldered their few belongings and headed for the farthest frontier—where opportunity might be better.

Big Matt said it never was better, but many had to learn that for themselves. The Captain claimed that a man could make it just about as well and as often in one place as another. The man who worked hardest, smartest, and longest got ahead, he stated.

Watching who worked as his father described, young Matt came to accept the idea, but misfortunes, like John McFee's unexpected death, showed that fate also had a hand, and Matt could only hope that good luck would keep coming their way.

When he was ready to talk about hotel building, the Captain included Alex Donovan and Lukey Bates. Big Matt called them together, and simply said, "Matt has a proposal that interests me. He can explain it, and you can all comment. If you approve, we will begin with the first freeze." Then he sat back, and Matt had the floor.

Where to begin? Matt had not expected his father to just drop the load on him. He had visualized hours of mutual planning and discussion—even then, he had supposed big Matt would have handled details. Well, he always wanted to be in charge, and this was his idea. Matt began.

"Except for a few older men with families and a few foremen who are better paid, our workers are living poor." Matt could sense a 'So what is new about that' feeling, and he hurried on.

"My plan is to have our best men begin sawing boards preparing to put up a number of worker lodgings. We can call them hotels for lack of a better description. There will be no direct payment involved. The idea is that we will let the men who are going to live in the buildings use the mill for free. They will use logs we have stored, and they will have to plan and construct the buildings they believe will best serve them. The hotels will be raised on the Miller land just beyond town.

"Those who build will be allowed to live in the buildings without cost through this winter. All others, and we must have room for about two dozen others, will pay ten cents a day for their lodging. If they are Miller Men, their payment can be deferred until they are again at work. Otherwise, rent will be collected once each week. No rent, no shelter, that will be the deal.

"After this winter, everyone will pay the same—whatever we decide is right.

"Now, understand that the Miller Company will own the hotels. The builders and occupants are only renters. I believe that everyone will gain through this venture. The first gain will be by Miller Men who choose to help in construction. They will have free housing through the freeze up."

Matt tried to judge the effect of his words on Bates and Donovan, who had not heard them before. Neither gave any discernable clues. So, Matt went on.

"I also plan to have the hotel builders establish a small store, perhaps within one of the hotels. The store will offer staples and probably a common room where hotel occupants can sit to eat and converse. A large stove will be provided, but if they wish to enjoy the stove, the hotel occupiers will have to collect the wood and feed the flames.

"Miller Men will have store credit payable in the spring when they return to work. Others will pay cash or barter.

"Finally, I intend to provide a one-meal-a-day food service where men can purchase an evening meal. Payment for meals will be handled the same as shelter. Whether meals will continue once warm weather returns will be determined by the demand."

Matt hesitated before adding, "It might turn out that lunches might be packed for men to carry to work. We might even . ." He decided to halt his dreaming.

Lukey Bates asked, "How do we know that most of the men who pay nothing all winter will not depart for other jobs when the weather breaks?"

Matt was ready for that question because the answer had plagued him since first imagining the hotels.

Matt said, "We will improve our chances of getting our money in two ways. First, those men who winter with us will be assured by us of work as soon as our spring hiring begins.

"Second, I will depend on Alex Donovan to choose men who are honest and dependable. I assume those men will have a record of work with us and provide indications that they will remain with the company for some time to come.

"We will not be dealing in dozens of workers. I expect that less than a dozen will be enough, but that will be up to Mister Donovan. He will be the man who hires and fires as well as sees that the work gets done and done right. Which is what he has been doing for Miller companies since before my time."

There was silence, and Matt waited for anyone to join in. He expected his father might break the silence, but it was Donovan who spoke first.

"Some of our men have spoken about going up to Millerstown for the winter. There are said to be twenty-nine hotels open to canal and other workmen right there in town."

As if choosing his words, Donovan took his time. "Up there, some of the hotels are just one room bunkhouses. I have seen them, and they are poorly built with bunks shoulder to shoulder. Most are two story buildings that have no heat, but some boast a stove somewhere in the middle.

"Speaking mainly for myself, I would not wish to winter in such a place, although it might prove better than the tents and shanties too many are living in. I would like to hear what you have in mind for buildings, Mister Miller."

Matt was uncomfortable with the "Mister Miller" from a man of Donovan's years, but he was set with his answers.

"I believe that two stories are better than one or three. One story wastes rising heat. Three stories is a pain climbing in and out, and three stories is more difficult to build.

"I think that partitioned spaces would be better than rooms because partitions that go neither to ceiling or floor allow heat or fresh air to circulate. We might wish to block out a number of rooms, however. Beyond there, I hope to have others' ideas in play.

"I think that a stove at each end of a floor would work well, although I worry about stoves sitting on wooden floors. Perhaps we could place them in sand boxes. Chimneys will be required, but they will not have to be fireplace size. Small stove chimneys should go up quickly, but . . ."

Matt stopped himself and shook his head at his own spill of ideas. "I have been thinking about this for a long time, and I admit to having schemes yet unannounced, but I do wish to turn the planning and building over to Mister Donovan. He can listen to my ideas or not, as he sees fit."

Matt added his last comment. "We have one other advantage in that men wintering up or downriver are unlikely to enjoy. Our sawmill has been producing for more than a year, and our piles of slabs are immense. That wood will be available to those living in the hotels, and in my estimation, there is already more than enough stove wood for two years. Our Miller Men will be warm and comfortable this winter. They will not be crowded in on each other, and with us, their quarters will be free."

Lukey Bates said, "We won't make a dime out of this."

Matt said, "Not in rent, this year—probably, but we will gain free buildings, and the store and food might bring in a profit. Next year, we will make some money."

Matt hesitated before easing into thinking that had been rattling around in his mind since he was a boy.

"The idea of Miller Men has worked well, and we have some of the best men around. They like working for us, and they are as dependable as the sun rising. Providing decent living places can only improve their attitudes and loyalty. That can pay somewhere along, I figure."

The meeting broke with no solid decision, but Matt believed his father would quickly announce a go ahead for the hotels.

On their way down the hill, Matt caught Alex Donovan alone. Matt was nervous with his request but plowed ahead, anyway.

"Mister Donovan, when you are considering the best men to keep on here more or less permanently, I wish you would give consideration to Mickey McFee. I know he is young and is annoying sometimes but, well, his family is in need, and I believe McFee has prospects—given the chance."

Donovan halted and fixed Matt with an annoyed and disgusted expression that resembled the one he had worn before throwing Matt into the canal those many years before.

"The plan is that I choose the men, young Matt. In hiring and firing I do the best for the company, not for the man or his family. If a man makes the measure, he will be kept. If he doesn't, he will be out."

Matt sunk into his collar in embarrassment, but Alex Donovan brought him back out.

"It happens that I already have McFee in mind. Unless he does something foolish, which with McFee is almost probable, he will be on the building crew, but do not think that it was your suggestion. I choose the men, not you."

Matt smiled within. Donovan probably did have McFee in mind, but now it would be sure. Mickey would be hired for the winter—and McFee would live at home with his family. They would not have to provide bunking for him. Good business all around, Matt figured.

Then he wondered, why did he care? McFee was an almost constant annoyance. He seemed to turn up everywhere, and Matt could feel McFee watching and judging him. A worker was not supposed to be hoping to fist fight his boss—at least he should not let it show.

Matt corrected himself. McFee did not actually let such feelings surface, but Matt knew they were there. McFee was just aching to square off against the Boss's Boy to see who really was best—Matt could sense it.

Matt guessed he might have to whack McFee a few times yet. He felt his fingers tingle and his arm muscles bunch.

11

The weather was summer warm and his father and Lukey Bates had gone to Philadelphia. Matt, with China looking over his shoulder, was in charge. He was almost twenty years old and . . .

Alex Donovan came into the office gripping a skinny child by his unkempt hair. What in. . .?

Donovan marched the child to a reporting position in front of big Matt's desk—behind which, Matt, the man in charge, tried to disguise his astonishment.

Matt managed a reasonably strong, "And who is this, Mister Donovan?"

Remarkably, the skeletally thin youth popped to a military attention and announced that he was Wilhelm Brado, formerly from Deutschland. The boy's English was poor, but he had understood Matt's query.

Matt looked questioningly at his foreman.

Donovan released his grip on Wilhelm Brado's scalp lock and examined his captive with a suspicious eye.

Donovan said, "This scarecrow has been hanging around the Irish camp like a starving hound. He eats what little is thrown out, and I do not care to guess where he sleeps."

Donovan again closed a huge fist within the boy's too long and thoroughly matted hair.

"The fact is, this boy is starving. Look at him, Mister Miller. I can see clean through his ribs. I figure we have two choices. The first is to just run him off and when we find them, we can bury his bones in the woods.

"The second, and probably best, is to turn him over to the sheriff for living in the county's poorhouse."

Matt was not fooled by the foreman's rough treatment or harsh words. Alex Donovan saw a youth in trouble and wanted something done about it. So he had come to the man in charge.

China was down at Mrs. Black's restaurant. Now that Matt thought about it, he spent a lot of time down there. So Donovan expected the Boss's Boy to handle the matter. Well, he had come to the right man—only young Matt had not the slightest idea what he could or should do with a woods-running orphan, or maybe a runaway indentured boy, or maybe . . . Investigate, that is what he would do.

Matt said, "Thank you, Mister Donovan. You are right; we can't have children starving in our woods. Leave him with me, and I will take care of it." Donovan released his hair grip and left wordlessly. Hard man, Donovan, but he had brought the youth in. Most would not have cared a lick what happened to the boy.

Now what? Matt studied the youth standing almost rigid, his heels together and his palms plastered to the seams of his ragged pants. Lord, but he was skinny—and he was shaking. With fear or from hunger? Matt had no idea. Probably both.

Matt pointed to Lukey Bates' chair and ordered, "Sit down."

The boy sat, and Matt saw his eyes pause as they passed over a remnant of cheese and some dried out bread that he and China had enjoyed. Was the youth really as starved as he looked? Matt let him suffer for a few moments while he examined possibilities. The boy's nose twitched, probably from the bread smell, but his eyes stayed on Matt.

Matt rose and started for the door. He pointed to the bread and cheese, and said, "Finish that up, if you want it." He looked back as he stepped out of the office door, but young Brado had not jumped at the offered repast.

A group of Germans was improving their road. It was Matt's idea, and he judged their rather amazing progress. All laborers worked hard, but the Germans seemed to accomplish more as teams than did the prickly Irishmen who argued among themselves almost constantly.

He called across, and one of the workers laid his tool aside and came to the office. Matt asked, "How good is your English?" The man's answer demonstrated that he was not a master of the language. Matt sent him to the German camp for someone who was. When he reentered his office, Wilhelm Brado was polishing off the bread and cheese with a gusto that indicated serious hunger.

Matt pretended to ignore the hungry youth while leafing through a number of Lukey Bates' ledgers, but he watched from the corner of his eye and tried to evaluate the boy's abilities. A skinny boy in wretched clothing who badly needed a bath was as far as he got before his German translator arrived.

The volunteer English speaker was the Baron, Deiter Haas, and that did not surprise the Boss's Boy. Von Haas often translated for the German workmen who stayed close to the Miller businesses. Haas spoke clearly if stiffly in English, and he was obviously smart and experienced. Matt regularly expected Haas's departure, but the Baron hung on, and, although he did not seize pick or shovel and therefore did not earn wages, Haas was often useful.

They exchanged handshakes before Matt said, "Alex Donovan found this boy hanging around the Irish camp, Deiter. The boy's English is terrible, and if I am to decide what to do with him, I must find out his circumstances.

"He may be a runaway that the law is looking for, or he could be simply lost. Most likely he is an orphan dodging some county poorhouse, and I do not wish that existence upon anyone. I would appreciate your interpreting what this walking skeleton has to say."

Von Haas began, and the boy's demeanor and answers demonstrated great respect. Germans recognized inherited nobility and authority. Matt thought them a disciplined people. There were a lot of them, and he planned to integrate more Germans into their labor force.

Von Haas was quick with his questions, and the boy's answers were rarely lengthy. Deiter turned to explain the youth's situation.

"This is Wilhelm Brado, Mister Miller."

Matt interrupted. "Deiter, I have asked you to call me, Matt. You are not one of our employees. I have not found it necessary to address you as Baron Von und Zu Haas, and you have not shown resentment to my calling you by your first name. Please use my given name from now on."

Without embarrassment, Haas began again. "Matt, this is Wilhelm Brado most recently from Philadelphia but originally from Kitzingen, Germany. In Germany, Herr Doktor Brado, Wilhelm's father had been a professor of mathematics at the university. A professorship sounds important, but times are difficult in Germany, and income was small. The Brado's started for this country in search of a new life, but both parents died aboard ship—a plague, I gather.

"The parents were buried at sea, of course, and there was no one at the docks to meet Wilhelm, so he continued on his father's plan to go to the frontiers where opportunities were said to be many. There his father hoped to obtain a teaching position, and the family would prosper."

Matt shifted uncomfortably. "That was a poor plan. Not many go to school in this country. This town has no school, and the closer you get to the frontiers the less anyone cares about schooling."

Haas nodded. "In Europe, there are many misunderstandings of this country."

The Baron smiled in his own amusement. "I have not found the land of adventure and excitement that I anticipated. In this, my second year in America, I have recognized that here, as it is everywhere, men prosper by hard work—especially from the hard work of others. Before long, I will return to my country rich with this new-found knowledge—that my father and grandfather had explained to me long before I was this boy's age."

Deiter added, "Young Brado understands English far better than he speaks it. I gather that his family was working on their new language for some time, but, as most youths do, Wilhelm had an ear turned away. I am sure that he now regrets his inattention."

Matt turned to Wilhelm Brado. "Why are you out here scraping food from poor men's leavings and sleeping in the woods, Wilhelm?"

Brado's answer was in German, and too fast for Matt to interpret. Von Haas explained.

"He says that he is going to the west seeking his fortune, and he expects that once he has reached the frontier, he will find a place where he can be of service." Haas avoided laughter, so Matt did the same.

The going to the frontier idea was extremely poor, but Matt Miller gave Wilhelm Brado high marks for working at it. The Boss's Boy thought the youth had been fortunate not to have experienced serious misfortune long before now. Perhaps he had, and they would discover details if the boy stayed nearby. Nearby? Matt pondered how that could come about.

The Baron was also considering, and he suggested, "If you can find nothing for him, we will take him in at the German camp, Matt."

Haas hesitated, as if weighing the child's abilities and potential. "This boy has been educated, Matt. He speaks High German, and he practices courtesies in his speech and posture that are uncommon to our peasantry."

Matt said, "He stands well, and he listens closely." Then he wondered, "Does he understand what we are speaking of now?"

Haas questioned and translated. "He understands and is pleased that we speak well of him."

Directing his words to Wilhelm, Matt asked, "Would you be interested in staying here and working as we see fit? Or would you rather enjoy a meal or two and continue on your way?"

Matt could sense Von Haas waiting, as he did, with intense interest in the youth's answer.

Wilhelm Brado did speak clearly.

"I have not done well in my search. I would be grateful for any work I could perform."

Matt spoke to Von Haas. "Well, that was excellent English. If he can speak that well on occasion, he should pick up the language quite quickly."

Deiter Haas agreed. "Shall I take him to our camp, Matt? I will see that he has shelter and food."

Von Haas's offer might be best, but Matt had another scheme forming. He studied the German boy for long moments before he had his words right. Then he wondered if his father might disown him over his choice. Orphans and runaways, although usually older than this boy, were everywhere. Why should he bother with this one? Matt had no special answer, but China Smith would have explained that "He just liked the cut of his jib."

Matt said, "I want him to understand exactly what I am saying, Deiter, so I will ask you to explain my words." Von Haas nodded acceptance, and they began.

Matt spoke to the boy and waited until the Baron re-spoke his words in German. "Wilhelm, you have three choices. You can continue on your way. You can go with Baron Von Haas and he will fit you in with the German men who work for us or work in this neighborhood. Third, I will hire you to work here in this office for our company.

"If you choose to work here, you will be given shelter in the building behind this office. You will eat when my clerk eats, and you will perform whatever work we ask you to do. You may shovel horse manure, or you may work at the company account books." Matt ruffled the pages of one of Lukey Bates' ledgers.

"You will receive a very small wage and clothing will be provided. You will be expected to learn English as quickly as possible, and you must learn to read, write, and figure in English so that you can work at these and other books."

Matt paused to allow Von Haas to catch up. The Baron nodded that the boy understood.

Matt continued, "Mister Bates, who keeps these records, will be your primary teacher, but there will be others. Mister Donovan, who brought you here by your hair, will be one, and if he is willing, Baron von Haas may also help."

Matt explained to Deiter Haas. "If he goes with us, I will be pleased to hire you as a tutor, Deiter. If this boy is going to be valuable to us, his retraining as an American should be swift and thorough, but I would not want him to lose respect for his homeland or to turn himself from his own people."

Matt had made his offer hard to refuse, and neither man was surprised when Wilhelm Brado chose to work with the Miller Company. Matt scratched out a note to Mother McFee asking that Wilhelm Brado, who spoke little English, be fitted with clothing so that he would not embarrass the company and be returned to the headquarters when he was ready.

Matt and the Baron exchanged a few of the mandatory German handshakes, and Matt believed the Baron to be pleased by the outcome. Matt did like the way it had gone, but he was still not sure just how young Brado would be worked into the company.

There were two other hurdles to be overcome. First, would be China Smith, who Matt expected would be more amused than exasperated. The father's response could not really be anticipated. Matt thought his best bet was to have the boy looking decent and gainfully employed before the Captain encountered him.

Gainfully employed would be the problem. How much did you pay a child like Willie Brado? Based on his own experience while growing up, Matt guessed darned little.

Surely not a dollar a week. Perhaps fifty cents a week? China would have advice there, but the less Brado was paid, the less likely the senior Miller would be to revoke the agreement.

Wilhelm would be eating with Matt or Lukey Bates and sleeping for free, Matt expected they could settle on five cents a day. Nothing for Sunday, of course. The Millers were not running a charity operation.

12

For a moment, big Matt listened to Willy Brado's twig broom industriously sweeping the dirt in front of the Miller headquarters. The Captain had not completely bought into his son's employment of the boy, but a week had passed, and big Matt had not shuffled the youth down to the German camp along Little Juniata Creek.

Matt Miller had been longer in Philadelphia than intended, and he had more important things on his mind. He had gathered his son, China Smith, and Lukey Bates to listen.

Big Matt said, "As you know, I have begun to separate this headquarters from my brother's operations in the east. The separation is more difficult than I had anticipated. Brascomb resents the change, and he makes everything painful. He hides papers, and he fails to remember important details."

The boss sighed, "Brascomb's irritation will only delay, but it means that I will have to be in

Philadelphia a number of times before everything is settled.

"For now, Matt and China will hold the fort out here while I concentrate on shifting things around. When I go back to wrestle Brascomb a few falls, I will take Lukey. Too much of that paperwork is beyond me."

The Captain scrubbed at his vest, as though he suffered chest pain, then he went on.

"Matt, when you were working with your uncle, how well did you get along with Scribner?"

Scribner had no commonly used first name, but the employment records listed him as Roger Scribner, age 37, single—clerk. Matt thought that description included almost all that any of them knew about the man.

Scribner had worked for Brascomb Miller since boyhood. He came to work on time and buried himself in his bookkeeping. Matt had examined the payroll, and he knew that Scribner, like his uncle's other two clerks, received less than his father would have paid. Lukey Bates was better rewarded, and Bates did not have to labor beneath the lash of Brascomb Miller's sharp tongue.

Once, when Brascomb's ire fell on Scribner's shoulders, Matt had caught his eye and winked at the abused clerk in shared understanding. Thereafter, when either endured specially directed tongue-lashings, exchanged winks eased tensions, and over Matt's two winters, became something silently shared among all the clerks. Matt wondered if the small bonding continued after his departure?

With those memories in mind, Matt made his answer pithy.

"Scribner works hard and well. He is easy to work with, and he knows the business. He is neat and on time. He is not first out the door at quitting time, and he is quiet and unassuming. Uncle Brascomb should pay him a lot more than he does, and, if I were Scribner, I would have long ago moved to where I was more appreciated."

Big Matt nodded. "That is good to hear. My opinion is much the same as yours. I ask because Scribner approached me with his request to transfer to this part of the Miller operations. Lukey already needs help, and . . ." big Matt gestured toward the hard-sweeping Wilhelm Brado . . . "that skinnied-down rag bag boy you hired may not be much use for a year or more.

"The problem is that Scribner has many years with this company. He has seniority, but I want Lukey as chief clerk without resentment from men working for him. How do you think Scribner would feel about being second man to someone younger and less experienced?"

Lukey tried to speak, but the Captain's raised hand made him wait. Big Matt said, "I know how you see it, Lukey, I want to hear Matt's thoughts."

The Boss's Boy had no doubts. "Scribner will hardly notice, Pa. He is not ambitious, and if it were not for Uncle Brascomb's barbed tongue, I doubt Scribner would be looking for a change. Out here, you will pay him what he is worth—which is a lot more than he is getting now, and our bookkeeping is not as intense. Scribner would be good for us, Pa." Matt glanced at Lukey Bates, "And I expect Lukey was about to say exactly the same."

The Captain asked, "Lukey?"

Bates nodded his head. Then he added, "Matt has it right, Captain. I did not realize that Scribner was interested, or I would have suggested he come with us. Your brother has few secrets from Scribner—not that he doesn't attempt to keep them to himself, but Scribner has been there so long that he knows almost everything." Lukey paused before suggesting, "What Scribner knows might come in handy, Captain."

Big Matt nodded acceptance, and little Matt assumed Scribner would soon be en route. Good! Bates did need help, and they had found no one else that looked promising. Uncle Brascomb might strangle himself because he would be acutely aware that Scribner knew details that he might not wish others—especially the company's senior man, to know. Matt liked that thought as well.

The Boss swung a thumb toward the company safe looming against the back wall. "As you know, I have transferred serious money from Philadelphia to our more handy safe. There will be more each trip until our separation is complete."

His chuckle was deep. "Getting cash from my brother is like pulling his teeth, but he has it, and he will cough it up." Big Matt shook his head in some awe. "You would think that our money was only Brascomb's money. Every dollar moved out causes him visible pain."

China added his thought. "You should have made this move years ago, Captain. Working with Philadelphia has always been a pain."

"You are probably right, China, but until Matt grew old enough to take hold, there was only Brascomb and me. We made a good team, and we have both prospered, but . . ." The Boss let it ride and returned to the conversation.

"I meant to speak about the safe. I do not like the way it sits in plain view. It almost challenges someone to try to break into it.

"Matt, I want you to have a couple of carpenters build a room around the safe. Make the entire back wall of this office a series of closets or something. The safe front will be hidden behind one of the doors—and it should be a strong door with a lock that will be difficult to break down to even get to the safe."

Matt thought that the best idea of the day. The huge iron box just sitting there, with other people's money in it, worried him. He had propped a loaded shotgun beside his bed, just in case.

The Boss continued with his son.

"So, Matt, beyond hiring some unusual workmen (his eyes again swung to the sounds of Wilhelm Brado's labors) what have you accomplished during my absence?"

Matt immediately felt nervous, but he believed his actions had been sound.

"Well, I spent some money, Pa."

The father threw up his hands in feigned despair. "Must you always begin with that particular statement, Matt? You always announce money spent. Instead tell me about money made. That would be a welcome change."

Matt hurried on. "This was a low water spring Pa. Only the earliest log rafts got down the river, so there were some raft breakups coming down that gave us a lot of logs to store behind Halderman's Island. We did especially well there, Pa."

The Boss nodded. "Money well spent, Matt. Sometimes, good logs are better than money."

Matt grimaced within and hurried on. "Well, I agree, Pa, but that isn't the money I referred to.

"A rafter was coming down the West Branch and got here more than a little too late. I got word passed to him that he had no chance of getting his raft through, and he pulled his load against the bank and tied it off while he looked for himself.

"I made it a point to happen along while he was staring at the bridge dam and the shallows below. He was finished, and he knew it. Unless there was a big river rising, he would have to hold his raft together for nearly a year until the spring rains and snow melt gave him water depth.

"I suggested that I lived nearby and might find use for his logs. I mentioned how hard it was to keep a raft together with the logs getting waterlogged and the ropes wearing and stretching.

"I told him how locals might see his logs as easy picking by just busting them loose and salvaging what they could off the dam and in the shallows.

"It took him three days, but he finally gave up, and I bought the whole raft for less than I could pay workers to gather individual logs. The logs from that raft have just about filled the channel behind Halderman's, Pa. We've got enough to last a long while."

The Captain nodded approval, and shook his head in some wonder. "You've got a knack for seeing opportunity, Matt. I assume there is enough money left in our safe to continue for a few weeks?"

Matt guessed he had done well. "There is more money now than there was when you left, Pa. Why we . . ."

The father held up a hand. "That will do for now on money reporting, Matt. I will look over the books. The more important question is, what is next? Have we got contracts waiting?"

China finally entered the game.

"There are important changes arriving, Captain. The canal construction work is more or less done. What is left has moved to the mountains, and the big contracts are out around Pittsburgh. We will have enough with Commonwealth maintenance contracts to keep our best men working, but there is change there as well."

Matt decided to take over. "Many of our Irish workers intend to move on, Pa. They seem to have developed itchy feet. They want to see the other side of the hill, or something like that."

The Boss grunted annoyance. "That's the Scots and the Irish for you. No matter how good they've got it, they move to the furthest frontier the first chance they get. Are they going as a bunch or just a few now and then, and when do they claim they are leaving? Some of them talk a lot and do nothing, you know."

China said, "Some have already gone, but not enough to bother our work. My guess is that the bulk of them will winter here in our hotels. Spring will see most of those that are planning to leave on the road." China looked thoughtful. "In fact, we might be a bit more careful to whom we give credit this winter."

Big Matt suggested, "We ought to have good men in mind to take their places. There is a lot of labor unrest taking place up in the coal regions, and it's the talk of Philadelphia. Men who have trouble in one place are likely to have it in the next. We don't want to hire malcontents that we will have to fire halfway through the summer."

Matt said, "I would like to hire Germans, Pa. There are some down in their camp that already consider themselves Miller Men."

The father's mouth set a bit grimly. "Like the ones you and McFee and a few others have been fist fighting?"

Matt hunched his shoulders readying himself for the anticipated onslaught. Sooner or later the fighting always came up. At least the slow-healing lump over his eye was completely gone.

"Most of the Germans are darn good workers, Pa, and I think we should tie them to us in some ways I haven't brought up. There are skills among them that we should have, and . . ."

"What skills?"

Ha, the Captain's mind had been diverted from fist fighting. "Brick making is one, and clay pottery is another. We should get dams across both Sherman's Creek and the Little Juniata before Harrisburg makes damming illegal. We can't get the speed we need on our water wheel at the mill to spin our saws the way we should. Dams can give us more power."

Then Matt went for his big one. "The fact is, Pa, we need at least one steam engine. Water wheels are passable, but they close down in the winter. An engine runs no matter what the weather. If we had a steam engine, we could spin two saw blades at once just about as fast as we want. We can have steel shafts and brass journals and iron axles that will last, with big screw nuts so that saw blade changing is quick and easy. We . . ."

Matt became aware of looking into widened eyes and open mouths. He dropped the steam engine and took up a more likely subject.

"Some Germans are terrific stone masons. We need them to get a foundry built to see if we can make use of that iron ore up on the ridge.

"We've got coal to burn in a foundry, and coal seems to be working as well as charcoal down the river. I think there is a market for ten plate stoves and big kitchen stoves with ovens. Everybody wants those, and a decent iron foundry could make them easily. One of the Germans I know about has iron casting experience, and . . ."

His father rose and walked out the door. China followed, but there was a smile on his face.

Lukey Bates said, "Sometimes you are scary, Matt. Your Dad was expecting that you might want to change the size of some lumber or something, and you laid out enough planning to employ every worker between here and York."

"Those ideas can make money, Lukey."

"And they will take money, Matt. And they will take time as well. A steam engine? Now where could we find a steam engine? Most people have never even seen one. Imagine what an engine could cost, if there was one for sale—which I have never heard of in all of my life.

"Talk sense, Matt; your father is not made of money. Some things are just beyond reach, and a steam engine is one of them." Lukey turned to his ledgers muttering about how he could use Scribner right now.

Matt heard his father and China trying to speak with Wilhelm Brado, and he hurried out to help translate the boy's words into English.

Wilhelm was standing at his usual attentive attention and answering the best he could. Matt judged the youth's English had already improved. Not letting him hang around with the Germans was a good decision. Immersed in English talk, Brado was progressing.

The young learned easily. Old folks, like China and his father clearly needed time to think through even the obvious things he proposed, Matt was discovering. The Boss's Boy decided to hold off on the other ideas he had until the Captain could digest what he had already been offered.

There was a bright side to their pondering. His father had not pursued the fist fighting, and every day further removed would make the incident older history. Maybe it would never come up again.

Never come up with his father, that was. China Smith enjoyed rehashing every detail about every bout, but China understood, and young Matt Miller enjoyed explaining how every fight had gone, especially his own—with all of the dramatizing possible.

13

China said, "I'm going up to the Irish camp to look around. I can feel something brewing that I'm not going to like."

Matt pondered aloud. "I haven't heard any extra grumbling. Is it something to do with the miners rioting up at Maux Chunk? What are you feeling?"

"Don't know, but I'll take a listen, anyway." Smith soft-footed away.

When Matt finished his paperwork he found Mickey McFee just outside the door. McFee's right hand was buried within a tight binding of cotton strips. No blood stained the cotton, so Matt guessed the reason for the wrappings.

"Broke your hand good, didn't you?"

McFee was clearly disconsolate, with the spirit taken out of him.

"Smashed it as bad as any I've seen. That's what I've come to see you about."

"What happened to it?"

McFee twisted in embarrassment. "Well, I've got an important bout coming up a week from now, and Klubber was fighting the other guy's style. I threw one at Klubber's chin, he ducked his head, and my fist took him smack on the skull." Mickey shook his head in misery. "Matt, I broke durn near every bone in my hand."

China re-appeared to stand just behind McFee. His voice held disdain mixed with a large dose of sympathy.

China said, "I just talked with Klubber, Matt. McFee's got it about right. Cole said he could feel McFee's hand bones crushing, and when he looked at the hand he could see it was all smashed out of shape."

Smith turned to McFee. "How long ago was that, Mickey?"

"Only been a half hour or so, Mister Smith. I hustled right over because I'm not going to be good for much the next week or so."

China snorted through his nearly blocked nose. "You won't be much use for more than a month, and it could be that you'll never have a strong grip in that busted up paw."

Mickey groaned, but Smith was not finished. "Likely all you did was wrap it in those cloths, that right?"

"That's right, Mister Smith, and that's another reason why I came over."

China's voice was expectant. "So I could tie it up right for you?"

McFee's voice was small. "I'd surely be grateful for anything you could do, Mister Smith."

China turned to Matt. "McFee won't be worth anything to us, Matt. You want to just turn him out for good?"

The silence was heavy with McFee's trepidation, but China Smith already knew Matt's answer and was just scaring McFee into compliance.

"Mickey stays, China. He's one of us, and we don't toss out our good men." Matt had heard his father say the same words more than once.

"Do what you can for his hand. I'm curious to see what a really broken fist looks like."

Gratitude dripped from Mickey McFee. Broken-handed and without a job, his future would have been bleak. As it was, he had other worries almost as great as holding his job.

When China gently unwrapped Mickey's broken hand, Matt took a lengthy look at the swollen and distorted knuckles that appeared to be shoved back into the back of the hand bones—two of which also seemed to be broken almost in the middle. It was enough to make a man shudder. Matt decided to take advantage of the situation.

"The fact is, McFee, there is one more thing you've got to agree to if we are going to keep you on in the shape you are in." He did not wait for Mickey's reply.

"The agreement will be that you've had your last money fight. You're all your family's got, Mick. You've had a run at knuckle fighting, and that should be enough."

Mickey groaned, and Matt thought China had hurt him.

"My broken hand isn't all of it, Boss."

McFee hesitated, "This is awful hard to say, but you've got to hear it."

McFee's explanation waited as China Smith examined the shattered bones. Klubber Cole had been right. The hand looked as if a horse had trod on it.

Smith scrubbed at his jaw. "If it were my hand, I'd straighten the bones until everything looked right, then I'd wrap it tight into a fist until it healed. That could be more than a month—more likely a month and a half. If you were going to fight again, it should be a lot of months before you began even gentle bag punching."

Matt was forceful. "The agreement is going to be that he doesn't fight again."

When he spoke, Mickey kept his head down, staring at his hand and not meeting eyes.

"I'm signed to fight in a week, and the money's been put up. That's the other thing I needed to talk about."

China said, "I'm going to start straightening and lining up bones now. The quicker the better, but it's been long enough that this is going to hurt like I was dipping your fist in fire. And, get something straight, McFee, you aren't fighting for a very long time, no matter how much you want to."

McFee's answer came in spurts interrupted by muffled groans and breath hissings. "Mister Smith, I've got to meet this man. The camp has put everything it could gather on me, and there's no way of getting it back."

China's voice was cold. "Then the camp loses. You can't fight."

McFee said, "There's more. I got suckered on this fight. We all got set up. What they did was ask me to fight a man named Percy Horn. They showed a picture, and Klubber almost laughed. The drawing was a young man, sort of short, but real pretty looking in the face. Nobody had ever heard of Percy Horn, and the men arranging the fight said he wasn't anything special in knuckle fighting. They said they were willing to bet because they figured Horn was about ready for a young fighter like me and would get better as time went on."

China's snort cut through McFee's words. "I suppose these men who set up the fight are gamblers out of a city, am I right?"

Mickey's voice was small. "That's what they are, Mister Smith, but I figured . . ." He looked a little confused. "I can't hardly believe that you didn't know about it, Mister Smith."

Irritation was in Smith's voice. "The Captain and I have been away, or someone would have told me."

China smoothed his voice. "You figured you had an easy fight and some easy money, and you agreed. So, who are you really going to fight?"

McFee chose to ignore Smith's question and turned his words to the Boss's Boy.

"Matt, I bet everything my family could put together. I even wagered Ma's gold ring and my sister Erin's brooch." Mickey's voice turned desperate. "I've got to fight and I've got to win, or we will be without anything at all. We'll . . ."

Pain cut off McFee's voice, and he writhed, his breath whistling under China's manipulations. As soon as he could, Mickey started again.

"What I need is for Mister Smith to wrap this fist as tight as he can, and I'll fight mostly one-handed. If I can just get one big one in I'm sure I can put him out."

It was Matt's turn to snort disdain, and China paused to examine his work.

Smith was ruthless, "McFee, all you've got is a right hand, and it is busted into bits. Your left couldn't jar a schoolgirl. One-handed, any mutt walking past could lick you."

China asked again, "Who is it you agreed to fight?"

McFee's voice was so low Matt could barely hear. "His fighting name turned out to be Boots Van Horn."

Van Horn meant nothing to Matt, but China Smith reared back in astonishment. "Good Lord, Bootsy Van Horn is older than I am. He's as old as Klubber Cole." Smith shook his head. "Hard to believe he is still fighting."

Despite the words, Matt could hear concern in China's voice. He waited for Smith's explanation.

"I heard part of this just a few minutes ago, but I didn't get much out of the men I talked to over at the Irish camp. The way I figure it now, a lot of our people have put most of what they've got on McFee whipping some boy-fighter that wouldn't be able to stand up to McFee's hard punching."

Mickey nodded. "Seems like everybody got took on this. We've all laid our money out, and if I can't win, this is going to be a poor camp."

Smith said, "They've got you two ways, McFee. First, you couldn't have licked Van Horn even if you were well. Second, with a bad hand he

162

would just pound you into the ground without raising a sweat."

China silenced Mickey's protest with a raised palm before continuing.

"I never fought Van Horn. He wasn't among the best, and you don't make serious money fighting second raters. But Boots Van Horn is a fierce spoiler. Even better battlers get hurt meeting Van Horn. His style is hard to fight, and he is as tough as a pine knot.

"Van Horn is below medium height, but he's thick all over. His head sits deep between his shoulders, and he fights with his head down looking only at the other man's legs. Van Horn never raises his chin. He holds his fists against his temples. He likes to lunge ahead and swing from in close. He likes that because his arms are short, and in tight, he hits like he had a club. If a man stands off and tries to pick at him, Van Horn dips his head and takes everything on his thick skull. Before long his opponent's hands are too sore to go on, and he quits."

Mickey said, "I'd get him with uppercuts."

China was disdainful. "That's what Van Horn is hoping for. You drop a hand to uppercut, and he steps in swinging like a gate. If he can, he will butt you, and if you go down he will keep pounding until you are flat on your back and not able to move. I never fought Van Horn, but he is known, and I've met too many just like him."

Matt said, "Well, it doesn't matter now. You'll not be fighting him." Then he speculated, "What they did was show you and Klubber a drawing of Van Horn when he was young, right?"

163

McFee was shame-faced. "That's what they did, but Klubber figured I could still beat him because Van Horn is old and fat. All I would have to do is keep him working till he gave out."

Mickey winced as Smith manipulated his fist wrapping. "That'll have to do. Don't try to use it, and keep it elevated when you can. It will feel better held high, but days will pass before the pain dies, and most likely an ache will hang on for a week or two. If you are lucky like I've been, you'll heal up and have a useful hand."

Matt said, "So what can we do about all of this, China? I don't much like our people being taken by this tricky stuff."

Smith lit his pipe and took one of the few drags he allowed himself. He offered the pipe to Mickey who shook his head.

China said, "Well, I can go talk to these people, but it's real doubtful that I'll get anywhere. Where will I find them, McFee?"

"They've gone back down to Harrisburg, Mister Smith. Klubber knows where they will be staying."

China thought for a minute. "Might be best if I go alone. You're so young they might not take you serious enough, Matt."

"I could go and show them my hand." McFee was again hopeful.

"That won't cut anything." Smith sounded certain. "They'd be glad to hear you're broken up. They aren't interested in the fight. All they want is the money, and if you don't show, the cash will be in their bag."

Then, why are you going?" Matt did not yet count himself out.

China was a little irritated. "I haven't figured anything out yet. Probably I will be wasting my time." Then he paused and appeared to ponder something.

"Where are you supposed to fight, McFee?"

"Along the river on that flat just below here. It'll be Saturday evening, and a good crowd should come."

Smith nodded. "Seems sensible and fair. Our people can be there in large numbers. So, who is holding the money?"

"Banker in the city. Klubber said that was all right."

Mickey was cradling his bandaged hand against his chest, and he rocked forward and backward, so Matt figured his fist hurt more than a little.

China saw it as well. "I expect we ought to give this bonehead either a dose of strychnine to finish him off or a swallow or two of laudanum to ease his pain. Which should it be, Matt?"

Matt grinned. "We're short of rat poison, so make it laudanum, China." Matt added, "Give him enough so that he'll sleep. Otherwise he might take to drink, and I'd have to go down and punch him unconscious."

Mickey stood and said, "I will appreciate the pain syrup." He tried to grin. "Only time you would ever dare to come against me would be when I had a broke hand, Boss's Boy."

Matt grinned back.

China got back from Harrisburg late in the day. He stuck his head in the office door and said, "Let's take a walk down by the river, Matt." He started off without waiting for a response.

When Matt caught up, Smith began without preamble. "Van Horn's backers are tough and experienced thugs. There's no chance that they can be interested in some sort of fair contest. With them, the fight's on. Be there and whip Van Horn, or the money's lost."

Matt thought about it, but no brilliant schemes surfaced. "So, what do we do, China?"

Smith had some ideas ready, and Matt was not surprised. First the old fighter asked a question.

"How determined are you on this, Matt? Men lose their money all the time either gambling or drinking it away. This isn't company business. Your Uncle Brascomb wouldn't give the problem a second of thought, and he could be right."

Matt had to answer slowly because he wasn't sure of his reasons or just how concerned he really should be. China was correct. His uncle would not bother with a worker's problem, but big Matt might, and what his father might do stood tall in young Matt's mind.

"I can't speak a lot of sensible reasons, China, but McFee and the others are our people. I know Uncle Brascomb doesn't feel that way, but our men work hard for us. We've brought them out here, and . . ." Matt's words trailed off while he thought some more.

"Mickey McFee and I have swung on each other a few times, but that was kid stuff. I don't dislike him for it, and I'm sure he feels the same."

Matt grinned at his friend and trainer. "When his hand gets well, I'd like to try him again."

China's return smile was hard. "That's no news. You've had McFee in mind ever since we first began, and if you fought smart, you could lick him, Matt."

China had never said that before, and Matt was pleased by the words, but maybe China was just saying he could whip McFee to give him confidence. Until the deed was done, neither he nor Mickey McFee would really be convinced.

They came to the fight area, and a few spots were already marked out. Matt saw a crude sign that read, "Saved for Barlow's." Barlow's was a popular saloon in Petersburg. The fight area had stakes placed so that vendors and other hopefuls would not have to be moved.

Matt asked, "What are we looking for?"

"Ideas, is all." China walked to where the bank fell steeply to the river and looked over. Matt joined him.

Smith said, "Wouldn't do to have somebody fall over there. Must be fifteen feet down and rocks on the bottom." Matt agreed. China said, "Hmm," and sounded thoughtful.

Away from the river the land rose in another steep bank, and some of the spectators would gather there where they could look over shorter heads to see the fighters more clearly. Big bettors and fist fighting fans would jam close to the squared off fight space, and if not kept at bay, they would crowd the fighters, sometimes attempting to trip one or the other and always willing to shove or even sneak a punch at a battler. It was not uncommon for a fighter to turn on an annoying spectator and deliver a few hard blows before the referee turned him back to his real opponent.

Lately, organizers had been stringing ropes between stakes to hold watchers out and fighters in. The common fighting circle that formed naturally around scrappers had become a square since it was easiest to plant four corner posts and to stretch a rope from one to another.

China had spent more than a little time teaching his protégé to stay out of corners because when a man was trapped against a post, sluggers ruled.

They were almost back to the office before Smith spoke again.

"There might be a way to turn all of this around." Matt waited expectantly, but China was not yet ready to announce any schemes.

They took seats on the small office porch, and Smith asked, "You willing to take some personal risks in this, Matt?" He paused before going on.

Apparently deciding, China said, "I'd best come straight out with it. Would you be willing to take on Van Horn in place of Mickey McFee?"

Goose bumps exploded all over young Matt Miller. His neck tingled, and he felt heat in his hands. Somewhere in the back of his mind Matt supposed he had wondered if he could, just maybe, toe-the-line in McFee's place, but facing the question of actually going knuckles to knuckles with a known slugger like Van Horn was vastly different, and Matt felt himself hesitate.

China sensed the uncertainty but did not intrude. The decision was demanding, and Smith would be just as content if young Matt was not interested.

Big Matt Miller had made it plain that China was not training his son to be a professional fist fighter, but Smith understood the youth's enjoyment of hard scrapping. He also understood that the hunger to know who was best could chew at a willing youth's innards.

China Smith believed there was a way to beat the professional. In fact, he figured he had two possible ways but, if Matt wanted to try, he would need to work hard on both before he met Boots Van Horn.

Matt swallowed his reservations. Fighting some over-confident farm boy or even a man like the Baron was nothing like squaring off against a professional prizefighter—especially one that certainly had more than one hundred fights under his belt. But, he wanted to!

Matt could feel a familiar hunger building. An equally familiar iron-like taste was reaching his mouth, and his heart had speeded up. How would it be to fight a pounder like Boots Van Horn? How would he, the Boss's Boy, stand when it got really tough? Now that it was in the open, how could he not want to punch Van Horn until the brawler quit or could no longer get up?

Suppose he said, no? Matt could feel himself cringe within. Matt knew China Smith would not send him in unless his chances were good. If China thought he could win, then he could.

McFee? It was past helping McFee. Matt recognized that he just plain wanted to do it.

Still, he had to ask. "Do you think I can take him, China?"

Smith sighed. "It will be tough, Matt. Reason it'll be tough is that Boots Van Horn will foul you a hundred times. He will hit when you're down. He'll butt, and he will knee you. Van Horn uses his elbows as much as his fists. He fights in close, and after he swings he brings his elbows back just like they went out, and an elbow smash can be worse than a punch."

"You taught me all about that kind of stuff, China."

"Knowing about it, isn't the same as facing it, and that is not all Horn will try. He will stand on your foot trying to anchor you for easier hitting. He'll head lock you, if he can, and punch your face while you are trapped. He'll bring his knee up into your face, and he will stick a thumb into your eye, every chance he gets."

Matt felt hairs stand on his neck, but the hunger to fight kept rising, and that strange joy that went with an oncoming battle began to tickle his nerves.

"So, how will I fight him, China?"

Smith laughed, but his tone was grim.

"You will beat him by being smarter and meaner. You will lure him so that he moves to where you want him. Then, you'll have one special chance to end it——and Matt, you will have to take your opportunity without hesitation. Otherwise, the fight will be just who can last the longest, and you can't fight a bruiser like Van Horn to a finish without taking a lot of punishment that won't just wash off."

Smith paused to stare more directly into Matt's eyes. "What I am going to plan isn't gentlemanly, young Matt, but prize fighting is the dirtiest game in town. It isn't for fun, no matter how much you think you will like it. Fighters like Van Horn get paid for winning, and they do not care how they win. The gamblers backing them care even less. Money has the voice in prize fighting, and it always will.

"Boxing, as some like to call it, is a mug's sport, Matt. The sooner you get it out of your system, the better off you will be. You think you've got a reason for taking on Van Horn, so now is as good a time to find out what bare knuckle fighting is really like. After that, I'm hoping you won't be so interested."

"There'll be a referee, China."

Smith was disdainful. "A good referee, like Klubber, for instance, does what he can, but all most can really do is try to drag a rule-breaker off his victim. If a referee called off a fight because of fouling or injury or anything else, the mob would beat him senseless, and the gamblers would shoot into what they left—unless their man was declared winner.

"Forget rules and referees. You will be out there all alone except for Van Horn, and I'm telling you now that he won't pay anymore attention to rules than would a wild bull."

"So, how will I fight him, China?"

"Before I get into that, we've got to face that we might not be able to make the fight. Right now,

171

those gamblers think they've got just about a sure thing. They've suckered a half-trained puncher into facing a spoiler who's been in there so many times he won't remember a lot of them. Why should they change anything?"

Matt had no answer, so China told him how they would manage it.

"We'll use Klubber for this, Matt. If they know I'm involved they will smell a hook and ignore the bait. You and Klubber will go see them. Klubber will tell how hungry you are to try professional fighting, and how you want to take McFee's place." Smith's grin turned wicked, "and that you are willing to bet one hundred dollars on yourself."

"One hundred dollars?" The sum was stunning, nearly five months of his pay.

Smith was unrelenting. "The game has to be sweet, Matt, or they won't come in. You've got to look like an innocent rich boy that hasn't any idea what he is getting into. Your face is smooth and unmarked, so that part will sell, but it will take profit to turn the trick.

"Klubber will hint that he, too, knows where to lay his money, and that he wants to get in on a bigger payoff when you lose."

"Who will Klubber claim he is betting with?"

"He'll leave it vague. Van Horn's managers won't just leap in, Matt. They'll ask around, and we will make sure that what they'll hear is that the Boss's Boy fought a few locals some time back, but that he is just a kid, and what could he know, anyway? What they hear will support what they see, and the money will lure them. There's a good chance they will take the fight."

Matt thought about it. He could see how it would work. Klubber Cole was known for handling all sorts of fighters, and the Boss's Boy would be just another hungry kid wanting to discover how tough he was and maybe gain a little local respect.

Was that what he was? Except for China Smith's training over the years, that would be about right. He had the excuse of wanting to help his workers, but really? Matt found he didn't care. He was going to fight Boots Van Horn, and he wished it were tomorrow.

Matt said, "So, Klubber and I will act just like you're describing, and the gamblers will agree, but to collect one hundred dollars I will have to put up my own money and some of the company's—which my father and uncle will take out of my hide when they find out, but how do I fight him, China?"

Smith nodded understanding. "This is my scheme, so I will put up what you don't have, Matt. We'll stay clear of the company's cash." He grinned almost evilly. "We don't want your uncle having some sort of brain collapse."

They moved around back to where Matt's punching bags hung from tree limbs and where the ground had been leveled and packed by their shuffling feet.

At China's direction, Matt took his stance. Left foot forward, balanced evenly on both feet, hands held high, both fists tightly clenched.

China got in front of him. He stood square facing Matt straight on. He crouched and ducked his chin onto his chest. He bent forward at the waist

173

and held his fists alongside his face peering at Matt's knees between them.

He said, "Now this is all you'll ever see of Van Horn except when he throws punches. What he does is charge forward, keeping his hands right where they are until he's almost against you, then he lets fly like a windmill. He never looks up, and he bobs up and down so that hitting what little you can see gets even harder.

"That's a tough system to fight against, but Boots got his nickname by carrying his charge right on through whoever he was fighting. He drives them backwards and off their feet. He likes to sort of accidentally stomp on feet and hands or anything else he can reach. If he can, Van Horn will also lean down and punch at his man's head before the referee gets him off."

Matt started to speak, but China was not finished. "You want to remember that bullet head of his when he charges. He will aim it right at your throat. If he gets in under your chin, he will keep butting and pounding away with both fists. Van Horn is smart enough to punch at your middle then go over the top of your arms to land along your head. All the time he will keep pushing, and if you get back on your heels you can't hit hard enough to break a cracker."

From behind his crouch Smith looked at his student. "How does that sound, Boss's Boy?"

14

It was not easy. Matt and Klubber Cole put on their show for the gamblers. Matt demonstrated his skills punching the air from a leaned back stance with his front leg stiffened and his weight on his rear foot. He held his chin high, as though keeping it out of the way, and he could almost taste the gamblers' satisfaction as they visualized Bootsy Van Horn's block-like skull jamming underneath while his sledging blows ripped into Matt's body.

Klubber proved unexpectedly skilled at convincing the gamblers of his underhanded interest in Van Horn's almost certain win and the extra betting money he could collect if the experienced fighter met the Boss's Boy instead of McFee.

There were two gamblers managing Van Horn's traveling fights. They moved ahead to set up bouts and secure the purses before their fighter appeared. The gamblers were not yet interested in individual wagering. Those smaller bets would be picked up shortly before the fights. The front money came as a combined wager from all sources interested. In McFee's case, the bettors included members of his working gang called Morgan's Men, and a horde of others who labored along the canals.

More than a few Petersburg residents who enjoyed rougher entertainments chipped in. All of those funds and the gamblers' matching money were placed in the hands of a Harrisburg banker who had served in a payout capacity before, and who guaranteed his appearance at the match with the cash for immediate payment to the winning party.

Because he had laid the bet and delivered the purse, the gamblers had no qualms about Klubber Cole changing the game, provided the changes were to their advantage, which always meant to their monetary profit.

These were careful men, however, and they chose to investigate. When Klubber and Matt drove their carriage back to Petersburg, they were accompanied by one of the gamblers. The man spent an evening asking around about the Boss's Boy. The answers were truthful—to the best of the teller's knowledge. Young Matt Miller had fought a few local youths and had done well, but he had no professional fights.

McFee? The Irish Hurricane, was discussed, and there was amused whispering among the locals about how Mickey was faking a hand injury hoping to deceive his opponent and perhaps gain an advantage.

Where was McFee? Why he had gone off with China Smith, the old fighter, and was training hard under Smith's tutelage. China, they believed, had some secret techniques to help beat the snot out of this Percy Horn. China Smith used another name for Horn and claimed to know him from way back, but it would not matter.

The mention of China Smith lit anxiety in the gambler. Everybody in the game knew about Smith, and he did fight in ways that no one else had mastered. It seemed clear that fighting the Boss's Boy could be safer than risking China's tricks.

Then, there was the money. A hundred extra dollars were not to be scoffed at. Boots Van Horn often fought for purses as small as twenty dollars with only small bets on the side

Even when they found out who Percy Horn really was, some of the woodsy muckers and choppers could be persuaded that an old pug like Van Horn was beatable. The locals were always wrong, but that news did not travel far, and the team of fighter and gamblers profited nicely from their small town bouts and steady betting with almost no chance of losing.

The gambler shook Klubber's hand almost eagerly, and the Van Horn versus the Boss's Boy fight was a deal. Explaining to the major backers who had raised the purse for McFee to fight was arduous, but when it was understood that McFee's hand really was broken and that it was Matt Miller or forfeit their money, most agreed—except perhaps

Mickey McFee, but he had been handled as smoothly as an ox led to the slaughter.

Alex Donovan had said, "McFee, with only one hand you're of no use around here, and Klubber wants you out of the way while he works something out on that fight we are all going to lose money on. You're to go with the survey party that's already started out. You can hold a stake or run a chain or anything else that'll pay your feed. Plan on being gone for nearly a month."

The headman had scratched at a bristly jaw and gone on. "If I was you, McFee, I'd try to learn something about surveying. Could be your mitt will never be good again, and the Boss will have to let you go. It'd be to your advantage to be able to do something other than swing a pick or carry a heavy load."

McFee had gone without complaint. Almost any other company would have already dropped him. No work, no pay, was the rule.

Losing fighting money would hurt. Mickey's regular pay was small and was most of what the McFee's lived on. The sideline of leather-patching worn knees and the seats of cloth work pants by his mother and sister helped more than a little, but even by putting all of their money and the goods they managed to barter into the pot, the McFees were struggling.

Mickey wondered a little about Matt keeping him on, but in his heart, he had suspected that the Boss's Boy would do just that. Now, why would he expect such a thing? McFee guessed that he and young Matt sort of liked each other—or something.

Mickey McFee planned on doing what the head bull had suggested. Surveying might be interesting, and although he had great faith in China Smith's wrappings, he could see that knuckle fighting wasn't all that he had once thought it might be.

A fist fighter needed a day free of training before a difficult match, so China had only four days to drive into young Matt all that he had to know. The Boss's Boy had to practice, and he had to drill until he could automatically adjust to the brutal assaults China believed were coming.

Then, there was the secret move that Smith planned, and as China had claimed, it was as mean as anything Matt had ever heard of.

China left no doubt about its use.

"You will do this, and you will do it exactly right with everything you've got, Matt, or I am quits on the deal right now, and you can take your chances on your own.

"I'll tell you one more time that this is not a sporting match. What you are into is a war. Van Horn will foul you every way he can. He will do his best to hurt you, and if he could, he would tear your head clean off your shoulders—and it would not bother his next meal."

Most of the words after that concerned making Matt move better, but the instructions were continual.

"The most important thing is that you don't get caught by Van Horn's charges, but if caught, you must do your best to tie him up by wrapping his arms within yours and dumping the both of you onto the ground.

"Hold him tight even after you are down. Watch his knees and even his feet, which he will try to rake along your shins. Jam your head tight into his neck and keep it there because he will slam his thick Dutch skull against your ear or nose or whatever he can reach. Don't let go until the referee pushes between you and him, and when you get up, come up fighting because he will be swinging before his knees leave the ground.

"You are young and he isn't, so you should be on your feet before he is, but do not change your game in any way. Fight the way we are practicing, and never do anything else no matter how safe or smart it looks.

"Boots Van Horn has fought every kind of man there is, Matt, and he has a bag of tricks to sucker you into doing something that he wants. Do what you are learning to do now and only that."

Then China grinned, "Well, maybe he hasn't fought anybody quite like me, and he won't be ready for what you are going to do. We are counting on that because if you fail, your fight will be terribly long and very brutal. Even winning, you will lose because a slugger like Van Horn cannot be held off completely, and when he breaks through, he will make up for all of the times you got away from him."

China fought like Van Horn. He weaved his way ahead holding his fists tight to his temples, and Matt tried to keep him away. The first trick was for Matt to keep his open left hand against Van Horn's forehead with his arm straight. As long as it was there, the short-armed Boots could not reach him.

The second trick depended on Van Horn getting tired of the hand on his head and trying to sweep it away.

China said, "That's when you strike, Matt. You know to stay balanced on both feet so that you can drop your right shoulder and come up with your right uppercut with everything you've got behind it. Aim for his throat, although it will be tucked behind his jaw. You do not want to land high on his head. That is a hand breaker.

"Now Matt, you hit once, and then you run. Do not wait to see how you did. Hit and get out. You will not knock him cold. Van Horn has been hit hard a thousand times. He will come back like a tiger. Do not be close to him. Get your hand on his head and be ready to move.

"Never move straight away from him or he will charge and drive you into the crowd where his short arms will work best. Move left or right, and mix them up—always with your hand on his head and the right fist ready.

"Your first right hand gave it everything you had, and he will remember it, but from then on, stay on balance and tag him when you can but do not take a chance on setting down and blasting him again. He will be waiting. What you must do is keep threatening his chin while you wear him down.

"Make him turn with your sideward movements and if he is slow, slide in from an angle and slug him as hard as you can hit. He will swing at you, and then he will backhand; if you are still near enough, you will get hit. If you can get behind him a little, punch him in the low ribs or in a kidney.

"When you come in from the side, punch once and get out because he will try to grab you. Get that hand back on his head with your arm straight. Drive him crazy with that hand. If he looks at you, stick your thumb in his eye. Not likely that he will, but that hand is going to bother him.

"Maneuver him, Matt. Remember that all you are doing is setting him up for a one-shot finish. Either you make it work, or you settle down to the longest evening of your life—unless he knocks you colder than an ice block."

They practiced, and it was hard. China left openings that Matt ached to try for, but he held off, and kept his left hand on Smith's bobbing head. China had footwork that Van Horn could never have, and he used it to get though Matt's guard. Then, the Boss's Boy had to grab frantically and battle to trip them both to the ground. Smith had no mercy for Matt's ribs and almost anything else he could reach. When he went over the top, however, he made his blows light, but they drilled home on Matt's head with more regularity than either would have liked.

"Tie me up, Matt. Smother my arms. Get your hands behind my elbows. Press tighter against me. Bury your head where I can't get to it.

"Watch your crotch, you are spraddle-legged!

"Slide to the left or right as you clinch. Don't stay in front of me. Heave me around. Tangle your foot behind mine, and when we go down, hang on and try to land on top. All right, we are down; now fight while we are on the ground. Get nasty, Matt, worse than Van Horn. Get him before he gets you."

The struggling was graceless and seemed endless, but Matt began to learn, and his successes became frequent.

China explained, "Sometimes, you will want your arms inside of Van Horn's. You do that so that you can throw him easier, and with your elbows blocking his punches, he will have no leverage, but you have to stay tight to him. We will try that for a while, and then we will mix clinching inside and outside together."

China said, "Don't let it happen if you can help it, but he could make you duck. What you do then is ram your front shoulder up and into him jamming with all your leg strength to throw him backward. Really slam him, Matt. Don't let him have his feet on the ground or be in balance when you are close in." They practiced shoulder slams.

Printed broadsides were appearing on trees up and down the Susquehanna River announcing the battle royal to be waged between the suddenly "almost champion" Boots Van Horn and The Boss's

Boy—the pride of Perry County and points east. Percy Horn seemed to have vanished, and The Boss's Boy was said to be a powerful hitter who had leveled the best brought against him.

Matt joked, "I didn't know I was that good."

China was dour. "You aren't. You have to be smarter, with your plan always in the front of your mind. He will tag you more than once. You have to keep maneuvering him and control your hunger to hammer back."

China sighed, "I've said that so often I don't want to hear it again, but there are a few more things.

"The first is that this fight will be using the Attack system. This kind of fighting has come over from England and is getting popular. Some over here call it Round fighting.

"You will each toe a line in the center of the square, and on the referee's command you will fight until somebody rings a cowbell. When you hear the bell, back aside. Not straight back, and move away, Matt, with your hands up and ready to hit.

"Sometimes, men in the crowd clatter their own cowbells hoping one or more of the fighters will relax. The referee will be slow, they always are, and Van Horn will pay no attention to the bell until later rounds when he'll be tired and pleased to hear it. Let's hope you end it before then.

"After about a minute's rest, you'll be called out to toe the line and go at it again. Go out with your hands up because Van Horn may not wait for a starting signal. Move fast and sideward out of his range. If Van Horn tries to cut you off or press you into a corner or against the crowd, go the other way, and get your hand back on his head. Never get cornered. You can get beaten into mush in a corner."

Matt's big question was, "When do I hit with my left, China?"

"In this fight, only when you have to, Matt. I know we've worked on left jabs and hooks and all of the usual punches and blocks, but this time do only what I am telling you. Keep busy turning him until the right moment comes. Then you know what to do," and they practiced the what-to-do many times.

Saturday was clear and warm. Work was slowed and some men were given the afternoon off. Most planned to attend the evening fights, and families would be coming for the festivities—although the ladies would retire before the fighting part began. That was sensible because it would also remove them before serious drunkenness, wild gambling, and foul language occurred.

Matt and China went in early to examine the grassy arena where Matt would fight. Someone had scythed the grass short, and the four posts had been moved closer to the river drop-off, so spectators could not endanger themselves by gathering on that side. Concerned citizens had suggested and finally demanded the change claiming fear that innocents would be injured by being knocked or simply falling over the bank and onto the rocks below.

Matt said, "It is a large square, China."

Smith agreed. "It is, and that is good for us. You can move, but Bootsy is old and heavy. A big square will help wear him out."

Vendors were already hawking wares. Gamblers had games of chance atop barrels, and a plank thrown across two barrels could constitute either a bar or a serving counter for foodstuffs and various liquors. A ladies' group was offering quilts and others displayed crocheted and knitted goods for sale.

The Petersburg cornet band was in evidence, and its warming flourishes added to a rising carnival-like din. The band's banner now read "The Duncannon Cornet Band" in expectation and support of the town's renaming.

A preacher, notorious for his endless sermonizing was flourishing his bible from atop a large packing box and exhorting passers-by to avoid the brutal goings-on and the godless rum and whiskey that was already beginning to flow.

A church ladies' organization planned to parade against the many evils exposed by the disgusting fist fighting. A convoy of four wagons had come from the county seat at Bloomfield, and the sheriff had ridden along, but only to observe—which was encouraging, because law officers often interfered with pugilistic performances in the name of peace and tranquility.

A small cannon was occasionally fired from the cliff above the river, and at each explosion the crowd cheered lustily.

There were wagons on the roads, and a few hopeful rakes pranced their horses where the town sports often raced their mounts. It was clear that the fine weather and excitement of prizefighting were turning the day into a memorable outing.

Matt got his first look at Boots Van Horn from a distance. To the Boss's Boy's eyes he looked a lot like Klubber Cole. He was shorter and thicker than the Klubber, but his close-cropped skull was scarred and lumped, and his face was a mass of scar tissue and crude, healed-over stitching, just like Klubber's.

Van Horn's nose was almost non-existent. That feature had been flattened until it lay squashed against his cheeks.

China Smith explained. "Uppercuts, Matt. Van Horn must have eaten a million of them. Most fighters get cut around the eyes, as he has, and they all have split lips and cauliflower-looking ears, but Bootsy's fighting style results in a lot of uppercuts being aimed at the middle of his kisser."

China grinned, "He hasn't breathed through his nose for a dozen years, and that will be to your advantage. To breathe deeply, he's got to open his mouth, and getting hit hard with your jaw not clamped tight isn't ever good."

Van Horn was carefully dressed and was surrounded by a contingent of supporters, including a pair of brightly dressed younger women.

China shook his head in wonder. "Every pug I know gets followed around by handsome women wanting his attention. It used to be the same with me when I was fighting. Something about the fight game that gets to them." He smiled humorlessly at the Boss's Boy. "Watch out for that, Matt. You stay in this business, and they'll be after you."

A number of Van Horn sycophants broke away and came to shake the hand of China Smith and to size up their fighter's opponent.

One said, "I didn't hear that you were working with the Boss's Boy, China."

Smith's shrug was eloquent. "I always have." He turned to Matt. "Been about three years hasn't it?"

Matt had a role to play. He held his chin high, the way he had when dancing around for the gamblers' benefit. He nodded agreement to the number of years but said nothing.

A man said, "Well, he looks nicely set up, China. Good muscles and all, but he ain't never fought nobody."

China's nod was solemn. "True, but a fighter's got to start somewhere."

"Bootsy is a pretty tough start, China." There were grunts of agreement.

Smith appeared worried. "Well, I told him that, but he's the fighter. What am I supposed to do?"

A Van Horn supporter sneered a little. "You got any money on him, Smith?"

China appeared disgruntled, and his voice sounded weak and insincere. "I don't bet anymore. Money is short these days."

They watched the group scuttle back to report to Van Horn and his handlers. Matt asked, "You think that did any good, China?"

"It won't interest Van Horn, but it might make for a few comfortable bets among our people." China thought for a minute before reconsidering. "You never can tell, though. Bootsy is already pretty sure of this fight, and seeing your unmarked face and straight nose, he might just relax a little bit more. We can use all of that we can get, Matt."

They walked back to the house to rest, and China reviewed what they had to do.

"Boots will try to grab your left wrist and pull you into him, Matt. Be ready for that. We've practiced against it enough. Use his pull to give your right fist momentum. Up you come with your right hand into the hole he left when he grabbed your arm, and you will have all you've got behind it.

"If you can't get the punch off, get in quick and tie him up. Then wrestle him down. Either be tight against Van Horn or back out of his reach. In between will get you hurt."

Matt lay down to rest, but China went back to spread rumors and smell the air. There would be preliminary bouts with local youths pounding on each other before the big fight, but Matt would see none of those. His task was to rest. He was to avoid thinking about Boots Van Horn and little about anything else until the fight began.

Matt wondered for a hundredth time what his father would say about all of this. There was no question that he would despise the betting, but he might be pleased by his son's willingness to stand by their men. The older Matt Miller placed great value on loyalty, but if the Captain had not been out of town, the Boss's Boy would not be fighting.

Of course, Matt knew how his Uncle Brascomb would react. The uncle would almost spit in disdain, and he would probably lay a small and very secretive bet on Bootsy Van Horn. That awareness brought a smile to Matt's lips.

Resting was not so easy. His mind roamed, and he found his fists and jaw clenched. China had taught him ways to relax, and Matt tried them. He deliberately relaxed his facial muscles followed by relaxing his hands and his arms. He worked for a while at letting his mind become vacant and managed a shallow doze for more than an hour.

As usual, China made a project out of wrapping protection around Matt's knuckles. Wrapping took time, but the work helped to ease the waiting. China had prepared a mountain of linen strips of various widths, and he applied them based on his own experience of hitting hard with brittle bones.

He covered Matt's knuckles, binding them tightly together with thinner strips running between the joints and far down the backs of his hands. China talked as he taped.

"This will feel too tight for a short time, Matt, but the cloth stretches, and unless it is tight, it doesn't help much. I'm padding your knuckles a little and wrapping them tight together. As usual, I'll wrap beyond your wrist so that nothing bends between your fist and your elbow. Wrapped right, your wrist won't give at the wrong time, and the wrappings will protect your hand and wrist bones from his fists when you block. When you hit, your arm and fist will be like ramming a log straight into his ugly mug."

The fight-gathering along the river resembled a carnival or a visiting circus. Prizefighting was rare in Perry County, but the farmers and townsmen took to it with hunger. A half-century earlier, the few oldest men present had fought hostile Indians, and many of their sons were veterans of the great revolution. Wild blood ran strong in the men of the north valley.

Of course, men fought without formalities. Men fought everywhere, but those were only mean and often drunken brawls that were hard to admire. Here men stood face to face, fought within agreed upon rules, and battled until one could no longer toe the line or the referee declared the fight a draw.

A draw was not considered shameful because fighters often punched until neither could raise a hand to knock the other into submission. Among poorly trained men, fights could not last long because the boxers became exhausted and simply leaned on each other trying to suck in enough energy for another ineffective blow. Those fights were draws.

Professional knuckle fighters sometimes fought for fifty Attacks, but bouts more often lasted only a few line-toeings because one fighter or the other managed to land a huge punch that flattened his opponent more or less completely.

China had guaranteed that Bootsy Van Horn was one of those blasting-powder hitters who preferred to win with quick violent and furious jaw-cracking blows. He had worked Matt hard to be ready for them.

The preliminary bouts were raucous affairs, some short and bloody, a few canceled in disgust when the fisticuffs sagged into exhausted clutching and wheezing. The crowd was ready for a real fight, the one they had bet their wages and savings on. The appearance of Matt in his boxing attire sided by the great fighter, China Smith, brought them to their feet howling and cheering in anticipation.

The shouted approvals of Boots Van Horn fans were insignificant in comparison, but the professional fighter's powerful physique and experience-battered features brought doubts to Boss's Boy supporters.

Here, clearly, was a battler who had seen the elephant. In contrast, Matt's muscled but youthful body and his unmarked features instilled serious doubts. Could a youth, almost a stripling in appearance, no matter how well trained, smash to the ground a brute like Van Horn? Perhaps they had been hasty in expecting that even the hard hitting McFee, much less the Boss's Boy, could toe the line against such a fighter.

The crowd made way for Matt and China to enter the square. Shouting and jostling drowned most of what was being requested, but Smith safely guided his fighter into the square where Van Horn and his handler waited. The handlers carefully examined the other fighter's hands for the presence of iron weights. Van Horn's man thoroughly felt Matt's wrappings grumbling about their extension onto his forearms but found nothing illegal. Van Horn wore tightly laced leather gloves that featured roughened leather knuckles. China ritually complained but could do nothing more.

Smith carried a bucket half-filled with water that he placed in the corner chosen for the Boss's Boy. A towel hung around China's neck, and he had certain helpful emollients buried in his pockets.

The fighters and handlers stood in their corners until the referee out-shouted the mob. China held the water bucket waist high, and Matt plunged his fists into it. At Smith's direction, he held his hands under his chin letting the excess water drain from his elbows. The wet linen tightened around his knuckles and seemed to bond his fists into solid and dangerous clubs.

The referee finally got enough silence to introduce the fighters, but Matt heard little of it. His mind seemed dazed, and he found himself intently studying unimportant things as if they were of special interest. He fought to focus his attention, and partly succeeded, but he felt astonishingly weak and incompetent. His heart pounded, his hands were chilled within China's wet wrappings. He had not suffered such debilitating uncertainties before other fights, and Matt suddenly feared he was about to make a fool of himself.

China demanded that a clutch of Van Horn supporters be removed from near the Boss's Boy's corner where they could flick cigar butts or spit tobacco juice at the resting fighter. Moving recalcitrant men took time, and there were demands to explain the Attack system and lengths of time for fighting and resting.

From a pocket, China withdrew a corked bottle of some kind of sheep oil that he spread liberally over his fighter's face. "The oil will help make his fists slide on your skin, Matt, and it'll make his handler mad."

Everyone's patience wore at the interminable delays, but finally all was ready. Matt found himself alone with Boots Van Horn and the referee, with his front foot touching a line scratched in the dirt.

Matt heard China's order. "Wake up!"

The command snatched Matt's mind from its wanderings, and he studied his opponent. Close in, Van Horn looked even worse. His gargoyle face had been beaten nearly inhuman, his head lacked a neck, and his shoulders bunched with immense muscle pads as high as his ears. The short but hugely thick arms were raised along the sides of his head, and even as Matt looked, Van Horn tucked his chin tight to his chest and appeared to gaze intently at Matt's knees. There seemed no opening large enough for even the straightest driven fist to get through.

Matt wore light, high-laced shoes, but Van Horn had heavy, hard-soled boots that China had warned could stomp and kick or scrape a shin to the bone. Fighters like Van Horn also used the heavy boots when stepping on and hold an opponent's foot while beating him thoroughly with fists, elbows, and head butts. All of those were fouls, but China said to expect them.

Still, Matt had a height and reach advantage on Van Horn. He was younger and expected that he was in better physical condition. He had a plan, and fair or not, he would use it.

The referee was a fat and mild looking older man neither he nor China had seen before, and they both doubted his ability to control the fight if things got nasty.

The referee cleared his throat in preparation, then announced the fighters in sonorous tones that belonged on a church pulpit. He explained most of the illegalities that Matt and China had already considered and warned that he would not allow them. Despite the strong words, Matt still doubted the man's abilities.

Gathering himself for the great moment, the referee surveyed his charges, raised a hand in warning, then dropped it with a shouted single word.

"Fight!"

The Boss's Boy hitched his body sideward, left foot forward, balanced with his weight on both feet, and with his arm straight as he could make it, he slammed his open palm against Bootsy Van Horn's forehead.

15

Boots Van Horn exploded! He burst from his crouch. His fists swung in tight vicious hooks. He slipped his head from under Matt's palm and drove at Matt's body. He grunted with each blow, packing all of his power behind every punch, intending that any that landed would flatten and finish the youth attempting to fight him.

Matt sucked in his gut to avoid the brutal swings and stepped sideward, fighting his left hand back onto Van Horn's head. The professional bobbed and weaved, and Matt danced left and right holding off the furious charge.

Gone were the butterflies in his belly and the weakness that had plagued him. There were no longer lessons to be recalled or skills to be pondered, only intense concentration on avoiding the wild man's slamming blows. Van Horn intended to end the fight quickly. He put immense power into stone-hard fists and grunted with every hook after monstrous hook that seemed to barely miss.

Spectators screamed and bellowed with excitement, expecting a blow to connect solidly and to see the youth smashed to the ground. Even the

Boss's Boy's strongest supporters realized that their man was running for his life.

Matt Miller felt the same. He could not plan. He shuffled and shifted. He faked and swirled away, struggling to keep his palm against the monster's head because if those hammer blows reached him, he would surely be broken and beaten. He threw no countering blows, and he blocked nothing. The Boss's Boy concentrated on keeping his elbow straight and his body beyond Van Horn's short-armed swings—as he waited.

It could not continue. Everyone could see that except China Smith, who judged the fight going exactly right, providing Matt could clear his mind and hold his balance for a few moments longer.

Van Horn snarled, and the ringside watchers heard a rumble of primeval rage that froze blood and made eyes smart. Some were suddenly fearful, but others licked lips in anticipation. A killer had been loosed among them.

Van Horn shrugged his massive shoulders and crouched lower, his head weaving a snake-like pattern. In irritation he flailed an arm at the palm holding him from his victim and lunged even harder into his attack.

Without hesitation or consideration of what he was attempting, Matt Miller dropped his right shoulder and drove his tightly clenched right fist upward into where Bootsy Van Horn's throat should be. He aimed at the open spot where Van Horn's thick arm had protected his face and chin.

It was not a vast opening, but the Boss's Boy had practiced, and he had waited for the target. His reaction to the opening was as instinctive as training could make it. Matt threw the mightiest right hand of his life, the punch that he and China had practiced for a seeming eternity.

This was not the calculated and powerfully balanced response that he and China had planned. Matt's blow was survival, and he spared nothing. If the blow missed, he would be wildly off balance and so committed that for terrible moments he would be almost helpless. Desperation added power to Matt's tremendous uppercut.

His shoulder low, Matt's cocked arm hooked upward, power exploding from a planted foot, through a driving leg and muscled back and shoulder into the water-saturated wrappings that froze his arm and fist into an almost oaken battering ram.

From his earliest training, Matt Miller had been taught to aim deep into a target. He did not point for Van Horn's buried jaw or the vulnerable throat behind it. His blow would peak at the back of Van Horn's skull—unless something stopped it before then.

Boots Van Horn's experience could not save him from something he never saw. Matt's fist struck like a sledgehammer against the professional's chin. It was a thunderous punch that drove Van Horn's head back, rocked him onto his heels, dazed his senses, and staggered him backward.

The crowd also exploded. Eyes glared and voices screamed in satisfaction or dismay. Men's fists were clenched, and their bodies heaved about as if they were part of the action.

Matt, too, was staggered by the effort, for a long instant his balance was gone, and he shuffled and bobbed regaining a fighting stance. A barely noticed ache blossomed in his hand and marched up his wrist, proving how solidly his blow had landed.

But Boots Van Horn did not go down. The seasoned warrior tucked back into his fighting shell and backed away beyond Matt Miller's reach.

With satisfaction, China Smith saw Van Horn's legs wobble, and judged that Matt had delivered a serious cautionary message,

He whistled silently to himself. That had been one hell of a punch, but he also sensed the Boss's Boy's desperation and awareness of fighting on the sharp edge of annihilation.

Now, Matt must not rush in. He must continue their plan because Boots Van Horn would be back harder than before, and with China's thoughts, Van Horn resumed his attack.

He lunged a bit more carefully, and he did not again paw at the hand on his head. He bobbed and weaved, he swung hard, and occasionally he brutally slammed a fist against Matt's straightened left arm. The Boss's Boy could not indefinitely stand heavy blows on his extended arm. The arm would tire; then Van Horn would break through.

A cowbell clanged ending the first Attack, and the referee pushed himself between the fighters. Matt Miller backed away, fists still cocked, and as usual, sliding sideward—this time behind the referee using him as protection against the raging professional.

Sure enough, Boots Van Horn tried to get around the referee and continue the fight. Not until Van Horn turned away and strode toward his corner did Mat Miller lower his hands and go to China Smith's ministrations.

An empty twenty-gallon beer keg had appeared in Matt's corner, and Smith sat him on it. The wrung-out towel was hung over Matt's head, and China mopped his charge's flushed features. He talked as he reapplied the sheep oil to Matt's face.

"All right, Matt, you're doing it just right. That uppercut was terrific, but do not try it again. Van Horn will be looking for it, and he might leave you a tempting opening.

"Relax and breathe deep and easy, Matt." China watched the Boss's Boy's breathing and judged the tension in his arms and shoulders. Matt's eyes looked clear, but China thought he looked a little scared. He should be. Van Horn was winging thunderous blows, and he would be able to keep throwing huge punches for more Attacks before he began losing steam. The time to strike was now, and China said so.

"All right, Matt, now is the time. When you go out there, start just like you did last time, but maneuver him to where you want him. Then, plant your feet squared away as if you were going to meet his charge and slug it out. Van Horn will see, and he will come like a wild bull."

Matt was nodding, so China added only, "Then, you know what to do."

A spectator deep into the crowd threw a wooden pail of beer across heads aiming for the Boss's Boy. As if he had been waiting for it, China Smith knocked the bucket aside and ignored the beer that splashed on them both. Spectators who had been drenched began shoving each other and voices grew angry.

China ignored the developing melee. He helped Matt to his feet. Across the square, Bootsy Van Horn was slamming a fist into his opposite palm and shrugging his heavy shoulders as if eager to begin punching.

China produced a small bottle from his pocket and waved it just below Matt's chin. The powerful sting of ammonia struck Matt's nostrils and traveled through his lungs and mind with a clarifying jolt. His mind seemed to refocus, his vision sharpened, and his nose cleared. The referee signaled, and the Boss's Boy stepped ahead to toe the line.

China wanted to curse; Van Horn had changed his style. Instead of rushing in with fists swinging, he stood flat footed and slashed at Matt's extended left arm.

How long could his fighter stand those blows crashing against his forearm? There were ways to respond, but he had never taught the Boss's Boy those moves.

Even while struggling to keep his palm against Van Horn's head, Matt could see inviting openings in Bootsy's guard. He could also judge the experienced professional's readiness to counter-punch the instant the Boss's Boy reached in to throw a fist through one of the tempting openings. Could he slide enough to hook a left hand up into Van Horn's liver or right hand around to a kidney? Matt shifted, trying each angle, but Van Horn turned with him.

Matt circled, and Boots stalked him patiently slamming a right or a left fist or forearm against the extended arm and the hand on his head. Matt let his hand move ahead of the blows, easing their impact, but instantly returning his hand to Van Horn's sweating skull.

Boots Van Horn never looked up. His chin was buried against his chest, and his eyes stayed on his opponent's knees. Matt wished mightily to drive another right hand up and into that tucked away jaw, but China had warned not to try it. What was he supposed to do, just keep letting Van Horn club his arm into uselessness?

The crowd did not like it. They had not come to study clever sparring. They wanted blood and fist-slamming, nose-to-nose battling until the weaker man collapsed helpless and beaten.

Their boos and cat calls rose, and as if responding, Boots Van Horn charged. A slap at Matt's extended arm led his attack. The charge was explosive and without hint of warning. Matt's hand slid off the dodging and sweat-slippery head, and Van Horn's first swinging blow slid across Matt's retreating body. Then Boots was on him. A fist drove in hard along his ribs, and Matt jammed his longer arms inside Bootsy's pummeling fists. He grabbed Van Horn's body. Heaving mightily, he hoisted the shorter fighter off his feet.

Van Horn's knees drove into him, and his boots kicked savagely at Matt's shins. Matt got a foot behind Boots' churning legs and toppled him backward. As they fell, Matt struggled to remain on top. He succeeded, and they landed hard with Van Horn's back striking with Matt's weight on top, but

Bootsy had been thrown a hundred times, and he barely slowed. His head butted Matt's face before the Boss's Boy could bury it alongside the fighter's neck.

Brutal knee slams came, but Matt slid his body to the side, and they missed their intended target. Van Horn's boots raked at his legs, and the powerful arms slugged anything they could reach. A fist struck the back of Matt's head and the other sought to reach in front and force Matt's face from the safety of Van Horn's massive shoulder.

It was like being beaten on by wild men using clubs. Matt hung on, and he could feel and hear the referee straining to separate them.

A little late, Matt Miller also began to fight. He slammed the side of his head against Van Horn's hard skull, and as the referee made progress moving them apart, he got his left hand loose and deliberately jammed his thumb into Bootsy's eye.

Van Horn jerked his face away, and Matt drove a knee into the professional's crotch. The blow felt solid and seemed to sink in. Matt's mind said, "Take that you . . ." but the referee was between them, and Van Horn was backing away and scrambling to his feet.

Matt scrambled faster. China had warned him to be quickest, or Van Horn would get him only half ready. He was on his feet, his hands up, left hand out front, but he was panting like a wind broken horse. The struggle on the ground had taken a lot out of him.

Van Horn seemed unaffected. He slammed around the referee and charged like a wild man. Matt held him at arm's length and danced sideward hoping desperately to position the monster for the final move, and Boots came on as if he was part of the plan.

It was right! The positioning was perfect. Matt squared his stance and was ready, but—at the crucial instant—Van Horn raised his eyes and his whole face as if seeking a clear look at his opponent. It was a chance too large to be missed. It was an opening to good to be ignored, and the Boss's Boy went for it.

Matt did it the smart way. He dropped his left palm in front of Van Horn's eyes to mask the straight right hand that he threw with everything he had directly down the pipe into Bootsy's battered features. Matt could almost feel the smash of his hardened fist—but the blow never landed.

Something exploded against the side of Matt Miller's head stopping his thinking and fogging his vision. The world tilted, and even the massed spectators wobbled. Matt's legs struggled to hold him up, but the earth and Bootsy Van Horn suddenly slanted the other way, and he was falling, helplessly weak, seeing Van Horn's fist coming at his head but able to barely move before it glanced from his temple, and he landed on the earth as limp as a dropped corpse.

China's mind had said, "Now!" but to his horror, Matt had thrown an explosive right hand into Boots Van Horn's trap.

It was a trap, of course. Shaken from muscle-straining ground wrestling and trying to reorganize, to get back to his plan and into his rhythm, the inexperienced Boss's Boy had been unable to resist Bootsy's perfect opening.

When Matt Miller dropped his hand across Boots' line of vision, Van Horn wove just a little so that Matt's punch would miss and launched his own devastating right.

Van Horn could hit. Power was Bootsy's major weapon, and his gnarled and battle-hardened fist sledged solidly just below Matt Miller's ear. China knew it to be a hell of a punch. He saw Matt's head jolt, he saw his knees buckle and his legs tangle, and he winced as Van Horn's second punch went in as if it were tied to the Boss's Boy's head.

Matt was already falling, but somehow he managed to cock his head enough that Van Horn's follow up almost missed. Matt landed soddenly on his side, and Bootsy Van Horn went down on top of him.

The referee tried, but Van Horn landed two smashing blows to Matt Miller's head or shoulders—who could tell in the moments of raging violence—before he dragged Van Horn's struggling body from his prostrate opponent.

Matt Miller felt as if he had been trampled by a horse herd. The side of his head was strangely numb, but his senses had cleared almost as Boots Van Horn had landed on him. Bootsy's wilder blows had not done measurable damage. One landed along his neck and another on his shoulder, but the Boss's Boy profited from the delay before having to regain his feet.

Could he get up? Matt wasn't sure. His legs were wooden, and he had little control over them. As he strained to rise, they became rubbery and were even worse. He doubted they would hold him.

Then he was up, and Van Horn came around the referee in a rush. Matt made his feet move. He fled at an angle, and as Van Horn closed he staggered away in another direction, and for an essential moment, Boots had not reached him.

Suddenly, the roar of the crowd returned to Matt's hearing. He had not noticed its absence, but it was back. He dodged away, sliding along a rope as hands from the crowd tugged and scratched at him, and a fist struck his back.

Van Horn marched forward in his crouch, his head again tucked and his clenched fists tight along his ears. Unexpectedly, the cowbell sounded, ending the Second Attack but, as China had warned, Van Horn charged.

The referee was taken by surprise, but Matt Miller was not. He had blundered once, but there would not be a second time—he hoped. Matt swiveled aside, and let Van Horn rush past. Then Matt retreated toward his own corner with his hands up and his eyes on his opponent.

Van Horn had missed the chance, and he did not even look toward the Boss's Boy. He sat down on his milk stool and a pail of water was thrown in his face.

Matt Miller almost collapsed on his upended beer keg. China Smith was not forgiving.

"That was stupid, Matt. You had him just right."

Matt began a gasping answer, but China cut him off.

"Save your breath. You're going to need all you can get. Take a few deep breaths. That's good, now relax your body, let your arms hang."

China appeared to study his fighter.

"All right, you're coming back fast, and maybe you learned something useful.

"Boots will come out ready to finish you. Move him around, just like you did before, but this time, do what you are supposed to do."

China rubbed on more grease, and stood the Boss's Boy up. "Do it now, Matt, while he is still willing and ready to charge like a bull."

Matt nodded, and the referee motioned the fighters forward. Van Horn toed the line and got his hands up. Matt made himself slow to arrive and managed a slight stagger as his toe sought the right spot.

China Smith saw the hesitation in the Boss's Boy's step just as everyone else did, but Smith recognized that Matt Miller was beginning to set up Boots Van Horn for a surprise ending.

The referee took an instant to warn both fighters that he would not stand for any more fouling. He got no acknowledgments, and he stood back, raised his hand, brought it down smartly, and called, "Fight!"

The Boss's Boy backed away in full flight. Boots Van Horn stomped after him, fists balled, his chin buried with his eyes on the other fighter's knees, his body squared to his opponent, ready to swing with either hand.

Matt Miller gave him a race, but Van Horn was edging ever closer, and most doubted that the Boss's Boy could dance much longer, and even if he did, sooner or later he would tire and the remorseless Van Horn would pound him into oblivion. Few believed otherwise, but China Smith waited expectantly.

The fighters had circled, and Matt again saw things as just right. He stopped moving and turned himself square to the advancing Van Horn. His fists bunched closer to his waist, and he bent a little forward, apparently forced to battle the heavy-handed Boots Van Horn to a slugfest finish.

Sensing a last desperate battle, the crowd roared approval. Van Horn took the challenge and marched in. The Boss's Boy retreated ahead of the menace of Van Horn's club-like fists. Then Van Horn charged.

Across the square they flew, Boots Van Horn closing hard, holding his punches until he was close enough to inflict brutal and crushing damage.

Spectators bellowed hoarse-voiced approval, and frantic or raging supporters screamed encouragement to both fighters.

Van Horn swung viciously, but Matt blocked with a forearm. Van Horn ducked his head even lower and plowed ahead in his wild bull style. Unable to face the overwhelming attack, the Boss's Boy scrabbled backward, and Van Horn pressed.

Matt Miller's feet tangled, and he tripped and toppled backward. Almost within Miller's arms, Van Horn leaped onto the falling fighter.

A Van Horn fist sledged Matt's ribs, but as he fell, Miller's hands clutched Bootsy's armpits, and within the same desperate and tumbling effort, Matt Miller's body extended its topple into a backward roll. His feet and legs jammed powerfully upward catching the leaping Van Horn below the waist while Matt's arms shoved Van Horn over his head as hard as he could manage.

Bootsy's reckless charge made the result even more dramatic. Propelled by Matt's driving feet, Van Horn's body soared as if levitated. Van Horn arced above the Boss's Boy's prone body and flew over the single rope to instantly disappear over the edge of the bluff above the river.

There was a sudden and disbelieving silence. One instant, Boots Van Horn was smashing the Boss's Boy. The next, Boots was gone as if vaporized. The crowd stood rooted. Men froze with their hands and arms in awkward positions, and faces wore blank or confused expressions.

China Smith was not among them. He had been ready and expectant. He ducked under the rope and into the ring heading straight for his still rising charge because China knew with certainty what was about to happen.

Smith's movement broke the spell, and almost as one the crowd surged into and around the roped-off square rushing to the bluff edge to see what had happened to Boots Van Horn.

The referee ducked under the rope to peer over the drop off and only belatedly realized what was happening behind him. He whirled and raised both hands frantically urging the crowd to halt, but few chose to wait. A wall of excited spectators boiled across the roped square, each seeking his personal look at the probably bruised or broken Bootsy Van Horn.

China reached Matt Miller almost as the Boss's Boy regained his feet. He placed himself protectively between Matt and the onrushing crowd and began to plow a way back through the thickening rush of mindless spectators.

China and Matt broke clear almost as the first of the bellowing herd reached the bluff edge, and they paused to watch the ensuing disaster.

Unwilling to miss anything, the crowd shoved ahead amid suddenly panicked squalling as those who had arrived first were pushed over the bluff edge and disappeared as swiftly as had their fighter.

The referee fared no better, and China and Matt saw his waving arms and white shirtsleeves disappear amid a dozen other unfortunates that reached the drop off too swiftly.

China did not waste time watching. He worked through stragglers who had been slower or luckier and were still heading into the chaos.

Matt said, "Good God, China, some of those people are surely hurt."

Smith's voice held no sympathy. "Surely are. Take it as a lesson, Matt. Never get caught up in a crowd. Not at a church rally, not at a lodge meeting. Crowds can become mobs in an instant, and people can get trampled or crushed."

Matt was slightly appalled. "You figured this would happen?"

"No way to be sure, but I'm not surprised. That's why I got to you so quick. Those excited people could have gone another way, you know. They could have mobbed you, and they still might.

"There will be sore losers. They might just try to even things up by beating the tar out of the fighter that threw their man over the cliff. That's why you're on your way out of here while I take care of collecting the purse and the bets.

A number of Miller's Men had gathered near the banker's wagon, and Matt realized that they did not just happen to be there.

China urged him away, and one of their workers walked up the hill with him. Matt turned before trees hid his view and saw China and the Morgan Men surrounding the banker who was standing on his wagon and gesticulating wildly.

China Smith was brooking no nonsense. His voice was loud enough for those nearby to clearly understand what was being said.

"Van Horn's got one minute to get back in the ring, Banker, and I figure more than half of that is already gone."

The banker's mouth worked, but China's voice cut through. "That's the rule, Banker, and we aren't changing it. When the minute's up, we want the money—all of it."

The banker said, "But men are hurt over there. Some probably fell on top of Van Horn, and there is no way he can climb back up that bluff in time."

China's voice held satisfaction. "I'm pleased that you see it our way, Banker. I figure another few ticks of our watch will make the time right. If you planned on delaying until a handful of that gambling crowd gets up here to argue and fight over how they would like it to be, change your thinking.

"We play by the rules, Banker, and you had best start laying out the money."

The moneyman moved slowly with many glances toward the milling, shouting, and cursing mob along the bluff, but no relief came.

The accounting took time, but it was nearly completed before the first of Boots Van Horn's gamblers appeared. The man began loud and bitter complaint, but Miller Men surrounded him. When he attempted to leave to gather reinforcements, the Irish workers hemmed him in while China and the banker completed the count.

Finished, China handed the purse to Klubber Cole who immediately departed accompanied by a number of Morgan's Men wielding ax handles.

The gambler tore away to inform his friends, and Smith and a solid group of supporters waited. China figured to have all matters concerning the fight settled here and now while he had the strength of numbers.

The gamblers and their cronies plus a large contingent of Van Horn supporters vented their rage with threats of violence and use of the sheriff's arrest authority. The referee, a bit battered from his tumble, announced that Van Horn had failed to toe the line and had still not appeared. The Boss's Boy had won.

A tall man among the Van Horn people offered his opinion as an attorney and a principled spectator. He said, "Van Horn's unfortunate fall negates all of the betting, and the fight should be ruled a non-contest. All monies should be returned to their owners."

The Van Horn men howled approval. China Smith stood on the banker's wagon, and they quieted.

China said, "This is how I see it, and I have been part of more fist fights than any of you have ever seen."

A heated but unidentified voice interrupted.

"You are the Boss's Boy's trainer, China. You'll be on his side."

China did not rise to the bait. He said, "You can listen and decide.

"One of you threw a bucket full of beer at the Boss's Boy. Suppose it had struck, and the Boy could not have toed the line. Would you have declared the fight a non-contest? Not in a week of Sundays."

A man shouted, "Those things happen, Smith. A fighter has to expect them."

China went on. "Suppose Boots Van Horn's head had struck one of the rope posts when he got thrown and knocked him cold. Would you have said a fighter should expect those kind of things to happen? Or would you declare the fight a non-contest?"

No one spoke up. China said, "The Boss's Boy's throw is within the rules, is it not, referee?" The referee allowed that it had been a legal throw.

"All of you examined the square. Did any of you request it be moved to a safer spot?" He looked around, "Of course you did not.

"Boots Van Horn is the fighter noted for charging wildly and slamming opponents to the ground. If anyone was going to go through the rope it would most likely have been the Boss's Boy. If he had landed among you, would any of you have kicked or punched him?"

Men snorted and vowed they would have gotten in a lick or two. China's smile was grim.

"And if it had been the Boss's Boy who had gone over the bluff would you be here now asking that the money be given back to those who laid bets?"

Smith did not wait for replies. "The Boss's Boy won with no rules broken. The money has been paid out, and that is the end of it.

"Most of you are in strange country, and there are not many of you. The local people might not take to you agitating around here, so my advice is that you mount up and ride. Load into your wagons and get gone while the mood is still good and you have daylight to see by."

There was ferocious complaining, but frenzy had gone from the moment. Boots Van Horn was brought up the bluff nursing a shoulder strained in the fall and many contusions from men falling on him.

China Smith stood in the box of the banker's wagon waiting until most of the crowd had departed. He wanted no rumors spreading that he had fled the scene or feared to face Van Horn's supporters.

A tall and powerful rider on a sturdy looking spotted-rump horse moved his animal close alongside. The rider wore leather and a rifle rode in a scabbard along his leg. Beneath a broad brimmed westerner's hat the man's eyes were coal black and matched the hair that fell to his shoulders.

He gestured to China to step closer, and his mouth smiled broadly.

"Mister Smith, many years ago, my grandfather fought a human giant not too far upriver from here. The gist of the many-times told tale is that my ancestor flipped the monster over a cliff just as your man did a half hour ago."

The horseman extended a large and powerful hand for shaking. "Whether it was planned or accidental, it was damned well done, and a pleasure to see. Congratulate the Boss's Boy for me, and when he fights again, I will be there to enjoy it."

China shook the offered hand. "Many thanks, sir. I will explain your appreciation to Matt. May I have your name, sir?"

"I am Rob Shatto from beyond Bloomfield. Mister Matt Miller, who I assume is the fighter's father, is well thought of in this county."

The man turned his horse, and China saw that the rider had a peg left foot that boasted a gold band below the knee.

A man of influence, China expected and filed the name Shatto in his mind. He stepped from the wagon, and the banker's driver hurriedly drove away.

China hustled up the hill to explain the outcome to young Matt. He figured he had better spend more than a little time making certain that the Boss's Boy did not begin to believe that he had whipped Boots Van Horn and go out seeking other professionals to throw over bluffs.

16

The winter had been brutal. Snowfall did not break records, but deep and bitter cold arrived and hung on week in and week out. Both rivers froze so solidly that loaded wagons crossed without maneuvering around thin spots.

Traveling was miserable. Stone-hard roads with teams slipping and sliding forced injurious falls.

The Captain and Lukey Bates spent most of January in the city because returning to Perry County—only to retrace their route in a few weeks—would be painful and wasted effort. Separating the businesses was proving far more difficult than big Matt had expected, and Brascomb Miller fought it all of the way.

With Matt Miller owner of everything except Brascomb's home, the transfer should have been simple. Big Matt saw the separation as giving both he and his brother even freer hands with opportunity to increase their profit. Brascomb saw the changes as reducing his importance and perhaps his income. The Captain could not know Brascomb's secret hunger to own it all.

Without important contact with the western projects, Brascomb believed his ability to influence Miller enterprises would be greatly lessened. How could he know what was happening out there? He knew that big Matt withheld profits and used them along the rivers, and Brascomb hated even that loss of involvement.

Brascomb Miller was not an evil man who regularly wished misery on others, but the thought of how he could take charge and move the companies forward if young Matt were not there to inherit appeared often. Brascomb knew with all of his being that young Matt Miller was not the man to run important and moneymaking operations.

Big Matt could prattle all he wanted about the ideas his son came up with, but ideas did not make money. Close figuring and careful bargaining did. Young Matt was a mere youth who liked (actually liked) to fist fight, who was pathetic with the accounts, and whose mind wandered instead of sticking to the figuring and calculating. If only . . . Brascomb did not dare think further.

Young Matt watched the rivers with trepidation. He had moved a small fortune in logs behind Halderman's Island, and they were tightly secured, but when the Susquehanna rose, anything in the river's way was likely to end up in

Chesapeake Bay. In full flood, entire islands and every log in the river could disappear downstream.

As the winter wore on and expected meltings did not appear, Matt measured the snowfall accumulations and judged that the approaching spring thaw might reach flood records. His logs should be moved to high ground, but the time and effort involved would be considerable. The Boss was again in Philadelphia, and Matt believed he should not wait for his father's approval.

Matt needed ox teams that could pull heavy logs from their frozen berths and drag them across the river ice into storage near the sawmill high above possible flooding. The oxen would have to come from nearby farms.

Most local farmers were German, and Matt had discovered that the Germans were as clannish as the Scots, the Scotch-Irish or the Irish. They trusted their own and looked with suspicion on all others. A stubborn German made a mule seem cooperative. When he bargained with the German farmers, the Boss's Boy met stolid resistance. Matt turned to the Baron.

There was information to be gleaned from the men tearing crop-yielding fields from virgin forests. In many times fought-over Germany, no such land existed—nor were there small landowners who owed nothing to governments or influential noblemen.

Such independent men interested the Baron. Deiter Haas believed he could enjoy meeting with local farmers. Haas spoke their language. He had the noble bearing and background that many German's respected, and he could summon comforting and interesting details of conditions and happenings in their distant homeland

Haas would speak for young Matt. The Baron would strike the best deals and might gain agreements that Matt Miller could only hope for.

Von Haas made a single request. He asked that Wilhelm Brado accompany him.

The Baron said, "I will return to Germany, perhaps this summer, Matt. I have already been away too long." Von Haas smiled a bit grimly. "I have relatives with hungry eyes, and they wonder if I will ever return or if I am really alive and writing the letters they receive." The Baron's teeth flashed, "It is time I returned to count my cattle and weigh my coffers.

"Young Brado will stay here and, in time, his language skills could be valuable to you. Now, we see a boy little more than a child, but before we grow much older, Wilhelm Brado will become a man, and you and your father should bind him to your company.

"I can begin Brado's introductions to the local farmers. The men will like Wilhelm, he will soften them, and the women will wish to mother him. He—and you—can build on those acquaintances until the farmers lose their ingrained suspicions and think of the Millers as trustworthy friends."

Matt could see the sense of it, and Wilhelm Brado, who was already filling out into normal appearance, went forth with the Baron to meet Germans.

Bargaining could become close, but the Boss's Boy's ambassadors had some things going for them. Draft animals stood idle in the winter months and turned little or no profit for their owners. Something coming in would have great appeal to farmers who struggled to more than feed their families.

The Millers paid in gold and silver, not in county scrip or through barter—unless a farmer requested boards or coal. The Boss's Boy wanted the ox teams cheap, and he wanted to gain the farmers' goodwill. Cash payment would speak loudly.

Young Matt had other plans not yet mentioned. Local farmers were forced to sell most of their produce in Harrisburg, which was not yet a large market. Downriver markets might prove better, and if the Miller Company provided a canal and river boat that would transport their produce of corn, wheat, or whiskey directly to Baltimore or perhaps to the Columbia railhead for sale in Philadelphia, everyone might find legitimate profit.

Over the winter, the Miller Company would become friendly with the Germans, and during the harvest, further mutual profit might appear.

With the departure to the west of many of the Irish and Scotch-Irish workers, one Miller hotel was unused, and a second was half-empty. Both were conditions the Millers abhorred. To young Matt's satisfaction, Germans again provided a solution.

As the winter bore down with exceptional cold, a delegation of Germans came to the Miller office. They were five in number, and Matt found their faces, if not their names, familiar. Invited in, the workers shuffled and twisted, apparently discomfited by the Miller Company's power and position.

Matt exchanged ritual handshakes, introductions, and short, almost military bows. He found the nervous workmen seats, offered a warm drink, and prepared to listen. Matt had called Wilhelm Brado from the attached quarters where they had their cots. Brado could provide interpretation of the often-polyglot language the workers employed. An uneasy spokesman began, and his English, to Matt's satisfaction, was reasonably clear.

The Germans came with proposals. The spokesman noted that the German workers living along the Little Buffalo Creek numbered seventeen. Three had wives and children. Two had families en route from Baltimore. With many of the Irish workers moving on, the German workers almost equaled the Irish Miller Men in numbers.

The Germans, Matt was informed, also considered themselves Miller Men. For more than two full years they had worked for no one else, and they believed they had demonstrated their worth and their loyalty.

The spokesman pointed out that living conditions were increasingly abysmal along the creek. In anticipation of moving on, the Germans had not built permanently, but they liked Perry County with its dominant German population, and they liked the steady work provided by the Millers—even if they did not always receive the Irishmen's wage of seventy cents a day.

That explanation out of the way, the crux of their visit was quickly described. The German workers wished to be considered Miller Men—to move into the empty hotel with the advantages of deferred rent until spring labor began and preferential hiring when work became available.

Matt had made up his mind almost before the request was presented, but he took his time, plucking at an upper lip, and appearing to weigh the proposal.

The actuality was—the Germans' desire matched his own. It was perfect! He believed that the Germans had skills he needed. The Company would require early-spring manpower, and it was increasingly clear that the Irish were heading west and would never return.

He pondered how best to bind the German contingent to him—to the Miller Company was a better way to put it.

The Miller Men concept held the best possibilities. Big Matt had never actually put the idea to the men or even into words, but Big Matt did hire the same men and, on their own, workers had come to believe that they were special. To be a

Miller Man held status, and to be accepted as one made employment steady, with proper payment always on time—a facet of labor many employers did not religiously observe.

Workers who stuck with the Miller Company through good times and bad had profited both the company and themselves, and they chose to call themselves Miller Men. The Miller Men concept was genuine.

As if still considering, Matt strode across the office, paused as if examining the building's wall, then returned to his seat seemingly decided and ready to speak.

As he began, Matt wondered how his father would react to his preemption of authority, but in the Captain's absence, he was in charge, and the Germans' request was fortuitous and needed an immediate decision.

Matt said, "As you know, our regular Irish and Scot workers are moving west, and they are unlikely to return."

Of course, the Germans knew, just as they knew of the hotel standing empty, but Matt wished to establish mutual understandings that he hoped would make his acceptance of their hopes even more important in their own minds.

"We are loyal to our workers—Miller Men, as many describe themselves. While they were among us, the Irish were given first hiring and a standard wage. Those who remain will continue to be Miller Men with whatever privileges that title provides.

"In the spring, we will again be hiring, We have, of course, noted the quality of your work and your willingness to provide a fair day's work for agreed upon pay."

Matt allowed a small smile to touch his eyes and mouth. "I also remember our Germans, you among them, standing ready to defend all of us after Boots Van Horn fell over the river bluff. Mister Smith and I have appreciated your willingness to act as Miller Men."

There was rough laughter. The Germans were relaxing, and Matt could feel anxiety thinning.

"Your proposal is well timed. We have been considering the best way to replace the men departing.

"Our Germans, including all of you, know how we operate and what we require. You have learned that we are fair in hiring and prompt in payment. You say that you like it here in the county, and that you would like to stay. We want workers who are likely to remain with us for many seasons, and we believe that hiring German workers would be most advantageous.

"So, here is my offer.

"The Germans desiring to work for us must be able to cooperate with our Irish. Old world disagreements must be laid aside. If difficulties between groups arise, I must be notified before rioting or Donnybrooks break out. We have no tolerance for Irish versus German disagreements. You must, as they must, be Miller Men first, and failure to follow that rule will mean departure for them or for you."

Matt found it necessary to rise and pace because he was now treading on personal ground. He chose his words with care.

"I am aware that I am speaking to fully grown and independent men. We Millers hire you to labor. How you choose to live your lives is not part of most labor agreements, but we see ourselves as a closely-knit company. As best we can, we look out for your welfare.

"You in turn are part of this company, this family, if you will, and you must blend in and strengthen us. In this manner, all will profit, and that, after all, is why we labor. Therefore, I have other, perhaps intrusive conditions upon which I insist.

"Perhaps most important is that everyone do their best to learn to speak English.

"That requirement is not frivolous. America will be an English speaking country. This is your new home, and if we do not all speak the same language, differences will multiply rather than diminish. If we cannot comfortably communicate there will be barriers of understanding between us. Instead of becoming one, we will remain a nation of many, and we will be weaker for it.

"Although I speak directly to you. The Irish, or the Poles, and the English, or the Dutch, or the Italians—if they appear, must work together in the Miller Company. They must work side by side without rancor over preferences or wages or ancient national traditions.

"That may not be easy, but it is essential to our progress."

Matt paused. "Is there agreement so far, or must you council with the others?"

The Germans turned to each other to exchange nods before acknowledging that they understood and agreed. Matt had expected no less. He could only hope that the stubborn Germans and the prickly Irish could perform as easily as they would agree.

The Boss's Boy sighed inwardly. Even if they fought, pushed, and shoved, eventually the troublemakers would be removed, and his workers would blend into one homogenous group of Miller Men—he hoped.

There was more. "Have you all worked for Alex Donovan?" Most had. "Mister Donovan will be foreman for most of the canal maintenance and repair crews. Some of you will work for him or for the sub-foremen he appoints."

Matt moved onto less solid ground.

"Since his father's death, Mickey McFee has acted as foreman for our headquarters crew. He will remain in that position. Can you all work for Mister McFee?"

Matt waited their reply with some trepidation. Mickey was young for the job, but he had been familiar with the projects, and the Irishmen liked him. It had been convenient to appoint him, and McFee had done well.

A German laughed and spoke in his language. The other Germans—including Willy Brado joined in the laughter. Matt turned to Brado for interpretation.

"The Irish Hurricane is well known, Mister Miller. The men say that if they did not work well for him, he would lump them as he did Frederick the Great. They will work for Mister McFee as they would for Mister Donovan."

Before the day ended, Germans were marching past the headquarters clutching their belongings or tugging them along in carts. The day was so cold that spit froze almost as it hit the ground, and Matt expected every German would bless the iron wood stoves that were already sending smoke spiraling into the still winter air.

Wilhelm Brado spent the hours making rosters of strange sounding names. Among the thirty or more names of new hotel occupants were five Fritzes and three Wolfs. No worse than the common English or Irish names, Matt supposed, but he wondered if he would ever sort them out.

Matt wondered how he would calculate rent for men who moved in with entire families? Wives and children would be a first for the Miller hotels. As none had significant money, Matt supposed, at least for now, a family would pay the same as a single man.

Early summer might prove interesting as Lukey Bates and Willy Brado struggled to square the German accounts and collect what they believed was owed.

Then there was Klubber Cole. Matt supposed that Klubber thought of himself as a Miller Man. At least, he had moved into a hotel alongside the first of the Irish workers, and he had been there ever since.

Klubber had knocked down a number of partitions in the second hotel and established a school for young men interested in learning the manly art of self-defense. Astounding!

Klubber made enough to pay his rent and to join the evening meals. Occasionally a stranger, sometimes a young gentleman of obvious wealth from a distant community, would appear to learn from the Klubber. Bare fist fighting had strange attractions and allowed odd bedfellows.

While the weather was cold, Matt took to working out on Klubber's weighted bags, using his Indian clubs, and skip ropes.

When Matt worked out at night, Mickey McFee appeared with some regularity to pound the bags and shadow box imaginary opponents.

Matt and McFee exchanged little conversation, but the Boss's Boy liked having McFee around, and at times, Mickey attempted copying China's footwork or bobbing and weaving as Matt did, but mostly he just blasted right hands and pawing left jabs at the heavy bags. McFee could hit; there was no doubt about that, and obviously his broken hand had healed, but Matt believed China had been right that Mickey McFee would not have gone to the top as a professional prizefighter.

McFee knew that he was being held to his promise to never again fight professionally, but he remarked regularly how his broken fist was stronger than before. Matt expected that the tough opponent from his youth wished dearly to be unleashed to try again.

Too bad! Mickey McFee was a foreman and sole provider for his mother and sister. As long as he stayed with the Millers, he would do no money fighting.

17

Matt complained that, with both Lukey and his father gone to Philadelphia most of the winter, paperwork was falling behind. Big Matt responded that, with this bitter winter, there was very little work of any kind to fall behind on, and that little Matt should spend less time punching sand bags and more hours seeking out new and profitable contracts.

Ignoring Klubber Cole's gymnasium in their second hotel, Matt pointed out that his athletic equipment had been put away and was obviously unused. With the world frozen solid there was little work to be found, and because of Lukey's absence, all of his time was taken recording payments to this and that with no time to seek new contacts.

The Captain conceded that his son's acquisition of German workmen was well done, but one success, he noted, did not provide them a livelihood, and the Germans would not create significant income until the Miller Companies put them to work.

The Captain also saw the importance of moving their logs to high ground. March had come in like the proverbial lion, but the month was half gone with no thaw in the air. It was claimed that in 1816 there had been a year without summer. Surely this would not be another, but who could know?

The ice was thicker than any recalled, and every snowdrop still lay upon the land. Those living along the rivers worried and planned to move quickly to higher ground if flooding began in earnest.

A final trip was needed to Philadelphia, and big Matt was again in the city. Because of little Matt's harping, big Matt chose to take Wilhelm Brado along for company. He had left Lukey Bates to his records and to help China keep little Matt in line.

The father had whispered into his son's ear that China was slowing down and seemed content to spend time sitting in the hotel parlor.

Matt wisely did not mention that he noticed his father slowing even more than China. It was clear that both men now enjoyed afternoon naps, and they retired early.

When they were alone, China said, "Your Pa wants to see his doctor in the city as much as he wants to finish up the Philadelphia work, Matt."

Immediately worried, Matt said, "I haven't heard him complain about feeling ill, China? What does he think is wrong?"

"He doesn't know. He says he feels tired all of the time and gets short of wind just walking up from the hotel. Anyway, he's got a doctor looking after him that is supposed to be good at curing such complaints."

"Do you think it is anything serious?" Matt did not like the sound of it.

"Hard to tell, but he has slowed down—which is probably a good thing. Have you given thought to how old your Pa is, Matt?"

Matt had to admit he had not given it much thought, but he could figure it out.

China had the answer. "Well, he's sixty years old. Most men his age are dozing by their stove, so he is doing all right, but more of the work will fall on you from here on out. You can depend on that, no matter how busy the Captain tries to be."

Matt wondered aloud. "How old are you, China? I've never heard."

The old fighter bounced on his toes and threw a few swift punches. "I'm still a sprout, Matt. I'll be fifty-five sometime this year. At least that is as close as I've ever been able to figure it. I've got no paper saying when I was born, and there never was anybody to tell me." China grinned almost fiercely. "I've got a big advantage there. I can claim almost anytime as my birthday, and nobody can prove otherwise."

Matt pretended to remember. "It seems to me that you had two birthdays last year that we had to celebrate." More seriously he asked, "How are you feeling these days, Young Sprout?"

To his astonishment, China Smith appeared suddenly discomforted. There was a long pause before Smith added explanation.

His color high, China said, "Well, Matt, I hadn't intended speaking on it just yet, but seeing it has come up, I've got an announcement or two I've been saving.

"The first fact is that I am planning on asking for Mrs. Black's hand in matrimony as soon as the weather breaks. The second thing is . . ."

His voice astonished, Matt interrupted, "You are what?" They found themselves halted, China examining the distant river shore, and Matt staring at his mentor as if he had never looked before.

China kept gazing away, but he spoke with intensity. "You think I'm too old or haven't got enough put away to have a fine wife like Mrs. Black, Matt?"

Flustered, Matt said, "I don't think any of that, China; you just caught me by surprise. I just never figured that you had any interest beyond what we've been doing, and I never noticed that you and Mrs. Black were . . ." Matt's words choked off.

China began moving again, and Matt found his feet going along.

Smith said, "Well, I've got other interests, and I've reason to believe that Mrs. Black might look kindly on having a strong man around. Her husband has been passed-on for more than six years now, and to my mind, she has been working too hard feeding a bunch of low-life Scotch-Irishmen for these past years."

Matt was doing some fast figuring. "But even if—or that is when—you are married, you will still work with us, won't you? And Mrs. Black—of course she will be Mrs. Smith then—will still run the restaurants won't she, China?"

Smith's answers were as shaky as Matt's questions. "Well, all of that isn't worked out yet, Matt. Off the cuff, I'd like to keep on with you and the Captain—especially as he is anchoring right here in Petersburg.

"I suspect, my lovely wife-to-be will want to keep busy, and I've not intended to claim that money coming in won't be welcome, but we haven't decided just how that will go."

China sounded a bit nervous as he continued.

"You can keep all of this to yourself for a few weeks, Matt. I think Mrs. Black's intention is to announce it in church at a time of her choosing. I probably shouldn't have said beans about it, but plans like marrying are hard to hold close to your chest."

As his thinking cleared, Matt recalled how often China was down at the restaurant. He should have noticed and realized . . . but he hadn't."

Then China nearly floored him.

"As long as we are talking about personal dealings, Matt. If I were you, I'd start paying a lot of attention to that gal who has her cap set for you. Being the prettiest and maybe the smartest eligible girl around these parts, she won't wait for you forever, you know."

Matt's feet halted. "Girl? What girl, China? There isn't any woman coming after me. Why . . .?"

China Smith's look of disbelief stopped Matt cold. His mind raced, attempting to discover who Smith might be talking about, but no one came to mind.

China said, "Matt, who is your best friend around here?"

Matt felt suddenly deficient, as if he had overlooked something really important. "Friend? Why I don't know that I have a real close kind of friend."

China sighed, "Well, you've always been slow about most things, Matt, but I'd have thought you'd have discovered who stands up for you if others speak badly about the Millers. I'd have thought you'd have figured who you should have backing you up if things got mean and you needed help."

Matt's blank look convinced Smith that he had to go further. "And I'd for sure have figured that you would have noticed that friend's sister who has been sneaking special looks at you for at least the last year.

"Great Scott, Matt Miller, if you don't know who I am talking about yet, I'm purely giving up."

China tossed his head in discouragement and turned off, heading for the livery and Bloomfield on business.

Matt watched him go, stunned by the marriage announcement and utterly confused by the revelation that one of the town girls was specially interested in him. Not that he hadn't looked them over more than once, but he hadn't seen anyone that particularly plucked at his heartstrings.

And the best friend part? Lukey Bates didn't fit at all, and Wilhelm Brado was just a boy. Who else did he know? The Baron? Hardly. Otherwise, the only name he could think of was Mickey McFee, but Mickey . . .?

McFee a special friend?

Matt had never weighed the possibility. Mickey had always seemed more of an opponent than a possible friend, and Matt had been away most of those earlier years when boyhood friendships formed.

Still, when he thought about who he liked, Mickey popped up first and—Great ghosts, Mickey had a sister. Matt saw her now and then, sort of just in the background when he had clothing repaired or maybe when she walked with her mother in the village, but he had never really looked. Why, she was just a young girl, sort of like Wilhelm Brado.

Or was she? Erin McFee. Matt knew her name, of course. She had always been around. Maybe Erin wasn't that young after all.

Bewildered and doubting mightily, Matt marched back to the office. Lukey Bates was hunched over his ledgers, and Matt went straight at it.

"Lukey, do you know Erin McFee?"

Bates glanced up and saw Matt's intensity. "Of course, I know Erin. Everybody does. Prettiest girl in the county, I'd say."

Then Bates stopped as if waiting, but Matt floundered, embarrassed and unsure of what to say next.

The silence wore on before Lukey tired of it. He placed wood in the stove and decided to offer Matt help.

"Matt, every Irishman in our camp knows Erin McFee. She is a beautiful and intelligent girl, and most of them have done their best to gain her attention. To my knowledge, all have failed.

"The German workers feel the same, and some of them have brought over flowers. One woodcarver made Erin three wooden spoons."

Matt was awed—and for no reason, irritated.

"She is one of my best friends, Matt, and she often asks me about you."

Asks about him? Ask what? He was around all of the time, so he must be familiar to everyone in the town.

Bates was willing to say what he thought.

"Erin likes you a lot, Matt. Why just the other day, she . . ." Bates paused, looking past Matt's shoulder and down the hill.

"We've got business Matt." He gestured toward the doorway and through the door's small window, Matt saw a sleigh pulled by a handsome pair laboring up the hill toward their building.

Business! Matt gathered his scattered senses. The safe was locked, but Matt motioned for Lukey to close the wooden door disguising its presence. The sleigh was pretty well buttoned up, but it looked like two men were inside.

Matt asked, "You know them, Lukey?"

"The sleigh is not from around here, and it is handsomely maintained. Business, Matt, that is for sure."

The team reached their road where Willy Brado had smoothed the snow, and it made better progress. Within moments, the rig had stopped in front. Two men dismounted, and the driver secured the team to an iron ring turned into the front of the building. The undoubtedly more important passenger waited, stamping his feet against the frozen ground, his breath steaming as strongly as the horses'. His hands were buried within a thick, beaver fur muff, and his nicely cut wool coat extended to the tops of his low-cut city shoes.

Lukey peered past Matt's shoulder. He said, "Money, Matt, and probably Commonwealth money." Bates scrubbed his hands in anticipation. "There is nothing better than State money."

Bates frowned in thought, "But what could bring them out this time of the year? It is too early to begin hiring." He shrugged, "Here they are, so get ready to deal, Boss's Boy."

Matt retreated behind his father's desk and motioned Lukey to handle the door. Bates stood ready, and as the driver's knuckles reached to knock, he opened and stood aside as stiff and erect as if on parade. Matt hoped he could look as impressive.

Introductions were swift and businesslike. Mister Horace Thorpe represented the Commonwealth and did the talking.

Thorpe said, "Your company has an excellent reputation with our department, and we are in need of swift action."

He added, "I thought you would be older, Mister Miller."

Matt smiled as if he had not heard it all before. "My father is the senior Miller, Mister Thorpe, but I can speak for the company. What can we do for you?"

Thorpe wasted no time. "This is Thomas Holcomb, our chief bridge engineer. Together, we have examined the Clark's Ferry Bridge discussing repairs needed before our spring breakup."

Thorpe shook his head in obvious dismay.

"There is no use beating around the bush, Mister Miller. Damage is unexpectedly great. Unless repairs to the bridge piers are completed before high water, floating ice slabs, and drifting logs batter the bridge, we may lose most of the structure."

Thorpe was clearly appalled and exasperated.

"We had expected our routine inspection to find the bridge little damaged and only minor and unimportant cosmetic repairs needed, but it seems that shoddy masonry work was included during initial construction, and now we are desperately short of time to make essential repairs."

The news was startling, and Matt envisioned the canal boats that could not cross without the bridge's towpath. His mind shifted to the practicality of the Millers providing river-wide tow cables or many-oared rowing craft to drag boats across. Thorpe continued.

"The winter freeze will break at any moment, Mister Miller, and we dare not wait for competitive bidding or even to move distant capabilities into position.

"My request is, can you provide the labor and the materials to immediately begin quality repairs to the bridge's stonework?

"And if you can, will you accompany Mister Holcomb and me in our sleigh to survey the damage without an instant's delay?"

Matt could see Lukey Bates shaking his head behind Mister Thorpe, and Matt understood his trepidation. If they took on the emergency labor and failed, the Miller Company's hard-won reputation could suffer serious degrading, and Commonwealth contracts might thereafter be denied them. Matt could easily claim lack of stonemasons and steer clear of problems.

On the other hand, if they could succeed, the contract would be more than lucrative. The overdue thaw could strike at any instant, and Thorpe was trapped. To lose the bridge would be crippling to the Commonwealth's profits from western and upriver shipping. Matt suspected he could almost name their price. Furthermore, the Commonwealth would, in a sense, be in their debt, and other business could come their way.

Where was China Smith? Matt felt his strong right hand's absence, but China was en route to Bloomfield.

Matt's hesitation had been only momentary. He nodded briskly and said, "Allow me a few moments to locate my chief foreman. He will join us in our own sleigh. If we can come to an agreement, we will wish to begin almost within the hour because you are right, Mister Thorpe, melting could begin tonight, and every moment will be precious."

Relief almost matched the hope in Thorpe's eyes, and Matt could see Holcomb, the engineer, relax. It appeared that the Millers really were their only hope—if they could do the work.

Alex Donovan's house was near the hotels, and Lukey Bates headed that way. A passing worker was sent to harness a horse to the Captain's sleigh and rush it to wherever Donovan wanted it. The man would also ask the Baron to join Donovan.

Matt expected his Germans would be important to any masonry being done on the massive bridge structure, and Von Haas could help translate the Germans' mostly incomprehensible English. Then Matt and the Commonwealth men turned their sleigh onto the river ice and headed for the bridge.

Matt saw the pier damage almost immediately. It was all out-of-the-water and upriver damage, for which he could be thankful because trying to replace giant stonework below the ice level would have been a monster, but when the river rose, everything coming downstream would crash into the damage he was examining and almost surely destroy more than one of the stone piers. Even a single pier loss would topple the bridge when the wooden structure sagged into the raging torrent of spring flooding.

Donovan and the Baron came quckly, and Matt asked, "Can we fix that, Alex?"

"I'm not sure, Matt. Getting mortar to hold and harden in below-freezing weather is not the right way. We might be able to heat the rocks over fires or maybe warm the mortar, but I would have to talk it over with our stonemasons before saying for certain."

"How about the Germans, Deiter? We have some that were masons in Europe. I mean the ones that have been cutting stone for our creek dam. They might know something."

The Baron said, "I will ask, but this is huge damage, and I would not accept the task until you are sure we can deliver."

Matt and the engineer Holcomb believed five piers were in desperate need of repair, and Thorpe made no argument.

"Can you take on the job and complete it in time, Mister Miller? Thorpe was clearly anxious—as he should be. Losing a bridge would not be a small thing.

Matt chose to speak honestly and without pretense. "I am not sure, Mister Thorpe. First, I will have to speak with my masons, and they will have

243

to come out and look over the task. That will take some hours."

Matt scrubbed at his chin in thought. "Give me those hours, and I will have a firm answer for you."

He added, probably unnecessarily, "This will cost money, Mister Thorpe. We must stop all that we are doing and planned to do. There will be teams to hire and men to relocate."

Thorpe gritted his teeth. "I understand all that you are saying and all of the thoughts behind your words, Mister Miller. If you do not grind the Commonwealth's nose in it, we must agree. We have no time to bargain, but Mister Miller, I can add that if you are successfully helpful in this matter, we at Harrisburg will remember, and we will be in your debt."

The man shrugged in resignation and acceptance. "Assuming it survives the spring floods, I can see that this bridge will be in need of great rebuild. When those contracts are issued, your companies will be remembered, Mister Miller."

Matt had only two foremen, Alex Donovan and Mickey McFee—plus the Baron. He gathered them at the headquarters and included one Irishman and two Germans who claimed to be experienced in cold weather building. He explained what was needed.

"Most of the damage is about five feet above the ice—above where most things hit during normal fast and high water. As long as the ice holds, we can work on that damage from sleds or rafts. If we are not done before the ice starts out, we will have to work from above, and I fear the water will come up fast and probably higher than it ever has before. That high water might help save the bridge because out-going ice and floating trees will strike above our repairs—at least we can hope that will be the case.

"Some rock damage is very high on the piers because stones closer to the water fell loosening everything above them. We will need a lot of stone to replace all that has disappeared, but I think we have enough at our dam site. We will use that stone, if you believe it is suitable."

Alex asked, "How many men do you want to put on this, Matt? If you are going to take the job, I think we should go at it as hard as possible." He paused as if judging the weather. "We could get a warming tomorrow, and if we do, we might have only a day or two to work."

Matt was clear. "We want everyone willing and able, Alex. You and Mickey choose five crews. Each one will have a pillar and, if we have them, each crew will need a man who knows how to build a stone wall."

One of the Germans chose to speak, and Matt recognized him as Fritz Frownfelter, a stone worker from their dam preparations.

Matt asked, "Herr Frownfelter?" But he had to wait for Deiter Haas's interpretation.

Frownfelter said, "We should use German mortar, Mister Miller. Nothing else will set properly in this cold."

Recognizing everyone's lack of under-standing, Frownfelter went on. "German mortar, as we call it, is used in the north of our country where it is often below freezing. The technique is to grind and filter the cement and sand even finer than usual. Egg whites in quantity are beaten into the water, but the mortar mix is kept very dry. The mortar must be so dry that it will only grip the stone. Wet mortar will freeze, and that means the mortar will swell in place and will be crumbly when dry. The drier the mortar we use, the less swelling will occur, and the stronger the stones will stand.

"That means that we must build genuine stone walls, dry wall you call it, that will support itself without mortar, and that will require careful stonecutting and fitting. Our mortar will add to the strength of our repair, but it will not be the walls' only support."

Matt asked, "You can mix this mortar, Fritz?"

"Yah, Herr Miller."

Matt turned to everyone. "Do we have enough stonemasons?" The foremen believed they did.

"All right, we will get started. Alex, you and Mickey divide up the men. I want you to choose a foreman for each team, and I want those foremen to meet me here at the sleigh in an hour.

"When they arrive, we will go out to the bridge and begin making plans and deciding how many teams of oxen or horses we will need.

"I will listen to those men and return to pass the word to Lukey who will relay it to everyone.

Meanwhile, get started on rounding up draft animals, sleds, and stones."

Donovan and McFee disappeared. The Baron went to add a second horse to the sleigh. Matt wished they had ice shoes for the animals. He wanted no broken legs or tangled harness.

Lukey said, "I've got to say that you make up your mind fast, Matt. I will add that you had better be right. This is going to cost serious wages and rentals for animals and sleds."

Matt tried to sound positive, but it took some stilling of the flutters in his breast. What would his father and China say?

Matt kept his words light. "Money is of no use unless it is used, Lukey."

Bates' words were heavy. "Your Uncle Brascomb would not exactly agree, Boss's Boy."

18

Mister Horace Thorpe had returned to Harrisburg to report their bridge findings and his employment of workers to begin immediate repairs.

The Miller Company had requested a high price, but without options, Thorpe had agreed. Now he would have to convince his superiors that his bargain had been necessary.

Examining the frozen river and the deep and hard-packed snow, the legislators and money dispensers would not be difficult to persuade. If the thaw arrived in full force, flooding was certain. On how high the flood would rise, no one dared gamble. Having been warned that the bridge could collapse, no one would dare to obstruct Thorpe's repairs. Of course, if Horace Thorpe's efforts failed, and the bridge was destroyed, the onus would be Thorpe's to bear.

Thomas Holcomb had remained behind to oversee the repairs. He had requested a room at the hotel on the Duncannon square, but none had been available. Young Mister Miller had offered the senior Miller's small apartment, pending his father's return from Philadelphia, and Holcomb had gratefully accepted.

The village was active throughout the night, and from his window, Holcomb saw fires built on the ice near each damaged pier. Sleds and wagons seemed constantly marching onto the river bearing loads that were unidentifiable in the wintry dark.

Holcomb carried a short spyglass, which he used to closely examine details beyond easy reach. With morning light and his glass to his eye, the engineer focused on the mile-distant bridge.

Astonishing! The structure crawled with workmen, and sleds were crossing the ice. Those going carried stones of great weight and were pulled by powerful horse teams or braces of oxen. Holcomb hurried his morning toilet and made his way up the slippery hill to the Miller headquarters.

On the steps of the headquarters, Holcomb again paused to use his telescope. From the greater height he could examine the ongoing work more clearly. He determined that workers were also moving along the bridge to assist in the repairs. Fires blazed on the ice, and Holcomb could see blackened circles where fires had been moved as ice melted. A few men had paused to warm themselves at the blazes, and the engineer saw a man toss large logs onto a fire to keep it high. How thick was the ice? Two or more feet, Holcomb surmised. That should require days of warm weather to break loose.

Within the headquarters building, Mister Miller and his clerk were absent, but a lean-figured older man with battered features warmed himself before the iron stove.

Holcomb said, "Mister Miller? I am Thomas Holcomb, Commonwealth Engineer."

The man smiled and said, "I'm not Miller, Mister Holcomb, I am China Smith, the Captain's right hand man. I just arrived from the county seat. Word that the Millers were tearing down the bridge came in before dawn, and I about wore out my animal getting back here." Smith again smiled and added, "I figured I had better find out what I was missing."

He gestured toward the river bridge, "I see that I am not needed. Matt has the situation moving and organized as if we had done the work a hundred times. If this cold will hold on another day or two, I judge Matt can beat the thaw and the breakup that will arrive shortly thereafter."

Again the smile, "That, I think, will be satisfying to all."

Holcomb was pleased by Smith's confidence, but his real interest lay in the work going on, and China Smith recognized his anxiety.

"Let's go down to the river and get a ride out to the work. Lukey Bates was here earlier, and I am repeating his thoughts to you, but we ought to see for ourselves, agreed?"

On their way to the river, Smith, who insisted on being called China—apparently a nickname in common use—brought them to a structure within which men labored industriously. The workers were German, and Holcomb could understand their language—acquired during engineering studies. German engineering was considered the backbone of the profession—at least until recent years it had been that way. The New York and Pennsylvania canal constructions and some of the bridges now being built surpassed many European projects of earlier times. American engineering was now being taught, but the German language was still essential to read the established books on the subject.

Miller workmen were regrinding masonry cement into dust-like consistency. The workman named Frownfelter explained again the concept of dry mortar, which was new to China Smith and particularly interesting to the engineer.

As kegs were filled, the powdery cement was transferred to a nearby shed where other men had sifted sand to a consistency almost as fine as the cement. The group combined the cement and sand in proper measures and mixed them thoroughly before bagging the mix and sledding it to the building sites.

At the bridge, everything was done at a trot, and Holcomb marveled. Commonwealth workmen were almost inherently unable to maintain anything swifter than a casual stroll. Miller Irishmen and Germans hopped about like fleas on a hot skillet.

Men shaping stone bent to their tasks and did not look up. Pails of egg whites were placed near warming fires, and Holcomb expected every laying hen in the county had contributed. Water was bucketed through ice holes, the eggs were added, and the mortar was mixed. Mortar carriers hustled, and there was no idle chatter. Smith and Holcomb found Matt Miller helping hoist a heavy stone into place. They watched as mortar was slapped on top of a lower rock and the new stone thunked solidly into place.

There were "Yahs" of acceptance, and the workmen went their way. Matt Miller turned to greet the arrivals.

Matt's face was lined with weariness, but his eyes were alert and intense.

China asked, "Have you been out here all night, Matt?"

"Almost." Matt turned to Holcomb and Smith. "Tad Shuler came in just before dark, and he said the weather will change today. We've no time to waste."

Holcomb had to ask, "Who is Tad Shuler?"

China answered, "Tad's an old woodsy who brings us fresh meat. He is one of Matt's finds, but you never know when he will arrive or depart. He lives over in Pfoutz Valley, has a cabin and a wife, but all he does is hunt and roam—I've heard."

"And he is a weather predictor?"

Matt had his turn. "Tad Shuler almost lives out-of-doors. If Tad says it is going to warm, I believe him, and we work as if he is going to be right. Getting started in the dark was hell, but these are Miller men, and they can do almost anything.

Now, we are well into it, and given decently cold weather today and tonight, we will do the job."

Holcomb noted that Miller spoke clearly and that nearby workmen heard his words. There was no telling how many of the laborers understood the English, but some would, and spirits would rise at their boss's appreciation and respect—and Matt Miller's men would work a touch harder to deserve it. Holcomb recognized good leadership, and his hopes also rose.

Men had chipped away ice around the base of the five damaged piers, and Holcomb saw them applying mortar to the lowest blocks they could reach. He said "That is not part of our contract, Mister Miller."

Matt did not need to look. "We are making mortar faster than we need it, and the stone cutting is slowest. There is no use having these men simply stand around waiting. That stonework can use the pointing up, and it will take nothing from our agreed upon repair. Consider it a bonus, Mister Holcomb."

Holcomb did, and his appreciation of the Miller Company leaped.

They visited each pier, and the work was organized the same at each. Men chipped at huge stones with chisels and sledges. A-frame hoists were positioned with their feet embedded in the ice and strong tackle rigged to lift the stones. Crude log scaffolding leaned against the piers, and men worked on them measuring and final-fitting stones of hundreds of weight.

A sand-filled sled arrived with fires built inside and stew boiling in huge iron kettles. The stew was ladled into wooden bowls and proffered to appreciative hands. Egg yokes were scrambled on a flat steel plate, and men shoveled hasty, on-the-move breakfasts. Men drank coffee or tea from Mrs. Black's white crockery cups that were hastily rinsed in ice water between drinkers.

Men relieved themselves on the ice, but always downstream with added comments of sending Baltimore special gifts, but the work never faltered. If a man took a break, another stepped into the job. Holcomb remained impressed and wondered how such willingness was maintained among men very tired from a day of work and then a full night on the bridge job.

Smith and Holcomb were picked up by Lukey Bates in his sled and transported to shore. Bates returned to the work site, and the older men dragged up the hill to the warmth of the headquarters where they sank gratefully into comfortable chairs, and China stoked more life into the stove.

China scrubbed his hands together and said, "I don't like the cold anymore, Mister Holcomb. When this bridge work is done, I will be glad to greet the warm weather, no matter how high the river rises."

"And this year it will rise high, China." Holcomb liked the easy familiarity of the nickname.

"This late in the year the thaw will come like lightning, and people living near the water are going to be flooded out. My guess is that the entire first street of this village will go downstream."

China agreed. "They've been told a hundred times, Mister Holcomb, and most have been flooded before. They just keep rebuilding, and they will again. It's their choice, so I don't worry about them."

"They will come to your door seeking help, China. Those kind always do."

"Yep, but they won't get it from me. God helps those who help themselves, and those folks don't hold up their end. It'd be best if they floated on down to Baltimore and didn't try rebuilding around here."

Matt appeared at noon with a crew of worn-down workers heading for their bunks until they replaced those who would build on until dark and into the night.

Before he flopped onto his bed in his room behind the headquarters, Matt asked, "Have you been outside in the last half hour?"

Neither man had. Matt said, "The wind is out of the south. It is warm, and the snow is already wet. The thaw is starting right now, so we haven't won this battle yet."

Holcomb said, "Oh my. I had hoped for a few days." He went to the door to feel for himself. After a moment he was back. "No question about it, if that warm wind continues, it will melt snow and ice as if it were a fire."

Matt stood in his doorway as he said, "We have two things going for us. The first is that it will probably get colder tonight as the sun goes down—maybe cold enough to stop melting.

"The second is that the warm air will help set our mortar and, we will need every minute we get. As you know, Mister Holcomb, fresh mortar is as weak as if it were only sand. We need a day, or better two days, for our mud to harden. After that? Well, we will see, won't we?"

Holcomb rose during the night. He saw lanterns on the bridge, but no great fires burned on the ice. He wondered why because firelight would have helped.

In dawn's light, the engineer discovered why there had been no fires. Inches deep water covered the river ice, and as he watched, Holcomb saw that the water flowed.

A river on top of the river; Holcomb had not seen it before, and certainly the permanent ice would be melting at a ferocious rate. The two-foot thick ice would soon burst free, rise to the surface, and perhaps come downstream in great rafts that would strike the bridge pilings with grinding force. The engineer feared their frantic work would be in vain.

When he stepped outside, Holcomb found himself in slush. Flowing water sliced small canyons in the deeper snow, and the small rivulets became rushing streams as they approached the river. Big flooding was about to happen, and anything on low ground along the Susquehanna River was about to be swept away.

A single sleigh remained on the river ice, and Holcomb assumed that the many rafts and sleds had been pulled to safety. They would be on high ground somewhere below Duncan's Island. No doubt the rented teams and wagons would already be on their way home to familiar barns and stalls.

Even as the engineer watched, the last sleigh slopped through inches of water and made its way almost to where he stood. Lukey Bates, appearing as exhausted as his horse, drove the sleigh ashore and halted beside Thomas Holcomb.

Holcomb asked, "How is it going out there?"

Bates shook his head in admission of not being sure. "We can't tell, Mister Holcomb. Our part is about finished. We are working almost at the top of the piers. If the water or ice reaches that high, the bridge will go anyway. Matt thinks we have done a good job, and the Germans have been challenging the river to bring on its worst. So, maybe the repairs will hold."

Holcomb asked, "Where is Mister Miller now?"

"He came off the bridge more than an hour ago. He walked in because he wanted to check on how the Juniata River is doing and to make sure the rafts and small boats are far up the banks. Matt believes this is going to be a flood beyond memory, and to my inexperienced eye it seems as if it would just have to be."

Bates considered a moment. "Matt says he expects the canals to flood and some of them to wash out." Holcomb saw the clerk's eyes squint.

"Whew, as terrible as that could be, there will be a lot of work this summer."

Holcomb climbed aboard, and Bates urged his weary animal up the hill to the headquarters.

Matt Miller was inside, and he had his leaders with him. Holcomb stood near the door and waited Matt's attention.

Matt said, "I know we are all tired, but some things have to be done right now.

"Alex, take some men and move the sawmill onto very high ground. I just looked at the Juniata, and the ice above the aqueduct has broken and upstream ice is pushing underneath it. That means we are about to have serious ice jams right there at Duncan's Island. The jams could get really bad, or they might just break up and float away, but my guess is that the ice will pile up into a huge dam, and at least some of the aqueduct will go, and when the backed up water hits the Susquehanna we will get flooding higher than we have seen around here."

Alex Donovan moved while Matt paused for breath.

Matt hurried on, "Mickey, take any of your crew that can get on their feet and have them help move our people and any property that is below High Street. Warn those that we aren't helping that big flooding is coming, but stay on our work, not someone else's."

Mickey asked, "Do you think it is going to get into the hotel, Matt?"

McFee rarely used Matt's given name, but neither noticed. "My guess is that Main Street will have deep water in it." Then Matt realized. "Move your family up here, into the back of the headquarters, Mickey."

He paused to smile grimly. "The first bunk is mine, and the one at the far end is Brado's. Move Brado's stuff, not mine."

McFee was gone in an instant, and Matt turned to Lukey Bates.

"Lukey, the first thing for you to do is put that animal in a safe stall and give it a good feed. That horse has put in a lot of hours and deserves attention.

"Next, go to bed. Sleep for hours. When you are rested, come back to work, but not before dark. I will be good until then, and China is as fresh as morning dew." Bates attempted to protest, but his heart wasn't in it. China said, "Follow the boss's orders, Lukey. You need the rest."

Baron Deiter Van Haas waited quietly. He appeared as unsullied as if he had slept the night away, and Matt grinned at him because Von Haas had done exactly that. The Baron had watched and helped a little here and there, but Von Haas had never hired on and was not being paid.

Matt shook his head. "Deiter, do all barons float around observing, enjoying, and joining in only when they feel like it?"

Von Haas smiled widely. "All that I know of Mister Miller. It is our duty to be informed and to encourage the peasantry."

China said, "When we get around to it, Matt and I and maybe McFee and Klubber Cole are coming over and stir your people into violent rebellion."

Von Haas laughed aloud. "Do come over, Mister Smith. My grandfather's dungeons are still ready for use."

More soberly, he asked, "What can I do to help, Matt?"

Matt was ready. "I have been hoping you would ask. What I would like you to do is gather every German that can still move and get them down to the Little Juniata. That creek will boil up as if a dam broke, and we do not wish to lose anything we do not have to."

Matt appeared finished for the moment, but China had something to say.

"The last thing, Matt, will be for you to go to bed. Mister Holcomb and I will keep an eye on the bridge and anything else around here that needs doing. If Lukey Bates needs to sleep, so do you."

Smith pointed at the door to the sleeping quarters. "Through there, Boss's Boy, and sleep soundly. You have done yourself proud—even if the entire bridge goes downstream."

China's laughter matched Matt and Holcomb's groans of despair.

19

The flood damage was almost beyond comprehension. From as far upriver as the new town of Lock Haven clear down to the Chesapeake, homes, businesses, equipment and people had been washed away. Coffins from eroded cemeteries floated down the rivers.

In Petersburg, two streets were flooded, with water in the hotel. Few dared guess how the canal had fared. The great waterways so laboriously cut along the rivers were still under water, but horrendous destruction was certain. Massive ice sheets had battered them. Some canal buildings were gone, and although the stone locks would stand, clay walls and smaller culverts might not.

The citizenry lived with mud. Roads were mires, and farmers had no hope of working fields for many days and perhaps weeks.

Mrs. Black's eatery was taxed to provide food for customers, and the hotels were filled with hungry workers to worry over. Workers ate heartily, and when they did not, their labor suffered. Going hungry was also devastating to spirit, and this year, in particular, the Boss's Boy did not want his men departing for greener pastures.

China first learned of impending food shortage from Mrs. Black. He spoke about it to Matt and, although the shortages did not apply directly to the Miller company, wheels began rolling.

There was food throughout the county. The problem was to get it to Petersburg. Matt dispatched wagons to farms and villages that were not along the rivers. He chose light wagons that could better plow their ways through the bogs that had once been roads, and he manned them with German drivers who would speak in familiar words to the often-stolid and always suspicious German farmers.

The wagons, and a few horse trains, would return with food because Matt provided silver for payment. The people in general hungered for real money, money that could buy manufactured goods instead of local scrip that no one believed was worth much. The produce brought in went on the company books. Matt charged it against Mrs. Black's account or to others who were pleased to buy. China Smith backed the restaurant account, of course; so Matt did not worry over that payment.

Many of the recipients worked for the Miller Company, and their pay could be fairly garnished. Others? They were few, and could be worked out later. Matt expected, that eventually, a fair profit would be returned from what he willingly provided for everyone.

And still the river roared. The mighty ice covering cracked and finally split into a thousand shards. Immense sheets of ice floated downriver, and the bridge repairmen watched their approaches with trepidation.

When they struck the piers the watchers winced, but the ice seemed to be rotten, and instead of solid smashes, the huge ice rafts crumbled, and their impacts amounted to little.

Other debris proved more serious. Uprooted trees were among the worst. Huge trees roared down on the bridge. Their massive roots and branches, borne high by the flood, threatened to tear away the wooden bridge structures, and Engineer Holcomb hired Miller Men armed with axes to chop away anything that struck and clung to the bridge spans. At times the axe man battled frantically, and the beams and trusses groaned and swayed from the strains, but the bridge held.

Then the barn approached!

The huge structure appeared far upstream and loomed like a floating island. A desperate cry rose among the men who watched the approaching behemoth with utmost certainty that this time they would lose.

It was a good German barn, built using giant timbers, each mortised to the next with wooden pins holding everything together. The building lay on its side, but even the roof shingles seemed intact on the high-floating juggernaut, and the wide-boarded barn floor looked undamaged. There had been hay in the loft, and strands and heaps of the sodden mass trailed and surrounded the obviously unstoppable monster.

Bridge defenders fled from where the barn would strike, and life poised as the massive wreck, looming high above the wooden bridge, made its final attack.

Thomas Holcomb's heart sorrowed as he saw the magnificent bridge, the pride of central Pennsylvania, about to be smashed into kindling. China Smith cursed aloud, and still on the bridge with his workmen, Matt Miller felt his emotions close down and his teeth grit in preparation for the rending of bridge timbers as none of the watchers had ever experienced.

Then, the barn was gone! Only yards from impact, the outwardly indestructible juggernaut simply vanished. Those on the bridge heard the popping of pins and mortises and saw the collapse, but to those further distant, the barn simply vanished.

Barn pieces floated through beneath the bridge spans, as most observers stared in disbelief. Matt found his jaw dropped, and appreciated the relief from teeth grinding in frustration.

The engineer said "Good God!"

China Smith asked, "Now how in hell did the Boss's Boy make that happen?"

Absolutely stunned by the bridge's miraculous escape, Holcomb was slow in grasping

Smith's humor, but when he did, his relieved and barely believing laughter joined China's.

Holcomb said, "That barn collapse must have been some reward from on high for all of the hard work the Miller Men put in on those piers. That, Mister Smith, was as close to a miracle as I ever expect to see."

It was not as good on the Juniata.

The ice dam below the Aqueduct piled ever higher and became hundreds of yards thick. Gigantic plates of ice slid up and sideward blocking the river's passage and forcing the flood across and inundating Duncan's Island. Upstream, the flood backed into the streets of Newport until the water touched Fourth Street. As long as the dam held, the water lay motionless, but if the ice dam went out in a rush, currents would roar, and loss of everything standing was feared.

The Juniata ice broke during the night, and the thunder of released water frightened those camped nearby. At dawn, the muddier water from the Juniata flooded far into the Susquehanna and stained the river as far as the eye could see. For many days, reports from up-river told of dramatic destruction from Hollidaysburg down to Petersburg, and all of the river crossings were said to be gone.

Matt Miller dispatched Lukey Bates on a saddle horse to inform big Matt of the extent of damage. He suggested that the elder Miller round up workers and begin marching them to Petersburg because emergency Commonwealth repair contracts were about to be floated as never before—and this time, because of their successful bridge repairs, the Miller companies would be at the front of the line.

It was a time of change. Engineer Holcomb had gone to Harrisburg with firsthand reports of the destruction and powerful recommendations for quick restoration of the canals. He and Mister Horace Thorpe had returned astride horses to allow quicker travel and closer and more thorough examination of the battered canals.

Canal contracts, in general, had been long issued, but in the emergency, there were many smaller contracts to be agreed upon and work to be started. True to his word, and because they stood ready, Thorpe worked closely with the Miller company. The dealing was fast and little argued over.

Matt Miller guaranteed to have the men and materials to take on all that he contracted for. Matt began to watch the bridge, anxiously waiting the arrival of workmen from Philadelphia. A letter had come explaining that the men were being gathered and would be en route within the week. Matt was to be careful to what he agreed, and he was to be sure that a profit was forthcoming. He was reminded that they did not work for glory or commendation. Money was what it was all about. There were also hearty congratulations on the bridge repairs so well done.

Then there was Erin McFee.

Matt could not believe that he had not noticed long before. He could not detect the interest in him that others saw, but Erin had become a woman lovely to behold.

Now he saw Erin often. The McFee's lived in the same open barracks room he occupied. The family had curtained off the farthest end of the room, but Matt heard their conversations and every rustle and clatter.

Mickey seemed to be continually clumping through, and Matt ritually complained that McFee should spend more time leading his crew of slackers and less slouching around his temporary quarters.

Far more often, Matt Miller was waiting for Erin McFee's passage in and out. He watched her dresses swish in movement. Her astonishing green eyes fell modestly away, but she often let her hair fall while indoors, and sometimes braided it into a single, thick coil that hung over a shoulder in the most enticing display Matt could imagine.

Occasionally, they shared a few words, but Matt Miller, dauntless leader of the mighty Miller Construction Companies, was at a loss on how to proceed. It was true that he worked from before dawn until well after dark, but there were moments when he might have . . . Matt was not sure exactly what he might or should or perhaps should not do.

He was drawn powerfully to Erin McFee—he guessed—but he had no direction in mind, except that, well, he liked looking at her, he liked talking with her, and he liked speculating on what suave and sophisticated moves he could produce that would make him attractive in her eyes. Discouraging!

Workmen arrived from Philadelphia, and Matt developed new crews and appointed foremen from the longtime Miller Men to lead and mould teams that could and would work in the Miller traditions.

Matt gathered his new foremen and made his speech. "You are all experienced in how we work and what we demand. As foremen, your pay will be increased accordingly, but I have two admonitions.

"The first is—do the job to my satisfaction or you will be relieved and someone else appointed. Your mission is to please the boss. For now, that is me.

"Second—make your crews into teams. If someone does not fit, remove him. If a man resists your orders, fire him. Take charge and remain in charge. Take no manure, and do not hand out a lot either. Lead by example. You, too, are a workman. Do not stand around and boss. Get in there and lead. You have seen how McFee and Donovan do it; follow their examples."

Finally, young Matt Miller made his biggest move of all. He doubted his father would cheer his decision, and he knew that Uncle Brascomb's soul would rot, but he went ahead.

He had talked it over with China who had been astonished at the idea. No one China knew of believed or acted in the manner Matt Miller intended, but Smith had seen the world from the bottom for more years than he preferred to remember. His experience told him that young Matt was onto something. That Matt's scheme would make them money, however, was, in China's mind, dubious, but . . .?

Matt was serious, and he intended to give his plan a try, so Smith stayed positive and swore he would stand with Matt when he explained his actions to his father.

With the flood still raging but with the rivers receding a few reluctant feet, Matt called a special Saturday night, after-work gathering. He chose to meet with all Miller Men in attendance, everyone jammed into Klubber Cole's hotel gymnasium and spread beyond into other men's sleeping areas.

Matt gave no explanation for his meeting, but it was plain that he wanted every long-employed worker present, and the foremen made certain that none were left behind.

It was an un-fragrant gathering that thickened the smoke-filled air with a sour stench of too long unwashed bodies. The men were used to the ripe atmosphere, but Matt believed he would be thankful when the weather turned enough for bathing in the rivers.

China Smith also noted the nose-wrinkling conditions and, as he often did, he whispered in Matt's ear. "This bunch stinks, Boss's Boy. You might consider making them bathe now and then as part of your conditions." With Matt's agreeing headshake, China added, "Do you notice that the Germans smell different than the Irish? Now why would that be, I wonder?"

Matt answered softly. "Different perfume, China," and enjoyed the older man's soft chuckle.

When he was ready, Matt stood, and the gathering instantly quieted. The immediate silence impressed, China Smith. Not all leaders gained such instant respect. Young Matt Miller had presence.

Matt's voice seemed conversational in tone and volume, but it reached the furthest listener. Heads cocked to listen, and eyes focused on the speaker.

Matt began, "Everyone here is a Miller Man. Your foremen have vouched for you, and most of you I know from times past and work performed.

"More than a few gathered here go way back. Some will remember when I was a young boy who had to whip Mickey McFee about once a week to keep him in line."

Matt's grin met his men's disbelieving laughter, and McFee balled his fists and shrugged his heavy shoulders in make-believe challenge. China thought that, too, well done. Matt had made himself one of them, and he had made them a memorable part of his history. The Boss's Boy had a gift. Maybe he should become a politician.

Matt went on. "I am proud of the work you men did on our bridge. Your work through the nights was beyond reasonable request, and there can be no doubt that we saved the bridge."

For a long instant Matt appeared lost in reverie. Then he shook his head as if disbelieving.

"When that barn came floating down I thought we had lost it all. When that huge structure just dissolved and slid underneath, I knew that someone up there was on our side." Men nodded in agreement and shook their heads in admitted astonishment that their work had survived.

Matt said, "We saved the bridge, and because of that success there will be rewarding contracts from the Commonwealth, and that means steady and profitable work for the Miller Companies."

Then Matt got to the heart of his meeting, and China felt goose bumps jump because this was something he had never experienced or heard of at sea or on land.

Matt said, "Our company profits will be strong this year, and I thank you for your labor that has made success almost common.

"For as long as I can remember, workers have earned seventy cents a day—no matter what the job. When we hire, that is what we pay, and if a man has worked for us for ten years, seventy cents a day is still considered fair pay.

"For all genuine Miller Men, I intend to change that system. I consider you special men because of your work ethic that makes you labor hard and at any task asked and because of your loyalty to the company you work for. Those are the reasons we employ each of you as steadily as we can.

"From tomorrow on, as long as this company can afford it, Miller Men will receive eighty cents a day, and as a bonus for the hard and successful work on the bridge, each Miller's Man who worked on that job will be paid an extra dollar."

Even China was shaken by the thunderous roar of approval. Men were on their feet applauding and slapping each other's shoulders.

Matt raised a hand for quiet, and despite the excitement, it came almost instantly.

"Do not misunderstand. When the company employs other workers, their wages will be the usual seventy cents a day. Only Miller Men will be paid the higher wage. Do not expect your uncle or your cousin to automatically be taken on as a Miller Man. Those positions will be rare and difficult to qualify for."

Matt closed his meeting. "I will add that it is my intent to have a company bath constructed. We will heat the water from beneath, and bathing will be free. Judging from the thickness of the air in here almost everyone will be glad to make regular, Saturday-night use of the facility." There was chagrined laughter.

"I thank you for your hard work in the past. I hope that we continue as a team for many long years." Matt grinned in shared entertainment, "You may use some of that extra money in paying overdue rent and spend the rest in our company store."

The
Boss

20

Matt studied the mighty Susquehanna with interest. How the water roared. The river was again within its banks, but the current seemed ever faster.

Before he left for Philadelphia, China had explained that during a flood, the river jammed and was held back at the Dauphin narrows only a dozen miles downstream. When the water was merely high, the current rushed through. Low water, of course, offered only a slack flow, and in some places a man could almost walk across.

Matt was slightly chagrined that he had needed China to explain something so obvious, but, he did not claim to know everything—yet.

A month had passed since the highest flooding had receded. Canals had reappeared and Miller crews were repairing and improving far up both rivers.

Mister Horace Thorpe had made numerous visits, and he paid promptly with Commonwealth bank drafts that Matt cashed in Harrisburg. The state was an excellent employer, and if the amount of money within the Millers' great safe had been suspected, Matt would have employed an armed guard.

Money came in, but money also went out—in sums that made Matt sweat.

On Saturday night, the workmen lined up for their pay. Following Lukey Bates' routine grumblings that a lot of paperwork could be avoided if the company paid every other week instead of each Saturday, Matt and Lukey sat at a table and paid off the workers. Miller Men were recorded in a ledger separate from other hired laborers. Bates announced the amount due, and Matt dealt the coins into the laborer's calloused palm.

Too many men immediately departed for a shacky saloon that had sprung up along the riverfront, and Matt, as ritually as Lukey's biweekly payment suggestions, exclaimed that the Millers should get into the beer and whiskey business.

Matt regularly claimed that if they sold liquor next door, they could simply issue coins to a worker, take payment for the beer or whiskey, hand the money back into the office, and re-issue it to the next man in line. Matt swore that all they would need would be a few dozen dollars—total.

China had gone to Philadelphia because big Matt had not come home. The Boss wrote regularly explaining that he was still feeling low, but his doctor was working hard for him.

Big Matt also sent money. Twice, armed guards accompanied money carriers who paused on their routes to dispense significant amounts at the Millers' western headquarters.

Big Matt was still dipping into the Philadelphia side of the business. The Boss's Boy was certain that his uncle Brascomb knew of the money transfers and resented them to no end. It was just as well that Brascomb Miller had no sense of the profits from the western contracts also piling up in the safe.

Big Matt saw that money and records sent east barely showed a profit. Soon, probably already, the east and the west companies would be separated in all respects except ownership. Big Matt Miller owned everything and would continue to do so.

China did not like the Captain's continued absence or big Matt's reports of feeling ill. Little Matt agreed, and China went to be at the Boss's side until he chose to return to Petersburg.

Petersburg—they had to stop using that familiar name. The town had agreed to adopt the name of Duncannon. Why? None of them knew, but the Irishmen liked the change because the new name sounded Irish or maybe Scot.

Matt always got the nationalities mixed in his mind. There were Scotsmen (most called them Scotchmen) and there were Irishmen. Unfortunately for clarity, there were also the Scotch-Irish who, Matt gathered, were Scots that had moved generations past to Ireland but retained different practices. Scots bragged about being highlanders, or were mildly insulted by being labeled lowlanders. Irish could be wounded by being termed Bog Irishmen, or . . . they also worshipped in different churches. Some were protestant Presbyterians and some were Roman Catholic. At any rate, Benvenue amounted to little, and Petersburg and Baskinsville were gone. They all now lived in Duncannon.

The current excitement was the impending arrival of the steamboat George Washington. Matt had already seen the boat tied alongside a dock in Harrisburg. Built for canal travel, the craft was almost flat bottomed and had its side-wheel paddles set into the hull so that they did not protrude and make the craft wider than the preferred ten feet. The boat drew only three feet of water when loaded, and Matt doubted it could carry significant cargo.

The foredeck was piled high with wood cut to fit through the boiler's small door. Wood was fed into the engine's firebox from the front, and Matt could see that leaving the door open while the boat was moving could create a draft that would stoke the fire and feed power to the engine. The massive and weighty steam engine filled the boat's middle, and passengers and cargo were carried aft of the boiler.

The George Washington was steered by a tiller attached to a large, catboat-like rudder that drew little water but extended well behind the craft.

Each paddle wheel could be slowed by a device called a friction clutch that could be eased in or out via long cords to the helmsman at the tiller. A skilled pilot could maneuver simply by slowing a paddle wheel. When wishing to stop, the clutches were allowed to slip, and the engine turned without transferring power to the wheels.

Matt could see the practicality of a steam engine in a large, perhaps ocean-going vessel, but within the confines of a canal, with extremely limited water depth? Until they were vastly improved, Matt doubted such a rig could return value.

Still, the vessel had appeal. It was claimed to be able to maintain more than eight miles an hour, and it could move upstream in almost any current. Most marveled—no horses to feed whether they worked or not, no long, shore-fastened tow rope to dodge and to wear through and part unexpectedly.

Truly marvelous machines, a few expected such engines were against God's will and nature's laws, but most, like Matt, believed that with more development, steam powered canal boats might, in some uses, challenge the towed barges.

Matt examined the George Washington's heavily built steam engine with envy. Eventually he planned to have such engines to turn the shafts and gears on a sawmill so powerful that it would fairly spit forth boards and planks to exacting dimensions.

The Boss's Boy also noted that the engine was not the best for its boat. On a canal boat of narrow beam, a steam engine should be built lighter and more compact, and the engine should sit very low. As it was, the steamboat was top heavy with a tall iron chimney hinged so that it could be lowered to pass beneath bridges—or just as probable in a canal, to avoid low hanging tree limbs. On land, excess size and weight mattered little, but afloat, extra poundage could degrade a craft's balance. The George Washington could never manage waves or seas of any size. The boat would always be a canal or small lake vehicle.

Matt had accompanied China to Harrisburg to view the marvelous invention. The old sailor had no good words for the brightly painted canal boat.

China said, "That bucket is so poorly built that not much more than the paint is holding it together. I'll be surprised if it makes it over the mountain in one piece. If that wreck gets to Pittsburgh it will be a miracle. The boat will never go further than the forks of the Ohio, that is for sure."

Matt saw most of what China did, but the modern steam plant colored his vision, and he wondered if they could buy a similar boiler and cobble together their own steam engine. The Boss's Boy resolved to look into that possibility.

China had gone on to Philadelphia, but Matt had stayed to speak with the boat's captain about his steamboat and steam engines in particular.

The boat's skipper was also the boat's owner. A flamboyant character, topped by the tallest double-beaver hat Matt had ever seen, the boatman lavished praise on his craft and his engine.

The longer the owner exclaimed, the more certain Matt became that the owner/captain actually knew little about either his boat or his engine. The man was more salesman than seaman. He owned the craft and had powerful hopes that he could convince individuals along his way to invest in his newly formed steamboat company—that was sure to return handsome monetary rewards. Matt returned to Perry County with visions of powerful engines but without steamboat company investments.

The McFees had returned to their rooms, and Matt saw Erin puttering with some flowers outside their door. He was tempted to stroll that way, but he had no handy explanation as to why he was out walking around. Matt scratched the idea and reentered the office.

Lukey Bates looked up from his books.

"Matt, it is Friday and tomorrow we have to pay half a hundred workers. I can't believe how the dollars run out our door. It seems that every day is payday around here."

His mind still on Erin McFee, Matt answered vaguely. "Well, money comes in more than it goes out, Lukey."

Bates sniffed. "It had better, we have the biggest payroll since I came on board. If business slackens we will have to lay off workers, Matt."

Matt remained undisturbed. "It has always been that way, Lukey, and it always will be. Workers know that, and perhaps you have noticed that more than a few of our contracts have come by way of Miller Men who told us about someone looking for labor."

Matt stirred restlessly. "I ought to hop a boat up toward Newport and look at that new iron furnace that is starting up a few miles this side of town. We should be getting into iron making, Lukey. Wood is going out, and iron is coming in. Machinery is all iron, and there is money to be made there."

Instead of going upriver, Matt stepped into their boxing yard and wrapped his fists to punch the heavy bag for a turn or two. Mickey McFee had made use of the equipment while his family was living in the headquarters, and Matt was impressed by the solid thumping McFee gave the leather-wrapped bag.

It wouldn't do to let the Irish Hurricane get ahead of him in the fist fighting game. The time might just come when . . .

Horses pulled up out front, and Matt heard Lukey's surprised and pleased voice. "Well, well, welcome home all of you." Fists still wrapped, Matt hurried inside.

Looking somehow uncomfortable, China and Wilhelm Brado stood just within the office door. Just outside, a man Matt quickly recognized as Brascomb's clerk Roger Scribner waited for room to get inside.

Matt supposed his father was just beyond, probably paying for the horse hire and looking over the rapidly enlarging community.

Before Matt could speak, China held up a restraining hand and motioned Matt into his usual chair.

Smith's voice was hoarse with emotion, and Matt felt his senses sharpen. Something bad was coming, and he tried to get ready for it.

China said, "There's no easy way to get into this, Matt, so I'll speak it right out." Still the old fighter had to clear his throat before continuing.

"Your Pa is dead, Matt. He passed away four days ago. It was sudden and unexpected. One moment he and I were talking. The next he was down and gone right there in Brascomb's living room." Young Matt's mind and body froze.

"There was no warning, and nothing could be done." China cleared his throat twice before continuing. "I'll save the details until you let this settle in your mind, Matt, but it is what it is, and I'll tell you straight out that we've got to go on without delay just the way the Captain would want it."

Smith shook his head in obvious misery and said, "I'm going down to the hotel and get myself cleaned a little. Willy can do the same here. I'll take Scribner with me. He can clean up there until you decide where he is to stay."

As if from a great distance, Matt heard Lukey Bates repeating, "Oh my, oh my," but he seemed anchored to his seat, and his hands had turned numb as if fallen asleep.

China and Scribner departed but Wilhelm Brado stood at his almost attention in front of Matt's desk—waiting, Matt assumed, for questions that needed to be answered.

Matt finally got his voice going. "Why did China leave so fast, Willy? I never even got a word out."

Brado said, "We decided I would explain what I could to you, Mister Miller because Mister Smith has been fired."

"What? My father fired China?"

"No, no, Mister Miller. Mister Brascomb Miller fired Mister Smith. He told him that he never was on the payroll and that his presence was no longer desired and that he was not to make use of Miller facilities and that when Mister Brascomb Miller arrived out here he did not want to find Mister Smith on Miller property."

Matt Miller grew even more numb. There were almost too many Millers in Brado's explanation, but the content came through. Uncle Brascomb had fired China? Absurd! Brascomb Miller could not fire anybody—but, of course, he could!

The realization struck Matt Miller like ice water. With his father gone, control of all Miller properties passed to Brascomb and would remain there until Matt Miller reached age twenty-one, still months away.

It was too much. Matt waved Wilhelm Brado away and hauled himself from his chair. Lukey Bates asked, "Where are you going, Matt?"

Uncertain of any destination, Matt twisted at a loose end on his fist wrappings.

"I'll be out back for a while, Lukey, I've got some thinking to do." Matt's voice sounded tinny and artificial to his ears, and he fumbled a little with the door latch.

Alone, Matt sat on a log China used when coaching Matt's boxing. The familiar surroundings helped, but an ache within his heart was developing, and young Matt Miller had no idea how to ease it.

He wished he could cry. The relief would be welcome, but no tears came. He tried to imagine his father dead and laid out for burial, but that picture remained blurry, and Matt put it aside for later.

Times past came more easily to his mind, and he allowed his memory to roam. How good he had had it with his father behind anything he tried, including forcing him to learn in school when all he wished to do was work with the Irish laborers.

The memories were calming, and after a while Matt rose and began the familiar routines of punching the heavy bag. The splat of his fist against the leather passed pleasurably up his arms and into his shoulders. He could feel his mind settling and organizing thoughts yet unannounced.

Then China was there. He took his usual position on the opposite side of the big bag and held it solid while Matt struck, bobbed and weaved, jabbed, and hammered hard with his right hand.

Matt judged he had consumed a lot more time than he had realized because China was shaved and in different clothing.

China said, "Keep punching, Matt. I'll talk while you work. Let your mind roam over what I am saying. We can talk it all out later on."

Matt's blows shook the bag, and China admonished, "Just lightly, Boss's Boy. Just tap at it, and let your body do its work." Then he began to tell how it had been.

21

China Smith worked at explaining his captain's death, and Matt could sense the loss behind his words.

China said, "As soon as I got to the city and saw big Matt, I knew something serious was wrong. The Captain slept more than he roused. He had lost too much weight, and he moved as if he had reached one hundred years.

"His doctors dosed him with some of the worst smelling stuff I have ever encountered. I can't begin to guess what it must have tasted like, but none of it helped even a little."

The old sailor paused to shake his head.

"These past days have been among the worst of my life. Your Pa was clearly going downhill, but Brascomb kept nagging at him wanting this cleared up and that understood until I longed to flatten him."

Again China paused, and this time he moved the bag so that Matt had to stop punching. He motioned them over to the sitting log, and Matt went along, anxious to hear but hating every somber and tension-filled word.

China spoke mostly to his feet thrust stiffly before him, as if avoiding Matt's eyes and adding his suffering to the Boss's Boy's obvious distress, but his words came clear.

"Your Uncle Brascomb is not a likable man, Matt. Your Pa described him as penurious, a word I hadn't known, and he had it right. Brascomb Miller places money above everything else in life, and his hunger for ever more money makes him resentful and envious and unpleasant to be around."

Matt already knew that, and he waited for his friend to go on.

"Your Pa had let Brascomb carry on until there was nothing more to be said. The day he died, big Matt announced that he was coming home, meaning here to Duncannon, and that Brascomb was to handle the eastern end of the businesses and report his progress and profits to him every few months.

"Your Pa made it clear that reporting would be a one way path. What went on out here would be his business, and his brother would have no part in it."

China sighed deeply. "Two hours later, big Matt was dead. He simply fell over, Matt. The doctor said his heart just gave out, and that sounds right. I doubt the Captain even felt the floor. That is the only good thing in all of this—in passing, your Pa did not suffer an instant.

"Then Brascomb took over, and I mean he didn't waste two minutes. His clerk contacted a funeral parlor, and your uncle ordered Brado and me into his office. He didn't even bother to close the door or let us sit down. He told Brado that he would be let go when he settled conditions out here because Brado could not perform a man's work.

"Then he reminded me that I had never signed on and announced that he owed me nothing, and that I was no longer welcome on or around Miller properties.

"If your uncle grieved for your Pa's passing, I missed it. I tried to talk about informing you before big Matt was put underground, but Brascomb had taken charge. He informed me that I had no say in the matter, and that he had heard my unasked for opinions for far too many years.

"He called a clerk and directed him to escort me, Mister Smith, from the premises. I grabbed my sea bag and left. Your Pa was buried the next morning with little ceremony, and I was able only to sprinkle a bit of earth on his casket."

China stopped and raised angry eyes to Matt's.

"We should go inside now, Matt, and let the others hear what comes next. From now on they will be involved."

Within the office, Lukey Bates, Wilhelm Brado, and Roger Scribner were waiting. Brado had also cleaned up, and Scribner looked as pressed and polished as if he had just risen from his Philadelphia desk. The clerk had brought a large bundle of notebooks and ledgers, and he appeared ready to immediately resume work.

Matt had sweat more than a little. He felt dirty and inexplicably exhausted. His mind again wandered, but he forced himself awake. When he sought his chair, Matt found his hand fumbly, and he thought he needed a whiff from China's ammonia bottle.

When all were seated, China took the floor.

"After I was ordered away, I had no more than walked out Brascomb's door when both Brado and Scribner appeared. Brado was packed and ready to come back here."

China was admiring. "Wilhelm can move fast when he's a'mind to."

"Scribner? Well, the Captain had planned on bringing him, and Scribner had planned on coming. Still, Brasomb Miller now ran everything, and what could I offer?" China's smile was grim.

"Right away, Scribner said, 'I'm going along, Mister Smith. The Boss's Boy won't stand still for Mister Brascomb Miller pushing him around, and I would greatly prefer working for him than for his uncle.'"

China's features relaxed a little. "Those were his exact words, but Brascomb has all of the law on his side—at least until you are twenty-one years of age, and he may not allow Scribner to hire on out here.

"I figured we had to be fast getting back because Brascomb will be close behind. Whatever plans he has for you and these businesses won't be pleasing, and if we are to do anything to back him off, we have to be ready and waiting."

China hesitated before adding, "And to tell you the absolute and complete truth, Matt, I haven't any idea of what can be done—assuming, of course, that you want to stand against your uncle."

Oh, Matt Miller would stand all right. He had plans, not firmed up schemes, but he had ideas that he had nurtured since his many months under Uncle Brascomb's thumb.

Growing boys planned revenges with utmost passion and luxuriated in their unfailing successes—if ever the opportunities appeared. Now the time had come, and the Boss's Boy would more than stand up. Using China Smith's naval terms, young Matt intended to sweep the decks clean.

First, Matt needed time to mourn his father's passing. He needed hours to gather his thoughts and organize his ideas into workable plans. He stood and explained the first part.

"You can bet your next pay that I am not going to roll over for my uncle. He is about to discover that this is not Philadelphia, and his rotten ways won't work with you or with me.

"We number five, and I will gather three or four more good men. Brascomb will not strong-arm us, that is for sure, but he may try. What I have to do is make sure that he leaves with no more than he should, and that he will not be back for more—ever.

"Right now, I would like to hear anything Scribner knows that might help, and I expect that some of it is within the ledgers he has brought along.

"Then we will separate until this evening. The men will be coming in from work, and I will want a few of them to sit in. Let's gather here at the office at thirty past the hour of seven. By then, I will have more to say."

Matt turned to his uncle's longtime clerk.

"The first point is that you now work out here for me, Scribner. Lukey will adjust your pay to what it should be and that will be a lot more than my tight-fisted uncle allowed. My father and I talked often about you joining us, and I am especially pleased to see you right now when difficult decisions have to be made."

Matt took a moment to choose his words.

"Do not feel that you have ingloriously abandoned Brascomb or are being somehow disloyal to him, Scribner. You suffered under him longer than most could have, and my uncle does not deserve personal loyalty, as he gives none himself.

"Welcome aboard. You are now a Miller Man, and out here, that stands for something."

Brascomb Miller left the Clark's Ferry Bridge angry almost to white heat. Their hurried travel from Philadelphia had been brutal with unrelenting crashing and banging on the almost impossible pike.

Nothing had gone right. A wheel had collapsed along the way, and almost a half-day had been lost replacing it. Moving by the canal would have been a hundred times more pleasant and far more dignified, but haste was necessary.

The disappearance of his clerk at the same time as Smith and the German boy's departure was highly suspect. Plots were being raised against him, Brascomb was sure.

Therefore, his driver was a hard man chosen for his reputation as an efficient protector of important people on their travels about the great city. Surely there could be no serious obstructing, the law was all on his side, but, as he saw it, Perry County was beyond the reach of civilized living, and his slugger would be there to prevent any lawless foolishness from his possibly unhinged nephew—or Smith, who might have rushed west to spread word of the Miller Company's changed leadership.

On crossing the last river bridge, his carriage driver had asked directions to Petersburg, and they were told to go north for three miles. Of course, Petersburg, or whatever its new name was, lay to the south, and the detour had been exasperating.

At the town edge a man had loitered. Again seeking directions, this time to the Miller Company itself, they had been directed through the town and across a stream to a large brick building on the right. There was no such building, and another hour was wasted turning back and finding the Miller headquarters.

Brascomb Miller was fit to be tied. He was physically exhausted and filthy dirty from long travel. To complete what he considered an utter

292

humiliation, a washerwoman stepped from a shack's side door and without looking hurled a bucket of filthy water into the street—and directly onto both Brascomb and his driver. The wretched peasant apologized to their departing backs, but Miller suspected he heard laughter within her voice. Could some of this infuriating humiliation been planned? By his nephew—who had always been a most irritating and irresponsible brat?

Unlikely, Brascomb decided. Young Matt Miller was still a boy in the law's eyes, and he could hardly have summoned townsmen to engage in petty harassments.

Matt and his accomplices watched from the safety of the hotel's upper porch. When Brascomb's dripping carriage and its soaked occupants had passed from view, Matt tossed coins to the amused laundry lady who had performed perfectly, and they gathered themselves for the confrontation Brascomb Miller thought he had planned.

China said, "I've got to admit that slosh bucket added a special touch, Matt. Brascomb looked about to explode. When he finds the office locked he will be ready to break down the door. Maybe we have thrown him off stride, but we'd better not linger too long."

Brascomb Miller was more than enraged. How could an office building be locked tight during the middle of a workday? It was no wonder that the western businesses had never returned their potential. He had suspected his brother of withholding profits, but perhaps casual working hours was equally responsible.

A group of men was working their way uphill, and after a moment Brascomb saw Smith, Brado, and young Matt among them. When he identified his clerk, Scribner, Brascomb recognized betrayal that would not go unpunished.

In fact, Brascomb resolved to hold Matt Miller responsible for everything that had gone wrong on this side of the river. His nephew would discover that Brascomb Miller was not a person to be trifled with. To his added chagrin, the group paused at the higher road to speak among themselves and to point out something across the river.

Surely, they had seen him waiting. The humiliation was deliberate, but young Matt Miller was playing with fire, and Brascomb resolved that this time he would get burned.

When he reached the door, Matt had his key in his hand. He said, "Good afternoon, Uncle. How did you get so wet?"

Brascomb thought the brat's voice was irritatingly knowing. He gestured at the door lock and said coldly. "Open up." Matt obliged and stood aside for his uncle's entrance.

Brascomb found his brother's office to be much as he expected. Two clerk desks and a number of filing cabinets were to a side, and a large soft wood desk (apparently home-carpentered) was centered with a chair behind it. Beyond the large desk a solid, new-looking wall featured a pair of doors leading to something behind the office building. Pathetic.

The large desk would have been his brother's, so Brascomb headed for it. A pair of side chairs was against a wall, but no one else attempted to sit down. The group stood and stared at Brascomb, but if they believed they appeared intimidating, they were mistaken.

The hired guard saw it differently. Two of the group had focused on him, and they were both fighters. Smith he had seen before, but he was old, and the Philadelphia tough could not recall what he had heard about the man. The second fighter was an Irishman. He was young, and although his face had suffered from hard-driven fists, he was rocking on his toes and was clearly willing to be turned loose.

There was a third man. A large and tough-as-a-nut Irishman with hands the size of mauls. He did not have the battered features of a bare-fist fighter, but he was the kind of man who drove other tough men. That one alone would be very difficult to handle.

The odds were not in Brascomb Miller's favor, and the brawler hoped that Mister Miller understood that, if fisticuffs began, their side had no chance at all.

Brascomb was finally pleased with his position. He sat, they stood, and he held all of the cards. His mind ignored the unpleasant looking workers and turned its attention to his nephew and the clerks.

His voice cold, Brascomb explained. "Your father is gone, Matt. Until you are twenty-one and your majority is recognized by lawful authority, I am your guardian. I control all of your father's resources—including everything out here in this wilderness."

There seemed to be no response other than interest, and that pleased Brascomb. He doubted he could endure juvenile outbursts. When they returned to Philadelphia, he would retrain young Matt's attitudes into those more befitting a young gentleman of position.

More importantly, he would reform the businesses to ensure his own profitability no matter what Matt chose to do when he inherited.

"You, Matt, can plan on moving to Philadelphia, unless you choose to proceed on your own, of course." Brascomb's smile was coldly inviting. It would please him greatly if young Matt just disappeared for the next half a year—or longer.

"Everything out here will be terminated as quickly as it can be managed. You, Mister Bates will be allowed to handle those closures. Your earlier performance in my office was adequate, and I will place you in Mister Scribner's position of responsibility—seeing he has so disgracefully abandoned my service." Brascomb Miller was almost luxuriating in his unchallengeable position of absolute control.

He gestured widely toward the other men gathered in the office. "The rest of you are not needed here, and you will promptly remove yourselves. Later today, Mister Bates will provide any payment due you." Brascomb focused his eyes on the hapless workers and announced, "That is all."

Matt wished to laugh. So he did. The laughter was not tension release or some sort of face saving. His laughter was full-throated and deep chested. Matt Miller was clearly amused. There was softer chuckling among the other men, including the still-hired clerk Lukey Bates.

Brascomb Miller was thunderstruck. He was being mocked, mocked by these uneducated of-no-importance laborers and his apparently deranged nephew. His head turned red, then sickly livid. His voice choked in his throat. His eyes sought his bodyguard, but young Matt's voice brought him back and the younger man's words further staggered his mind.

Matt spoke as if explaining to a recalcitrant child. His words were deliberately patronizing, and like razors they slashed Brascomb Miller's pride and self-importance.

"Uncle Brascomb, you have been a self-serving jackass for as long as I can remember. For just as long, you have been aching to control Miller businesses. Now you think you have the chance.

"Well, Uncle, yours is not even the chance of fat in a fire. I have other plans, and I will take them up with you in a moment.

"First, I must thank you for burying my father with such loving and tender care and for offering me, his son and your nephew, such heartfelt condolences on his passing. Your sensitivity and compassion are gratefully accepted."

The sarcasm was blatant, and Brascomb sought words, but Matt did not pause.

"I hope that you enjoy sitting in my father's chair because your honor will be short. That chair, and all that goes with it, is now mine."

Matt turned to Brascomb's bodyguard, and again his words bit like knives.

"The gentleman standing slightly behind you is China Smith, one of the world's great fist fighters. This is Mickey McFee, the Irish Hurricane. I sometimes fight as The Boss's Boy.

"I offer you the opportunity to wait for your employer at your carriage. If you choose to remain, we will immediately beat you so thoroughly you will be unable to perform any duties for many days." Matt waited.

The wait was short. The hired muscle was not stupid. He nodded acceptance of an impossible situation and stepped outside.

Brascomb Miller exploded. He surged to his feet spitting his words. "You young fool. I will have the law on you so heavily that you will beg to be freed from confinement. You . . ."

Effortlessly, the huge man with immense fists pressed Miller back into his chair.

Matt said, "This gentleman is Alex Donovan, Uncle Brascomb. If you do not control your outbursts, he will pummel you until you decide to listen and absorb what you should already understand."

Matt chose to stride a little while arranging his words properly. Everyone, including Brascomb Miller waited.

"Uncle Brascomb, this is not Philadelphia. In this county, we are strong. Out here, your name and position are unknown, and no one will care what you think about anything. You speak loosely of confining me?" Matt turned to Wilhelm Brado and nodded. Brado stepped outside, and they heard his voice.

A form filled the doorway. The man entered and, dressed in a worn business suit, he appeared larger than anyone already present. The stranger was of middle years. His shoulders were immensely developed, and his arms were almost waist-thick. Eyes as hard as steel focused on Brascomb Miller as if hungry to begin punishing, and large crooked teeth appeared behind drawn lips.

Matt pointed to a glittering silver star on the man's chest. "This is Sheriff Timothy Cameron. He represents the law out here."

Matt's lips smiled, although his eyes did not.

"Sheriff Cameron has been informed that you might attempt a completely illegal takeover of my father's business, and if such an attempt were to develop, he is prepared to place you within his jail until the matter is thoroughly settled, including lengthy appeals, within the court system.

"Believe me, Uncle. You will not like our jail. As you have too often noted, we are primitive west of the Susquehanna, and we are not willing to sacrifice much of anything for individuals accused of wrongdoing."

Brascomb Miller's voice had grown defensive, but he did not surrender. "You cannot get away with this travesty, you whippersnapper. You will pay a hundred times for your threats and insults. You . . ."

The large and powerful man that had sat him down said, "Shall I hand him over to the sheriff, Mister Miller?"

Matt appeared to ponder, and Brascomb belatedly realized that he really could be jailed in a small town hell hole and that other authorities might be long in being notified and much longer before securing his release.

Who would come to his aid? He knew no one in Harrisburg, and despite rapid thinking, no one in Philadelphia came immediately to mind. He could rot in whatever Petersburg called a jail for months. By the time he was released, Matt Miller might have reached his majority, and where then would Brascomb Miller stand? Nowhere was the answer. He would be jobless with bills overdue, and—Brascomb Miller's certainties fled as if they had never existed. His soul longed for the security of his ledgers and his Philadelphia office.

What could he do? Nothing, it appeared. Somehow, young Matt had effortlessly gained the upper hand, and he doubted the youth's charity would run strongly in his uncle's favor.

Matt pulled a chair close to the desk and seated himself facing his uncle.

Settled, he said, "We will hold the sheriff off for a short spell, Mister Donovan. I have a proposition to offer my uncle. If he is wise, he will take it and shortly be on his way home. If he does not like what I offer, then we will call in Sheriff Cameron."

Donovan nodded to Sheriff Cameron who stepped outside, closing the door behind him.

The Irish prizefighter called The Hurricane placed a pair of heavy, wrought iron shackles on the desktop. He said, "I brought these leg irons up for the sheriff in case we needed them."

Brascomb Miller stared at the shackles in poorly concealed horror. He had seen criminal wretches confined in such devices, but for himself? It was beyond comprehension and far exceeded a person of dignity's toleration.

Matt ignored the leg irons and spoke as clearly as he could. This was the heart of their effort, and he wished to do it right.

"Uncle Brascomb, I have no interest in anything you are doing east of the Susquehanna. I repeat—no interest at all.

"When I gain control of the businesses, I will liquidate all that you have developed back there, much as you intended to do out here.

"As you know, that will occur in the fall on my next birthday. When those businesses are closed, you will have nothing with which to earn a living. You are a clever and diligent man, and I am sure that you can reestablish yourself within a year or two—or three. I doubt, however, that you will ever again prosper as you have until this moment.

"I do not wish you harm, and beyond disappointment in your attitudes and efforts to wound me, I can wish you well. Therefore, I have prepared an offer that will require immediate acceptance or rejection.

"Accept, and you go your way. Reject, and you will reside with us for as long as we can manage. I expect that I will be near my birthday by the time you will again encounter fresh air and sunlight. In the meantime, I will assume control of all business ventures and begin dissolving yours immediately."

Matt reached below his knees and recovered two of the ledgers Scribner had brought from Philadelphia. He placed them on the desk, and Brascomb's gasp was obvious to all present. Then, Matt seemed to ignore them and their contents.

Closely in front of his uncle, Matt placed three carefully drawn documents. He explained as his uncle read.

"Mister Lukey Bates and Mister Roger Scribner have worked diligently preparing these agreements so that escaping from any of their requirements would prove difficult. As you will see, however, each is fair, and the result will allow you to continue much as you have been—although your personal coffers will be seriously depleted."

The Boss's Boy waited as his uncle's eyes roamed the pages. Satisfied that Brascomb had the gist of his proposal he clarified.

"This paper releases you of responsibility for me and, until I am twenty-one years of age, assigns guardianship of my person and all that I possess or may possess to Mister "China" Smith.

"The second document grants you immediate and irrefutable ownership of all Miller businesses and possessions in and around Philadelphia. It will be signed by me.

"In the final agreement, you pay me fifteen thousand dollars in gold for your purchase of those businesses and properties—and," Matt made his pause significant, "in return I will deliver to you the ledgers now on this table."

Brascomb's mind had weighed all of the possibilities before Matt stopped speaking. He could manage it all, but the defeat was stultifying and the immense payout approached pauperizing. He would not simply succumb.

His voice distant and strange to his ears, Brascomb said, "How could anyone manage a sum of fifteen thousand dollars? No one in our circles possesses that kind of wealth. Men retire on less than fifteen thousand dollars—and in gold? To raise that sum would beggar the businesses and me. I would have nothing."

Matt was unbending. He tapped the ledgers on the desk suggestively.

"Uncle Brascomb. Let me remind you of what these records contain. This is your secret set of books. They show clearly, in your handwriting, the amounts you have withheld from the Miller companies over the past twenty years. You secreted the ledgers in your safe, but you also underpaid, overworked, and demeaned your best clerk, so that he was willing to bring them with him when he left your service."

Matt seemed to weigh the amount of money involved. "It is no secret that you spend little and hoard what you make. My father often joked that you, the bookkeeper, could probably buy him out.

"Of course, the Captain did not know of the serious amounts you skimmed from company profits. If he had, you would have been disowned and shown the door."

Matt again tapped the damning ledgers.

"You have been a thief, Uncle Brascomb, and this evidence, shown to proper authorities, can put you in a state penitentiary for many miserable years.

"You have my proposition. If you accept, you can put all of this behind.

"You will meet with me in Harrisburg one month from now with payment in full, all fifteen thousand dollars in gold, or I will immediately thereafter deliver these ledgers to the proper magistrate in your city."

Matt paused, and then quietly added, "Uncle Brascomb. You must sign my person and property over to China right now. Those present will witness your signature.

"I will sign the eastern businesses and properties over to you, as witnessed by the same individuals, but that paper will remain in my possession until I receive full payment.

"Decide now, Uncle, or immediately go to jail."

Matt added a clincher. "If you do not comply, my next stop—while you languish in our jail—will be to Philadelphia with these ledgers in hand to report that the culprit is even now imprisoned in Dunncanon awaiting higher authority's actions."

Matt accepted an inkwell and pen from Lukey Bates and placed them on the desk within Brascomb's reach.

His voice a snarl, Brascomb Miller took up the pen and dipped it in preparation for signing.

"You are still a minor, young Matt. Your signature means little on anything."

Matt remained cold. "That is all you will get, Uncle, but you have one solace. My word, unlike yours, is my bond. Deliver the money, and you will have the businesses and the ledgers."

Brascomb signed, and three men witnessed. Wilhelm Brado held the door, and the uncle entered his carriage and was gone.

China watched the carriage out of sight. "He might change his mind, Matt. Fifteen thousand dollars is a pile of money. And he is right. He can claim he was coerced, and your signature would not hold if it was challenged."

"Correct, China, but if he even flickers, I will hold the ledgers over his head. Thanks to Scribner, we have him. He will scheme, and he will squirm, but there is no escape. If he signs, he has something. If he does not, he really will go to prison."

The participants grouped within the office to exchange congratulations.

Matt said, "Building a wall in front of the safe was nice, Lukey. If that big iron thing had been there for my uncle to wonder about, he might have put up a lot more resistance. The less he saw to like or be curious about, the better off we were."

Bates shook his head in wonder. "Your uncle came prepared to destroy everything out here and fire us all, Matt. Then, he folded up and melted away as if all of his bones had been pulled from his body. He didn't even argue."

"Brascomb Miller is cunning and clever, but he is no fighter, Lukey. His mind is quick, and he realized he was helpless and in a very bad position. My uncle would never be one to fight for principle. There was no profit in continuing, so he gave up. But, he will be planning and scheming. Do not doubt that for an instant.

"Until I get the money, we cannot be certain, and when I go to Harrisburg to collect, I intend to be surrounded by a dozen or more Miller Men. I would not put it above Uncle Brascomb to appear with officers of the law planning to jail me until I gave up—or even have highwaymen waylay me somewhere on the road or even in the city streets."

Matt smiled grimly, "Put these ledgers in the safe, Lukey. They are as valuable as gold."

Matt shook Cameron's massive paw and enjoyed the man's huge Scottish grin. "You make a magnificent sheriff, Tim. Our enemy never thought to question that you might not be the real thing."

Matt fingered the shiny star. "Where did you get this badge, anyway?"

Clearly proud of his wordless performance, Cameron said, "I made it down at the shop. We cut the star out of iron and silver-coated it at the furnace. I soldered a pin on the back and hung it on my coat."

Cameron admired the result before adding, "I like being sheriff. I think I will run for the office."

All present agreed to vote for him, and Cameron left to resume his blacksmithing work.

Matt returned the leg irons to Mickey McFee. "Where on earth did those come from, Mickey? I could hardly believe it when you dropped them on the desk, and they about took my uncle's breath away."

"Klubber has had them for years. They are so rusted they won't open, but Tim Cameron thought they might be a good idea, and he was right. I figure they punched another hole in your uncle's scheming."

There was more shared laughter before the meeting ended. Matt, China, and McFee went out the back door into the boxing yard. Mickey hammered a series of hard right hands into the heavy bag.

Matt grumbled, "Don't think you have the day off or something, McFee," but his mind was already moving on.

He needed time to digest his father's death and the fact that everything now rested on his shoulders. He believed he could handle it, especially

with the help he had at hand, and the Irish Hurricane
was one of them.

22

China had brought Matt a gift from the city. The old sailor presented it almost shyly. Young Matt Miller was now the boss, and that made things a touch different.

The gift was a pair of leather gloves. China held them out, but Mickey McFee, who had come by on business, grabbed them. China growled, but Mickey ignored the threat. McFee was obviously not overly intimidated by China's minor irritation or by Matt's new authority.

McFee tried the gloves for size, but his fist was too large. Mickey said, "I have heard about these, China. These are just what I need."

His words died in his throat, and he fumbled to restate. "What I meant was, these would be perfect if I was going to be a fighter again."

Matt extended a palm, and McFee handed over the gloves.

The gloves had no fingertips, but they fit snuggly, and they could be laced tightly high on the wrists. Matt could feel how they would tighten and protect his knuckles in a fistfight. There was a row of very rough stitching using hide thong across the knuckles. Another crossed the back of each glove, and a roughly whip-stitched line was included on the heel of the palm. The gloves were not pretty to look at, but it was no wonder that Mickey McFee had snatched at them. Matt had heard about gloves like this, but he had never seen a pair as finely made.

China said, "You'll recall that Bootsy Van Horn wore tight gloves instead of hand wraps. I don't believe much in gloves for formal fighting. Wraps are better, but where a man can't walk around with his hands wrapped, he can usually pull on a pair of gloves without much comment.

"I hope you have given up on the bare fist fighting, Matt, but the time might come when you will want to paste someone squarely in the chops. Then you slip on these gloves, which will offer some knuckle protection and cause a lot of damage.

"If a fist is twisted just as it strikes, the hide stitching across the knuckles will rip skin like a flail. The hide across the back is handy when you are separating or throwing a backhand. The palm stitching is for scrubbing into a man's face when you clinch."

McFee said, "I want a pair, China, where do I get them?"

China glowered at him. "You are through fighting, McFee. You gave me, and Matt, your word."

Mickey glared back. "And I keep my word, but I might run into someone just like Matt might. Then I could need a helper like these gloves."

China had to admit that could happen. "I'll measure your fist and wrist, and get a pair made for you. I know the man who makes them, but I doubt you would ever encounter him."

China warned, "I'm not buying them for you, McFee. Have your money ready, and they aren't cheap."

The gloves provided a respite from the problems of the day, but Matt had to get back to the worries. He was now the decider. The livelihood of many lay on his shoulders, and he felt burdened by the responsibility.

He had to find the work that employed his Miller Men, and times were changing. Brascomb Miller might consider Perry County a frontier, but civilization had arrived. Matt's association with Horace Thorpe, based on their successful bridge repair, would reap benefits, but with the canals completed, Commonwealth work was drying up in the area, and large contracts were fewer.

Miller Men expected to work, and young Matt Miller had to be up to the task of providing those jobs. Right now, there was work at hand, but Matt knew he had to plan far ahead or he would come up short.

Because their work had been steady, Miller Men were bringing their families from the cities. A few were building homes. Alex Donovan was one of them, and Matt had examined his foreman's house plans. His father had promised to sell Alex a five-acre plot separated from the section on which the hotels stood. When Donovan was ready, Matt would, of course, honor that promise.

There was the matter of not enough water to properly spin his sawmill, and his creek dam was far behind schedule. They had done nothing about iron furnaces, and he had never gotten around to having tree stump pullers built.

Matt was positive that he could permanently employ a number of stump pulling crews. Matt judged that the county would never run out of tree stumps, and as the communities grew and the population burgeoned, farmers and townsfolk alike would want the pestiferous stumps gone from their fields and streets. Matt made a mental note to go up the Little Buffalo Creek and speak to Mister Shatto who had the only iron stump puller he had seen.

China had gone down to the restaurant, probably to court Mrs. Black, who, Matt judged, was about to announce her betrothal to Mister China Smith.

He and McFee had punched the bags a little because they liked doing it. Mickey was still loitering as if he had something on his mind. Matt walked them through the office where Lukey and Scribner worked on books with Willy Brado leaning close to learn and out the front door to examine the river and the town laid out before them.

Out front, Matt sat on a ladder-back rocker that China had positioned for river watching. McFee still stood around, so this might be the right time to approach him about courting his sister.

Before he could begin, Mickey said, "Do you know Alex Donovan's daughter, Matt?"

Surprised by the subject, Matt said, "I've seen her off and on. Her name is Bridgett, isn't it?"

Mickey's nod was deep, and his sigh was long. "Matt, I'm planning on asking for her hand in marriage, and, well, I've run aground right there."

Matt thought—Perfect! I'll have my say on his problem; then he will have to consider my request."

Matt urged McFee ahead. "You would make a good husband and father, Mickey. Why are you hesitating?"

"Because of Alex, Matt. I can't guess how he will react." Mickey laughed ruefully. "I don't want him to throw me in the canal again."

Matt joined the laughter. "He would find it harder these days, Mick." Then he became serious.

"Look at it another way, Mickey. You are a responsible man that he knows and has known since you were small. That has to mean something to a father who will be worrying about some Fancy Dan soap salesman coming to town and spiriting his daughter away."

McFee was nodding, so Matt went on. "You have steady work with pay as good as his own, and he will recognize that if he can raise a family on what he makes, so can you. You go to the same church, and that is important."

Matt winced mentally at his own comment. Unlike the McFees and the Donovans, he rarely attended church services—and when he did, he varied his denominations, so that his men would not suspect he was partial to one group over another.

Mickey's thoughts were moving on. "I've got a mother and sister to support, Matt. Alex won't like that part much."

"Everybody brings along some baggage, Mickey. Seeing Alex hasn't gotten tired of that punched-up Irish mug of yours over the last dozen years, I think he will look kindly on you—assuming Bridgett and her mother see it the same.

"Just go ahead and ask him, Mickey. You are a grown man by any measure, and most would say that you are already late in settling down."

McFee snorted. "I'm no slower than you are Boss's Boy. I haven't heard your excuse for camping all alone up here in that drafty barracks we shared during the flood. I've just been waiting for the right girl."

Now was the moment, and Matt seized it. He would have to hurry because China was coming back up the path.

Matt said, "It happens, Mickey, that I've been meaning to speak to you—speak with you as the man of your house, that is."

McFee looked suspicious, and Matt felt his head turning red with embarrassment. Over what? He didn't know, but it was always this way when he tried to speak about personal things.

Across the river, a steam whistle screeched wildly and black smoke rose skyward in an almost vertical pillar of soot. The George Washington was coming, and the salesman skipper was throwing fat and green straw into the furnace to create an eye-catching column of smoke.

Everyone's attention would be on the steamboat, and . . . Matt saw China pick up his walking pace. God, at just the moment he was trying to talk seriously to Mickey McFee. Matt plowed doggedly ahead.

"The fact is, Mickey, I am asking your permission to court your sister Erin, and I have no more idea how to proceed than you do with Bridgett."

McFee shifted his feet, squaring his body as if he were about to begin swinging. He did not ball his fists, so Matt did not raise his, but . . .?

Mickey McFee said, "Well, it's about time! Erin has been brooding over you for more than a year. It is terrible around our house with worrying over the right headscarf or if her nose is shiny. I told her that men didn't even notice such things and that you were just slow and dopey, but she has been irritable about it just the same.

"Matt, everybody's seen this coming. Your Pa mentioned it to me last fall, and China was there to hear—you can ask him right now if that isn't so."

"Ask me what?" China had arrived.

Matt suspected his head might explode. He was grateful and relieved that McFee appeared to hold no resentment or reservations about his courting, but all this about him being slow or that they had all talked about them as if they were a couple?

China Smith repeated, "Ask me what, McFee?" He cocked his head to the repeated whistle blasts from across the river. "Mrs. Black is busy cooking, but I'll bet that noise will bring her outside."

Matt hoped the steamboat's approach would become the subject, but Mickey answered.

"That big Matt and I spoke about little Matt and my sister Erin being just about a perfect match and that time was running on for both of them."

China saw Matt's embarrassment and chose to shift the attention a little. "Well, Mickey, that conversation did take place, but as I recall, we were also speaking about you and Bridgett Donovan and how you couldn't walk past her without turning as red as a boiled beet."

McFee said, "I didn't remember that part, China."

China said, "So, is that what you two are wrangling about now?"

Matt forced himself back into the conversation. "It's that neither of us knows what to do next, China. I tried to speak to Mickey because he is head of his home, but he started calling me slow and probably stupid and . . ."

Mickey said, "I did no such thing, China. I do not speak to my boss that way, but Matt is right that we don't know what to do next."

Smith seemed to study the smoke column rising across the river. He spoke as if to himself. "Being young is a horrible condition. I'm glad I don't have to do it over again."

Then he turned to Matt and McFee. "What you do is, you each gather an armful of those wild flowers growing against the bank. Squeeze them into a bouquet. That's a French word for a bunch of flowers.

"Then you march down to your chosen gals, hand them the flowers, and invite them to accompany you to watch the George Washington cross the river.

"If they agree to come with you, and they will, then you invite them to ride in Matt's carriage to the aqueduct and perhaps go aboard the marvelous steamboat as your guests.

"If they agree, and they will, signal me, and I will have Mrs. Black make up a nice lunch for four that you can take along, and I will arrange for the carriage to be brought around."

China said, "That's as far as I can take it right now, boys, so get at it."

He thumbed Matt from his chair, sat down himself, and waved them away.

"Get your flowers and get at it before that boat moves too far and you've lost your chance."

23

Across the river, the George Washington found it necessary to stop at every pullout in the canal to allow admirers to come aboard (for a one-cent fee) and listen to the skipper-owner's fervent descriptions of his boat's unmatchable abilities.

Impatient spectators were lined along the Susquehanna's west shore to watch the boat's crossing of the swift and high water. Seated in his father's carriage (Matt supposed that the carriage really was his now) the four young people hoped the boat would take its time while they, for the first time together, were able to enjoy each other's company.

Bridgett Donovan was clearly discomfited by the presence of her father's boss, but Erin whispered (so that all could hear) not to be upset. Matt was no different than any of them.

As Matt Miller was also his boss, Mickey McFee was daring in suggesting that if the Boss's Boy gave them difficulty he, the Irish Hurricane, was there to defend both ladies.

Oblivious to the detail that his sister was present and being courted by his boss, McFee was little deterred by Erin's reminder that it was Matt who had first flattened Mickey's nose all over his face.

Erin's pointed and pithy defense pleased Matt. Until he learned who really was the better man, McFee might yet need to be punched around.

Mrs. Black's tasty lunch (via China Smith) was devoured with appreciative comments, and still the steamboat loitered on the far side.

Mickey hazarded, "Maybe he's afraid to cross with the river running so strong."

Matt did not share the doubts. "Oh he'll come across. I think he is loading wood for his boiler right now, and he is squeezing all of the attention he can out of all of us."

McFee said, "Well, he's got mine. I've never seen a steamboat. In fact, I've never seen a steam engine up close." The girls admitted their own lack of steam power experience.

From his position of experienced steam engine examining, Matt described what they would see.

"This boat is quite ordinary. It was made narrow so that it could use the canals, and the paddle wheels on each side do not stick out beyond the boat the way they should. That means that the wheels grab water only along the bottom tips where the paddles stick below the keel. The boat also has to be very shallow draft so that the paddles will not strike the canal bottom and either break or tear up the canal."

McFee sought to get in the information game.

"That sounds to me as if the boat cannot carry much weight, and with its load of wood for heating the engine boiler there won't be much flotation or room for either passengers or cargo."

His audience listened with some awe, but it was Matt who broke their silence.

"Flotation? Where did you get that word, McFee? Have you been studying my books when I wasn't looking?"

Erin was quick to her brother's defense. "He reads all of the time, Matt—everything except his Bible, that is." Her displeasure at her brother's lack of Bible study was clearly a point of contention.

Mickey came to his own defense with his usual twist of humor. "I learned that word and five others just as hard to drop into conversations. Everybody knows I am smart, but occasionally I like to demonstrate my brilliance."

"Brilliance? Occasionally? Mickey, you are dazzling us all. I didn't know that you spoke much—other than vile and ungentlemanly curse words, that is."

McFee's retort was halted by Bridgett Donovan's excited announcement. "The boat is moving again. I think it is coming out of the canal."

And it was. Whistle shrieking and black smoke towering, the steamboat thrust its nose into the Susquehanna's powerful current. The pilot/owner angled his boat's nose upstream so that the current did not push them down the river. Moving as smoothly as if it were on rails, the George Washington effortlessly breasted the flow and moved smartly toward the western shore. Still, Matt thought that the boat's owner and operator should have hired one of the regular Clark's Ferry pilots to see the boat safely across. Towed canal boats used crossing pilots and, despite the unusually deep water, this stranger-to-the-river just might need someone with special knowledge.

Passengers aboard the craft waved and spectators on the bridge flailed their arms and added excited calling to the spectacle. The captain and owner stood at the stern handling the long tiller, repeatedly doffing his tall hat in appreciation of the enthusiastic reception.

Although enjoying the show, Matt was most interested in the performance of the steam engine itself. More compact than the giant engines he had seen at the coal mines or the monsters on the canal that hauled loaded boats up the railroads and over the mountains, the engine turned the paddle wheels with a solid and certain power that Matt Miller found impressive. He saw the boat's captain adjust the clutch on the upstream paddle shaft slowing it a little so that that the opposite paddle would help turn the boat a bit more into the current and better drive the boat ahead. Very well done, and a simple and effective system Matt believed.

Then Matt saw the log.

In retrospect, he believed he might have been the first to see the huge and waterlogged tree trunk coming down the river. Barely breaking the surface, the floater rolled slightly as it plunged ahead almost like a giant ram and, from a quarter-mile distance, Matt judged the boat was the monster's target.

Matt found himself standing. He was pointing and shouting, but even those in his carriage missed the terrible danger heading for the steamboat. Mickey McFee came up beside Matt his big fists clenched and his eyes darting, asking, "What?"

But it was too late for anyone to do more than watch. Playing the crowd, the helmsman did not see the sodden log coming, and Matt expected it was already too late for the boat to swerve aside.

The ram came under the bridge, and as it passed, spectators on the span finally saw. They screamed and pointed, but not realizing that disaster approached, the boat's helmsman waved and smiled in return.

Matt doubted the people on the steamboat ever saw the log, but the three or four foot giant smashed end-on into the frail watercraft, striking almost amid ship.

The impact of the horrendous smash could barely be heard, but the result was stunning. The vessel buckled in on itself, and bits of boat flew into the air. A blast of released steam joined the smoking funnel as the boiler burst from the impact—and that explosion, spectators clearly heard. Stacked firewood flew before falling into the river as if raining from the heavens.

The craft was driven sideward, but the massive tree trunk imbedded itself within the wreck of the demolished George Washington and momentarily held everything afloat.

Passengers had been propelled from the wreck and floundered in the water. Matt's eyes were torn from seeing the end of the George Washington to the desperate struggles of survivors to grasp anything floating that would help keep them above water. Matt doubted many could swim and, despite the cords of firewood floating among them, he knew in his heart that all would not survive.

A head floating free of the sinking wreck caught Matt's eye, but within the moment, he identified the object as only the tall beaver hat that had been worn by the helmsman.

Then the remains of the George Washington struck something solid and further broke apart. The deadly log floated free, and the tall iron funnel supported by something unseen floated for another few moments, but the heavy iron engine with the ruptured boiler sunk from sight as if they had never existed.

Downriver, rowboats were pushing out from the Duncannon waterfront. Matt judged they would save some of the survivors, who had managed to grasp or climb upon debris that would keep them afloat, but the water was numbingly cold, and the swift current was rushing those adrift far downstream. The boats had better hurry.

As suddenly as it had happened, the river was again smooth and empty. The stunned and silenced crowd gradually dispersed. The four in the carriage watched until there was nothing more to see.

They spoke about the tragedy until the words became repetitive and stale. Then Matt drove the girls home, and he and Mickey stabled the horse and went to the hotel to listen to the gossip and to hear survivors speak of what they had seen and felt.

Within the hotel's sitting room a dozen voices vied for attention. Survivors and spectators mingled and repeated what they had seen and their version of how the wreck could, or could not, have been avoided. Listeners waited impatiently for their turn to expound, and most estimated the number of passengers aboard that would not be rescued.

The former owner and captain had been saved, although his magnificent hat had not. He huddled close to a fireplace, sucking in warmth, a broken man, arms clutching his ribs, his bowed head sunken between hunched shoulders. A blanket had been provided, but his clothing remained soaked, and Matt thought he would be wise to remove his shoes and stockings, so at least his feet could dry.

China Smith sat close to the shattered boat owner, and Matt judged that he did his best to soothe the man's emotions. Losing a boat would be especially meaningful to the former sailor, and Matt guessed that China had seen it more often that he cared to remember.

The situation was terrible with reports of bodies recovered coming in. It was no time to broach business subjects, but Matt signaled to China who, after carefully reserving his seat, came to where Matt and Mickey stood.

Matt asked, "How is he taking it, China?"

"Bad, Matt. Everything he had was invested in that boat, and it is gone for good. Most of it went downriver with the log still driven inside. Nothing has been salvaged, although the end of the funnel is sticking out of the water just below town—for whatever it would be worth."

Matt cleared his throat in minor embarrassment. "Could he talk business, China? I would not want to push him over an edge or something."

China's eyebrows rose. "What business, Matt? The man hasn't got a place to lay his head. He's wondering how he will get back to Baltimore where he has family."

Matt gritted his teeth and stuck to his interests. "The steam engine, China. It is sunk, but I know exactly where, and when the water goes down we can get it. The boiler must be split wide open or it would have floated, but that can be repaired. The rest, including the shafts and clutches, should be there somewhere. I want to buy it all."

China began to nod. "By golly, you are right, Matt, but I hope you can spot the sinking really close, that engine should not be left underwater too long, and it's a big river."

Matt warmed to his subject. "After the log hit the boat, the wreck smashed into something just under the water. What it hit was that big rock in the bridge dam. The one that sticks up high when the water is low. There is a deep hollow washed out just below the rock. That will be where we find the engine and probably the rest of the iron parts."

China listened carefully before pointing out, "One of the paddlewheels left the scene, Matt. I saw it rolling as if it were still attached—going down stream a-helling. Lord knows where that ended up."

Matt hurried him on. "So, can he talk business now, China? I want to get to him before someone else does, and of course, I want to drive as hard a bargain as possible."

Smith considered for a long moment before answering. "He can talk. He's more worried about being broke than he is about the boat itself. I gather that he has not been successful in gaining backers, and this wreck will not be forgotten, even though it was not the boat's flaws that demolished it."

Before Matt could speak, China said, "It might be best if you let me make this deal, Matt. We've been talking personal and close, and he might see me as a sort of acquaintance and perhaps more friendly than a stranger."

China leaned closer to be even more confidential. "How high are you willing to go to own this wreck?"

Smith's tone suggested that the sum should not be high, and Matt agreed. Too much money offered might waken the boatman's awareness of what he was selling and raise resistance. Too low an offer would be insulting, but the fact was, Matt Miller did not have the slightest idea of how much he should pay to own the wreck. He needed a steam engine badly. Should that make him offer more? Matt did the wise thing. He left it to China Smith.

China grumbled, but he went back to his seat beside the owner, and they spoke together before Smith motioned for Matt to join them.

China spoke as if he and Matt had not discussed the matter in any way. Matt played along. This was business, and he had already been at it for a few years.

China said, "The skipper here might be interested in selling his damaged boat, Mister Miller. He lives in Baltimore, and salvaging his craft could be inconvenient. Would your company be interested?"

Matt made his eyebrows rise in astonishment.

"We don't buy boats, China. We build them."

He pretended to look out the hotel door and added, "What boat are you talking about, anyway? What is left of the George Washington is passing Harrisburg about now, and the rest of the boat is sunk somewhere between the bridge and Dauphin. The engine exploded in a hell of a blast, and it is a wonder that people weren't badly burned."

"The iron is out there somewhere, Matt. That should be worth something." Smith let his voice sound uncertain, as if he wanted to help but feared claiming too much. The owner simply sat, leaving his immediate future to those bargaining.

Matt scrubbed at his jaw and tugged on his upper lip. Then he addressed the boat owner and made his words as believable as possible.

"Mister Smith is right. The iron is worth something, but finding and raising it will not be easy. I'm not sure that we can make out on the deal."

China interrupted. "Come on, Matt. This gentleman is in dire straits. He needs to get back home and get on with his business. You are the only person along this part of the river that could use the iron. Make an offer."

Matt said, "All right, I will make an offer. If you, China, agree to take charge of raising the iron and whatever else I may find, I will pay this gentleman one hundred dollars for what is left of his boat." The owner groaned aloud, and Matt added, "Iron is not rare as it was even twenty years ago, so I can go no higher."

China turned to the distraught owner and they spoke softly together. Then he again turned to Matt.

"I will agree to handle the salvage, but only if you add fifty dollars to your offer, Matt. Without my services you will have a difficult time even locating the wreck. I can provide the flatboats and rig the tackle to raise whatever we find. Fifty more dollars for this gentleman, and you have an agreement."

After appropriate weighing and complaining, Matt gave in, and they struck hands on the deal. Matt went to get the dollars, and China stayed to help the former owner accept that he had made the best bargain possible.

McFee walked up the hill with Matt. He said, "So that is how business is conducted. I've got to say that you and China worked smoother than sliding on ice. That poor slob never had a chance."

Matt nodded agreement but added, "Bargaining like that is peculiar business. After it is over, both sides should feel that they did the best possible. The maneuvering, disclaiming, and grumbling is all part of making everyone believe they did their best and struck a hard and close bargain. He got enough money to get out of town and to arrive home with something in his pocket.

"I got a steam engine. Assuming I can find it—which I can, also assuming that Tim Cameron and his iron hammerers can repair the boiler—and I believe they will do that easily, I will have gained an engine worth two thousand dollars.

"That, Mickey McFee, is what business is all about."

24

Matt had brought Erin to Lover's Rock that overlooked the village and the rivers' joining. The view was spectacular with the Susquehanna curving into a bow and the Clark's Ferry covered bridge crossing only a mile or so upstream. The rock dam that created the slow-water pond below the bridge could be seen from this height, and Matt wondered if there might not be Commonwealth work available in maintaining or improving the dam. He would remember to ask Thomas Holcomb the next time he met with the engineer.

The walk up the mountain had taken a half hour, but the view was worth the effort. Matt could appreciate why some called the lookout on Cove Mountain "Hawk Rock" because looking across the river valley one could feel almost like a bird on the wing.

They rested in the shade of a giant oak that tilted dangerously over a long fall to the river's edge. Over the years, trees did lean too far and crashed onto the narrow river road below.

Falling trees and loosened rock hurt or killed people with some regularity, but everyone except farmers loved trees and grew them too close to their homes. Farmers were the exception, and they continually complained that encroaching trees shaded fields and diminished crops.

Matt had brought his telescope, and they shared peering through the magnified viewing, but Matt feared that they chose different details as most interesting.

Erin liked finding birds roosting on the small islands, and logjams with water swirling caught her eye. She enjoyed watching men working in fields and women at their washing and cooking. In this warm weather almost everyone cooked outside, so Matt's lady had much to see.

Matt closely examined the roof of the distant Clark's Ferry Bridge. He had won the re-shingling contract, and his new mill was cutting squared cedar logs into suitable shingle-lengths.

The shingling job was immense. The entire bridge was roofed to prevent decking and underpinning from harsh weather and eventual rotting. A wooden towpath was attached to the south side of the bridge for canal boat mules and horses to use. That towpath was being considered for a shingled pent roof that Matt hoped Miller Men would construct.

For shingling, Cameron's blacksmithing shop had produced a half-dozen two-man froes that could split shingles from straight-grained cedar boards at a record rate. One man placed a froe across a cedar block, and, using a hardwood maul, the second man struck it a single sledgehammer blow that split off a perfect shingle.

Shingles could be made more uniform by sawing, but sawn shingles were prone to warp because they were not shaped along natural grain.

Within the week, he would have men ripping off old shingles, drawing all of the wrought iron nails—most of which could be straightened and reused—and another team would immediately begin re-shingling. Older structures had shingles pegged into place, but the Clark's Ferry Bridge was more modern.

Old shingling could not be dropped into carts waiting on the bridge because traffic would be too often blocked, and nails sticking out of the broken shingles would threaten the hooves of teams using the bridge. The simplest answer was to drop discarded shingles into the river.

A pair of flatboats could be moored on long lines to the bridge pilings and maneuvered downstream to recover the battered shingles as they fell into the river. Some shingles would get away, but in the slack water above the dam, dozens of boatloads would be salvaged for fire building at the hotels during the cold months.

There was other and better scrap hardwood available, but old pine smelled especially good burning in either stove or fireplace, and thin shingle strips were the best there was for fire starting—as long as too much was not used. Pine resin could coat chimneys and cause serious fires.

Matt's old men would do the shingle recovery, and expenses would be small. The once-used but thoroughly seasoned wood would also be sold as kindling in convenient-size bundles, and the Irish and the German workers, as well as the town folk, would buy—as long as he kept the price in the single or two penny range.

Erin had begun to doze, and when Matt lightly squeezed her hand she barely responded. He too would relax and enjoy the warmth and mountain-clean air, but he would not doze. There were things to think about, and he enjoyed that part as much as relaxing with his bride-to-be.

Cameron's ironworks merited thought. The business was Matt's idea, but Tim Cameron had jumped on it.

The Miller businesses needed ironwork from tool sharpening and animal shoeing to special tasks like mending the recovered but badly blown apart steam boiler. Yet, too often, company iron work was slack. The blacksmithy stood idle, bellows did not pump, and the forges were cold.

Matt's proposal was that he would turn over all of the company's tools to Timothy Cameron and provide anything else Tim might need to open his own iron working shop. In return, the Miller Company would receive extremely low rates and immediate service.

The offer appeared generous, but to be sure, Lukey Bates and Scribner had worked out the figures. Matt would profit from not employing a full time ironmonger and his assistants.

Cameron remained a Miller Man, and he was welcome and expected at gatherings or business meetings. Tim Cameron, business owner, responded to the generous arrangement with innovative iron work, like the two-man froes, and he had requested the contract to make and straighten the nails needed for bridge shingling. Matt willingly placed that order, and Cameron's forges were already pounding away.

Matt had met with his uncle Brascomb. He accepted payment for the Philadelphia business and handed across the bill of sale.

Matt had arrived with eight Miller Men in wagons, all armed with adz handles, and two men wearing deputy stars (made by Tim Cameron that looked impressive but remained unexplained) who were carrying short-barreled shotguns that some called "murderers."

None of the Matt Miller contingent smiled or offered friendly comment. Brascomb Miller also came prepared, but his four bullyboys were clearly overmatched, and business remained orderly if limited, and conversations were terse.

Matt had been short with his uncle because the Susquehanna had fallen, and China was recovering the remains of the steam engine from its resting place on the river bottom. Matt's interest lay there, but fifteen thousand dollars was vastly important as well, and he welcomed the final separation of the businesses.

The recovery of the engine proved almost perfunctory. China hooked flatboats together, anchored them securely, and eased their lines until he believed the boats to be above the sunken engine.

China raised a strong log A-frame above his rafted crafts and mounted a windlass on one boat. A few shallow-water dives secured the main engine weight to his ropes, and men windlassed the iron from the bottom and onto the flats.

The ruptured iron boiler was an immense worry with a split running along one curved side, but Tim Cameron appeared un-intimidated and scrubbed his hands together in hunger to start repairing.

A number of other worthwhile items were located and also raised. Both iron clutches with their axles intact were important, and after everything in mid-river was brought ashore, China raised the tall but crazily bent iron funnel that had floated down river within the wrecked boat before sinking near the west shore.

To Matt's eyes, the salvage appeared seriously damaged, but Cameron and China Smith had few doubts. Cameron went to work rebuilding a powerful steam engine from the piles of, to Matt's eyes, barely identifiable metal.

Matt liked to watch the iron masters work. He saw the great rent in the boiler repaired by riveting a wide metal plate over the straightened metal. Leaking was prevented by heating the entire patch and soldering all edges from both inside and outside the boiler.

Matt discovered that boilers had a door let into one end that was secured by massive bolts. The nuts for the bolts had been silver soldered to the inside of the iron boiler so that screwing in the bolts from outside was practical. The door on his boiler was removed, and a small workman wearing padded leather clothing to prevent burns went inside to buck the rivets and returned later to solder the patch firmly in place.

Riveted in place, the patch and surrounding metal were heated until solder ran freely. Solder was then laid into all gaps, and the heat melted and sucked the silver and tin into every crevice.

Cameron noted that the silver soldered patch would be positioned away from the fire box where it would not overheat and melt the solder.

Working fast, the inside man choked and coughed. He sweat an ocean and was burned here and there as well. Matt bought him a bucket of beer and paid him fifty cents extra.

The notice and extra pay sat well with the workers, and a fat man from the village, who could not have fit through the small boiler entrance, swore that at that pay rate he would be the next volunteer to work inside the boiler.

Work on the engine was steady, but there were other tasks that took the Boss's attention. Matt was surprised and gratified to hear the George Washington's steam whistle sound off to announce the engine's first firing, which also meant the completion of the new sawmill using it.

The whistle had not been mentioned in the salvage report, and Matt recognized its installation was meant to please him. He made much of his pleasure, and his men appreciated that as well.

The new sawmill had been built along Sherman's Creek where there was deep water for floating in logs. Recent Commonwealth legislation had limited dam building across creeks because boat travel was being restricted by dam after private dam.

If a canoe could make headway, even ridiculously shallow streams were declared navigable waterways, and across the Commonwealth, dams were ordered removed.

Without a dam, Little Juniata Creek at Duncannon's south end had little to offer. Rather than battle authority to get a dam approved, Matt moved a few hundred yards further south and made the larger Sherman's Creek their mill site.

The steam engine had been mounted and the opposing side-wheel shafts had been hooked to four-foot diameter circular saw blades. The engine was fitted with a giant bronze flywheel and spun the blades with awesome momentum and power.

Boards and planks virtually sprang from the saws, and Matt's expenditures in purchasing and restoring the engine were being repaid at a phenomenal pace. It was good business that big Matt would have been proud of, the Boss's Boy believed.

With the new mill spinning, China had come to Matt with a request that changed many things.

China said, "Matt, I'm getting older than I like to believe, but age being a fact I cannot really ignore, I want to make a proposal."

Smith sat down opposite Matt's office chair, wrinkled his nose in preparation, and began.

"Your Pa pulled me out of being just another beached sailor and gave me a living as his right hand man. I enjoyed every minute with him as my boss and my friend.

"I've enjoyed teaching you and being your friend for all of these years as well, but now I want to trim sails a bit and set a new course. So here are my thoughts on the matter.

"As you know, Mrs. Black and I will be married soon. Of course, we will live together in her home, and I will help her in her business where I can.

"However, I need work of my own. Not only for money, Matt, but for something worthwhile to do. I have plans in my mind for a sleeping boat to move along the canals for workmen or road travelers to stay in. A sort of floating hotel, you could say.

"I would like to construct a mess boat for rough eating that can move with the workers. I have dozens of ideas that have been brewing in my mind since I first began standing beside big Matt.

"The sharp point is that I would like to buy the old mill from you. I will pay what I can immediately, and the rest as I make money. In turn, I will, as Tim Cameron does, give Miller work lowest rates and quickest service.

"I will always be near to give a hand, as I always have, and I will hope that you will find me useful for many years to come."

China sat back, relaxed, without tension or agonizing. Whatever Matt decided, that would be China Smith's course, and he would sail it unremarked and without regret.

Although surprised by the direction their talk had taken, Matt was swift with his answer.

"If that is what you want, China, that is the way it will be." Matt thought for a short moment.

"The mill and its improvements are yours without cost, but frankly, everything has been used hard and is well worn. I fear there will be more repair and maintenance than profit. The land I will sell to you for whatever my father paid for it."

Matt had to pause for more than a moment because his throat had tightened. When he was ready he asked, "But what am I going to do without you at my side, China? You have always been there making sure I did not do too many dumb things and teaching me the best ways—including all of the fist fight training."

China grinned as if he had been waiting for the question. "Why Matt, what you will do is get someone else, and I can think of only one man for the job. You know the name as well as I do. He will take the job, and he will be your strong right arm for as long as you want him."

Matt did not answer, so Smith laid it out.

"Mickey McFee is your man, Matt. He has been around you as long as I have. You have liked each other since before you got tossed into the canal all of those years ago.

"Now, Mickey is grown, just like you are. He has worked at about everything there is. Workmen respect him, not only for his fighting ability, but because he can lead men like a boss should.

"Mickey is your age, and together you can do great things. Bring him close to the business. Give him a place that he can be proud of and that will reward him in life.

"You are good at that, Matt. Look at how your Miller Men idea has worked. Those men want to work for you. They will do anything within reason to move you and your company ahead. Mickey will be the same. In fact, he already is."

China paused. "Mickey will be your brother-in-law, and that can bind you even closer, if you allow it.

"The Irish Hurricane is your man, Boss's Boy. Round him up and offer him the job. It will be the smartest move you will make this year."

Resting with Erin far up on Hawk Rock, Matt considered China's opinion, and he found it as sound as usual.

The more he weighed the idea, the better Matt liked it. He could get along with McFee—to tell the truth, he did like having Mickey around. They shared similar points of view, and they attacked problems in much the same manner. Mickey could handle men as if they had all grown up together. He could tie the headquarters closer to the manpower, and that would grease the working wheels, making everything better understood and smoother moving.

China wanted to get on with his mill and boat building plans, and Matt believed the time was right.

When they came down, he would talk to Mickey. He would make him a good offer, and if the hardheaded Irish Mick did not jump on the deal, he, the Boss's Boy, might yet have to pound sense into the Hurricane's thick skull.

25

Mickey McFee's gang was improving the road north of Duncannon. The village, the township, and the county had managed funds for the rebuild, and Matt Miller had bid the job.

Rebuild was probably not the right description for the work. The road from the Juniata River into Baskinsville had never been planned or graded—much less surfaced. Travelers had followed the old Indian path until they wore it into a road. If a wallow became too deep, someone threw in stones, dirt, or perhaps log slabs until passage was again possible.

Matt had agreed to improve the route until it could be considered an all-weather road that would join Duncannon to the canal system at Benvenue and Clark's Ferry.

Matt had hired three heavy farm wagons, their teams, and their drivers to haul shale from a bank handy to the road. Miller shovelers loaded the wagons, and others emptied the loads where Mickey McFee called for them.

The plan was to raise the low spots until the entire road was above ground level. Shale fill allowed packing, easy leveling, and good drainage, but a number of small stone culverts had to be built to allow uphill water to pass under the road and reach the river. There were also two bogs that defied attempts to fill to road level, and those seemingly bottomless wallows, McFee was making corduroy.

Sumac logs were squished into the muck one upon the other until the fill seemed solid. A new surface was leveled using shale. Then logs were laid cross-wise side by side with shale packed in to fill hollows and gaps. Corduroy roads stayed flat longer than the leveled up shale roads, but when they fell apart, the corduroy was hard to repair.

Matt watched Mickey work—giving directions and jumping in to help when he could be useful. Work gang leaders did not just stand around giving directions. Theirs was a hands-on, example-setting kind of leadership, and McFee did it well.

Matt waited until Mickey was not engaged before calling him aside.

Matt said, "Put your best man in charge here, Mickey. I've got a proposition to talk over with you." McFee called a name, gave a few directions and came to sit on a nearby stump beside his boss.

Matt had thought he would be awkward and self-conscious speaking with McFee, but to his satisfaction he found his words coming easily without expectation of smart-assed retorts or some sort of knee-jerk rejection of his proposal.

Matt said, "Mickey, China wants to retire. He intends to buy the old mill and spend his time building special canal boats he has designed. Of course, he will still be around if we need him, but he will be on his own and no longer standing at my shoulder.

"I need a man I can trust to take his place, Mick. I want someone I know well who will understand how I think and what I want without me having to explain every detail."

Matt still felt good about his offer and went ahead. "I would like you to take China's place, Mickey. You know as well as anyone what China's job was, and you know how this company works and what we do better than anyone, except maybe Alex Donovan. I figure we can get along, and I know that you are as dependable as the sun rising."

McFee appeared stunned by the offer, and Matt thought he might settle a point before Mickey had to raise it.

"Alex Donovan would also be a good choice, but I am looking for someone who will be with me for a long time.

"Alex is a lot older. I would guess he is almost China's age. Before we can hardly turn around, Alex will be asking to be let go, so that he can go over and work part time at China's boat building."

Matt nodded his head in agreement with his own words. "That is the way it should be. The old move on, and we young guys move up, but it could prove valuable to have the old men nearby. They know things that we haven't yet seen, and we can turn to them when we have to."

Matt said, "I am assuming that you and Alex can work out you being both his boss and his son-in-law. I doubt he will have trouble with either, but you would know most about those details.

"You don't have to decide at this moment, Mick, but the sooner the better. Just let me know when you can."

Mickey McFee felt success and a recognized contentment blossoming within his soul. In a single instant, he had gone from being one of the better men to almost exalted leadership with financial security in hand. In his line of work, which was hard, physical construction laboring, no position could be more rewarding or more permanent in nature than standing at Matt Miller's shoulder.

Mickey had, of course, dreamed of such advancement even before he had become a full time worker (who did not, after all?), and Mickey had long recognized that young Matt and he had, somehow, forged bonds of friendship (beyond the boyish who-was-best fist fighting) that he highly valued.

Mickey McFee did not waste time or inject foolish speculating. He bobbed his big square head in understanding and appreciation. He thumped a fist into an open palm to show sincerity, and his words were clear and positive—the way Matt had hoped they would be.

"There's no wait needed, Boss. I've been eyeing either Alex or China's job ever since China first muttered about retiring."

Mickey shrugged his shoulders in reflexive surprise adding, "I really thought you would want Alex for China's place, Matt. I make no claims to knowing anywhere as much about anything as he does, but if you want me, I am your man, and as you know, I will do my very best at it."

Matt said, "Then you've got the job, Mick."

They shook on it, and Matt was pleased that McFee did not begin asking about how much he would make or what his hours would be. Men hiring on who asked those questions too soon rarely worked out. Matt wanted men who wanted the job, not men who wanted just the payday. Wages were important, and the money would be on McFee's mind.

As a laborer, Mickey had earned his seventy cents a day—until Matt had raised all Miller Men to eighty cents. Big Matt had paid regular Commonwealth wages, and as a foreman, McFee had made one dollar and twenty-five cents per day. At Matt's side, he would have to make as much as Alex Donovan, which was supervisor's pay at two dollars and fifty cents six days a week. Mickey McFee was getting up in the world.

Matt rose and dusted his pants' seat with his hands. "Stick with this gang today, Mickey, and start with me tomorrow.

"Pick your replacement, but remember that whomever you choose will be taking your place all along the line, not just finishing this road."

Matt was walking away when he added, "And don't expect to use my boxing gear, McFee. If you have to punch bags, keep going over to Klubber's—after your work is done."

Mickey's retort was, of course, instantaneous.

"I'm glad you brought that up, Boss. Now that China is retiring, I'm wondering if I am free of my 'no professional fighting' promise? It seems as though I might be . . ."

Matt's answer was short and extremely clear.

"No!"

He did not pause or look back, but he could sense Mickey's grin. Yep, he was going to enjoy working with the Irish Hurricane.

26

They had ridden a canal boat to Newport. The only livery in the town rented them a horse and wagon along with directions to Rob Shatto's home on Little Buffalo Creek.

The creek road was worse than either Matt or Mickey McFee had expected, and their rattling and bumping passage along the barely passable trace made them further appreciate their own recently improved road.

"Maybe Juniata Township would put up money to have this route made tolerable." McFee added, "We could all retire on the profit from changing this mess to a road."

Matt said, "We should have rented horses, and I'm not sure we are out of Oliver Township yet. This road is terrible."

McFee complained, "Newport, if that is the name they are going to stick with, is one of the prettiest layouts in the county. The gentle slope to the river is purely handsome. They have a creek upstream and another below the village. They should have bridges. Reider's Ferry is slower than pouring molasses in January, but they do not get anything done."

Matt was not supportive. "Good Lord, Mickey, almost nobody lives in the town yet, and most people cross the river upstream below the rope ferry—where the canal crosses.

"When they get more people, more work will get done. Look at our village. Even with all of the Susquehanna traffic and business, we can't lay out a decent borough square or get a permanent horse water built."

McFee remained unsympathetic. "Horses can water at the river, so I'm not for spending money to build horse troughs. Anyway, a man can't go a mile in this county without crossing some sort of running water."

Mickey proved his case. "This trace we are on is a good example. We follow the stream so close we can water this nag any time we want to."

Matt changed the subject a little. "That's another thing. Roads should follow the Indian paths, and you will almost never find an Indian trail running along a stream. The land is driest and smoothest half way to the nearest ridge, not down here in Bogsville. The Indians discovered that about a million years ago. I don't know why we can't stick to those routes."

"Well, Matt, mostly we do, but Indians just lived where they stopped. We civilized people reshape everything so that it fits what we want. A hundred years from now all of these roads will probably be cobblestoned, and a man won't hear anything except iron horse shoes and wheel rims clashing on the rocks."

They had gone to discuss stump pullers with Mister Rob Shatto, who owned the only decent puller Matt had ever seen.

Shatto had willingly shared his knowledge, showed them his magnificent mountain horses, fed them a noon meal, and urged them to reach Newport before dark caught them on the road. The Shattos, Matt gathered, were busy training horses and wasted little time gabbing.

Rob Shatto was big, physically powerful, and carried a gun at all times. He had also lost a foot in a shooting and wore a gold-rimmed, wooden peg leg.

Shatto commented on the various bare fist battles about the area and remarked how he would like to see the Irish Hurricane take on his boss in the squared circle.

McFee announced that they were both retired from professional fist fighting—which surprised Matt because he had made no such promise.

Banging and crashing back down the miserable road, both ex-fist fighters believed the trip had been worthwhile. Mickey would go to Philadelphia and have the same skilled mechanic that Shatto had used make him three of the powerful screws that were the hearts of the iron stump pullers.

Matt planned on laying out drawings of the massive iron tripod that supported each screw for Tim Cameron's perusal. Cameron could then visit his iron master contacts downriver and contract to have three tripods cast.

Matt expected that within four or five months, probably in the spring (when the earth was soft and roots would pull easily), he would have stump-pulling crews working steadily. That would be good business.

They reached Newport before dark. There were no canal locks en route to find closed until daylight, and an ark was heading down-canal with intent to travel through the night and layover at the aqueduct turning basin. Matt chose to go aboard. He and Mickey could walk home in the dark or in early morning light on their greatly improved road.

A few miles below Newport, Matt pointed across the river. "Do you recall that clay bank they hit when building this canal?"

"Of course, Matt. Some of our people helped clear the river bottom right below here so that clay-loaded wagons could cross easily. The canal we are running in right now is lined with that clay."

Matt said, "I've been talking with the landowner, and I've about closed a deal. The canal section superintendent is boating in clay for maintenance and repair, so the landowner can't profit from that business anymore. He's a farmer, and the clay pit is useless to him."

McFee's eyebrows rose. "But it isn't to us, Boss?"

"Bricks, Mickey." Matt Miller seemed to savor the word. "We all want bricks. Sheriff Hipple floated in seven thousand of them from way down river. I want a pile for the house I intend to build for Erin and me. You will probably build out of straw, but your father-in-law would like to build with bricks, and if we can make them fast and reasonably priced, a lot of people that are planning on stone houses will use bricks."

McFee pretended indignation. "I would pick bricks, like most would, but a clay bank doesn't make a brickyard, Boss. I don't know anybody that knows about brick making, so I hope you do."

Matt's voice was unworried. "I can't say that I know a brick maker, but I know a potter who is a Miller Man—Emil Bower, you know him, Mickey.

"I can't see that making bricks is much different than turning out clay bowls. I spoke with Bower about it, and he is working on ideas for brick furnaces and a huge bunch of brick molds made out of wood that China will make at his mill.

"Bower said that the secret is to make the molds exactly the same and dovetail all of the edges so the molds last a long time. The molds, he says make the bricks."

Matt was clearly enjoying his explanation, and McFee listened carefully because, as sure as he listened, most of the actual construction and organization would fall on him.

"Bower says we will need huge mixing vats above ground where we can blend water with the clay. The vats should be close to the building platform where greased molds will be filled on a flat surface.

"When a mold is filled, it goes aside to air dry. Once the new brick is set up a little, the mold is knocked off, and the green brick sits for many days until most of the moisture is gone and the brick feels dry and hard.

"Bower will make some kind of beehive furnaces out of green bricks and harden the furnaces by firing inside. When he makes bricks, the green ones will be stacked inside in special ways that allow air to pass between them. The fire in the furnace will be built low and stay that way for days so that the bricks dry all the way through before they are fired with a hot fire that will harden them, like bricks ought to be."

Micky said, "It sounds slow and a lot of work, Matt."

Matt nodded. "It sure does, but once the bricks start coming out the end, they will pile up at a hellish rate. We will have to float or drive the brick loads across the river and shift them onto canal boats."

Matt pointed to a wide spot in the canal with dock remains alongside. "The flood took the dock, but right there is where the clay wagons off-loaded onto boats and carts. We will use the same place."

McFee said, "Then you had better arrange to buy or rent that ground, Matt."

Matt grinned, "Big Matt bought that land and a lot more along the canal from the state way back, Mick. Most of the land between the canal and the river is state owned and cannot be purchased, but big Matt knew someone who knew someone, and we got the land.

"Pa claimed that someday people would want to live along the river with the canal protecting their backs or making transportation easy from their mill or river landing."

Matt pondered, "It could be that our brickyard will be the first of such businesses put up all along the river."

McFee suggested, "That potter could make crocks and jugs as a sideline, Matt. Miller Pottery could be shipped all over the country."

The canal boat had been late in arriving at the basin. A horse had thrown a shoe and then fought the replacement as if it were a deadly enemy. Again underway, the second animal had begun tossing a hoof and examination showed that it too had loosened a shoe.

McFee groaned and sought a more comfortable position among meal bags stored on deck. Dawn was near when the boat pulled close to the bank above the basin docking, and the two men hopped ashore.

Tired and irritable, both had sought their comfortable beds and planned on speaking to no one before noon. Matt had hardly fallen asleep when Lukey Bates knocked vigorously on his door. Matt vowed that it had better be important.

Lukey was fast and clear. "I'm glad you are back, Matt. There are two men at the hotel. They are down from the coal regions near Maux Chunk."

Matt grumbled, "Who cares, Lukey. They won't have business for us. What are they doing down here, anyway?"

Bates was firm with his explanations and made his words serious enough to catch Matt's attention.

"They call themselves Organizers, Matt. They are here to talk with our men, and they have been doing just that for two days."

"Talking about what?" Matt reached for his pants.

"They claim that workers are being cheated out of decent living by greedy owners who pay them about half of what they are worth. They say that by organizing, they can force bosses to pay more, a lot more, because contracts have to be filled, and businesses can't wait. They say . . ."

Matt was short. Pulling on his shoes he said, "I know the rest of it, Lukey. I heard those kind of people pushing their unions and clubs up at the coalfields a few years back.

"Some of what they are saying is true, but they agitate and cause troubles that you would not believe. A lot of men have been injured, and a few have already died in the rioting their organizing caused, but I didn't see any improvement in working conditions despite the dues miners are paying to their unions."

Matt scratched at his unshaven chin before asking, "So, why are they aiming at our people? We pay more than most around, and we provide a lot of benefits others do not."

Bates had no certain answers, but he had ideas. "I think they figure if Miller Men, who are better paid sign on, about everybody getting less will line up."

"Are they getting listeners?"

"Well, they buy a few beers and speak long to anybody that is handy. I can't tell if any of our men are interested, but about everyone likes to hear that he should get paid more. They won't be doing us any good, Matt."

Matt nodded. "Get Mickey up, and . . ." Matt hesitated before adding, "Tell McFee to bring his gloves."

"His gloves?" Bates did not follow.

"Yes, his gloves. Mickey will know. I'll meet him here." Matt thought for a moment. "Once McFee is on his way up here, have Willie Brado round up those two Organizers and invite them to stop by and talk to the head men here at our office."

Bates hurried away, and Matt located his own leather fighting gloves and stuffed them into a rear pocket. He did not expect to fight anyone right away, but he had seen union organizers work up at the coalfields, and they could be brutal and overpoweringly demanding. Mine organizers called Molly Maguires had been locally infamous and particularly rough in their dealings. The odds were that these two Organizers had been through those sometimes-bloody insurrections, and Matt planned on being ready.

McFee came at a trot. He was already wearing his gloves and was clearly ready to begin battling.

McFee said, "Who are we fighting, Matt? How soon will they be here? How many of them are there? Have you sent somebody for China?"

Matt got him calmed and explained in detail.

"What these men do, Mick, is stir up workers until they hate everybody in charge of anything. The workmen begin by slowing their work while they make demands for more of this and a lot more of that.

"As it goes on, and the owners or foremen do not comply, they break equipment and send things to the wrong places. They rarely get caught or punished because while one is doing something rotten, others are watching out, and no one ever admits to anything. Guys like these Organizers do all of the talking, and they do not honestly bargain."

Matt paused to gather his breath. "This may not be like it was up at the mines. Miners were and are treated like dirt. Organizing was grasped by darn near everyone, but mine owners could outlast workers who already owed them for food and lodging, and needed all of their pay just to stay alive. So far, unions have caused a lot of trouble, but they haven't done much good.

"Mine owners easily hired other workers because there are so many looking for work—any kind of job. The regulars causing trouble ended up fighting the new men in brawls that broke bones.

"Real work darn near stops, and off and on, times have been desperate up in the coal regions. I don't know when it will get straightened out, but I don't plan on any of that happening here—not to our men, not to our business, and not to those around us."

The Organizers arrived wearing open smiles and offering hearty handshakes. They were large, strong, and experienced, men who had done their time in the coal pits but had now moved on to better lives. If they were surprised by the young men waiting for them, they disguised their satisfaction. They seemed not to notice the greeters' thick and rough gloves.

The two had clearly done organizing work before. Their words were smooth and honest sounding. Many would believe they spoke from the heart, and that their efforts were about to produce marvelous rewards for common working men.

Matt Miller was not among those believers.

Joseph Boleski was clearly the front man, but Frank Pavlovic nodded at every word. Many of the laborers at the mines in Carbon and Lackawanna Counties were Polish. Most were peasant immigrants who struggled with the English language and marginally survived on pittance wages paid to coal miners. The Organizer leaders apparently shared the Polish blood, but these men were of at least a second generation and were born to English speaking.

Matt nodded seriously as the Organizers made their pitch. They came, they said, for the benefit of the laborers whose work made profit possible. They asked only to be heard, and they hoped fervently that Mister Miller would not be one of the obstructionists who blocked their honest and honorable messages from reaching his men's ears.

Matt nodded understanding and furrowed his brow in apparent concentration. His announced decisions suited the Organizers as few had before. This, they recognized, was going to be easy.

Matt Miller said, "Workers should be treated fairly. A dollar's pay for a dollar's work should be the rule." Boleski and Pavlovic beamed. The hard young man wearing gloves beside Mister Miller (Boleski tended to remember only the important names) appeared noncommittal.

Miller said, "It would be only fair that all of our men hear what you have to offer, and that can be arranged without your having to rush about disturbing men at work or speaking to some deep into their cups or too weary to care."

Young Miller examined a calendar on his desktop. "Today is Thursday. Suppose that I gather our Miller Men at Klubber Cole's gymnasium in the second hotel up the road on Saturday evening. I will have the meeting announced and call work off an hour early. You can make your presentation to everyone at once."

Pleased almost beyond beaming, the Organizers departed. Business leaders never cooperated. That was the expected condition, and both Boleski and Pavlovic were always prepared to be harder and rougher than owners and their hired goons who kept miners from asserting their rights.

Talking uneducated and unsophisticated laborers, who usually were abused and cheated, into joining their unions and contributing to the good of all was often easy—providing bullyboys were not employed to drive away the Organizers. The Miller Company, with its cooperative owner, would fall like overripe fruit.

The Miller headquarters watched them go, and not until they were well down the hill did Matt speak.

"All right, we've set the stage. We will have everybody in and listening. After they are done talking, I will have my say. I want to end this organizing here and now, and I plan to do it so thoroughly that Organizers, or whatever they call themselves next time, will not come here."

Lukey said, "There is a chance that the men will like what they hear, Matt. We could get the word out that we do not like what these Organizers are proposing and that Miller Men should stand against them."

"No, Lukey, We will take this head on. Our men deserve to hear all sides of arguments like this. If they buy into what these men offer I will be astonished, but if that happened, I am prepared to change the way we do things—but probably not to many's satisfaction.

"Big Matt and I have tried to treat our men fairly, and I believe you will agree that we have.

Anyway, I will make all of that clear when I talk after the Organizers have finished."

Matt urged them all to lean closer, just as China Smith came hurrying in.

"Damn, Matt. I was out on an ark and was hard to find. What did I miss?"

"Nothing, China. Everything is going to happen Saturday evening, so sit close and listen to my plan."

Matt Miller talked for some time before sending listeners to perform various tasks.

27

This would be the best attended meeting yet, but Lukey Bates studied the gathering with some trepidation. He feared that Matt was allowing the Organizers to gain control and the opportunity to sway Miller Men with blandishments and promises of personal gain that could never be.

And there were more than Miller Men here. China and Tim Cameron with their workmen were to be expected, but Bates saw canal boat pilots and even the old men who shoveled river coal into flatboats and dragged logs into storage behind Halderman's Island. There were two farmers who often rented teams and wagons to the Miller Company, and a small group of ladies gathered to one side. All would be influenced by the polished presentations of the Organizers, and Bates doubted anything good could come of that.

Before the meeting Matt had spoken with the Organizers. He had talked of the men he hired and how well they labored for their common good. He spoke about a new breed of workmen living here in the hills where hostile Indians had been fought and from where two generations of military heroes had volunteered and served in the new nation's wars.

These immigrant Irish and Germans, once peasants with intolerant overlords, were changed, Matt claimed. They were now free men, and they thought and acted in independent ways. Matt warned that these Perry County men were not likely to listen to improbable arguments or to believe otherworldly promises of unearned rewards.

Matt suggested that whomever did the speaking use care because these were not men to insult or false promise.

Matt quieted the meeting by standing as if ready to speak. China Smith again admired the persona that allowed just standing up to control a bunch of Irishmen who were rarely willing to be directed under the best of circumstances—plus the Germans who were most likely to be sullen and obstinately unresponsive. But here they were, going as quiet as if in church just by the Boss's Boy being ready to start.

Matt looked them over, unsmiling and serious, introducing the talkers without supporting or condemning what was to be presented.

Matt announced, "These gentlemen are Organizers from up in the coalfields around Hazleton and beyond. They wish to speak to Miller Men about their efforts and suggest certain directions to everyone gathered here."

Matt paused to let his eyes roam the assembly. "When these gentlemen have finished, I will pass voting ballots to everyone, and we will vote on acceptance or refusal of the ideas they propose. No names will be taken on how anyone votes. This is an opportunity to express your personal feelings, nothing more.

"Before the vote count is announced, I will say a few words that will include my personal opinion on all of this. I will wait until that time so that my thoughts do not influence your decisions."

Matt introduced Mister Joseph Boleski who would speak for the Organizers.

Boleski was a powerful and experienced speaker. His voice thundered and his finger pointed. He accused business owners of foul deeds against honest and reliable employees. He blamed deaths, injuries, and overwork on greedy employers who forced exhausting labors but paid less than living wages.

Boleski explained the labor unions now forming at the Pennsylvania mines. He described the improved conditions about to appear and the handsome wages that would, almost immediately, be forthcoming.

Boleski encouraged his listeners to join him in stamping out the abuse of workers by banding together and demanding fair wages, safer working conditions, and shorter working hours.

Boleski claimed that when those in this audience led, other suppressed multitudes along the rivers would leap to follow their sterling examples.

Following lurid descriptions of vile employers abusing human decency and the abject degradation by devil-led employers of men just like themselves, Boleski closed with his explanations of how—if just and fair requests and demands were ignored—common men could control their destinies by standing together through work slowdowns, even strikes, and if all else failed—but only with great reluctance—by damaging or even destroying property that would force greedy and uncaring bosses to pay more and demand less never-easing labor under foul and degrading conditions.

The Organizer's final remarks repeated his assurances of better times with milk and honey for all—including sharing out the overpayment of foremen and supervisors' huge wages among the men who produced all products and services—the workers.

Boleski thanked his audience for its attention and sat down. To his astonishment the room remained tomb quiet. Had he stunned them into undivided acceptance? Or did the silence bode something less acceptable? Faces told him nothing, but the voting was what would count.

Young Miller was a fool to ever allow laborers to discuss a company's direction. Once a foot was in the door, the unions would rule. It had not happened yet, but Boleski could sense progress in the coalfields. It could happen here even more quickly.

Frank Pavlovic congratulated his companion on a terrific speech, but he too was worried by the lack of response. Neither recalled any such reaction. Still, the vote would tell. They waited.

Seated in the front row among his men, Matt Miller gestured for Bates, Scribner, and Brado to pass a single small paper square to each person present. Matt took one himself and chose a charcoal bit from among those offered.

Rising, Matt said, "This paper was salvaged from Scribner's secret diary, so use the side that has no writing on it, and do not read what is on your scrap." His explanation avoided the almost bitter detail that few of his men could read, and even fewer could read in English, but they understood his weak humor.

Matt waited for the chuckling to die down. "Draw an 'X' if you are interested in joining or hearing more. If you have learned all that you wish to know about unions and workers' clubs and do not like what you have heard, scratch a circle on your paper."

Matt again smiled and added, "One paper per man—watch your neighbor. We do not want any vote padding going on."

Now there was talk and some laughter. Wilhelm Brado collected the votes in a large hat and retreated to a table where he, Bates, and Scribner prepared to separate and count the ballots.

Matt observed with some astonishment. The hat, a bit worse for wear, had been the steamboat owner's magnificent double beaver. He had believed the hat long gone, but here it was again being useful.

Pavlovic came over to watch the count, but Matt was again addressing the crowd, and the Organizer turned to listen.

Matt's tone, which had been pleasant had turned surprisingly chill, and his eyes glittered more steely than any could recall. The tenor of the meeting changed dramatically, and the Miller Men felt their senses sharpen.

"I choose to speak now, before the voting is announced, so that no one will believe that the outcome influenced me.

"I do not doubt the vote result because I know the men gathered here. I know your loyalty, and I respect your work as you respect mine—which means that you will ignore foolishness that does not apply to you or to me, and you will vote against the Organizers."

Boleski's and Pavlovic's heads snapped up, and their mouths opened in surprise. This, they had not expected. Never had an owner, supervisor, or foreman spoken as openly or as confidently to his workers.

"However, men like these Organizers will come again and again, and I want everyone to know how I feel about these men and the trouble they have caused in the coal regions—and how I will act if any of them ever gain a foothold among Miller Men."

Matt went on, "These Organizers speak truly about the mines and the conditions faced by those who work there, but we are not miners. I am not an evil and greedy boss, and you are not fools or incompetents who work for poor pay under rotten conditions.

"I resent hugely their implications that I bully those who work for me, and that you are dull, trod-upon peasants without will or brains enough to act for your own benefit without fast-talking strangers appearing to instruct you and promise rewards that are beyond possibility.

"Miller Men are special. You are chosen men, and you are few. Miller Men are treated with respect and paid decent wages with decent hours, and when it is needed, they—meaning you—have decent housing.

"If work is available, Miller Men are hired. If there is no work, credit is offered, and no man is abused, insulted, or driven from his job by any foreman or supervisor. As Miller Men, you know that I can be talked to—as can Mister Smith, Mister McFee, or Mister Donovan. We listen, and we do our level best to do what is right."

Matt strode closer to his audience, and their eyes followed.

"There is more that you should understand.

"The Miller Company is mine and only mine. No one else will ever control how I conduct business, how much I pay, or how I treat my workers.

"Unions or the clubs might succeed at the mines because those workers produce a single product from a single source. Abusing equipment or slowing work would cause loss.

"We are not like that. Our jobs are many and diverse. We do not have a single product to bind us here or anywhere else. If workers refuse their work, I can walk away and begin somewhere else. I can move my steam engine or saw blades to another creek and hire new men. China Smith can build canal boats anywhere. Mister Donovan and Mister McFee can, at any time, hire crews to do new work at wages lower than Miller Men are paid.

"That does not happen to you or to this company. As you trust your welfare to me, I trust my company to you. Together we prosper, but never doubt that if I am abused or crowded or imposed upon I will depart this scene taking with me only those I still trust. Complainers, plotters, malingerers, and union men will not be among them."

The silence had become heavy. Matt believed he had left little doubt as to his feelings. He turned to Wilhelm Brado.

"Announce the voting, Willie."

Brado's piping voice said, "All but one vote is against the Organizers, Mister Miller."

Even Matt was a little stunned. He had not expected such a clean sweep. Boleski and Pavlovic were on their feet, their eyes glaring and their mouths turned down. Shouting and whoops of satisfaction rose in a wave. Matt raised a hand in shared satisfaction and marched to the hotel door. Mickey McFee was instantly at his shoulder with China pushing to get through excited workers to catch up.

They stepped outside, and the Organizers were quick to arrive.

Pavlovic raged silently, but Boleski stood too close, and his words were snarled.

"You set us up for that, Miller. You primed those fools like you would a gunpowder charge. We aren't taking that vote as meaning anything, and. . ."

Matt interupted. "The voting is done, Boleski. There will not be any more. You had your chance. I warned you fairly about the kind of men who live up here. They bow to no one, and in your annoyance, keep in mind that I am one of them."

Matt closed strong. "Now, you will leave us, and if you are wise, you will not come this way again."

Joseph Boleski had trod hard paths, and he believed he knew men, but this baby-faced youth had suckered him and made him look foolish and small. Now the brat ordered him away as if he were one of the dead-brained peasants he claimed to help.

Boleski's rage blossomed and ballooned beyond caring. He had had enough. His face turned red, his body swelled, he raised a fist—and Matt struck.

Matt Miller had listened to his character being insulted and stepped upon—and he despised it. He almost expected, or perhaps he had hoped, Boleski would wish to fight. The Boss's Boy had always been willing, and this time he was almost anxious to begin.

Matt's blow took the short route. It started at his waist and slid upward between them. He had made his balance right, and his tightly gloved left fist moved as if on a track. Matt whipped his body weight into the uppercut. His straightening leg added power, and set his balance for the follow up.

Boleski's blow was still threatening when Matt's gloved fist sledged him under the chin with bone breaking force. The stunning impact fogged Boleski's brain. His head snapped backward, and his eyes looked dazedly skyward.

Frank Pavlovic flinched. He recognized the meaty crunch of a solidly delivered punch, and his partner's head snapping backward made the power of the uppercut plain.

Pavlovic had expected that Boleski would turn physical. As Organizers, they often did, and thoroughly hammering young Miller would impress the rebellious part of any crowd—as well as ease their personal embarrassment at having been so easily duped.

Pavlovic hauled back his right hand and aimed his hardest punch at the side of Miller's head. Pavlovic was fast, and he was ready. He had engaged in many brawls over many years. He knew how and when to hit. His fist drove like a ram at Matt's unprotected ear.

Still too far away, China saw Matt's punch, and as he pushed aside the slower moving, he admired the power that drove Boleski's head almost off his shoulders. He also saw Pavlovic's fist coming from beyond Matt's vision. Too far away, China Smith could only watch.

Mickey McFee was right where he wanted to be. Slightly to the left and a half-step behind, Mickey saw Pavlovic draw back and swing like a rusty gate. The blow was a monstrous overhand right—the kind of punch the untrained throw, but powerful enough to stun and floor whomever got hit.

McFee went underneath. He struck from a crouch and drove his right fist into Pavlovic's unprotected liver, just below the short ribs on the right side was the spot. His was a trained fighter's blow, and Mickey's fist went in deep. Pavlovic's punch halted in flight, and the Organizer folded like a punctured pig's bladder. He sagged to the ground, his mouth hung as agony swept his body, and his lungs struggled for enough air to stay alive. Pavlovic moaned, gripped his side, and passed out. Mickey turned his eyes to the Boss's Boy.

Matt's uppercut was simply his beginning. Because he chose to again punch Boleski in the face, Matt too resorted to an overhand right. Unlike Pavlovic's swing, Matt had his shoulder behind the punch, and he rolled it and his hand as the blow landed with crushing force. Blood spurted from split skin, and down and out went Boleski.

China quit hurrying. The action had taken barely an instant, but the fight was over. Both Organizers were unconscious, and Matt's man was bleeding profusely from a cheekbone that had ripped wide open. China thought—good gloves!

He watched to make sure that no one jumped out of the stunned crowd onto Matt or McFee's back, and sure enough, there was old Klubber Cole doing the same.

McFee had already turned to order the crowd to move back and quit crowding into everything before Matt took his eyes from the unconscious Organizers.

Whew, McFee had hit Pavlovic with about the hardest body punch Matt had ever seen. Even China would have to admire that one. Pavlovic was curled into a fetal ball, and Matt wondered if Mickey had burst something important inside the man.

Hurt or not, the Organizers were leaving the area. Matt called to Alex Donovan who had worked his way to the front.

"Alex, round up some men and have them haul these carcasses down to the hotel so that they can grab their belongings. Then have them loaded into a wagon and driven to the canal. Dump them there and have them watched for a while to make sure they keep going north. I don't want to wake up tomorrow and have to do this all over again."

Willie Brado made his presence known. "I'll get the wagon and drive it, Mister Miller." He was off before anyone could comment.

Matt's voice had been strong and his directions clear, but the Boss's Boy could feel tremors in his muscles.

Flat out fighting was different than bare fisted box fighting. By finishing his man quickly, both he and Mickey had avoided the wrestling, biting, kicking and slugging of a common street brawl—but it was still nerve-straining work.

Loud voices from the crowd pushing and shoving to see better caught Matt's attention. Men shouted "Good job" to him, and one complained that Matt had done what he had intended on doing.

Matt turned to Mickey McFee. "Thanks for the help, Mick. That bozo would have nailed me sure."

McFee was still excited by the action, and he shifted his weight from foot to foot, his fists clenched at waist level, and his eyes peering as if other enemies were about to pounce.

Mickey said, "I nailed him good, Matt. One clean shot from The Hurricane's Irish Cannon, and he was down to stay." McFee brandished his right fist as if it were a club.

China looked over and said, "Too bad you don't have a left hand to go with it, McFee. One-hand fighters do not get far—unless they are hitting men who aren't looking."

Mickey remained pleased with himself. "If he isn't looking, that's his problem. Hit 'em when you can is my motto."

Matt said, "Mine, too, Mick."

China smiled and claimed, "That's a good policy. I've used it for years."

The crowd was long gone, but Matt, Mickey, and China were still in the office, calming themselves by talking about old fights and fighters when Wilhelm Brado returned from delivering the Organizers to the canal.

"They went north, just like you wanted, Mister Miller." The boy sounded worried.

Matt thanked him and asked him to put the horse and wagon away.

"That man that Mister McFee hit was still holding his side and groaning, Mister Miller, but the other one, the one named Boleski was madder than a wet hornet.

"His face kept bleeding from where you hit him, and . ."

McFee broke in. "That glove about wiped his face off, Matt. You ought to pay China for them, like I had to for mine."

Smith said, "People punching unsuspecting men in their soft bellies don't need fighting gloves, McFee. Now stay quiet and listen to what this boy has to say."

Brado did not have much more.

"All I can add, Mister Miller, is that Boleski told me to tell you that you would see him again, and next time it would be you that would bleed."

China Smith laughed, Mickey McFee shook his head and snorted. Matt smiled grimly, "There isn't much else he could say, Willy. A man that just got whipped and run out of town can't do much more than threaten, but I heard what you said, and we will take Boleski's words real serious.

"If the Organizers come again, we will be waiting, and next time we will mark them so that they remember their visit and will never want to repeat it."

28

There was a fall nip in the air, and Brado had lit a warming fire in the headquarters stove. Matt stood with his back to the blaze, heating his behind while rereading the Baron's letter.

Deiter Haas had returned home and was again ruling his people, but he had not forgotten his American time, and his first letter had a proposal that needed answering.

Matt handed the letter to Willy Brado who was helping Lukey Bates with the weekly payroll.

"Read the second page, Willy. It has to do with you."

Brado read, *If Wilhelm Brado wishes to return to his fatherland, I have a place for him. His position would be within my household and much like his work with Lukey Bates. If he elects to return to Germany, I will see him through proper schooling and have him tutored in the ways of German gentlemen.*

Please inform Wilhelm that if he chooses to remain in America I will understand and wish him well. Your country, too, has much to offer.

Matt waited expectantly, and Brado did not disappoint him. "Will you answer for me, Mister Miller, or should I write to Baron Von Haas myself?"

"Whichever way you prefer, Willy, but before you announce your decision be aware of how fine a future you could have with Deiter. The Baron can offer a thousand comforts that you are unlikely to discover in this country."

Matt smiled broadly, "On the other hand, in this young nation, who can tell what opportunities may appear. In Germany, you will be what tradition and custom allow. In this country you can rise—or you can fall—as your skill, your determination, and your luck provide.

"There is no hurry, Willy. I will not answer Deiter for at least a week, or you can write your own letter at any time."

Brado assumed his usual position of attention and answered clearly. "I do not need time, Mister Miller. I do not wish to return to Germany," the boy pondered, "except for a visit or two when I am much older."

Matt nodded his agreement. "I am pleased to hear that, Willy, but if you are staying with us, I have plans for you that will begin almost immediately."

Brado appeared worried, so Matt hurried on.

"If you are to succeed in this modern world, you must have schooling." Matt grinned openly. "When my father forced education on me I resisted as powerfully as I could manage. I was dead wrong, but I do not expect that response from you.

"Within the month, a school year will start at the academy over in Bloomfield. I will expect you to attend and to do well. That means that you will return to us here in Duncannon only on vacations. I may drop by during the year, but your full attention must be on what the professors are teaching."

Matt pulled his lip and added, "I may send Lukey now and then to check on your progress. He is a graduate of that academy, and you have seen how much more he knows than do the rest of us.

"Do you agree to that course, Wilhelm?"

Brado did with apparent pleasure. Matt reminded the boy that he would still be a Miller Man, and he would be expected to add luster to the company's reputation.

Matt broke the conversation as the sound of stumbling hurry and heavy breathing approaching their door.

The door burst open, and one of Matt's ancient river rats entered. Matt had stationed a number of the old timers on probable approaches from upriver. This one, Old Ben, had been living in Port Treverton for almost a month. His job was to observe everyone who came downriver. If Organizers, whether familiar or new faces, appeared, he was to beat them to Duncannon.

Judging Ben's urgency, Matt guessed that he had figured it right. Joseph Boleski was returning—and he would have people with him.

Old Ben had worked at getting to Matt first. He had seen the Organizers, eleven of them counting Boleski, on a packet boat heading south. He had climbed aboard and yarned with the helmsman and steered when the man needed natural relief clear to New Buffalo. There, while the ark laid over, he had rented a horse and come a'helling on down to the Miller Company headquarters.

Matt sat him down and asked Willy to fetch a beer bucket from the hotel. While the old timer regained his limited vigor and waited for the beer, Matt gathered more information.

"How far behind are they, Ben?"

Ben figured. "I'd say, they won't get to Benvenue until, maybe, late this afternoon, Boss."

He expanded his chest and set his shoulders more squarely. "I hustled more than a little getting down here, Boss. We'll need some time getting ready for them."

Ben twisted his worn features into a fighting mask. "They've all got pick handles, Boss, and when they were drinking, they were loud about the damage they were going to do to the people that had insulted their organization and jumped their leader from behind."

The beer arrived, and Old Ben swallowed and lip-smacked his pleasure over his German-style stein while Matt began his preparations.

First, Brado was set to bell ringing. The youth worked at it, and there could be no mistaking the clanging urgency. The steam whistle at the mill followed suit, and from distant places Matt heard conchs and at least one coach horn adding to the din.

Good! Taking Boleski's parting threat seriously, he had made careful preparations. The loud warnings were step number one.

As they arrived, Matt huddled with his foremen and a few selected Miller Men (plus Klubber Cole) chosen to directly participate in their Organizers' reception.

Frank Pavlovic was not along, and Boleski resented his absence. True, Pavlovic still complained of pain in his liver, but he had stopped peeing blood, and Boleski believed he was fit to take part in their carefully arranged revenge.

Boleski was want to touch the scar along his cheek where Matt Miller's blow had split his skin and possibly fractured a cheekbone. Unlike Pavlovic, who Boleski believed had given up—the head Organizer sought payback.

The Organizers marched eleven men strong. Armed with pick handles, they intended to do physical damage to anyone between them and Miller, who led the company. After they had thoroughly pounded Miller and whomever else was handy, they might burn a few buildings or even a boat or two before they left town.

Smashing the Miller Company would send warning up and down the rivers and through the coalfields that the worker organizations were powerful with long arms. Other laborers would gain courage to stand and resist. Uncooperative companies would think again.

Few beyond the men in Boleski's group would know that Joseph Boleski had spent personal money hiring his ten thugs—none of whom worked regularly at any employment.

Boleski had planned a withdrawal march up the Susquehanna's east side where they would be out of Perry County jurisdiction and pursuit would be unlikely.

He, of course, would not walk the many miserable miles back to the mines. If Frank Pavlovic was unwilling to fight, he could still be useful. Pavlovic would even now be riding south with an extra horse in tow. When he met the victorious Organizers, he would turn an animal over to Boleski, and they would ride the rest of the way.

When their packet touched the wharf at the Duncan's Island lock, Boleski organized his men and immediately set off on the short march to Duncannon. Surprise could be as valuable as the strengths of his men because the Miller Company had already demonstrated its ability to rally a crowd of sympathizers.

Boleski would not wish to encounter the mob of Miller Men present at the voting. Boleski sneered to himself. Those Miller people would not be as admiring when their boss lay broken with their headquarters burned to the ground. That thought reminded Boleski to check that each of his men had his heavy scarf about his neck so that it could be pulled across its owner's face disguising features and making positive identification improbable.

Boleski judged the time of day and believed he had chosen well. There would be daylight for their vengeance. Miller's laborers would still be scattered at their work, and by the time Miller Men could rally, the Organizers would be gone and dark would be descending. Men who had already worked a full day would not be anxious to chase a strong enemy through the night.

Boleski almost wished some Miller Men would attempt to run them down. His thugs would hammer those unfortunates into the dirt—just as they were about to batter and pound Matt Miller himself.

He had considered sending a scout into town to make sure Miller was there, but Duncannon was a small community, and if detected, their plan would be ruined, and they might have to run like frightened children. Not this time! Boleski's fingers touched his scarred cheek.

A half-dozen loggers bearing their axes and adzes had boarded Boleski's packet a pair of miles earlier at Amity Hall, but they had purchased transport to Harry McKee's hotel across the Susquehanna. Boleski gave them little thought. As soon as its river pilot boarded, the boat would resume its passage. His attention was focused on what lay to the south, not across the river.

Joseph Boleski believed the Gods smiled on him. His group of sluggers had barely broken through low growth that had replaced trees once covering flat ground all along the river to enter a decent-sized clearing where a number of men were clustered around a large iron kettle held above a fire. With astonished pleasure, Boleski recognized Matt Miller and the fighter who had, with a single punch, taken the heart out of Frank Pavlovic. The other three men Boleski did not know and were of little interest.

Here, delivered unto him were the men he most wanted—the devils he had come to repay. Boleski's satisfaction could not have glowed brighter.

Boleski immediately fanned his men in an arc around the Miller Men who seemed to ignore their presence. He had them pinned against their fire, and none of the Millers would escape. His men flipped their scarves across their faces disguising their features. Boleski did not. He wished to be known.

Matt Miller finally looked his way, and Boleski was astonished by the calm acceptance of what must surely seem like impending disaster. Miller's fighter moved to his side, as he had before, but the three others at the fire stood relaxed and outwardly unworried.

It might be that they did not know what was about to happen. Boleski spared no sympathy. These hapless fools were probably among those who had voted against him the last time he had passed this way. His bruisers would punish them as well.

Because he was silently enjoying his sluggers' supremacy and their forthcoming beating of Miller into mush, Boleski had not spoken. Matt Miller did.

Miller said, "I warned you not to return, Boleski. You have made a serious error."

Boleski was prepared to laugh, but apparently on signal, a row of a dozen men armed with tool handles stepped from the brush along the road to Duncannon. Boleksi felt his men freeze in place and his own nerves twanged with instant recognition that it was he who had stepped into a trap.

From the way Boleski had come, the six loggers who had boarded the packet at Amity Hall stepped into view blocking the only route back to the canal. The loggers had knocked off their metal tool heads and were also armed with the ash ax and adz handles. Boleski felt sweat pop, and he could sense fear beginning to challenge his hired toughs.

Boleski's shifty mind went to work, and he forced a crooked smile. He intended to explain that he was only passing through and that he had no bad intentions, but Miller was not yet finished, and from the brush beyond the fire, more men emerged. The man Pavlovic had claimed was a famous bare fist fighter named Smith led them. Poleski did not bother to count. They were more than a dozen, and their faces were as ungiving as the tool handles they gripped in work-hardened fists.

Boleski feared his panic showed. One of his men swore, and the sluggers milled uncertainly in the face of overwhelming odds.

Again Miller spoke before Boleski could reorganize his thoughts.

Miller spoke to Boleski's lumpers. "You men were hired to attempt an impossible task. You have two choices. The first, and wisest, is to lay down your clubs and march yourselves back to the canal. If your boat is there, board and leave this place. If there is no boat, begin walking north or across the bridge. Do not turn back, or you will regret it forever.

"Your second choice is to stand and fight beside Boleski, who will not be going with you. He will not win, and you will not either. That decision you will certainly regret as long as you have memory."

Miller's voice was iron hard. "Choose now. Fight or depart."

Tool handles struck the ground. There was no hesitation, and no blustering in the face of overwhelming force. No sluggers asked what was going to happen to their leader. En masse, they dropped their clubs, turned on their heels and strode back the way they had come. Matt's six blockers stepped aside to let the intimidated bruisers pass.

Boleski, too, tried to depart, but one of the fire tenders stepped into his path. Boleski recognized him from the voting meeting. He, too, was a former fighter, and his features had been bashed and reformed many times. Boleski felt his soul wither. His was not going to be an easy departure. Neither his clever words nor his experience in brawling would help him a lick. Matt Miller would do as he wished, and Joseph Boleski had no hope that his treatment would be mild.

The mass of Miller Men closed around their captive, and Boleski saw no sympathy in any eyes. He said, "Now, Mister Miller, there is no need for fisticuffs here," but he got no further.

The face-battered old fighter gripped Boleski's right wrist, and another man stepped forward to secure his left arm in the same grip. They were powerful men, and Boleski stood helpless to make more than token motions.

Matt's cold voice said, "Coming downriver you and your men boasted about how they were going to smash the Miller Company."

Boleski's soul writhed, God, they had been watched all the way.

"You, Boleski, described how you would beat me to a helpless pulp and break a few bones so that I would remember your visit. Those were your words, Organizer."

Boleski knew his voice whined, but he was beyond caring. "That was just talk, Miller, we had no such intentions."

"You said you might burn buildings and leave these men out of work, Boleski. Miller Men take such threats to heart."

Boleski had no more explanations to offer. He stood mutely while Miller studied him.

Matt surprised him. "There will be no fisticuffs, Boleski. We have a better way to deal with trash like you."

Boleski's hope rose a hair. He did not believe Miller would kill him in front of so many witnesses, and . . .

As if sensing his thoughts, Miller said, "You will probably survive this time, Boleski, but if you are found south of Clark's Ferry again, your bones will rot on the bottom of the Susquehanna.

"I warn you once more, but for the last time. Do not come this way again." Miller turned away as if uncaring, but Boleski's hopes vanished as the grips on his wrists tightened, and men stepped forward brandishing sharp knives. He heard himself whimper, but the men ignored his sounds. They slashed his clothing and cut everything above his waist away until the rags hung below his belt, His hat had been knocked away, and he stood naked to the waist.

The old fighter on his right said, "I would close my eyes if I were you."

Not understanding, Boleski asked, "What?"

Then he saw the men at the kettle dip long-poled swabs into the bucket and bring them out soaked in something evil. The smell reached him. Pine? It was pine that clogged his nostrils and melted all hope. Boleski knew what was about to happen. He had heard of it, and he had considered its use up in the coalfields, but it was an awful punishment, and now . . . now he was about to experience it.

The swab men stepped close, and one moved out of his view behind him. The man in front slapped his pitch soaked swab up under Boleski's chin, and the heat and stickiness of the heated pine pitch seemed to shrivel his skin. The heat was not boiling, but it felt as if it were.

The pitch flowed downward and across his chest sticking as it traveled, but before Boleski could judge how heavily he was being coated, the man behind flopped his pitch swab onto Boleski's head, and the Organizer understood why he had been advised to close his eyes. The pitch was searingly hot, and the men wielding their terrible mops were unmerciful.

Boleski howled in anguish and thrashed frantically. Other willing helpers reinforced the men holding his wrists. The swabs were returned to the cauldron for redipping, and back they came to add misery in a sticky coating that burned like liquid fire.

Finally the swabbers stopped, and Boleski dared to open his eyes. His face had been spared, as had his hands. Otherwise, he was a mass of rapidly cooling pine pitch that would resist removal like skin itself.

Men stepped forward with handfuls of something Boleski could not make out. When they hurled their loads onto him, Boleski knew, and believed he should have expected it—feathers and perhaps goose down. The feathery mass coated him, sticking to the pitch as if it had grown there.

The ring of tormentors stood silently, but the men holding his wrists stepped away, and Matt Miller again appeared in his view.

Matt's words were few. "Get out of Perry County, Boleski, and never return."

Miller and his helpers gave him their backs as they walked away toward Duncannon.

The Miller Men circling him were not as generous. They voiced their threats and promises of death if he was seen again in Miller country. They said that they knew him and would never forget what he looked like. They, too, ordered him away, and Boleski began to totter in the direction of the canal docks.

Someone urged him faster, and a stone bounced from his back. Panic struck Boleski. These men were willing to kill him right now, and Miller had walked away leaving them free to do as they wished. He broke into a frantic if wobbling run and left the clearing behind.

Matt listened to the shouting and threatening coming from the clearing. He asked, "Do you think we've convinced him, Mickey?"

"Convinced him? Matt we just convinced every bad guy in Pennsylvania to avoid Perry County." Mickey laughed, "Once this word gets around, I doubt anyone in the whole county ever drinks too much or hits his wife."

China said, "I hope someone will tell Boleski not to scrub too hard removing that pitch. Turpentine can help, but not much else will. He will wear that stuff for weeks until his skin just naturally lets it go."

McFee said, "When it comes to doing miserable things to people, you are the master, China. I would have just licked him good, maybe broken up his face a bit, but that hot pitch treatment was the perfect answer. Nobody would ever face that a second time. Boleski will never approach the county line."

They walked in silence, each deep in his thoughts. Matt's mind had moved on. He had his forthcoming marriage to ponder, and the need for bricks to be ready by spring when he would build their home. The potter who would run the brick factory was also interested in producing and selling his pottery. Miller Pottery, as McFee had suggested? Why not? Business was business.

Then there were the stump pullers. He expected to have teams pulling stumps for as long as he lived. He expected that he had better corner that market before others jumped in on him. Once Cameron's designs had proven themselves, he would have more pullers made. They would own the molds for casting the tripods and only the turning screws would be expensive. Matt figured on.

China Smith marveled at how the boy he helped grow to manhood took hold. Young Matt was willing to try anything sensible. He had turned over the old mill, and they both prospered from the transfer. China's new boat would be the fastest packet to ever hit a canal, and Matt was co-owner.

They had already contracted for replacement towing teams all the way up past Lock Haven. On the other hand, there was the option of carrying fresh teams along on the fast boat and swapping horses when animals tired.

Matt planned to station the lean and swift packet in Harrisburg, and China expected that he had better begin design on another boat. When Matt Miller found a good thing, he was prone to run with it.

Mickey McFee strode in contentment. He walked beside a boss he could like and admire. He had a job anyone would envy. With Matt Miller running things there would always be interesting work—and other activities. McFee grinned inside as he thought back on the humiliation of Boleski and his thugs.

He had hoped that he and Matt might punch holes in the Organizers the way they had the first time, but Pavlovic had not come, and Old Ben had reported that the man was peeing blood. The pine pitch was better, anyway.

Matt Miller had heard Ben's report, so he must have been impressed by Mickey McFee's punch. McFee had noted that Matt was wearing his fighting gloves while they had waited in the clearing. So had Mickey—just in case.

For as long as he lived, Boleski would wear the scar from Matt's punch in the face. Matt Miller could hit, too.

Mickey McFee couldn't help wondering—if silently—just how The Irish Hurricane and Matt Miller would come out going toe to toe.

Mickey would bet his last dollar that the Boss's Boy was wondering the same.

The End

The Canals

Although *The Boss's Boy* is not a book about canals, those wonderful Pennsylvania waterways are engaged within the story, and readers may wish to know more about them.

Oddly, interesting construction details and even stories about canaling days (particularly on the Juniata Branch) are difficult to find. Research New York's Erie Canal, and information flows like water. Yet, the Pennsylvania system, which was vastly more extensive and a greater engineering feat, receives little literary attention.

I have often confessed that I, as an author, rarely conduct original research. My writing relies on what I can extract from what others have written or have told me.

Operating secondhand, as I do, offers opportunities to make inglorious errors of serious importance, and, as we all know, it is almost impossible to repeat a story exactly the same even twice in a row. Therefore, what I now record as fact may not actually be the final word, but the maps and the details should give anyone less dedicated than a canal scholar a pretty clear picture of the

Pennsylvania canal system. I wish that I had had at hand all that I now record.

It would be discouraging to list all of the digging and scratching I went through to discover how little I knew about the canals—waterways that I have admired since I was a wee lad growing up on the canal banks at Lewisburg.

Canals were built along both the Susquehanna and Juniata Rivers. The entire canal system was built, by hand labor, between 1827 and about 1834. The "about" got in there because when a canal was completely-completed depended on who judged and reported on which was the final shovel-full removed or the last stone laid.

The canals were built to move inland goods to cities along large rivers, bays, and oceans. We, who enjoy easy road travel, must remember that before pavement, roads and pikes were simply awful. Use of any road in the world was a miserable experience. The only fact making such travel tolerable was that there was nothing better.

The Commonwealth of Pennsylvania had two major cities—Philadelphia in the east, and Pittsburgh in the west. All produce and manufacturing west of the Allegheny Mountains (that split the state into halves) went down the Ohio River and was lost to Pennsylvania use and profit.

If canals could join the cities, the entire state would profit via shipping back and forth. In those pre-industrial revolution days there were no giant corporations (like the railroads that came later) that could undertake canal building efforts of such magnitude. So, the Commonwealth chose to pay the costs, to design and build, and to operate the complex waterways. Their payback (a modern term) would come from tolls, taxes, and increased revenues from more business.

The first section of the canal transportation system was actually a railroad (using horses to pull the cars) between Philadelphia and Columbia on the Susquehanna River. That sixty-plus mile long railroad dramatically reduced the shipping of goods on down to Baltimore and beyond Pennsylvania use.

Note: A wagon on rails could move about five times the weight as the same wagon could on a road—and in about one half the time.

In that era, serious river traffic could occur only during high water. The Susquehanna was a shallow and obstacle-filled river, and only in the spring could steady shipping be accomplished. River shipment (due to sinkings and groundings) resulted in lost boats and destroyed cargoes almost as often as safe arrivals. Good canals could avoid most of those misfortunes.

Canals began at Columbia and stayed on the east side of the Susquehanna all the way north to Clark's Ferry—Dauphin County to the east and Perry County to the west.

At Clark's Ferry (earlier called Green's Ferry) the canal crossed the river into Perry County and separated into two canals. One branch went north on the west side of the Susquehanna, and the other branch traveled northwest along the south (west) side of the Juniata River.

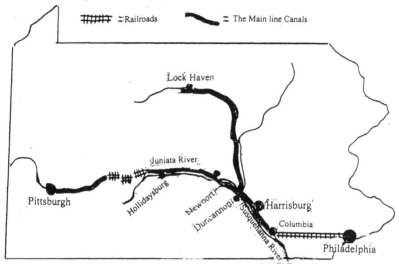

The Commonwealth of Pennsylvania

The Susquehanna branch was important to Perry County and towns such as New Buffalo and Liverpool were built along its route. Those somnolent villages were, in canal days, thriving market ports with six canal locks within Perry County, and—believe it or not—Liverpool boasted two canal boat building and repair yards.

The second canal boat built and launched west of the Susquehanna River came from Liverpool (the first was built and floated at Millerstown on the Juniata Branch).

The Juniata River splits Perry County, and following that river's rush from the Allegheny Mountains to the Susquehanna River, the canal opened interior Pennsylvania commerce to the outside world.

When the Juniata Section of the canal reached the Allegheny Mountains, an engineering feat deemed impossible by some was accomplished with barely an eye-blink.

A series of short, steeply rising railroads were built leading up the otherwise impossible mountainside. A boat with its load intact was floated onto a submerged rail car. Car and boat were hauled to the railroad's highest point by use of a steam engine implanted near that high spot. The boat-bearing car was then transferred via simple shunting and switching onto a parallel railroad that went higher on the mountain using a second steam engine at that road's summit. So the rail car with the boat as cargo went over the mountain and descended the same way on the west. Thereafter, the canal resumed its downstream flow all the way to Pittsburgh.

Describing the canal routes is not the same as digging them, and the labor of those unnamed multitudes of Irish, German, Swede, Polish and—who knows who else—laborers would alone be a tale worth recording.

Canal workers labored twelve-hour days, six days a week. Their pay varied from seventy cents a day to eighty-five cents. Other benefits of any kind were unheard of!

A workman was expected to move 15 cubic yards of dirt each day and/or excavate three linear feet of canal each day.

A contractor (like Matt Miller) bidding on canal work was offered ten cents per cubic yard of earth removed and forty-five cents per cubic yard for solid rock removal.

Put another way, a worker was paid seventy cents for removing 15 cubic yards and the contractor—who provided and paid the worker—was paid one dollar and fifty cents for the work.

There was a surplus of workers, and every laborer was a recent immigrant battling to gain a foothold in his new land and to inch forward, just a little, in material possessions.

One might think that payment of seventy cents a day was miserly, and it was. Bosses existed (and still do) to make money, not to perform social services. If laborers could be hired for seventy cents, why would they be offered more?

As this is written, the United States is faced with illegal immigration by hundreds of thousands of Mexican citizens who will labor at wages far below the demands of American workers. Should businesses pay them more?

Historians will examine labor parallels between the earlier 1800s and our early twenty-first century. I will suggest only that hiring cheaply is part of our capitalist system, and that, in the long view, cheap labor has worked well for the country and for almost everyone passing through or assimilated by the system. *But, there are other, less easily measured, social costs, and, if empowered, I* *would put an end to all <u>illegal</u> immigration using any means possible!*

Low wages can only be maintained where goods are also cheap. As examples, of costs during the canal building era, a gallon of Applejack (brandy) cost twenty-five cents, as did a gallon of Blackstrap, a mix of rum and molasses. A glass of either popular drink cost three cents.

Here is an interesting price that might prove more comparable. A 2" x 12" plank cost four cents per running foot. Almost all of that cost lay in the sawing or hewing of the plank, which was not accomplished as conveniently as it is today. Today (May 2006), a similar 2" x 12" plank would cost one dollar and eighty-eight cents per foot.

Household goods, flour, meat, cheese, beer, and such things as salt and fish could be shipped via canal for two cents a ton per mile.

Coal and iron shipped at one cent per ton per mile, and sand and clay cost three-fourths of a cent per shipped ton.

A packet boat hauling passengers was charged twenty-five cents a canal mile. A passenger aboard the packet paid a toll of a half-cent a mile.

A canal boat captain was paid about sixty dollars a month, but if he provided all of his help, his horses and their feed, etc, he received two hundred and twenty dollars a month. A steersman on a boat made twenty-five dollars, a cook made twenty dollars, and a driver (of the animals on the towpath) was paid ten dollars per month.

A short note about these drivers is in order. Most drivers were boys. They worked six-hour days without breaks except for halts at locks, farmer's landings, or to water or feed the animals.

During those six hours, a boat might travel ten miles if heavily loaded or as much as eighteen miles if running light. If using one and two horse teams, the drivers walked. If four horse teams were hitched, a driver sometimes was allowed to ride the last horse.

I note here that more than a few canal boats carried their relief teams (as many as six horses) along on the boat. It was found to be more certain and often cheaper to carry teams than arranging for them en route. Carried horses could be swapped with working animals at any point, which could prove advantageous as an animal tired.

In the census of 1830, Pennsylvania had four hundred and three slaves. Some of those slaves were worked as cooks on canal boats, and some free Negroes were also employed as cooks.

I use the term "Mucker" in this book. Mucker was a disparaging name for someone who dug the accumulated muck from canal bottoms usually while they were drained during winter and before reopening in the spring. Mucking was a bottom-paying job. Imagine the filth that drained from fields, canal-side villages, and all that was dumped from the boats (garbage and sewage). When carbide lamps came into use, ashes from the lamps were dumped into canals to help reduce the growth of weeds. It worked but, of course, it killed all of the fish.

One might wonder how busy the canals actually were. A recorded example is that in one season (usually 36 weeks) thirty-six hundred boats arrived at Huntington from the east. Persons living along the canals noted that, "A boat hardly got out of sight before another hove into view."

A boat every twenty minutes was recorded. That spacing was often determined by the time required to cycle and pass through a one boat lock.

Canal shapes are discussed within this book, but more can be said about the boats themselves. As examples, it should be pointed out that square-ended boats and rafts were common, and they could be brutal to the canal banks. To reduce damage by all boats, a speed limit of four miles per hour was established.

Speeders could receive a ten-dollar fine. However (there is always a however where speeding is concerned), publications note that fast packets reached eight miles per hour. Packets carrying passengers (their primary function) traveled eighty to one hundred miles per day where a freight boat might make twenty-five.

Interesting rules of the canal era include that every boat was required to have a light on its bow at night. Square-ended boats and rafts were supposed to have curved platforms added to their bows to keep from damaging canal banks with their sharp corners.

As "sharp" is mentioned, the law required every decked boat had to have a knife-edged instrument fixed to the bow (or stern) to cut a towrope that might inadvertently pass over the boat. A towrope could virtually behead someone caught by it, or a rope could destroy structures above the deck—such as cabins. A caught towrope could also injure the pulling animals, and horses were known to be pulled from a towpath into the water by a caught rope and a boat's momentum.

It is interesting to know that packet boats were scheduled to travel from Pittsburgh to Philadelphia in four days. The actuality might be six days. Canal breaks, bad weather, and delays at the inclined-plane railroads and at ordinary locks were to be expected.

Canal boats were not all eighty and ninety-foot long monsters, and most boats were under fifty feet in length. Despite ninety-foot long locks, there were even a few one hundred-foot long boats that managed to pass through. How, one could fairly wonder, could that be done?

The first way was to allow part of the boat to overhang a lock's doors. If the rise and fall of a lock was not too great, a large craft whose deck extended past stem and stern waterlines could overhang both lock doors and so travel up or down river.

The second method was to have an oversize boat enter a lock and then close the doors tightly against the sides of the craft. By allowing the water in or out at a rapid rate, the boat rose or fell about normally despite leakage and scraping between lock doors and the boat hull. Obviously a flat-sided barge-like boat would use that method more effectively than a rounded-hull boat. The practice was not common, in part, because of the terrific water waste involved.

Two river crossings concern the Perry County canals. The smaller was the crossing of the Juniata above Newport, almost to Millerstown. We now call that spot Old Ferry.

Our Old Ferry was known as the Rope Ferry in canal times. An endless rope was hooked to the ferry and through pulleys on each bank. A water-driven windlass was turned on one side (the north bank), and the boat was pulled across the river.

The other canal/river crossing was, of course, at Clark's Ferry. As described within this book, the boats were towed across the Susquehanna by animals on a towpath attached to the downstream side of the bridge.

Before the canals, Clark's Ferry (once Green's Ferry) had constructed a river dam by piling rocks high enough to raise the water level a foot or two.

A sluice at one end of the dam allowed river craft passage around the dam. When the state took charge of the crossing to provide passage of canal boats, they also gained responsibility to maintain the dam. At low water, the remains of that dam can be seen and will probably remain evident for another hundred years.

A similar dam was in use below the Rope Ferry on the Juniata River. The purpose of these low dams was to create a pool of water, almost without current and of sufficient depth to float canal boats even when the rivers were low.

An aqueduct was, and is, a canal raised above or below ground level. The Romans built aqueducts to transport water, and these two thousand-plus years later, some still stand. Our aqueducts were built to float canal boats across streams and rivers.

Our biggest aqueduct made of wood on stone piers was at the junction at Duncan's Island near Amity Hall where the Juniata Canal crossed the Juniata River. Nothing remains of that structure or any other aqueducts known to this author, but every stream emptying into the river had an aqueduct. If the stream was tiny, the method of allowing the water to flow beneath the canal and continue on its way to the river was called a culvert. A lot of those still exist.

The canal years lasted only sixty years, and were at their most powerful for only their first twenty years—1830 through 1850. Arrival of the railroads reduced and finally destroyed their usefulness. By 1890 the canals were finished.

If viewed from a comfortable distance, theirs was a romantic era. The actuality was that all of the 1800s were violent and struggling years for the canals, the nation, and our people.

By any measure of any condition, we are far better off now than we were then—except perhaps in personal freedom to do as we wish and to keep what we earn.

If one desires to know more about our Perry County canals, turn to Harry Hain's *History of Perry County*. His is a marvelous work and worth reading by anyone interested in county history.

There is another book titled *The Pennsylvania Main Line Canal* (author unknown) that is powerfully informing, but the book is available only through library transfers from BIG libraries—meaning that it is hard to find and must shortly be returned. Pattee Library at Penn State University has a copy.

RFC